Dream a Little Dream

Sue Moorcroft

First published 2012 by Choc Lit Limited
Penrose House, Crawley Drive, Camberley, Surrey GU15 2AB, UK
www.choclitpublishing.com

A CIP catalogue record for this book is available
from the British Library

ISBN-978-1-906931-90-2

Printed and bound by CPI Group (UK) Ltd, Croydon, CR0 4YY

For the two men I've known longer than any others
– my big brothers
Kevan Moorcroft and Trevor Moorcroft
Thanks for being there when I need you.

Acknowledgements

My thanks, as always, to the fantastic Choc Lit team, because working with you is such a pleasure. Also to my buddies in the Romantic Novelists' Association for the support and the parties.

A host of people were kind enough to help me with this book and I'm deeply grateful. Joan Innes at Moulton Therapies, who armed me with a wealth of information about treatments and let me talk to her reflexology students at The Academy of Reflexology and Massage. Liz Rhodes of BBC Radio Cambridgeshire let me sit in on her show whilst she explained the clever stuff radio presenters do. Gail and Alex Willis invited me onto *Half Century,* Gail's lovely river cruiser, so that Alex could teach me to drive it. Clorissa Paul gave me dog-training advice and a dog I saw skateboarding in Brighton gave me the idea for Crosswind. Kathleen Mears shared her experiences of living with a narcoleptic. Dave Lowry provided great insight into air traffic controllers and then magically arranged for us to meet Paul Templeman, General Manager, NATS, Stansted, who took us into the Stansted Tower – my thanks to those on watch that day, for not minding my questions. Also to everyone on Twitter and Facebook who advised me on what's hot in Halloween costumes and where to secrete a phone and wallet in Lycra leggings, especially Mark West for his specific and enlightening knowledge, and Dan Moorcroft for letting me borrow his middle name.

A special mention for my valued beta readers: Dominic White, Mark West, Joan Innes, Dave Lowry and the late and much-missed Roger Frank. I can't tell you how much I appreciate your time and expertise.

I'm indebted to Narcolepsy UK (www.narcolepsy.org. uk) for its clear and authoritative information about the rare sleep disorder, narcolepsy, and to John Cherry and those on the message board who gave me help and advice. At Narcolepsy UK's conference I was grateful to have the opportunity to ask questions of the clear and engaging Dr Emmanuel Mignot, Director of the Stanford Sleep Sciences, Stanford University School of Medicine, California, thus straightening out my backstory.

There's one person without whom this book could not have been written. When I asked for help on Narcolepsy UK's message board I said that my hero, Dominic Christy, was in his thirties and had narcolepsy. Amongst several responses was one that began, 'My name is Dominic, I'm in my thirties and have narcolepsy ...' Since then, he's answered a thousand questions by e-mail and in person, supplying intelligent, articulate and good-humoured insight into the fascinating, frustrating life of the narcoleptic, read my manuscript twice, allowed me to bug him endlessly without apparently losing patience, and helped me empty a satisfactory number of wine bottles. Dominic White, you are a star. If the goblins sent you, they obviously knew that writing this book was important. Thank you.

Narcolepsy is bittersweet. I hate the way it controls how I live, my job and what it's done to my relationships. But I realise that it's inescapably part of me. I have – almost – come to terms with it, and I know I have to value it however I can. The silver lining is that narcolepsy's given me a unique perspective. Often, I have had to sit back, but I've seen more than most people notice: the way they behave towards each other and what they do when they think no one's looking, the small movements and the secret brief glances filled with anger, uncertainty and, sometimes, love.

Bitter or sweet, narcolepsy's in every part of my life and it touches deep emotions: when I first meet someone or, later, really start to fall for her – that growing connection, being almost physically drawn her way – it affects how a woman thinks and feels, and whether she falls in love with me.

And, of course, if I meet you, your reactions to me, knowing I'm a little different to almost everyone else, will affect me – and whether I could, possibly, fall in love with you.

Dominic

Prologue

Liza wasn't dancing-on-the-table drunk. But she'd spent the evening getting stuck into the Friexenet with Rochelle and Angie.

And Adam's mum, Ursula Überhostess, was semaphoring disapproval across the room with frowning eyebrows. *You're drinking too much, Liza.*

Liza sent back a cheery wave. *No, I'm not. Leave me alone.*

Rochelle nudged Liza, raising her voice to be heard over the aunties and uncles singing along with Rihanna about her umberella-ella-ella. 'Do we have to stay? If it's supposed to be Adam's birthday party, why are hardly any of his mates here? I've wasted an updo on rellies.' She pulled at one of the blonde tendrils that had been allowed to escape artfully from the roll on the back of her head.

'Because it's a "do",' Angie put in, wisely. 'Friends know there'll be stacks of rellies, so they stay away.' She drained her wineglass and Rochelle immediately refilled it from the satiny black bottle of Friexenet – the fifth of the six they'd brought from Liza's fridge.

Glumly, Liza extended her glass for refilling, too. 'The others are already clubbing at Muggies, waiting for us. They keep texting.' She could see Adam, over the heads of those on the dance floor, on the stage, talking to the DJ – one of his army of cousins – and laughing. Adam wouldn't hurt the family's feelings by making an early escape. She sighed, tragically. 'I'll have to stay till Adam leaves. You two can go, though. I'll survive wasting a new dress and pin heels on a hall full of balloons, paper tablecloths, cardboard plates and homemade buffet.'

Rochelle and Angie rolled their eyes but remained in their seats under the bobbing *You are 30!* and *30 Today!* balloons as red-faced, laughing relatives gyrated on the dance floor under a glitter ball. 'Booooring,' Rochelle muttered.

'Sorry, hon.' But at least relieving boredom was one of Liza's talents. Her gaze fell on one of the blue-and-silver foil balloons. Reeling it in by its slinky satin ribbon, she put its seal to her mouth, and giggled.

Rochelle brightened immediately. 'Yeah, Liza, do duck-voice.'

The foil made Liza's teeth feel funny as she bit down, but soon a little puff of helium hissed out and she could put her lips over the hole and suck, until her head gave a tiny telltale spin. *'Hello Rochelle, hello Angie!'* Her voice felt curiously smooth as it hit a note at least an octave higher than usual.

Angie giggled. 'Hello, Donald Duck!'

Liza laughed – like a cartoon duck – which made Rochelle and Angie snort Friexenet bubbles of mirth. She inhaled again. *'Maybe I should talk duck to Ursula?'*

'Yeah, yeah,' they gurgled. 'Ursula will love you talking duck!'

Squeezing the deflating balloon, Liza sucked her hardest, trying to see how high she could make her voice go. Then, suddenly, relatives began shouting and looking at her, beaming and applauding.

'What's up with them?' she quacked.

Rochelle shook her head, unable to speak for laughing, wiping at her mascara with a fingertip.

Adam, still up on stage with Cousin DJ, boomed through the microphone. 'Liza? Come up here, sweetheart.'

'Oh. Shit.' Suddenly duck voice didn't seem such a good idea.

Rochelle laid her head on Angie's shoulder and sobbed with laughter.

'LIZA!' Adam insisted.

'*Oh, SHIT!*'

Clutching her stomach, Angie began to slide sideways off her chair.

And the relatives clapped harder, shouted louder, 'Lie-zah! Lie-zah! Up on the stage, Lie-zah!'

'You … you've got to!' wept Rochelle. 'It's a "do". Adam's going to make a speech.'

And a scrum of relatives descended, arms outstretched. Liza, drink-drenched and helium-headrushed, was powerless to avoid being hoisted up the three wooden steps and left teetering at Adam's side. He smiled, boyishly, taking her clammy hand in his warm one.

The room fell into waiting silence.

Adam pressed his lips gently to her palm then suddenly – hideously – dropped to one knee, dark brown eyes smouldering up at her. Enunciating every word, he said into the microphone, 'Liza Reece, will you marry me?'

People whooped and began to clap. Others shushed, wanting to hear Liza say, 'Yes!'

'I think it's what we both want.' Adam held the microphone up to her lips and winked, playfully.

Liza recoiled from his hand and the spongy microphone that smelled like bad breath. In what universe did he think she'd want to be publicly cornered into relinquishing Singledom? Had she missed a discussion about radically changing her life? Tying herself to Adam? Her heart pounded in her ears, making it impossible to think logically about the audience, the occasion, or how to handle a delicate situation so as not to hurt Adam.

She just opened her mouth and the truth quacked out. '*No, I don't want to marry you.*'

Chapter One

PWNsleep message board:

Tenzeds: Just found this forum. It's not long since I was diagnosed and, coincidentally(!), not long since I came out of a relationship. How easy will it be to hook up with someone new?

Sleepingmatt: Hmm, can be tricky. Try and find a hot woman who understands about meds, naps, sleep hygiene and that you're not just being dull when you need rest ...

Tenzeds: Wow. That's all, huh?

Not exactly the reassurance he'd been looking for ... Dominic Christy shut down the People With Narcolepsy Sleep message board and passed his iPad to Miranda. 'Can you keep hold of this for me while I have my toes twiddled? Which is going to have zero effect, by the way.' He leaned back in the seat he'd been shown to by the teen receptionist. The room was airy and warm, though October rain beat on the window. As well as two chairs and a desk, a black leather treatment couch extended diagonally into the room, its back raised. A holistic centre. So not him. 'I don't even like people touching my feet. Does reflexology tickle?'

'Of course not.' Miranda peered at him over the top of her glasses with her I'm-the-slightly-older-and-wiser-cousin expression, no less irritating now than it had been twenty years ago.

Dominic grinned. 'Nutty vegetarian idealists, like you, think anything can be cured through massage and green tea.'

'And illogical people dismiss complementary medicine without trying it.'

He narrowed his eyes. To cast a slur on his logic was to hit him where he lived. Much as he loved Miranda, he couldn't let her get away with that. And he knew exactly how to invoke cousinly rage in return ... 'Reflexology's only going to help me if this therapist of yours is young, gorgeous and has a chest like a shelf full of melons.'

But Miranda actually smiled. 'Big oops, Dominic. Big, big oops.'

And a new voice came from behind him. 'Tick one, tick two. Three, I'm afraid, is just your sad fantasy, unless you revise downward to grapefruits. But my appearance doesn't affect your treatment.'

Dominic froze as a woman stalked into his field of vision. Slight and blonde, a cross between a nurse and a nymph in dark green trousers and tunic, she seated herself in the other chair and directed a sweet smile at his cousin. 'Hello, Miranda.'

Despite dancing eyes, Miranda somehow managed to return a smile of studied sorrow. 'I apologise, Liza. My cousin can't help his shallow maleness.' She tucked Dominic's iPad under her arm. 'I'll wait in reception – unless you feel you need a chaperone?'

Liza turned to her desk. 'I'll shout if I do.'

The door closed. Dominic found himself torn between running after his cousin to demand her instant return to explain that he'd only been pretending to be a sleazebag.

And just running.

Liza consulted a clipboard, then glanced up between twin wings of blonde hair that curved to points exactly level with her chin. 'Dominic Christy?' Her voice and her smile were polite but in her eyes lurked something unspoken. Probably: *I'm being professionally polite. You try to be the same.* They were the bluest of eyes, lined with turquoise, lashes thick with mascara.

He tried to regain control of the situation. 'I can't apologise enough. You overheard macho crap meant only to infuriate my cousin. That's not the real me, I promise. You must think I'm a moron.'

'I'm Liza Reece. Shall we talk about what's brought you here, today? This is your first reflexology treatment, I gather? I'd like to get an idea of your history and circumstances, so that my treatment can be informed and the reflexes will make sense to me.'

Evidently, she'd decided that the best way to deal with his motormouth moment was to ignore it, but he wanted to protest, *'C'mon, if you can't reassure me that I'm not a moron, at least acknowledge the possibility that I was only winding Miranda up!'* But he sighed and played it her way. 'Miranda thinks that I ought to, um, open my mind to complementary medicine. I've already been here for aromatherapy and ear candling.' Only because Miranda badgered him into it, but Liza Reece didn't need to know that. He needed the brownie points.

Her eyebrows rose, as silky and fine as a child's. 'And how did you find those therapies?'

'Interesting.' A non-reply, but better than lying. Or telling the truth, as one of the words he'd used to Miranda had been 'nonsense'. The other had been basic, but descriptive.

She began to take details about his age, past or planned operations – sending dark thoughts Miranda's way, he was tempted to say he needed a cousinectomy – was he a diabetic? Epileptic? Did he suffer from high blood pressure? She moved quickly down a questionnaire, glancing up politely for his answers, until, finally, he responded, 'Yes.'

'Sleep disorder?' She stopped, and let her gaze rest properly on his.

'I was diagnosed with narcolepsy about ten months ago.'

Instant interest blazed in her eyes. Stunning eyes, and even though he realised that her interest was engaged by his weird condition, not him, he still found himself wishing that he'd worn something newer than the comfortable shirt Natalie had bought him because she'd said its dark purple made his grey eyes look silver. When she'd been his girlfriend, not his ex.

'Narcolepsy?' Liza Reece propped her chin on her fist. 'That's a rare one. How's it affecting you?'

'It's no fun. Daytime sleep attacks are the worst, they just suck me down. And I have vivid dreams, which can be disorientating.' As if he'd taken something. A bad something.

'How's your night-time sleep?'

'If I'm feeling OK and I follow my routines, it's usually good. It's forcing myself awake in the mornings that can be next to impossible.'

She made notes, frowning in concentration. 'Isn't there some muscle weakness associated with narcolepsy?'

'Cataplexy.' He nodded. 'It's occasional. And just a fuzzy feeling around the knees, usually, and a sort of glimmer to my vision. It's only occasionally that my legs really disappear.'

'Medication?'

He gave the details of what he usually referred to as 'the yellow pills' and 'the white pills', and watched her hands as she wrote. She wore no rings and her fingernails were clean and trim. White, soft skin. No watch on either delicate wrist. 'My condition's mild, compared to some, and I'm a bit drug averse so I try to take only what I absolutely need, and accommodate the condition with lifestyle.'

'How does that work?' Her blue gaze was intent. It might have been alluring to be subjected to such scrutiny if only it was him prompting it, rather than his bloody narcolepsy. But at least she was engaging with him. And if he kept on talking, she'd keep on being engaged, and he could watch the way she moved and the expressions flitting through her amazing eyes. 'Scheduling controlled daytime naps and keeping my sleep routines regular – you've probably heard it called sleep hygiene. Eating well. Exercise. Avoiding soporific situations. Avoiding stress.'

The frown slotted back between her fine eyebrows. 'But isn't narcolepsy neurological?'

'Yes. For me, it's a genetic thing combined with an autoimmune disorder, where the wrong cells were killed in the part of the brain that governs sleep. In hindsight, I've fought mild narcolepsy symptoms for ages. Wild dreams right from childhood – you know how kids think there's something under their bed? For me it was a goblin, slurping away. And I once did genuinely believe that a dog had eaten my homework. Variable energy, not hearing alarm clocks, being late. I went into a profession with a rotating shift pattern and a doctor taught me to manage my sleep by splitting it. I was operating in a fast-paced environment, which is helpful, and I coped until pneumonia triggered narcolepsy and then it was like someone had cast a spell over me. I needed to sleep and sleep and I just couldn't get over it.'

'Where does the stress come in? Are you stressed?'

'Only to head-exploding stage.' The attempt to get her to smile didn't work. But, hey, she was great to look at even when she was solemn. 'High anxiety increases the frequency and intensity of episodes. Diagnosis and the end to my relationship came in quick succession, which was pretty stressful.' *Personal relationships can be affected*, it had said, in the information he'd been given. Slowly, he breathed in, willing himself not to betray by so much as a tremor how much it hurt to say the next words. 'And I had to leave my job.' Another long, slow breath. 'I'm … I was an air traffic control officer at Stansted Airport. Pilots prefer us to be awake.'

She still didn't smile. But that was refreshing, considering how many people seemed to think narcolepsy a joke. Maybe she even had a handle on how unfunny it was, because her gaze softened. 'That's tough on you.'

He kept his expression neutral. *Depression and feelings of isolation are common* ... 'No matter how many naps I schedule, I can't be relied upon to operate efficiently for the necessary spans of time. Lives are at stake and controllers have to pass medicals, so I lost my licence. I'd just passed a board to become a deputy watch manager and my employers wanted to keep me but all they could offer was Air Traffic Paperpusher in the offices at the bottom of the control tower while people did my dream job, up top. Narcolepsy is no place for sissies.'

'I can see that.' Chin in hand, she clicked her pen in and out, thoughtfully. Then, when he volunteered no more, she completed the rest of the form, which only involved him in saying 'no' a lot. She flicked her hair back and put down her pen. 'So Miranda Sheldrake's your cousin but you don't share her interest in holistic medicine?'

'I don't, but she's trying to convert me while she gives me and my dog houseroom for a few weeks.'

She finally managed a smile. The backs of his hands tingled as he smiled back. Not just a Pavlovian response to anyone hot and female, but in real pleasure at the way even a therapist-to-client smile made her beautiful. Her skin was fine and white, her mouth drawn by an artist, her eyes as blue as a summer sky. For the first time since Natalie did what she did, he felt a proper tug of attraction.

'Perhaps she's already explained that complementary medicine is exactly that. It complements allopathic medicine, it doesn't replace it.' She talked about pressure points, releasing blocked energy channels, stimulating circulation, removing toxins, promoting healing and relaxation. 'I may be able to help you in terms of relaxation and wellbeing – reducing stress and improving the quality of your night-time sleep, which may help your daytime issues. But I can't cure you and I'm not going to be able to make those irresistible daytime sleep urges magically disappear.'

'Nothing does.'

She recommended six treatments – if he didn't perceive a benefit in that time there wouldn't be any point in continuing – asked him to sign her notes and then moved her clipboard to a trolley beneath large multi-coloured diagrams of feet and hands. 'Would you like to take off your shoes and socks?'

He fumbled with his laces, feeling unexpectedly uncomfortable, even vulnerable, though she was washing her hands and not watching him. He'd received no complaints about cheesy feet or gnarly toenails but he could think of better first physical contact with a woman.

She settled him on the couch with his back angled comfortably and a light blanket across him, talking about the background music as she raised the couch via an electronic control. Her voice filled his airspace. Her eyes were on him. She saw to his comfort. He lay back to enjoy being the centre of her attention.

She began by cleansing his feet. Although he'd showered only an hour ago, he couldn't help a thread of unease.

But part of him – a significant part – found it intensely erotic.

He knew he wasn't meant to be fascinated by her slender white hands sliding the cool wipe up his instep and between his toes, tracing the sensitive soles of his feet with long, soothing strokes, but he was suddenly glad that he had another foot waiting for the same treatment. In fact, he wished he had a couple extra.

He watched as she pumped cream from a large white dispenser, spread it between her palms, and seated herself on a stool. 'First, I'm going to relax you.' She cupped his heels. Mmm. Then, wrapping his left foot in a soft towel, she passed her cool fingers smoothly from his right ankle over the top of his foot to his toes, her thumbs sliding along the sole. Reversing, she swept her palms down from toe to heel – and the movement went straight to his groin.

In fact, the wave of pleasure nearly whooshed him vertically into the air. He actually had to grip the sides of the couch. He'd never suspected there might be an upside to sensitive feet but ... *whooh*. He wasn't sure that sensation was legal.

'Try to sink into the couch and let go.' She'd obviously spotted that he hadn't relaxed. Her thumbs began circles just below his anklebone. 'Perhaps if you close your eyes and drop your head back?'

He did both, while her hands continued to sweep over his foot. Not tickling. Definitely not tickling. Whoa ... Not relaxing, either. Yeah, he *liked* this. He could lie here with Liza Reece's hands on his feet until the end of time.

'And now I'm going to begin to apply pressure. Just listen to the music and enjoy. Feel free to share with me anything you're experiencing but we'll talk after the treatment.'

'Mmm.' If he shared what he was feeling, she'd scream for Miranda. He checked that the blanket covered his lap.

Her hands had warmed. She began, delicately, to manipulate his big toe and, unexpectedly, relaxation did begin to take over. He would never have anticipated that 'toe twiddling' would make him feel as if layers of tension were flipping from him in slow motion. This was great.

She began to press his toe tips. 'Is this pressure OK?'

He opened one lazy eye. 'Bearing in mind how this meeting began, I'm quite relieved you're not digging with your nails.'

She smiled. Not the formal bending of the lips she'd sent

him earlier, but a fleeting grin of sparkle-eyed mischief, though her tone remained strictly professional. 'If you feel as if I'm using my nails then you're experiencing tenderness, which might reflect an issue in your body.'

'OK.' He digested that idea. 'Is that how you diagnose—'

'Assess.'

'—assess, what the issues might be?'

'Mainly, I pick up reflexes. These could feel like grittiness or bubbles, hardness or hollowness.'

Silence grew for long minutes, except for peaceful music rippling around the room. The base of his toes. The ball of his foot. As she worked along the side of his foot she paused to pay attention to one area, provoking a strange sensation. 'That prickles.'

'I'm picking up a reflex from your shoulder. Has it been injured?' She paused, leaving one hand on his foot. He heard the scratch of a pen. Then her fingers went back to work.

'I cracked my right shoulder in a fall. But it's healed.' That was weird. He considered and rejected the idea of Miranda feeding Liza information about his shoulder. Miranda might be utterly convinced of the efficacy of alternative medicine but cheating wasn't her style.

Then his thoughts parted and floated away as Liza's fingers sang their lullaby. Flesh heavy. Bones melting—

The headset was so familiar that he hardly felt its weight. The aerodrome spread out below the tower like a scale model, aircraft glowing spectacularly white in the sunlight, taxiing, or drawn up in orderly rows between the stands. Sebastian, in the left-hand seat, saw the aircraft safely between ground and air and Dominic, in the right-hand seat, watched his 'strips' progress across his screens as he delivered the aircraft between runways and stands.

But he became aware of an incident. Ryanair 9272 had a medical emergency. He strained to hear the pilot, holding all other aircraft on Delta apron as he anticipated a request to return Ryanair 9272 to its stand. Sebastian stared at Dominic. Looking, not speaking.

Relief flooded over him as he saw the problem. He should be in the deputy watch manager's seat, further back. 'Ryanair 9272, stand by.' He unplugged his headset and moved to his correct station where he could see the runway over the heads of the controllers or glance left at the inbound aircraft hanging in the clear blue sky on approach.

A warm tide of satisfaction rolled over him. He was back where he belonged—

Liza rose, wiping her hands on a paper towel. She studied the tall man lying on her couch, his breathing deep and even. His streaky dark blond hair shone softly under the lights, tumbled, as if he'd combed it with his fingers. His mouth was set in a line of determination, even in repose, beneath hand-carved cheekbones. In other circumstances, she would have liked him a lot.

His chest rose. Fell. One hand twitched.

She washed her hands at the basin in the angle of the wall behind a curtain and readied a tall glass of cold water. He hadn't moved. She watched him uncertainly. She knew you weren't supposed to wake sleepwalkers. Was it the same for narcoleptic nappers?

At least Miranda was in the waiting room.

Then his eyes flickered open. For several moments she was stranded in his gaze, the pale eyes emphasised by eyelashes and brows darker than his hair.

'OK?' She smiled, not sure whether offering him the water would help him rouse, or if it would embarrass him if he had trouble gripping the glass. He seemed to be taking a little time to surface. She waited, giving him time. Letting him collect his thoughts.

Finally, he blinked, and stretched. 'Can I take you out to dinner, some time?'

Her heart gave a tiny lurch. Obviously he was back on Planet Earth. She made her voice light. 'Sorry – I don't. Just stay where you are for a few minutes. Perhaps you could drink this while we talk? It'll help with detoxification.'

He took the glass of water in both hands. 'Hydration's always good.'

She resumed her seat beside the little desk, picking up the blue clipboard. 'How do you feel?'

'Great. Very relaxed. That trick with the shoulder was impressive.'

'It's not a trick.' She added a smile, with an effort. 'I picked up a reflex, explained by the fact that the shoulder was injured in the past.' Bloody man. 'I also picked up quite a top-of-the-head reflex, on both feet, which might correspond with your narcolepsy. I'd be interested to know whether you notice any improvement in your night-time sleep, but feel that's more likely to happen after several treatments. Is there anything you'd like to ask me?'

His grey eyes sparkled. 'I think I just asked you about dinner?'

Her smile fell away. 'If you'd like to discuss your treatments, later, ring the front desk and if I'm with a client they'll arrange for me to return your call.' Giving him a Stables Holistic Centre card, she touched the electronic control. Gently, slowly, the couch hissed back to disembarkation height.

Dominic pulled himself upright, slipped into his socks and laced his black Timberlands. He paused on the side of the couch, then stretched, until he was on his feet, smiling down. 'I know we got off on the wrong foot—'

'Ho ho,' she interpolated, obligingly, as if she hadn't heard all the puns a thousand times.

He grinned. 'Thank you for the feeble joke appreciation. The dinner invitation is an apology for what you overheard, which was, honestly, just the remnants of years of winding each other up—'

'You've already apologised.' She opened the door and stood aside to let him pass. 'If you decide to have further treatments, I'll do some reading on your condition.' And, as he didn't seem inclined to move ahead of her, she stepped out to the short passageway to reception.

That did draw him out, but only to position himself between her and the waiting area. 'You're in a relationship?'

She looked up into his eyes and wondered if he was always this focused on what he wanted. He reminded her of a lion, tawny, stalking, watchful, but with the potential to explode into action at any time. 'No. By choice.'

'You're going to be single for life?'

'Yes. I'll probably get a cat.' Not a lion.

He laughed. His eyes narrowed, as if he was trying to weigh her up. 'Implying that a cat would be better company than me isn't enough to put me off. What else can you come up with?' His gaze became thoughtful. 'That I'm your patient? Then I won't have further treatments.' His face fell easily into a smile. His teeth were white, his cheeks smooth and his jaw line firm; his feet had been long and strong in her hands. He was easily the hottest man she'd treated this week. This month. This age.

She held his gaze. 'It's not because you're my client.'

Slowly, he settled a shoulder against the wall, cocking his head to study her. 'I won't fall asleep and drool in my gravy. Or feed the goblin at the dinner table. Probably.'

She flushed. 'It's not that!'

His smile gleamed. He probably thought that her refusal was a form of flirting and she had to admit that something breathless and skippy was going on. It had been ages—

But remember Adam.

Her breath took a longer pause. Adam shouldn't matter now but ... But hideous experiences had a way of piercing vital organs with a pain that was designed to educate the brain to avoid similar situations. She made her lungs work. 'I make a bad girlfriend.'

His eyebrows lifted. 'I only asked you out to dinner.'

'And I don't do one-night stands.'

'Look, I know what you overheard didn't present me in my best light—'

'No. And macho bullshit is something that no amount of reflexology can help you with.'

Chapter Two

A horrified glimpse of his face, blank with shock, then Liza was scrambling back inside her treatment room, slamming the door and leaning on it, eyes screwed shut. Why had she said that? She'd meant to defuse the situation with humour, but it had somehow got mixed up with an instinct to claw like a frightened kitten.

Fear. Rage. Perfectly reasonable reactions to what Adam had done and the knowledge that she'd made him do it. Not reasonable to project that fear and rage onto a completely different guy.

A tap fell on the other side of the door, loud beside her ear. 'Are you OK?' His voice was deep, hesitant, bemused. 'Liza? I didn't mean to— Oh, bollocks.' Then Miranda spoke, muffled, distant. Dominic raised his voice to answer. 'Yeah. I think it's fairly certain that my treatment's over.' His voice receded down the corridor and Liza took a huge breath as her shoulders sagged, swallowing a swelling ball of tears.

Seconds later, a king-sized rat-tat-TAT-TAT-TAT sprang her away from the white-painted wood an instant before Nicolas burst into the room, dark eyes blazing. 'What did I just hear?' The door snapped shut behind him like an exclamation mark.

Liza dropped her gaze, guiltily.

'Did you suggest a client was talking bullshit?'

'I'm sorry.' She swallowed. Then, weakly, 'He wanted me to go out with him and I thought I was handling it, but—'

'You decided to insult him? How likely is he to come back to the centre, now? Haven't you listened to anything I've said about us needing every scrap of business that we can drag through our doors? You know that this place works on a mutual business model. If you lose a client, you lose a potential client for everyone.' His jowls trembled with every rising accusation. 'I'm in my office tearing my hair over rent, business rates, insurance and bills, and have to listen to you driving clients away!'

Liza bit down hard on her lips before it burst out of her that Nicolas was full of bullshit, too, as all his money worries arose from not doing his sums properly before he took The Stables on. Instead, she made her voice calm and reasonable. 'We could get more clients if we tried new ideas, Nicolas—'

He threw up his hands as if warding off the devil. 'Don't! Not that same old stuff, Liza! New ideas, new ideas,' he mimicked. 'What you mean is five-minute wonders and faddy crap.'

She clenched her fists in frustration. She knew how to put the fucking place in profit if he'd just listen. But it was useless to try and force her views into his closed little mind.

Moving her practice to The Stables had seemed such a great opportunity. She'd been looking for a house in Middledip village and to have a treatment room near the neighbouring village of Port-le-bain, rather than in Peterborough, a fifteen-mile, traffic-angry drive away, had made the house purchase financially viable.

But the lucrative horde of clients spilling across the lawns from the luxurious hotel rooms of Port Manor had proved to be a figment of Nicolas's business plan; and sometimes Liza found herself shuddering at visions of bailiffs turfing her out of her house, snatching her little black-and-purple car and sending her down Port Road to beg a room in her sister Cleo's house. A house that would have no spare rooms, soon, when baby Gus's cot was moved from beside his parents' bed to the last available bedroom.

So Nicolas had a point. Insulting clients was idiotic.

She breathed in slowly, from her abdomen, to steady her voice. 'I'm sorry. It sounded jokey in my head but it was inappropriate. I'll apologise to him—'

'I don't want to hear it.' Nicolas passed his hand over his face. His skin gleamed white and unhealthy, like overcooked pasta, and his voice came perilously close to wobbling. 'You're repentant now but in five minutes you'll be making jokes about me coming the big boss. Overreacting. Having a hissy fit. Because respect and supportiveness are pretty much absent in you, aren't they? What was yesterday's little love bite? Oh, yes. "Nicolas practises seagull management – getting into a flap and shitting over everything".'

Liza winced. 'I didn't mean it in a horrible way.' Which sounded feeble, even to her ears. 'We've always exchanged friendly insults. You call me Stroppy Knickers.'

'Well, you are.' Finally, Nicolas smiled. But Liza didn't like the smile. It was as if he actually felt sorry for her. 'And the longer I know you, the less friendly I'm finding your insults. Of course, anyone who's drowning in financial mire is likely to have a sense of humour failure when he hears you pissing off paying clients.'

Heaving a big sigh, he steered her to her chair, before perching his beachball behind on the desk. He looked like a man determined to tick a bad job off his To Do List. 'You've had your practice here a year, Liza, and it's been stormy. I made allowances when you explained what had happened in your personal life. You're a great therapist and we've all put up with your "friendly" insults, because the clients love you and I thought you'd mellow as you left your problems behind.

'But the centre's bookings are dropping.' He checked his watch. 'It's nearly four. Do you have any more clients today?'

She met his eyes, stricken. 'What do you mean, "all"? "We've all put up", you said.'

Nicolas shifted, looking suddenly uncomfortable. 'We're only a small team here, aren't we?'

'Imogen and Fenella? Even Pippa?' Young Pippa, on the reception desk, had only left school last year and still seemed to Liza like a baby animal, all big brown eyes and long legs.

Nicolas sighed, pushing back a lock of lank hair. 'I'm afraid so. Do you have more bookings today?'

'No,' she admitted, voice small.

A long silence. She looked down at her white, ballet-slipper shoes. Nicolas's brown shoes faced them, as if the footwear was having its own confrontation. 'I'm sorry,' she muttered. 'I hadn't realised I was taking out my problems on you all.' She and Nicolas always sparred, but Pippa? Fenella? Imogen? She'd thought they were a sisterhood.

Clumsily, Nicolas patted her hand. 'I think you've had plenty of opportunity to realise before this, Liza.' He hesitated, before adding, heavily, 'I'm sorry if this seems unsympathetic after what happened with Adam but my back's against the wall and I can't afford your erratic ways. I'm fighting to build the centre and the rest of the team doesn't need a difficult person.' He paused again, as if bracing himself to say what had to be said. 'The centre needs investment and more clients and I'm meeting some people tomorrow morning who might bring both. So, I'm putting you on notice to move your practice elsewhere by the first of December.'

Liza's stomach flipped like an acrobat. '*What?*'

Nicolas went on relentlessly. 'I'm just glad that you're working the afternoon and evening tomorrow, because at least I know you won't come out with some outrageous crack whilst they're here.'

She found her voice. 'Nicolas, things aren't working out as I hoped, either, but you can't possibly expect me to find new premises and move in less than eight weeks!'

'Actually, I have your signature on a piece of paper that says I need only give you four. I'm sorry it's come to this, Liza.' He didn't waver, even though he must know she was staring disaster in the face.

But, belatedly, she realised that Nicolas was going to do whatever it took, because he had his own disaster to stare at. And it was every bit as big as hers.

Driving through the gates of Port Manor and along the lanes to her house in Middledip village, the late afternoon sky suited her mood. Cold and grey: darkness on the horizon.

She parked her black-and-purple Smart car outside 7 The Cross, which waited, cosy in the gloom.

The Cross, which, having only three legs, wasn't a cross at all, marked the centre of the village. Familiar with Middledip from the years Cleo had lived there, Liza liked that, in contrast to her anonymous former life in a modern box of a flat in a suburb of Peterborough, any villager might be encountered at the nearby shop or garage, or at the pub.

Number 7 was attached to its grand neighbour, The Gatehouse, which had been empty, but was currently showing a light in every one of its windows. The new people must have moved in.

The Gatehouse dwarfed dear little number 7 and, since its render had been painted blinding white and the stone sills and lintels shiny black, outshone it, too. Liza was glad her house still wore its unpretentious red brick, shaded with age, even if its two storeys were squat beside the Gatehouse's lofty three. It seemed bizarre that the two houses were joined – like the local squire marrying his kitchen maid. But, there they were, sharing a wall. Goodness knows what gate The Gatehouse had ever been the house to, unless it was some relic of the Carlysle estate. More likely, some earlier occupant of The Gatehouse had simply decided it was posh for a house to have a name, rather than a number. And it did have a garden gate; maybe that was it.

As Liza slid from the car, huddling into her coat for the brief journey up number 7's six-foot front path, an iron-grey middle-aged woman appeared through The Gatehouse's imposing black-painted front door. 'Good evening.'

Although she didn't really feel like going through the friendly neighbour ritual, Liza paused, key in hand, and summoned a smile. 'Just moving in? Welcome to Middledip. I'm Liza. If you haven't unpacked your kettle yet, I could make—'

'I'm Mrs Snelling,' the woman interrupted. 'Is that your little house? It adjoining ours was nearly a deal breaker.'

Any intention of offering a cheering cuppa instantly vanished from Liza's mind. 'It's been "adjoined" for about a hundred-and-fifty years. It didn't grow overnight, like a zit.'

Mrs Snelling somehow managed to make her unsmiling face smile even less. 'But then I realised that we could make you an offer, and break through – it'll be useful space. My mother might like to live downstairs and we can make the upstairs a guest suite. If we paint the exterior, the two properties will blend nicely.'

Liza laid her hand protectively on her plain front door. 'It's my house, not useful space. And painting these lovely bricks would be vulgar.' Stabbing the key into the lock before Mrs Snelling could reply, she almost fell into the sanctuary of her hall, trying not to wonder how much longer her house would be her house. No practice equalled no money; if she couldn't manage the mortgage payment she'd have to sell. And now here was bloody Mrs Snelling waiting to annexe it. She flipped on the sitting-room light. 'I won't sell you to that rabid old bat,' she reassured the room. But if she let the bank repossess it then they wouldn't care who they sold it to, which would probably mean a delightful bargain in Snellingland. Useful space for people who already had acres of it.

Dropping her ski jacket over the back of the sofa, rubbing her chilly hands along the radiators, she made for the primrose-yellow kitchen and warming ginger tea, sitting at the small pine table to drink and think. Above her, the ceiling airer was hung with three copper saucepans, a dark blue glass ball, a drying top and leggings, and a bunch of lavender that, though it bathed her in its scent, failed to soothe her. She stared at the rain pattering at the window and wondered what the hell she was going to do. Her reflection stared back, pale hair and pale skin above dark green uniform. 'Liza Reece,' she asked it, 'how has this happened? How could you upset your workmates? You need to return to the sunny, cheerful Liza that everyone knew and loved, this instant. Smile!' She gave a great cheesy grin. 'Wipe those frowns from your forehead.' She smoothed with her palms, physically reminding her brow how it was meant to be. Unlined. Serene. 'Stop worrying.'

How? The frown tried to repucker. Hastily, she plastered her forehead flat again. 'By doing nice things.' She summoned up a fresh smile. 'Like ringing Angie and Rochelle.' The smile became real and she reached for her phone.

Two hours on, curled in a corner of a leather sofa amongst the bright lights and chatter of the coffee-fragranced Starbucks in Long Causeway, she was glad she'd made the effort to jump into artfully frayed jeans and blue cowboy boots and drive to Peterborough. Angie and Rochelle were curled into the brown-leather tub armchairs opposite, hair long and highlights blonde; Angie a sort of sixties' bouffant puff at the back of her head, Rochelle a cheerleader's ponytail. Today's look was ripped jeans and flat shoes—one pair grey, the other a pleasing purple.

Rochelle beamed over her latte. 'This is mega. We were beginning to think you were avoiding us.'

'It's only a few weeks since you came over,' Liza protested.

'Yes, we go to Middledip.' Angie cradled an Americano. 'It's you coming to civilisation that doesn't happen.' She waggled her eyebrows. 'Give us an update.'

Liza felt her smile stiffen. 'A bit crap – I've lost my treatment room. I was hardly making enough to get by, but it'll take ages to find a new place, so I'm not sure how I'm going to pay my mortgage. Or run my car.' She tried to think her brow flat. But it might have puckered, just a bit.

Rochelle looked aghast. 'Are you being made redundant?'

'The self-employed don't get made redundant – or get redundancy payments. They just go bust.' Liza sighed.

Angie's eyes brimmed with sympathy. 'Is Nicolas having to close the treatment centre? I saw on *Look East* that everyone is cutting down on non-essentials. I can see why alternative therapies might be losing money.'

'He's not shutting down.' Liza had ordered a frappuccino, though the weather was miserable and the caffeine and calorie count must have been enormous. But there was something about the cream whirl and the spiral of chocolate sauce that made her feel better about finding herself in such a complete mess. She ducked her head to the straw and sucked up icy coffee spicules from beneath the flamboyant topping, then stirred slowly, watching the cream and chocolate sauce mix with the coffee slush.

When she lifted her eyes, Angie and Rochelle were waiting like parents who knew the weaknesses of their child and were creating a silence to be filled with the appropriate confession. She sighed. 'Nicolas wants me out.'

'What?' breathed Angie. 'Liza, you're brilliant! Has he gone insane?'

Liza shook her head. She had to suck up a little frappuccino before her throat would allow her to speak again. 'He heard me swearing at a client – the client asked me out and I seem to have lost the knack of gracious refusal. And Nicolas told me' – deep breath, swallow – 'that everyone's fed up with me making them the butts of my stupid jokes, and now that I've moved into driving clients away … He's got someone lined up who, apparently, has both money and a fresh client list to bring to the party.'

Silence.

'Was he creepy?' Rochelle frowned.

'Nicolas?'

She waved her hand. 'No! The customer who asked you out.'

'Client,' Liza corrected automatically. 'No.'

'Smelly?'

'Ugly?'

'No, he was pretty hot.' She paused for thought. 'He's got this kind of young Kevin Costner streaky dark blond thing going on. Or Eric from *True Blood* – kind of golden. Leonine. With Daniel Craig eyes.'

'Ooh, dirty blond.' Angie shivered. 'I love a dirty blond. What else?'

'He's obnoxiously, quietly overconfident.'

'Like Spike, from *Buffy*?' suggested Angie, hopefully.

Rochelle snorted. 'Spike's platinum blond, not dirty. How can someone be quiet and overconfident?'

Liza shrugged. 'It's like anything he says, he expects to happen. He did deign to discuss why I didn't want to go out to dinner with him but it was plain that he thought he could find a way to make it happen. He has a determined mouth.'

Angie made wide eyes. 'Pass him my way.'

Rochelle was more cynical. 'Married?'

'No,' Liza had to admit, 'he's fresh out of a relationship. But that wasn't the point. I just didn't want to go out with him. And knowing I completely overreacted makes me feel like an idiot.'

Drawing her frappuccino glass a little closer, she sucked the creamy coffee goo up, tiny sip by tiny sip, signalling how much she no longer wanted to talk about Dominic Christy.

Rochelle hooked Liza's hair back from her face. 'You used to love being asked out.'

'That was then.'

Angie frowned. 'Why have you been horrible to the others at the centre?'

'I hadn't realised that I had. But now Nicolas's brought it up, I'm going to have to talk to Fenella, Imogen and Pippa.' Liza groaned.

'And isn't it up to you how you speak to your clients?'

'In a way. But the benefit of having several therapists under one roof is the potential for sharing clients around. Having – hopefully – loved their reflexology treatment, a client might be receptive to trying ear candling or Indian head massage with Fenella, or hot stone therapy and aromatherapy with Imogen. Nicolas says that me chasing away custom risks dragging the whole centre down. And, of course, we pay him a commission on every fee, so the fewer I receive, the less I pay him.'

Rochelle snorted. 'Just don't swear at any more customers. Go to work tomorrow and apologise, be repentant, penitent, whatever you think it needs. Sorted.' She sat back, draining her cup.

'And what about the mad fools Nicolas's got lined up to take my treatment room? No. The whole Stables set up isn't working for me, not just because Nicolas wants me out but because he's a crap businessman. It ought to work, to have a treatment centre in the grounds of a posh hotel, with all those guests coming and going, but Nicolas has this stodgy old business model and doesn't want change to come within shouting distance of it. He likes to present himself as the boss, but he's just a glorified landlord, managing the premises, contributing little but taking a salary out. I know that Fen and Immi are worried, too, but they're being a bit ostrich.'

Rochelle frowned in thought. 'Can you become the investor? To keep these other people out? Then you could make all your whizzy changes.'

'I might be able to raise some money, but that doesn't resolve Nicolas being dead weight, or us pulling in different directions. Getting more deeply involved with him and his finances would make everything worse.'

Angie patted her arm. 'You should at least try and stay where you are until you've got somewhere lined up. I'm sure the others realise that you're not yourself. Everyone knows that Adam did this to you, Lize.'

'It wasn't his fault,' she said, automatically.

'Yes, it was!' they chorused. 'It was the way he and his nightmare of a mother handled the break up that knocked all the stuffing out of you,' Rochelle added. 'What does Cleo think about what's happened?'

'I haven't told her. She's got her hands full with baby Gus suffering from horrible colic. She and Justin haven't had a night's sleep since he was born and she's extended her maternity leave. She'd probably tell me that I need to get out more.'

Angie dropped her cup back to the table with a clatter, eyes shining. 'Yes, you do. With us. We'll take you to clubs—'

'Pubs to start with,' Rochelle amended. 'Let her work up to clubs when her good-time muscle memory comes back. Friday, Liza?'

'Um ... OK, thanks,' agreed Liza, not feeling equal to resisting, but wondering if she really felt thankful. Friday was only two days away.

Angie twinkled at her. 'And you ought to see men again, Lize, just to cure yourself of Adam.'

Chapter Three

Hands slid from Dominic's feet, to his legs; stroking, trickling. The woman was working her way up his body. Hands cool. Mouth hot.

In an instant he was hard and aching. He wanted to move, to pull her closer, to get her out of her clothes ... but his limbs were disobedient: light yet heavy, as if he both floated in water and was pinned to the bed. He was aware of his nakedness, of her hair falling over her face, brushing his skin, tingling, prickling.

He watched. Wanting her. Wanting more.

Slowly, slowly, she turned her face and she was Liza Reece, wearing that grin that he'd glimpsed: conspiratorial, mischievous, lighting her eyes. Blue eyes. Laughing. Small soft hands. Stroking.

Waiting.

He wanted to say, 'Don't stop!'

He wanted to rise up and over her and find her mouth with his.

He wanted her out of that damned green uniform so that he could explore her body, in turn. He was definitely a gentleman, like that.

He could smell—

And then he was sitting up in the darkness and Liza had gone. His heart was pounding, his body was throbbing, but he was alone except for the shape of Crosswind curled into his doggie beanbag on the floor. The rectangle of light that outlined his bedroom door was from the lamp that burned on the landing so that Ethan wouldn't be frightened if he woke in the night.

He was in Miranda's spare room.

'Damn.' He fell back onto the mattress. His heart was trotting and his skin damp. His groin was heavy. He flipped his pillow, closed his eyes and tried to fall back into the erotic, arousing world he'd just left, where Liza Reece worked him over with her soft, supple, knowing hands.

Those skilful fingers could read his feet … what could they do to the rest of him? He ached to find out.

But dreams weren't like that. His mind just fell into blackness.

Chapter Four

Tenzeds: I'm finding a career break difficult. Unless there's something to stimulate my interest, I can lose hours.

Nightjack: Set your alarms and get up at the same time every day, like you're at work. And if you're snoozy in the day, set your phone alerts to go off every half hour.

Sleepingmatt: Outdoors! Get out there.

Miranda's and Ethan's voices filled the kitchen as Dominic paced around the table, into the hall and back. After the noontime thirty-minute nap his neurological consultant recommended as "scheduled sleep" – Dominic, less clinically, called it catching zeds – he'd been refreshed. But, as the afternoon was wearing on, the now-familiar wooliness was trying to cloak his mind. *Resist it.*

Patiently, Crosswind paced after, nails clicking on the quarry tiles. Named for the fact that anything could happen when there was a Crosswind about, his square face, amber eyes, tan-patched body and upright tail were all fox terrier, but his sandy bandy legs betrayed a mixed marriage somewhere in his pedigree.

'Take you out after dinner,' promised Dominic, bending to ruffle the dog's wonkily folded ears. Crosswind had been all Dominic had bothered about holding onto as his relationship broke and failed. Natalie hadn't put up a fight. Crosswind knew who his human was.

Ethan's small-boy laughter burbled into the air and Crosswind turned to listen. Crosswind approved of Ethan, always good for a bit of needless charging around or a carelessly sported biscuit.

Ethan had lately joined a playgroup and was all high-pitched excitement about it. 'Dommynic!' he shouted as Dominic paced back into the kitchen, shouts being Ethan's usual conversational mode. 'Today I painted my hands, then I pressed yellow paper and every time it made a hand shape!'

Dominic grinned. 'Wow! Every time?' Ethan's pint-sized personality had kind of snuck up on him. Until Dominic had moved into the spare room of Miranda and her husband, Jos, Ethan had just been Miranda's kid; they'd met every few months and forgotten one another between times. But now he was coming to appreciate the developing brain, the entertaining child's eye view, the cute pronunciation, the importance of packing a red *Cars* backpack with 'stuff' for outings.

'Your hand's always hand-shaped, Ethan,' Miranda pointed out, reasonably, which somehow prompted Ethan, the natural enemy of silence, to thunder down the hall screaming, 'Cheee-arge!' Crosswind raced, barking, behind him.

In front of the Raeburn, Miranda stirred a sauce of tomatoes, courgettes, red cabbage and sweetcorn, a pan of pasta verde bubbling on the next burner. Mentally, Dominic sighed. Miranda was a great cook and he must be incredibly ungracious, but he just couldn't share her joy in vegetarianism, even if he knew that fruit and water-rich vegetables were great for energy levels. Pity Liza Reece hadn't agreed to have dinner with him. His mouth watered at the thought of a huge, overdone steak. Or a big, juicy mixed grill. With garlic bread. Bread made him drowsy but that didn't stop him wanting it.

His mouth watered at the thought of Liza Reece, too, but that was a waste of good saliva. He wouldn't be surprised if she'd rather eat rat salad alone than eat steak with him. He hoped it had more to do with the stupid remark she'd overheard than with his health or employment. Lack of. Or maybe he'd just opened up to her about the goblins too soon.

So that Miranda wouldn't think he was hanging around just to sound her out, Dominic began to set the table with three full-sized place settings and one smaller set, red, Ethan's 'favouritist' colour. 'So, what do you know about Liza Reece?'

Miranda gave him a malicious grin. 'Breasts about the size of grapefruit.'

He winced. 'I'm surprised she didn't call the police.' He took out the wooden pepper grinder from a cupboard – Miranda didn't believe in salt, which was another good reason to eat out, and soon.

'Actually, I only know her to chat to if I see her around the village. Hope Jos comes soon, the dinner's ready.' Miranda stirred the pasta, fished a twist out, blew on it, then popped it in her mouth. 'I'm friends with Liza's sister, Cleo, so I know that Liza was in a relationship that ended badly.' Reaching down the colander from its hook, she peeped at him questioningly over her glasses.

He put three plates to warm and fixed Ethan's red bowl to the table with the rubber sucker that stopped it from whizzing off under the stresses of inexpert chopping and shovelling. Crosswind, an expert at recognising behaviours, took up strategic station under the table. 'I asked her to dinner. She couldn't have turned me down flatter.'

'Dom! Are you nuts?' A cloud of steam enveloped Miranda as she plopped the colander into the sink and poured in the contents of the pasta pan.

'What?' Innocently.

'Tomorrow, you're going to meet the owner of The Stables

with a view to buying into it! It's a business – not a personal harem.'

He blinked in mock surprise. 'In that case, I'll have to reconsider.' Then he became serious. 'Miranda, you know and I know that I'm not going to buy into a holistic treatment centre – it's you that's into all the complementary stuff. It's just one of several business opportunities that the crap Peterbizop agency has waved under my nose, in a misdirected attempt to earn a commission. I'm only looking at The Stables because I like where it is, not what it is.

'Liza treated me like a predator, and now you are. Get over yourselves! She's hot and I'm single. The whole point about being single is that I can date anyone I want. Except if I've offended her with "macho bullshit", of course,' he added, reflectively.

Miranda laughed, wiping steam from her glasses with her cuff. 'Actually, I think Cleo mentioned that Liza's on some kind of celibacy kick. Cleo thought it was stupid – completely foreign to Liza's personality.'

He winced. 'And a crime against nature. She's amazing.'

'She's an intelligent and capable young woman,' said Miranda, severely, as if Liza being amazing was something it was not politically correct for Dominic to notice. Then her voice softened. 'Aren't you interested in the treatment centre, really, Dom? It would be fantastic to have you living nearby.'

'Thanks,' he said, neutrally. Of course, Miranda intended to train in therapy when Ethan was older and so Dominic having a therapy centre would be convenient. Before motherhood she'd had an incredibly sensible – read: soul-destroying – job as a supervisor in a call centre, and had no intention of returning to it after a career break in which she'd embraced all things holistic, complementary, green, alternative or conservationist. But Miranda also had mother-hen tendencies and he hoped she didn't want him nearby so that she could cluck over him, because, much as he appreciated her, another benefit of being single was avoiding conversations that began, 'How are you?' and progressed through, 'Taking your meds? How difficult are the mornings? How hard is the daytime sleep hitting you?'

'Miranda,' he began. He paused to soften his tone; she didn't know about all the irritating things she'd just said in his head. 'Mi, I've lost my ATCO licence, my driving licence has been suspended, my GP won't pass me medically fit for scuba until "we've had a good look at how you go on" – and I can't imagine an insurance company wanting to cover me or a divemaster wanting to take me down – and almost all my friends were in aviation, my lost world. It's incredibly nice of you to want me living locally and invite me to stay while I try and sort myself out, but I'm not going to shoehorn myself into some touchy-feely business that so isn't me. Can you really see me as part of the new age music and pretty uniforms?'

Miranda tipped a tiny amount of sauce onto a teaspoon, to taste it. 'I didn't think the uniform was particularly pretty. And not all your mates are in aviation. What about Kenny King?' Kenny was Dominic's oldest and quirkiest friend, the yin to Dominic's yang, Dominic excelling at maths, science and technology and Kenny compensating for his dyslexia with superhero performance on the sports field. Being brought up within a few streets of both Dominic and Kenny, Miranda had known larger-than-life Kenny King since childhood.

'Yeah,' said Dominic. Pulling out a kitchen chair, he dropped into it. 'What about Kenny? An Outward Bound instructor in North Carolina, every day a new adventure. Loving life and getting paid.'

Miranda halted, spoon halfway from her mouth, eyes full

of compassion. 'Sorry. I'm so used to you being stubborn that I forget that sometimes you might have a point. I'll shut up about you buying into the treatment centre. The premises are in a fantastic spot, though, aren't they? Must be a lovely leafy place to spend your days. Fantastic views.' She lifted her voice. 'Eth-an, din-ner!'

'Couldn't agree more. Although I'm more interested in actually being outside than just looking at it.'

'You outdoorsy guys. It's not enough just to stroll around the park in your lunch breaks?' She grinned as Ethan raced in, 'Cheee-arge!', Crosswind skittering to meet him and escort him to his chair. 'Would you put Ethan on his booster seat, for me?' She took down the plates with a tea towel.

Swinging Ethan up, Dominic didn't bother reminding Miranda that being outdoors made it easier for him to be alert. 'C'mon, Ethan, bend.' Ethan had a strange habit of making himself the wrong shape for the seat by pointing his toes and sticking his legs straight down, like a human golf tee. Dominic's training having involved a lot of problem solving, he simply tickled Ethan's legs to make him giggle his knees up to his chest, *'Eep!'*

Miranda made sure Ethan's food was in manageable pieces before putting it before him with an affectionate pat to his round cheek. 'But I am sad if you're still prejudiced against alternative therapies, Dom.'

'I'm never prejudiced, it's unscientific.'

'Didn't you enjoy the treatments?'

Dominic took the chair next to Ethan's and prepared to help him dig pasta out of his red bowl with his red spoon. Beneath the table, Crosswind edged closer. 'I didn't enjoy the ear candling nonsense.' Dominic laughed as he watched Ethan tutting over the challenge of capturing pasta on a spoon. 'Use your fingers, Ethan, it's more efficient. I did enjoy the reflexology.' Oh yeahhhhh …

'Yes, well, Liza's a lot prettier than Fenella.' Miranda ladled pasta and sauce onto the rest of the plates.

And then Crosswind barked and whirled to face the back door an instant before Jos, dark hair tied at the nape of his neck, walked in, bringing with him the scents of rain and engine oil. Crosswind woofed and wagged and Ethan squealed, 'Daddee! Dad-deeeee!'

'Hey, my little Ethan!' Jos made a kissy noise at Crosswind and grabbed Ethan up for a cuddle, dislodging several pasta twists from various nooks, which Crosswind snaffled before they could even bounce.

'Hiya, Jossy!' Miranda gave her doe-eyed husband a dazzling smile, a soft kiss on the lips and a plate in his hand in a flowing series of movements, and the subject of Liza Reece was forgotten.

Except by Dominic.

Chapter Five

PWNsleep message board:

Tenzeds: I want to just sleep without my brain talking to itself. Dreams are vivid and weird right now.

Inthebatcave: Lucky you! I get dreams that are mainly dull ☺ But dropping really quickly into REM sleep is what makes our dreams difficult to tell from reality.

His new alarm clock was shrieking, *beeee-beeee-beeee-beeee*. He slapped at the black plastic box until he hit something that stopped the racket.

In the silence, he jumped up, threw on a sweatshirt with his boxers and padded along the landing to where a small white goat watched him with malevolent eyes. Natalie stood with a hand on the goat's curling left horn, staring, her hair a sheet of silk over one shoulder. Every nail on every finger was inches long and bleeding. Apprehension broke sweatily on his chest and put pressure on his lungs. His breathing faltered—

Brrrrrrr! The next alarm. Ringing. Drilling into his ear. 'Shit.' Landing, goat and Natalie flickered as he dragged himself towards wakefulness. The weight on his chest stood up and became Crosswind, and Dominic tamped down the now familiar wave of frustration as he realised he'd sunk back into sleep after the first alarm and not jumped out of bed at all.

He tried to haul an un-cooperative arm free from a ton-weight quilt. A snuffling cold nose touched his chin and the prospect of being French kissed by Crosswind gave Dominic the incentive to heave his upper body sideways from the bed.

Gravity took over and he banged uncomfortably onto the carpet. Crosswind landed lightly beside him, giving him a 'job done' lick on the ear and running to the bedroom door. Rolling onto his side, Dominic fought against the warm fuzzies coming back to shove him under. The alarm was still blaring. The carpet had grazed his knee. But, on some level, he was awake.

A knock fell on his bedroom door. 'Dom?'

'Um up,' he managed, thickly.

'You're up? OK.' Then, 'But your alarm—'

He forced his arm into the air and finally landed it on the big blue clock button with all the dexterity of a baby trying to play Pin the Tail on the Donkey. The *brrrrrr* stopped. 'Goddit.'

A pause. 'Are you still up?' Miranda's voice was muffled, through the door.

'Yeah.' *Just leave me alone a minute for FUCKSAKE!* But he didn't let the anger become real words. It wasn't Miranda's fault that mornings could be so miserable. Crosswind scratched the door and whined.

'Shall I let him out into the garden?'

Slowly, his stone legs began to flex. 'I'll do it. Thanks.' *In a minute*. Gradually, Dominic forced himself to his knees and onto his feet, checked that he was really wearing boxers, pulled the sweatshirt he'd left out last night over his top half, and fumbled with the blister packs he kept on a shelf out of reach of Ethan for his first tablets of the day, one yellow, one white. Swallowed the yellow one, dropped the white one on the bed. Sucked it up directly from the sheet. Waited, whilst his head cleared some more, and opened the bedroom door. Crosswind whipped past and galloped downstairs.

Miranda was lingering on the landing, her eyes smiling through her specs. 'I don't mind letting him out for you if—'

Battling the impulse to snap, 'I'LL DO IT!', when snapping

would probably be impossible, anyway, he managed, 'Um fine. Ull do it.' And, ignoring his own need for the bathroom, he followed Crosswind past where the last tendrils of his dream still wanted to put the goat and Natalie, holding on to the handrail as he persuaded his gradually co-operating feet to take the stairs.

Ethan shouted, ''Lo Dommynic!' from amongst the toy-car traffic jam he was happily creating on the floor in the sitting-room doorway.

''Lo, Ethan.' Dominic trod his feet into the trainers he'd left in the hall before attempting the frozen wastes of the kitchen's quarry tiled floor. Pushing open the back door, he knew he was really awake when a frozen blast of rain slapped into him. '*Whooh*, shit!' He checked behind him to see if Miranda had heard him swear within Ethan range. Nope. Safe. He turned back to the frigid morning. He could have sheltered behind the door while Crosswind cocked his leg over Miranda's statue of the green man, but, instead, he let the wind sear the sleep from his mind and dispel the remnants of anger that something as simple as getting up in the morning should feel like struggling out from under a hot, heavy monster.

OK. Brain was engaging. Today was Thursday and he had an appointment with Nicolas Notten of The Stables at half-ten, which created welcome feelings of focus and anticipation. He turned to check the kitchen clock: eight-fifteen. So far, so good. He had something to do and he was awake in time to do it. Result. His aggravation with the getting-up process began to subside.

The leather of his trainers chilled his sockless feet as he reviewed his situation. Peterbizop had proved to have an inadequate level of personal service behind their flashy website, the agency/client interaction consisting of e-mail and telephone contact. Empathy and common sense were absent as other businesses they'd suggested included rodent control and modular building erection – don't think so.

But perhaps they'd inadvertently done him a favour, reinforcing what he'd long suspected: he'd have to start his business from the idea up. He tingled with the need to find something to replace the precise, focused and rarefied atmosphere of the air traffic control tower. He'd taken courses in business start up, management and finance. Now he was bursting to put what he'd learned into practice, to create something worthwhile. What he'd done at The Stables so far had been time inefficient, but today that might just change.

By the time Miranda had walked Ethan across the playing field to the village hall for playgroup and Dominic had taken Crosswind for a run, showered and dressed in something approximating office clothes, the appointment with Nicolas Notten was approaching. Miranda had dusted off a dress and jacket that were not ethnic print and, whisking her mouse brown hair up in a bronze butterfly thing behind her head, looked as if she attended business meetings every day. Dominic felt a twinge of regret that he wasn't going to be able to buy into the treatment centre, a ready-made opportunity for Miranda to begin the new career she saw for herself in her not-too-distant future. He smiled at her calmly, although he was feeling an unexpected humming of his nerves. 'All set?'

Beaming, she jingled her car keys. 'Let's go.'

It was less than a ten-minute drive to the black iron gates of Port Manor Hotel. Once through, Miranda following a white signpost, swung her car left off the wide hotel driveway, taking a smaller track, curving uphill under the green light of a tunnel of trees. After half a mile, they returned to sunlight at the rear of the hotel, greensward running either side.

Perched on a crest, in the days when Port Manor had been the residence of some minor aristocrat and The Stables had been the stables, they would have been sufficiently distant for the smell of horse not to sully the house.

The buildings edged three sides of the stable yard. On the fourth, the park swooped down towards a lake that reflected a coppice and racing grey clouds. Beyond, the countryside raked uphill again until it met the sky. Dominic paused on the rim of that giant, green, grassy bowl for a big beautiful blast of fresh air. Maybe that's why it was called 'the great outdoors' – because being there could make him feel great. He'd love to put a kayak on that lake and practise rolls. He could almost feel the water, cool and silky—

'*Eek*! Wind!' complained Miranda, clamping both her hands over her hair.

'You're such a girl.' The imaginary kayak vanished from the ruffled lake and Dominic followed his cousin into The Stables's reception area, with its counter and three chairs, manned, as it had been the day before, by a gangly girl who looked too young to be anybody's front-desk presence. She regarded Dominic and Miranda with a hint of surprise. 'Hello, again.' Her gaze flicked to her computer monitor, as if to match them to one of that morning's bookings.

Dominic smiled. 'Nicolas Notten's expecting us.'

'OK, Pippa, I'm here.' A lank-haired man in his early forties barrelled down the corridor, oily face split by a grin of welcome, hand extended. Dominic shook it, introduced Miranda, and resisted the impulse to wipe his palm on his trousers.

'Why don't we go into my office?' Nicolas beamed.

Dominic followed Miranda and Nicolas, crossing the spot where, yesterday, Liza Reece had left him standing like a buffoon. The door to her treatment room was shut and he wondered whether she was behind it, bringing bliss to some other lucky bastard's feet. In the office, he took the seat nearest the door, a blue vinyl-covered chair that wheezed when he sat on it, and waited through the ritual of Nicolas offering coffee and Miranda's, 'Do you have any herbal tea?'

'I think the girls keep camomile in the kitchen.' Nicolas beamed again, rubbing his hands as he bustled his bulk back out through the door.

'I'll stick with coffee,' Dominic called after him. 'Strong, if possible.' Dominic grinned at Miranda, knowing Nicolas had gained no points with her for referring to adult females as 'girls'.

A few minutes later, Nicolas returned on a whoosh of words. 'Here we are, here we are, here we are!' He deposited three steaming mugs on the desk and plumped down in his seat. 'What I'd like to tell you about The Stables is—'

Armed with his shot of caffeine, Dominic sat back to listen as an obviously prepared pitch spooled out. And out. For a heart-sinking hour. Although he was beginning to feel guilty at how far Nicolas seemed to have got his hopes up, it would have taken a harder heart than his not to hear him out.

Miranda, who, no matter how much of a force she was in her own home had never got over a childhood shyness with strangers, contributed nothing. The office was overheated. Dominic opened the door to let in fresh air, glad that he'd set his phone alert to go off twice in case he got sluggish. Rising on the pretext of depositing his empty mug on the desk, he remained standing, to keep his head clear. 'So, how is your income generated?' he put in, when Nicolas paused to sip his lukewarm coffee.

Nicolas folded his hands. 'Each therapist pays me rent for their treatment room and a small commission on every treatment.' He moved smoothly into a practised speech about how an injection of working capital would revitalise the business, replenish the promotion budget and encourage the business to make a profit.

'How, exactly?' Dominic pressed.

Nicolas's hands tightened. 'With the, um, greater promotional budget to, er, bring in more clients to each therapist, so building commission.'

Dominic began to feel a bit sorry for Nicolas, so nervous, so transparently desperately searching for funds with no real idea how to plug the leaks through which money was gushing. But he felt even sorrier for everybody who worked at the treatment centre, as Nicolas's hopelessly unrealistic outpouring made it ever clearer that his business enterprise was doomed. He was chin-deep in financial sewage. And, any moment, someone was going to come by in a speedboat.

Still, Dominic's agenda prompted him to say, 'Yes, please,' when Nicolas heaved himself from behind his desk and offered to show them around The Stables.

First port of call was the room in which Dominic had met Liza Reece, yesterday. Without knocking, Nicolas thrust the door open. 'This is one of our treatment rooms.' Dominic's skin prickled at a flash vision of white hands on his feet.

'We have three treatment rooms – the other two are in use but are similar.' Nicolas listed all the therapies the centre offered, which he'd said at least eight times already, and waffled about equipment, which, so far as Dominic could see, wasn't much: the couch, two chairs, a desk and a trolley. As Nicolas talked, Dominic's gaze ran along a row of framed certificates on the wall, each bearing the name of Liza Reece: maternity reflexology, baby reflexology, vertical reflexology and foot reading.

Nicolas was already moving on, towards the other wing of the building. 'Back through reception, we have the staff room, kitchen and cloakrooms.'

Dominic's interest was caught. 'Does the kitchen need to

be so large?' The square room accommodated a washing machine, dryer, hob, microwave and fridge, with acres to spare.

Nicolas beamed proudly. 'It was all in place before my time here. The hotel converted the stables with the idea of creating a spa, with a pool, hot tub and everything. Then they decided the economic climate wasn't right so looked for someone to lease the premises and run a facility that would be an added attraction for the hotel.' He swelled a little. 'Mine was the successful proposal.'

Dominic processed the layout of the building through his mind. 'Where would they have put a pool and a hot tub?'

'The pool was going to be dug behind, on the other side to the stable yard. The hot tub was to go in the wing I didn't take on. There are showers and changing cubicles,' he took a few steps to the end of the corridor and rapped on a door, 'just behind this.'

Slowly, Dominic nodded. 'So the empty part could be leased from the hotel, too?'

'So far as I know, yes.' Nicolas shuffled his feet, the beginnings of bliss dawning on his round face. 'Were you— were you thinking of putting in enough money to expand? Gosh, that's something to talk about.'

The moment of truth was obviously arriving at a gallop. Dominic jammed his hands in his pockets and sighed. 'I think that's too much to hope for. Shall we continue this conversation in your office?'

But the damage was done. Nicolas bounded back to his room, throwing an airy request for more coffee and camomile tea at Pippa, rattling on about always wanting to do more with the place but needing the investment.

Finally, when Pippa had delivered a tray of gaily spotted china mugs, Dominic had to interrupt. 'Nicolas, hang on a minute.'

Nicolas halted, mid-sentence, glancing between Dominic and Miranda.

Dominic hesitated. None of his courses had armed him with the kindest way to crush hopes.

But Nicolas was nodding understandingly, a smile lifting his jowls. 'I think I already know what's worrying you – you can't see a place here for your partner.' He beamed at Miranda, who had worn a speaking expression of wistful longing during the tour.

Taken aback, Dominic said, 'Partner?'

Nicolas tapped his nose. 'The guys at Peterbizop made me aware of the situation and I've already taken steps. Things are a bit rocky with one of the therapists, so I've given her notice that she has to relocate her practice.' He beamed at Miranda. 'The treatment room right across the hall, the one we looked at, would be yours. What are your therapies? Something that isn't already offered by the others would be best, of course.'

'What?' In her shock, Miranda found her voice.

Nicolas began to repeat himself, but Dominic cut across him. 'Wait. I had a treatment with a therapist in that room, yesterday – Liza.'

Nicolas, nodding, 'That's ri—'

'And you've sacked her?'

'Well, no.' Nicolas laughed. 'I can't sack somebody that I don't employ. I've just given her notice to relocate her practice.'

'Why?' Dominic and Miranda demanded, in unison.

Nicolas's brow creased uncertainly. 'I don't wish to be unsympathetic because Liza has had some difficulties in her personal life. But something happened, yesterday, that gave me the opportunity to give her notice.' He picked up a copy of the details emblazoned with the red logo of Peterbizop Agency. 'I have explained, and it does say in here, that all the therapists are self-employed.' He glanced apologetically at Miranda. 'The only person I directly employ is young Pippa. Each therapist pays a premium on her rent to cover Pippa's wages—'

'Why?' Dominic repeated.

Nicolas looked up questioningly.

'Why did you give Liza Reece notice?'

'Well.' Nicolas folded his hands. 'Let's just say ... it was a straw that broke the camel's back situation.'

'Did it involve a client?'

Nicolas's brow lifted, as if grateful for Dominic's understanding. 'I'm afraid so, yes.'

Oh crap. Dominic rose, glad to leave the unpleasant vinyl chair. The furniture seemed to have its own sweat glands; no wonder Nicolas looked as if he'd just left a sauna. 'OK,' he said. 'Let's move on to why you think my cousin is my "partner" and that she wants to come here as a therapist? Or even that she is a therapist?'

'Cousin? The guy at Peterbizop called her your partner.' Nicolas blinked.

Dominic turned to Miranda. Eyes wide, she shrugged. 'When he rang when you were asleep, I did tell him what I've told you – that I'd love to train in a couple of years, when Ethan's at school. I suppose he could have assumed that because we're living in the same house, we're in a relationship.'

Nicolas cleared his throat. 'Peterbizop rang to run through the possibilities. You know, they,' he cleared his throat again, 'help you to prepare. To explore scenarios and have answers ready to likely questions. He said it was in the notes he'd been given by his colleague that Miranda wanted into the business, as a therapist,' he added, with an air of injury. 'He encouraged me to have a solution ready, because that kind of thing could be a deal breaker.'

Dominic snorted. 'Sounds as if the staff at Peterbizop make up what they forget to put in their notes. I can't believe you gave Liza Reece notice on such a bogus pretext.' He jammed his hands in his pockets and, feeling less need to be careful of Nicolas's sensitivities, continued, 'I'm afraid we're wasting each other's time. I can't see that there's an income to be made, here. I'm sorry.'

Bewildered, Nicolas clambered to his feet. 'I've obviously been fed duff information and if I've done the wrong thing about Liza, we could always tell her she can stay—'

'You have done the wrong thing and you should tell her that she can stay, but it doesn't make any difference. I'm not able to invest in your business. Coming, Miranda?'

Outside, Dominic breathed in deeply of the fresh air. He checked that Nicolas hadn't followed them into the stable yard. 'Oily little oik.'

Miranda's eyes were guilty. 'I'm sorry if I said anything that has made things difficult for you, Dom.'

'It's not your fault! But Liza Reece must want to eviscerate me.' He paused as a titchy black-and-purple car swept up and halted beside the building. 'Great,' he sighed. 'I think we're about to find out.' The sound of the car door echoed around the stable yard and Liza Reece headed towards reception, pink skinny jeans and blue sequined trainers showing beneath her jacket, with no sign of the clinical dark green. She began to smile. Then she saw who it was and stopped dead.

For several seconds, Dominic and Liza gazed at one another. Her eyes widened and he was caught, baked in her gaze. Her soft lips parted. She was hot. Hotter than hot. Hotter than he'd remembered. Imagined. Dreamed … his dream of her working her way up his body floated gently through his mind, and he smiled, forgetting for half a heartbeat that it hadn't been real.

Warily, she stepped closer, so obviously squaring her shoulders to attack a job that had to be done that he almost laughed as he snapped back to reality. 'I suppose I owe you an apology for yesterday. Sorry.'

Dominic had seldom heard anyone sound less sorry. 'I owe you one in return. Nicolas stupid Notten's just told me he's asked you to relocate your practice – and I'm afraid it's all down to me being so outrageous as to ask you out.'

She flushed. 'He considers the whole thing my fault, not yours.' With an obvious effort, she added, 'He has a point.'

'But he might be prepared to reconsider, now because—'

She made an impatient gesture. 'It would have happened sooner or later. Things aren't working that well for me here. Got to go. I have a client at two.' She checked her watch and started toward the door.

'Wait!' he protested. 'There's more I have to tell you.'

'What?' Her baby-doll blue eyes flicked from him to Miranda and then back to her watch.

'I think we could usefully exchange information. Is it too much of a cheek to ask to meet you, later?'

'I'm booked through until nine.'

'I could pick you up after your last client— Oh, shit. No driving licence.' He felt his face burn, as if his licence being suspended was his fault. Losing the use of his car had been like losing a limb. He took a breath. Calm, Dominic. It's not your fault. Work around it. 'How about I meet you at that pub in Middledip, on Main Road?'

A glimmer of sympathy had dawned in her eyes when he mentioned his licence, or lack of, but her shrug was still ungracious. 'The Three Fishes? I suppose so.'

He tried his best slow smile, right into her eyes. 'I won't mention the word "dinner" in case it triggers your fight-or-flight response, but I'll be eating. I'm really not shy but I don't like to eat alone so it would be great if you'd eat, too.'

She didn't smile back. 'I noticed you're not shy.' A blue Golf whizzed into the stable yard. 'Here's my client. See you just after nine.'

It was good to be busy, helping people to relax and seeing the lines and puckers fade from their faces as she set her sensitive fingers to searching out the gritty, bubbly areas of their feet.

After her last client, Liza washed her hands, stuffed her towels into the washing machine and prepared to file the day's notes. She'd just posted a Newton Faulkner disc into the stereo and opened her filing cabinet when Nicolas slid around the door. She sighed.

He hunched his round shoulders. 'I've been thinking, Liza. I feel bad about blowing up at you, last night. We're all under a lot of stress.'

Oh, really? She gave him a thoughtful stare. Sweating, fidgeting, Nicolas showed all the signs of a man in a bit of a spot.

He shuffled further into the room. He wore a smile, but his eyes were unhappy. 'You know I wouldn't really chuck you out, don't you?'

The beginnings of relief washed through her. If she wasn't being ousted, then some of the pressure was off her whilst she decided what to do next. She cocked her head. 'But aren't I too unpleasant for everyone to work with?'

His laugh was forced. 'I didn't say that! Or, if I did, I was angry and I probably said too much.'

'No luck with the investors?'

His smile stayed pinned in place. 'Early days, early days.'

Slowly, she closed the filing cabinet drawer. Such a feeble justification for this about-face brought with it a whiff of rodent. 'Have Imogen and Fenella finished with their clients?'

'I don't—'

'Let's see.' Dodging past him, she whisked down to reception. 'Pippa! Have Fenella and Imogen finished their evening sessions?'

Pippa was already zipping herself into her coat, hooking her ponytail out of the collar. 'Yup, all the clients have gone.'

'Good. Can you just hang on a sec? And you, Nicolas.'

'But—!'

'Won't take a moment.' With a brilliant smile at Nicolas, Liza shot off in search of Fen and Immi and vitally illuminating feedback.

Once everyone was assembled, still in the despised forest green tunics and white shoes, Liza turned to face them, clasping her hands and assuming what she hoped was a desolate expression. 'I'm really sorry,' she began. 'I had no idea I was being so horrible to you all and now it's been pointed out to me, I feel awful. Nicolas has given me the chance to stay at the centre, but I don't feel I can unless you guys are all OK with it. It wouldn't be fair. I apologise for my behaviour, of course.'

Silence.

Nicolas shone with sweat. 'Well—'

Imogen's dark hair was threaded artfully into a beaded circlet at the back of her head. She tucked away an escaping tendril, frowning. 'When were you horrible?'

Fenella gave a bemused shake of her head. 'What do you mean, "a chance to stay"?'

Pippa just looked confused.

Liza gazed around, as if in surprise. 'Nicolas explained that I've been upsetting everyone; that I go too far with my friendly insults. He didn't seem to think he had much choice but to ask me to go.' Then watched, with satisfaction, three pairs of astonished eyes swivel towards Nicolas.

Nicolas backed up like a cornered fox. 'I may have overreacted to something Liza said to a client.'

'Liza's had a hard time, she's a bit sad sometimes, but I don't remember her insulting me.' Fenella folded her arms.

'Me, neither,' Imogen agreed.

'I may have blown the incident up.'

Liza gazed at him. He shuffled. Finally, he muttered, 'Sorry.'

And all there was left for Liza to do was heave pretend sighs and hug, kiss and thank everyone in turn as they reassured her. Except Nicolas. Nicolas just gave her a look that seemed to say he knew perfectly well he'd been punished.

Now all she had to do was work out why she'd had to do it.

Chapter Six

PWNsleep message board:

Nightjack: Yesterday evening was so crap. I was talking to a hot girl and I couldn't clear my head. She must have thought I wasn't into her at all.

Inthebatcave: Would it work to take your meds a bit later, to keep you with it, if you know you're going to be out late?

Nightjack: Yeah, but I hadn't known I would be. It was, like, a developing situation ... ☺

Tenzeds: Were you really that into her, if her conversation didn't keep you alert? Talking to a woman I like has definitely kept my eyes open, so far ... ☺ But it's scary to think it might not.

Liza, huddling into her jacket, was grateful to step into the beery warmth of The Three Fishes after the raw autumn chill of the evening. Locals gathered near the bar and grouped around the tables under the darkened beams. A blazing log fire danced its welcome with the cosy smell of wood smoke. And it was inexplicably comforting to find Dominic Christy lounging at a brass-covered table, his jacket a similar harvest-gold to his streaky hair. His glance was a flash of silver.

She dropped into the chair across from him. 'Bloody Nicolas! Did you think I wasn't coming?'

His smile was slow and lazy, tugging suddenly at her insides. 'The possibility occurred. If you want to eat, we need to order right away and there are only three things we can have this late: chicken korma, goat's cheese and pear salad or tuna pasta bake.'

'Is the korma with white rice or brown rice?'

He rolled his eyes. 'You're not going to go all Miranda on me and extol the virtues of brown rice?'

She sighed. 'But it is better for cholesterol, energy … Never mind. I'll have the korma, please, I'm starving. And one of those passion-fruit-and-pomegranate drinks.'

Whilst Dominic ordered at the bar, Liza hung her ski jacket around the back of her chair, rubbing her hands, wishing he'd chosen a table nearer the fire. She glanced around, smiling and waving at people she knew, enjoying the gentle buzz of conversation, the occasional laugh, the crackle of the fire. Three men at the next table, flushed with alcohol, halted their conversation to look her over. One sent her a wink. She acknowledged him with a tiny smile. Angie and Rochelle may have been right that she needed to put some life back in her life, but red-faced pub bugs had never been her type.

Dominic returned and slid two glasses onto the table. His held Guinness. 'Bloody Nicolas what?'

'Bloody Nicolas came to talk just as I was leaving.' She sipped at the drink, sweet and tart together.

'Let me guess.' He drank from his black beer, returning it to the circle of moisture it had left on the table. 'He's reconsidered giving you notice on your treatment room?'

She propped her chin on her fist. 'Good guess. Now it's my turn – you and Miranda are the investors he'd arranged to meet today? That's why you were leaving as I arrived?'

He was nodding before she'd finished speaking.

What did that mean? Where did he fit into her picture? 'You haven't opted in yet, and he's realised he needs my rent a while longer?'

'I'm not opting in with him at all.' His grey gaze was steady. 'He got some dodgy information from the business opportunity agency that made him think I'd make bringing Miranda in as a therapist a condition of my investment.'

'So he put me on notice in case he had to get me out to make way for her, knowing he could pretend a change of heart if he needed to?' A lick of anger. 'But Miranda's not even a therapist.'

'Nope. I've delisted from the agency, because it's obviously staffed by monkeys and gibbons, quite unable to understand the concept of losing a dream job and having to find a new one. I'm glad Nicolas isn't turfing you out.'

'It does make life easier.' She blew out her cheeks. Last night she'd tossed and turned over whether to find a treatment room in Peterborough, where population would be dense and trade more plentiful but she'd have a fifteen-mile drive each way, or to try to drum up enough business around the villages. It would mean being a mobile, as Mrs. Horrible Snelling might report her or object or whatever it was you did to stop people if they tried to trade from home. And she didn't know anyone who was making being a mobile pay as a full-time business. 'It's nice not to be up against a deadline, but it doesn't solve the underlying problems.'

His gaze was thoughtful, focused. 'I presumed from what you said this afternoon that there are some. Am I allowed to ask what those problems are?' His eyes smiled. 'I do have a reason for asking.'

She shrugged. 'When I moved out of Peterborough I knew I'd lose existing clients, but there was supposed to be a flood of guests from the hotel to more than make up. But it's been more of a trickle than a flood and, of course, many are only around long enough for single treatments. But the premises are fabulous and I keep on at Nicolas that we need to get creative to capitalise on them. We need new ideas and I've got loads. But he only has to hear the word "new" and his mind clangs shut.'

She paused as Janice from behind the bar brought two steaming oval plates of fragrant curry on fluffy pillows of rice – white – with hot naan bread on the side. Dominic thanked her with a smile. Janice smiled back in a way that suggested that, although she had two decades on Dominic, she wasn't impervious to his charms.

Liza propped her head on her hand. 'Suddenly I'm not certain whether I'm starving hungry or can't eat for worry.'

'Still trying to get out of having dinner with me?' He assumed an expression of injury.

She managed a sort of laugh and stripped the paper napkin from her cutlery. 'Being credit crunched isn't good for the appetite.' Which she proved when she pushed away her plate with half the food still remaining. She waited until he'd cleaned his plate before picking up the conversation. 'So. Are you going to share your reason for asking about my problems?'

Leaning back, he stretched his legs out beside the table. 'I need to find a new career. Narcolepsy has made certain options no longer viable, including shift work, which would turn me into a zombie. Becoming self-employed seems a good way to go. It makes it easier to schedule my sleeping pattern and I've always enjoyed leading projects.' He smiled crookedly. 'Miranda wanted me to give The Stables a look.'

'So you did and you hated it,' she supplemented, drily. 'I think I got that.'

'I'm certainly not tempted to train as a therapist.' He stared pensively at his drink, making patterns in the condensation with the pad of his thumb.

She waited, thinking, absently, how unlike Adam he was. No endless patience or gentle light of adoration in this man's face. Dominic's habitual expressions were determination, laughter or thoughtfulness. But at least what showed on his face seemed real.

Whereas, Adam's adoration had disguised the mechanisms he employed to make things what he'd like them to be …

Resolutely, she dragged her attention back to the moment.

'So why the need for information about The Stables, if you hate the idea of being involved?'

He fixed her with his grey gaze. 'It's only reasonable to research an idea before accepting, rejecting or modifying it. There are some things I don't understand. Like, how does Nicolas make any money out of the place?'

Janice returned to clear the plates. Dominic asked for water. Liza ordered coffee. 'I think your question ought to be, "Does Nicolas make any money out of the place?"'

He sat up, planting his elbows on the table. His phone sounded an alert and he fished it from his jacket pocket and silenced it impatiently. 'Does he?'

She shook her head. 'Not enough, I don't think.' It probably wasn't ethical for her to publicly paw through Nicolas's business, but neither had been giving her notice in case he could move a new therapist in. 'I'd been living and working in Peterborough, but my sister lives in Middledip and I wanted to move to the village. The hotel wanted a treatment centre, Nicolas took up the lease and advertised the rooms. The premises were great, and I fell for Nicolas's rosy view of the future. I suppose it didn't occur to me that he could get it quite so wrong. I should have been like you – all research and logical. I'm learning the hard way.'

Her coffee arrived. 'I suppose,' she continued, slowly, scooping up the spinning-froth island on her teaspoon before licking it off, 'that Nicolas is basically lazy. He wants the traditional model of obliging clients who make appointments, turn up for treatments, pay and book again. But there just aren't enough.

'I – and Fenella and Imogen – suggested bridal pampers, hen parties, new treatments and stuff, but he says they're not true to the ethos of alternative medicine. They're crossing over into beauty treatments and gimmicks.' She gave a sniff. 'Frankly, we're prepared to sacrifice his principles to make a living but it's in our agreements that he makes the decisions about the centre as a whole. Which is why we're all wearing those gross green NHS reject tunics.'

She sipped at the hot, sweet coffee and noticed his gaze fall to her lips as she licked away the froth. Maybe he was regretting ordering water but, too bad, she didn't allow herself much skin-dulling caffeine and she wasn't sharing. 'Also,' she continued, 'Nicolas doesn't bring any money to the party; he just wants to take it out.'

His gaze shifted to her eyes. 'Clarify?'

Rather than being irritated by the way he rapped the word out, she found herself admiring his focus on the conversation. It felt good, to be listened to as if every word was of vital importance, and a stark contrast to the way Nicolas dismissed everything she said. She liked intensity, she decided. She liked this man, brushed by gold under the lights from the bar, his intellect almost a palpable thing, his attention all on her. 'He's not a therapist. He doesn't have clients. What we pay him buys us the use of the general facilities – the building, the electricity, water and the receptionist, Pippa, though I've never known another centre with a receptionist to make appointments and show clients into the treatment rooms. It's a luxury. Most therapists use voicemail and return calls to manage appointments. And Nicolas draws a salary, too. He sits in his office and does the admin but that doesn't bring in fees. To run Nicolas's kind of operation would need the clients and prices you see at a top-end spa. I wish the hotel had made the stables a spa, as they planned, and we'd rented the rooms from them. They could have sold spa breaks and attracted the upscale clientele that would expect those kinds of fees. Right now, things are not working out for Nicolas and not working out for us.' Dominic was so still as he listened that she flushed, suddenly self-conscious. 'Sorry, I must be boring you to death.'

'No.' He stirred only to down the last of his water, not removing his gaze from her. 'It's not boring. What you're saying fits in with what I observed. Nicolas seems to have a novel view of business. He's got nothing to offer and apparently thinks an investor is an angel who'll swoop by with a briefcase full of money, mysteriously providing the therapists with so many clients that he'll be raking in the dosh.'

Liza let out an inelegant snort.

'What do you think will happen to the centre? And to you and the other therapists?'

For a moment, she let her eyes shut against the spectres of a dwindling client list, dwindling income, her car and house gurgling away down a great economic plughole. 'I don't know about Immi and Fenella but I intend to start looking for better premises after Christmas and hope to limp along until they're found. Unless Nicolas gets to the stage where he can't make his rent. In which case we all shut down.'

He nodded. 'So you've got to relocate, whatever? There's no chance of you making things work with Nicolas?'

'I don't see one. But at least I can do it at my own pace now Nicolas isn't giving me notice.' Liza finished her coffee and smothered a yawn. Many of the locals had drifted off and Janice was washing glasses. Tubb, the landlord, came through from the mysterious area only ever referred to as 'the back', assessed the scene through narrowed eyes, checked his watch and said something to Janice. Probably that he was going to watch Sky Sports and she could ring last orders and cash up. 'Being self-employed has its drawbacks,' she mused. 'I sympathise with your medical needs but running your own business seems a long way from the career you've been used to, with paid holidays and sick days and never having to go out and find business.

'There will be no guaranteed pay cheque at the end of

the month. Nobody to do your work when you're away. Bank holidays might be a thing of the past. Whatever your business is, you have to make that product or service sell, collect the money and do all the paperwork.'

He grinned. 'But I like a challenge. I'm sure I can make a business work – it's just a case of finding the right business.'

Chapter Seven

Liza had agreed to meet Rochelle and Angie in Peterborough at a wine bar on Friday evening.

'I know that pubs are in your comfort zone, but they're too weekday,' Rochelle had pre-empted her protests. 'Friday counts as the weekend. It's only Ruby's on Thorpe Road. That's not even properly in the city, Liza, and it does food so it's not binge drinky. Don't worry – we won't make you enjoy yourself too much.'

At least Liza knew where there was parking on Thorpe Road. And it was good to wear something other than her uniform or jeans, even if she'd gone for a cover-up, but mildly sexy, option of musketeer boots with silky leggings and a floaty blue-checked overshirt with a waterfall hem that swished around her hips. She'd even had time to apply lilac smiley transfers to her nails.

And when she burst in from the cold, Rochelle and Angie were waiting on chrome-back, tall stools with an air of expectation; their hems high and their necklines low.

'Here's Liza. Whoop! Squee!' Angie sometimes talked like a Twitter update. She waved at the stubbly young barman. 'What are you having, Liza?' All in white, except for a green tartan bow tie, the barman hovered for Liza's reply.

'I'll have a sparkling mineral water, please.'

'No, she won't, she'll have a little pinot,' Angie said to the barman.

Rochelle snorted. 'Don't say things like "little pinot" to a man, Ange. You'll give him a complex.' She exaggerated the two syllables, *pee-noh*, and giggled.

Angie began to giggle, too. 'OK, she'd like a large pinot, then.'

'Fizzy water,' Liza repeated to the barman, who had the hunted look of a man being teased by politically incorrect women.

By then, Rochelle had grabbed the wine list. 'Look! A *big pink* pinot! We'll have that.'

'Yeah, quality *and* quantity!'

The barman's colour heightened. Liza took pity on him. 'They mean that they'd like a bottle of pinot grigio frizzante blush, please.'

Rochelle leaned off her stool to plant a kiss on Liza's cheek. 'Spoilsport,' she said as he busied himself with selecting the bottle of pale pink wine from the chiller, polishing three flutes and standing them on the bar.

Angie snatched one up. 'Wow, you're only going to be able to put a really tiny pinot in there, aren't you?' Without answering, the barman flourished his cloth and popped the cork, splashing a taster into her glass. Angie downed it and motioned him to splash more. 'Fantastic. It's pretty and it matches my outfit.' She sat up to give him a view of her pink crocheted dress and the body it took three gym sessions a week to maintain. Then, when he stood the frizzante in a wine cooler, looking more embarrassed than enticed, she sighed and turned to Liza. 'C'mon, Lize. Just half a glass.'

'Water, thanks.' Liza smiled at the barman, who smiled back, probably in relief that she wasn't intent on teasing him for entertainment.

Rochelle rolled her eyes, outlined with jade green eyeliner and gold shadow, and snatched up a menu from the bar. 'I hope you haven't gone all boring with food, too? Because we're doing desserts.'

'Excellent! What do they have that's chocolate?' Liza grabbed the menu to dispel the impression that a 'wet blanket' sign flashed above her head. Doing desserts with Angie and

Rochelle was harmless. If you considered subjecting your body to an entire meal of sugar did no harm.

Rochelle and Angie emptied and replenished their glasses with automatic efficiency as they pored over their menus, never allowing more than an inch of frizzante in their glasses, so as to retain the chill. Rochelle was the first to announce her decision. 'I'll do tiramisu for my starter, something more substantial – yes, a crumble – for main course, and a nice chocolate mousse for dessert.'

'I'll start light, with champagne sorbet, then New Yorker cheesecake, finishing with ...' Angie's eyes ran up and down the list, '... chocolate indulgence.'

'Pig,' said Rochelle, admiringly. 'C'mon, Lize. I'm hungry; choose, so we can order.'

'I'll give the starter a miss—' the others groaned at her lack of commitment

– 'and go straight for chocolate melt-in-the-middle pud with chocolate ice cream, then pot au chocolat.'

'OK.' Rochelle was grudging. 'But we'll have after-dinner mints between courses, as *amuse bouche*.' She beckoned the barman with a slow smile. 'We're ready to go through.'

'I'll show you to your table.' The barman looked relieved to be getting rid of them.

The dining area was impressively done out. Polished black marble gleamed against ruby red carpet and snowy white tablecloths. Benefitting from enthusiastic promo in the local press aimed at those who loved to be first to try somewhere new, it was also impressively full. The barman passed them and the remains of their wine to a waiter, who, as Rochelle explained their liking for large pink pinot and Angie chimed in with the wine/dress co-ordination factor, seated them towards the back of the room, next to a long table of partying women under a golden foil banner saying *50 Today!*

Around them, heads turned as the waiter pulled out chairs and flourished napkins. 'I'm Darren, and it must be my lucky night because I'll be looking after you.' His uniform included a long white apron secured by an incongruous tartan cummerbund to go with the tartan bow tie. His gaze snagged on Liza and he paused to let her register his appreciation. 'Good evening.' He had the golden skin and bottomless dark eyes of a Mediterranean ancestry.

Liza felt the old Liza flicker inside her; pre-Adam Liza, hanging out with Rochelle and Angie and flirting with hot men. She smiled. 'How good?'

His voice dropped. 'Getting better by the moment.' Producing menus from the oversized front pocket of his apron, he began, 'Here are your menus, ladies—'

Angie beamed at him. 'We've chosen. We're doing desserts.'

He paused.

'Dessert for starter, dessert for main course and dessert for dessert,' explained Rochelle, raising her voice over a burst of laughter from the fiftieth birthday party. 'And we're ready to order.'

Darren produced a pad. 'Fabulous idea! Can't think why more people don't do it.' And, when Liza only ordered two desserts to the others' three, 'A lightweight! You really don't need to watch your figure, you know.'

Liza let her smile tell him that, actually, she did know. But she appreciated the validation. Yes … she was beginning to get in the swing of the evening.

The first desserts arrived quickly and Liza picked and stole from the others to cries of, 'Hey! Get your own!', until her own 'main' dessert, chocolate melt in the middle, complete with chocolate sauce and chocolate ice cream, arrived on white porcelain in Darren's lean brown hands. '*Mm.*' She dug into moist sponge and set free a river of melted chocolate. '*Mm-mm.*'

Darren paused in whisking past to dip his head close to Liza's and, under cover of the noisy birthday bash, murmured, 'Very *When Harry Met Sally*.'

Liza laughed and watched him hurry away, letting herself notice the width of his shoulders and the neatness of his behind. An inch of pinot blush had somehow appeared in her glass in front of her. It was tempting. A couple of mouthfuls surely wouldn't hurt—

But as she picked up the glass, cool between her fingers, the hubbub from the fiftieth birthday party table died. It was almost as if her ears had popped.

And Rochelle and Angie stopped eating, spoons poised, staring at a spot above Liza's head.

'What?' Like a child left alone with bedroom monsters, Liza didn't want to turn and look.

'Hello, Liza.'

Her glass clunked down.

The voice was syrupy with meaning. 'Looks like you're having your usual good time – drinking. Flirting with waiters.'

Somehow, Liza forced herself to face the monster: a tall woman with corned-beef cheeks and a hair colour at least two shades too dark for her skin. 'Ursula,' she managed, dry mouthed under Ursula's flinty stare. 'How are you?'

Ursula smiled tightly. 'Oh. You know. Managing.'

Behind, the entire fiftieth birthday party, of which Ursula was, presumably, a part, craned closer. Liza's heart flopped like a fish as she wondered frantically whether she should ask about Adam.

At her silence, Ursula began to back away. 'Have a lovely time. I know you know how to party.'

She returned to her own table. The conversation in the room picked up to replace the buzzing in Liza's ears. Boiling with mortification, repelled, now, at the mere thought of the delicate pink fizz in front of her, she poured iced water from the jug in the centre of the table, the lip chattering against the glass.

Rochelle slipped a consoling arm around her. 'Ignore the witchy old bitch,' she hissed. 'It wasn't your fault.'

'Don't think she'd agree.' Liza tried to laugh but the evening had been poisoned. Butterflies were aflutter in her stomach, and even they felt sick. Jerkily, she pushed away her plate, fumbled for her purse and dragged out a couple of notes to throw on the table. She couldn't look at her friends, knew she'd read sympathy beneath the meticulous make-up, mingled with exasperation that Liza had let Ursula get to her. 'Sorry,' she mumbled.

'Oh *Liza* —!'

Hurrying back to the car along damp pavements, she selected *Cleo* on her phone. When her sister answered, she made her voice as light as marshmallow. 'Hi! Just had a brainwave – I'm not tired and you and Justin are so sleep deprived you're like sleepwalkers. I'll look after Gus for a couple of hours while you have an early night, because it's my Saturday off, tomorrow.'

'Sleep would be bliss,' Cleo acknowledged, slowly.

'I've got your spare key.' Liza checked for traffic and crossed a side street. 'So you could even leave a bottle of milk in the fridge and go straight to bed and get a head start. I'll let myself in and be there when Gus wakes.'

But, half an hour later, when Liza turned the key quietly and crept into Cleo's house in Port Road, she found Cleo curled up on the sofa in her silent house, waiting like a parent for a child who'd missed curfew. She uncurled, climbing to her feet as Liza tiptoed in. Her dark hair was messy and her eyes were weary, but she smiled. 'I've sent Justin up to bed and I'll bring Gus down here to you in his Moses basket when I go up. What's the matter?'

Liza opened her mouth to chirp, 'Nothing!' But the word lodged, quivering, in her throat.

Cleo opened her arms and dragged her in. 'What?'

'I saw Ursula—' She gulped.

Cleo pulled her down onto the huge sofa, nestling her cheek against Liza's hair. It felt warm and safe. 'It wasn't your fault. It really, really wasn't your fault. It was horrible, but you've got to let it go. We all want the old Liza back. This new Liza you're pretending to be, who never has a drink or goes out with a man, she's a stranger.'

Liza let herself cling, comforted by knowing she could say anything, anything, to Cleo, who would never fail in her big-sisterly duties. 'I'm still me,' she protested, swallowing so hard it hurt, 'but I just can't bear to be the pre-Adam clubbing and drinking Liza. That was then.' She nestled her head more comfortably into the hollow of Cleo's shoulder, being careful where she put her weight out of respect for a breastfeeding mum. 'You wouldn't believe what happened at the centre. Nicolas tried to get me out.' She reeled off the whole sorry story.

Cleo's arms tightened. 'Is this how you distract yourself from the Adam situation? Worry about your business going down the drain, instead?'

Liza managed a laugh. 'It's not a planned strategy. But I've got to find a way of changing my life.' She stopped. Slowly, she pulled away, until she could see into her sister's face, struck by an idea so clear and fine and obvious that she couldn't believe it hadn't come to her before. 'We could try and get Nicolas out,' she whispered. 'Wow, Cleo, why didn't I think of it? I'll talk to Fenella and Imogen. But it's a no-brainer! If Nicolas can't keep the centre going, we'll take over the lease – then we can bring in whatever business we want and he won't be draining it like a vampire.'

Cleo seemed to be having no trouble keeping her

excitement under control. 'Sounds like a workable solution. If you think you can pull it off.'

Liza tried not to feel hurt. 'I won't be "pulling it off". I'll be executing a well-thought-out business plan.'

'Sorry!' Cleo grinned. 'If you say you can do it, you can do it. And it's easier than sorting out your heart, pesky thing.' She sighed, scooping Liza back into the safe haven of her hug. 'Lize, you don't even seem to meet a man you fancy any more. It's as if you've given up.'

'I haven't! I've just met a man who asked me out, and I liked him.'

Cleo's voice suddenly rang with pleasure. 'Great! So you're seeing him?'

'Well, no,' Liza owned. 'He's the one I said the bullshit thing to, when Nicolas overheard, the one who looked into investing in the centre but decided against it. I did meet him for a quick meal at The Three Fishes but it was just because he wanted to interrogate me about The Stables. It's not the beginning of something.' She refused to indulge herself in speculation about what it would be like if it was. Too dangerous. Too scary. Too tempting.

Cleo shrugged. 'OK, forget about beginning anything. Just for the emotional exercise, tell me why you like him.'

Liza groaned. 'You're using your training techniques to make me think positively, aren't you?'

'Yes. Is he attractive?'

'Awesome,' Liza answered, honestly. 'He's a streaky dirty blond, with spooky light grey eyes and dark lashes. Heartbreaking smile. Single. He's Miranda Sheldrake's cousin.'

'Oh, Miranda told me he was staying with her.' She paused. 'He's got a medical condition, hasn't he?'

Unexpectedly, Liza found herself being defensive. 'It's just a kind of extreme sleeping. It doesn't affect who he is and he pretty much dares anyone to think that's all there is to him.'

'And you like that confidence?'

'It's deadly. And he looks at women as if he appreciates them.' Probably better not to tell Cleo about the shelf-full-of-melons thing. She knew that that hadn't been the real Dominic Christy.

'And he asked you out?'

'Yes.' The series of questions suddenly made her feel like a participant in a Top Tips for Effective Active Listening workshop. Most of the time, she didn't even acknowledge her attraction to Dominic to herself; spilling her heart to Cleo would not only make it dangerously real but provide Cleo with ammunition in her Liza Must Get Over It mission. She clammed up.

After a silence, Cleo gave in gracefully over the questions and offered an opinion. 'I think that would do you loads of good. Loads. Why not tell him you'll go?'

'It's probably too late. I might never see him again.' Liza tried to see herself chatting over lamb and asparagus. Or with Dominic in a car, at the end of the evening. She sighed, heart shifting as much at the unsettling prospect of entwining her life with a man's again as at the imagined pleasure of the warmth, the proximity, his smile and the intensity of his gaze. 'Relationships all go messy. What if he likes me more than I like him? Or I like him more than he likes me? What if it all gets deep and complicated? What if we hurt each other?'

Cleo didn't answer.

'What if he brings out the worst in me?' Liza prompted, for sisterly devil's advocacy.

But Cleo remained silent, and when Liza sat up to look, she saw her eyelids had closed and her face slackened in sleep. Grinning, Liza nudged her. 'Go to bed, Cleo. You're shattered. I'll come up with you and get Gus.'

Cleo blinked awake. 'Sorry! What were you saying?'

'That you need to get to bed. No, I don't need a drink or a quilt or anything. Nor am I going to have Gus in the spare room so that you can still hear him cry. We'll be fine down here and you can get some sleep before you have a nervous breakdown. Go to bed!' Dragging her sister from the depths of the sofa's embrace, Liza hustled her up to her bedroom door and shoved her in, receiving in exchange her tiny nephew in a basket with a blue-and-purple striped lining. As if transporting a million fragile eggs, she glided with the sleeping baby back down the stairs, slowing where the staircase wound round, so as not to wake him with sudden changes of directions.

Gently, gently, she floated the basket onto the floor of the sitting room. Gus slept on.

Liza turned away to fetch a pillow – and Gus made a thin, distant noise. She froze. The distant noise swelled like an air raid siren, stronger, higher, louder, until there was no room left in the air for anything but the wail of baby.

Hastily, Liza closed the door to the hall then scooped Gus from under his blankets, soothing him as he squirmed against her and tried to force angry fists into his tiny, screwed-up face. A crying baby held no terrors for a cool, hands-on auntie like Liza, though. 'Noisy Gus,' she crooned, heading through the kitchen door to the fridge, as he rooted and squalled in despair that no one would ever feed him again. 'Hungry, hungry Gus-Gus. Your mum needs sleep, so you're stuck with me, kid.' The information did little to soothe Gus's anxiety and she extricated the chill bottle from the fridge with her free hand and dropped it into the bottle warmer, joggling him against her shoulder. 'I know, you're not used to waiting, but you're on the bottle tonight, mate.' She propped her behind against the kitchen units and settled Gus in the crook of her left arm, catching one flailing foot and easing off its drunken blue sock to cup the warm, soft baby skin. 'Chill, babes, your belly will soon be full.' Gently, slowly, she began tiny circles with her thumb tip, just level with Gus's perfect baby metatarsal notch, following the curve where his heel met the waist of his foot.

Gus's face became a couple of shades less puce. The end of his world seemed less nigh.

When the warmer bleeped, she carried him to the sofa, settling comfortably in the corner before she let him latch onto the bottle with mouth and both hands like a milk monster. Once he'd established that the synthetic teat was a reasonable food source in place of the human version, Gus heaved a big sigh. And ... relaxed.

Liza gazed down at the miracle of humanity as she worked on his other foot, the miniature features that blossomed and changed every time she saw him. The gossamer hair. The satin skin. The huge eyes, already dark, like Cleo's, staring back at her. The perfect fingers that searched out one of hers and held on, as if he already knew and loved her.

By the time the bottle was empty Gus's eyes had shut, his mouth, hands, whole body, loosened with sleep. She turned him gently onto her shoulder until he burped mightily, then replaced his socks and laid him on his back in the basket, tucking the blankets around him, holding his heels whilst he settled.

Feeling virtuous and cocooned in intimacy with the sleeping baby, she heaped up the sofa cushions, wriggled out of her boots, and dragged her coat and the sofa throw over herself to nap until Gus woke again. Cleo had left only one bottle, so Liza would have to wake her for the next feed.

But, for a few hours, everyone could sleep.

Chapter Eight

She awoke, stiff and cold, to Gus's siren impression. Daylight edged the curtains and Cleo's boyfriend, Justin, stood grinning down at where she was curled tightly on the sofa, his baby son once more writhing in the throes of starvation. 'You're an absolute star, Liza. Cleo and I got eight hours' sleep. Did Gus only wake once?'

She yawned and stretched. Sleeping in her clothes made her feel like something discarded too long at the bottom of the laundry basket. 'Yup. I got your babe trained, Daddy.'

'Not kidding. You know where the kettle is if you want coffee. I'm taking Gus up to Cleo. I think he's ready for breakfast.'

Blearily, Liza hauled herself up. 'Where's Shona?'

Justin's sharp features creased into an even wider grin. 'Watching cartoons in our bed. She hates being left out of a Saturday morning cuddlefest.' His eyes were bright. 'By the way, we're finally getting married. Soon. Registry office and village hall.'

Liza clicked properly awake, aghast. 'Cleo didn't tell me!'

He laughed. 'She couldn't. I'm only telling you as a trial run for telling her. I'm tired of putting it off because we need to spend money on the house and Cleo's on maternity leave. It'll have to be cheap and cheerful.' Then he was gone, Gus's diminishing wail marking father and son's progress up the stairs.

Liza stared after them, trying to envisage how Cleo would take her wedding being thrust on her like that. Concluded she would probably take it in her stride, because nothing about Cleo and Justin's relationship had been orthodox.

Yawning, she considered the coffee situation. She might as

well wander home as drink down here, alone, Liza-no-mates. She tried not to feel miffed that Shona hadn't run down to fling herself on Liza with the million degrees of excitement she usually reserved for her favoured auntie, but ... a cuddlefest is a cuddlefest. Liza imagined the whole family squeezed into Cleo and Justin's bed, the warmth and morning smells, the sinking pillows and the fighting over the quilt, Gus making sucky baby noises while Shona – and probably Justin – laughed at Sponge Bob Square Pants on the TV.

She sighed, yanked on her boots and let herself quietly out of the house.

It was her weekend off and as she progressed through laundry, Saturday shopping and Sunday coffee at Rochelle's flat, her mind worked on her amazing idea of taking over the treatment centre. Excitement puckered the back of her neck. A hurdle was, obviously, Nicolas, who might not wish to relinquish his tenancy. On the other hand, if he was near to going under he might be glad of armbands and a rubber ring. Nicolas presently took care of all the admin. But Liza, Imogen and Fenella could do that between them. They already managed their own businesses; how much more work could there be? Her mind cannoned around like a marble in a tin.

And she forgot to brood about Friday night and Ursula. Or Adam. Mainly.

All three therapists had elected to make Monday an afternoon/evening day, so the centre would shut at nine. Liza grabbed Fenella and Imogen in between clients and invited them for tea and biccies at her place after work. In her meal break, she wrote a list of discussion subjects.

What is monthly rent compared to sum of rent we three pay Nicolas?

Bring in another therapist in Nicolas's room?
Other bills. Rates, water, telephone, electricity
Increased insurance? Paid monthly? Check public liability/
buildings/contents
~~*Nicolas's cut*~~
~~*Pippa?*~~ *OMG*
Cleaner. Weekly. Cleaning supplies
Accountant. Annually
Solicitor—but only for lease legals?
Maintenance. Us or hotel?

She racked her brains for expenses, either hidden or obvious, that she'd overlooked, and added supplies for common areas, like loo rolls and soap. She tapped her pen and scratched her head and really couldn't come up with another thing.

So her opening remark, when Fenella and Imogen were curled up in her chairs, yawning with end-of-day fatigue, drinking jasmine tea and eating Jammie Dodgers, was an impetuous, 'I think Nicolas is ripping us off.' Then, at their frozen expressions, modifying it to, 'Perhaps not ripping us off exactly, but at least on a cushy number.' Deep breath. 'I think we three could go into partnership, offload Nicolas and make more money. He's deadweight because he brings no clients in – just takes our rent and pushes a bit of paper.'

Silence.

Imogen's eyes were like saucers. 'Where's this come from? Why would we want to cut out Nicolas?'

On a lurch of disappointment that they hadn't leapt on her masterly plan with cries of joy, Liza tried to sound persuasive. 'Lots of reasons. For one thing, he says he's in the poo, financially. If it gets so that he can't afford the rent, what will happen to us? Will the centre close while we run around looking for new premises or try and work from home?'

Fenella dropped her Jammie Dodger in shock. 'He isn't going to close, is he?'

'I don't know that he is.' Liza had to be honest. 'But he showed some investors round, on Thursday.'

'Pippa told us,' said Fenella. 'So they might invest.'

'They've already said no. He said they were his last hope.' Liza relayed what Dominic had told her, including the bit about investors not being angels with briefcases full of cash. 'I think it's possible that Nicolas is going to have no choice but to give up the lease. And we'd be the obvious option to take it over.' She brought out her list. 'Look, I've been brainstorming things we need to investigate.'

But, barely sparing the piece of paper a glance, Fenella screwed up her nose. 'There's bound to be something you have to pay Nicolas.'

'Why?' demanded Imogen. She'd released her hair from its daytime knot and was combing it with her fingers.

Liza remained silent. Hmm. Pay Nicolas?

'You know,' explained Fenella, vaguely. 'If someone owns a lease, they own an asset. If you want it, you have to buy it.'

'Oh that,' said Liza. She added, *buy lease?* to the list.

Imogen's hair raking grew agitated. 'But that would take money we don't have.'

'We might have to borrow a bit,' Liza agreed, as if borrowing was no big deal, even though she already had her mortgage and her car payments. And credit cards that were OK but not what you'd call clear. 'But think about the big picture! We already have our businesses intact. Each of us has our equipment, our supplies, our insurance, everything. All we'd be doing would be cutting out the Nicolas factor. And he doesn't bring money in – he just takes it out.'

'But he pays all the bills.' Fenella seemed unable to conceive of The Stables without Nicolas sitting like a butter ball in his office.

Liza fought to stay patient. 'But he pays the bills out of our rent. If he can pay it out of our rent, we can pay it out of our rent. That's only reorganisation, not extra money.'

Imogen had turned Liza's list so that she could read it. 'Why have you crossed Pippa out, too? And written "OMG"?'

Liza went all hot. She looked down at the damning line through little Pippa's name. 'I don't think we can afford her,' she admitted, sadly. 'I think we need to each meet our own clients in reception and show them through to our rooms. It'll save mega money.'

'Ow!' Fenella sounded as if it was she who had just received Liza's dagger in her back. 'We can't sack Pippa!'

'And I don't want to borrow money,' finished Imogen. Sitting back, she folded her arms.

A pause. Heart sinking, Liza took up her mug. 'So where will you begin looking for your new treatment rooms? I might try Bettsbrough, because it's closer than Peterborough. Driving in and out to Peterborough every day's ridiculous, in view of fuel prices, even in my little Smart.' Bettsbrough was the nearest town to Middledip.

When the other two glared at her, she gave a great, exaggerated, sarcastic shrug. 'What? You might want to shut your eyes to the fact that Nicolas's business plan was a fairy tale, but I'm sailing dangerously close to not making a living. Once Christmas is over, I'm going to start looking around. I'm not going to lose my house and my car.'

'So you'll clear off and leave us with even more rent to find!' wailed Fenella.

Liza's heart sank a few more inches. 'I'm free to leave at a month's notice, as Nicolas so kindly reminded me last week. But, yes, he'll have to get another therapist in, if the centre goes on. I'm really sorry if you think I'm baling out,' she added. 'Probably you guys aren't feeling the pinch so much, because you have partners to share your living expenses.'

'So maybe there would have been advantages to marrying Adam, after all?' Imogen snapped.

Liza breathed in slowly and deeply so that she didn't go off like a faulty firework. Imogen was upset and probably didn't realise how bitchy she sounded. 'I don't need a man,' she managed, eventually. 'I can do this. But it might mean some hard decisions.'

Chapter Nine

PWNsleep message board:

Tenzeds: I get really p*ssed off if I go to my room to work on my computer. Without the bustle of a workplace environment I can just stare into space or drop off.

Inthebatcave: At uni, I used to keep alert by working around the noisy bastards. Sounds counterproductive but it's better than sliding into sleep every half hour.

Dominic gave himself a week to think. He spent a lot of that time at the kitchen table, reading websites, making phone calls, guarding his iPad from Ethan's sticky little hands whilst Miranda created veggie meals or baked.

On Thursday, he e-mailed Kenny King. In the confusion of learning to cope with narcolepsy and Kenny going off to lead wilderness expeditions and Outward Bound courses in North Carolina, communications had lapsed. But now he felt as if contact with Kenny was exactly what he needed. Kenny was fun, lively, alive.

Hi Kenny,
Seems ages since I heard from you. What's going on in
your life?
Dom

Kenny's reply came quickly, hardly punctuated, and littered with the usual hope-spellcheck-puts-me-right word choices that he relied on to make his dyslexic way through life.

Hey doc! Haven't herd from u 4 so long I through u
weren't talking 2 me its 5am here just getting ready

*2take a group of teenagers into the swamp n Carolina
fantastic apart from heat and bugs but my time hear
is nearly up & ill have to leaf the US and look for a
job. Have put a few feelers out but nothing coming my
way yet
Ken*

Dominic grinned. Nobody but Kenny ever called him 'Doc',
a nickname that came from Dominic's initials, adopted by
Kenny because Dominic was what Kenny termed 'brainy'.
Dominic replied:

*Been getting my head around all the crap that came
with my diagnosis. Where are you going next? If you're
coming back to the UK I might have something to
interest you.*

He sketched in a few details, added *Dom* and touched *send*,
then slid his iPad on top of the fridge out of Ethan's reach
and took out the ordnance survey map he'd ordered from
Amazon. He spread it out, taking pleasure in the thickness of
the paper and its fresh smell. Ordnance survey maps evoked
orienteering and climbing weekends. When he'd sorted his
life out, he'd get back to those.

Ethan threw down the Duplo bricks he'd been forcing
haphazardly together and clambered up onto the chair
beside Dominic. 'You got a big picture.'

'It's a map.' Dominic let Ethan slide onto his lap. 'It's kind
of a picture of the ground, from above.'

Ethan smelled of the porridge he'd eaten at breakfast.
'What's that?' He stabbed the map with a pudgy thumb,
which he often stored in his mouth between sentences,
leaving a damp thumbprint.

'The green bit? Grass. The blue patch, here, is a lake,

these spiky things are trees that don't lose their leaves and the cloudy shapes are trees that do.'

'And what are they?' The thumb besmirched the paper at a different spot.

'Buildings. And see these black lines? When they get close together, it shows that there's a hill. The lake's between two hills and the buildings are on top of one.' After breathing hard on the map and adding an artistic array of thumbprints, Ethan wriggled back down to his Duplo, leaving Dominic to study the no-longer-pristine map in peace. But when he folded it into a clear sleeve and rose to extricate his walking boots from the pile of footwear beside the back door, he found not only Crosswind dancing around his legs, but Ethan, too. 'I come wid you, Dommynic?'

Dominic met the little boy's eager eyes regretfully. 'Sorry, Ethe. I'm going too far for you this morning. But I'll take you to the swings this afternoon.'

The little face sagged into instant misery. 'Caaaan't I coooome nooo-ooow …?'

With an apologetic look at Miranda, Dominic repeated, 'Later, mate,' tucked a bottle of water guiltily into his hiking jacket, leaving his cousin to cheer her son with a story from Ethan's favourite book of folk tales which, from Ethan's grumpy face, didn't make up for Dominic's monstrous betrayal.

Crosswind bounced like a toy along the narrow pavements of the village, jumping up every few strides to nudge Dominic's hand with a wet nose. But, as soon as they cleared the houses and Dominic unhooked the lead, the little terrier settled down to the serious job of snuffling the hedgerows, tail quivering with joy, leaving Dominic free to fall into the rhythmic stride that he could keep up for hours, first along the verges and then onto a footpath. He breathed in the sharp air, enjoying the feel of his muscles bunching and blood pulsing through his veins.

After a couple of miles he took out the map to compare it to the land he was approaching: a coppice, then coniferous trees that looked as if they ought to have a star on top for Christmas marching up packed contour lines of grassland from a pale blue comma lake. The big slope that rose up to The Stables. The small dash footpath that Crosswind was happily exploring by nose was joined by a larger dash bridleway where the hawthorn hedges funnelled the wind, combing Crosswind's fur and rattling streams of dry golden leaves along the ground. At the lake, Dominic clicked the lead back onto Crosswind's collar and climbed the steep greensward, breasting the hill in front of The Stables, pale grey stone sparkling with lichen in the autumn sunlight. He took the water bottle from inside his jacket, along with the small collapsible bowl that lived in one of the many mesh inner pockets. He took a couple of swallows from the bottle, expanded the bowl and poured Crosswind's drink, then tied the lead to a drainpipe. 'Crosswind, down. Stay.' Crosswind lay down slowly, too well mannered to complain, but eyes full of wounded reproach.

Dominic rubbed the dog's silky ears. 'Yeah, I know. I won't be long.'

Through the black-painted door, and Dominic stepped into the cool and quiet interior, smiling at Pippa at the front desk.

'Hiya!' She beamed, obviously beginning to view him as a regular visitor.

'Is Nicolas in?'

'Let me find out.' And she disappeared up the short passageway. Dominic's eyes followed her so far, but then slid to the closed door of Liza Reece's treatment room.

Pippa bounced back. 'Nicolas says to go in.'

So he turned his mind away from Liza and to the task in hand, shucking out of his jacket to enter Nicolas's overheated office, receiving a sweaty handshake and a beaming, hopeful smile. 'This is a pleasant surprise! Coffee?'

'Not for me. I've got a dog waiting outside.' Dominic didn't take the seat that Nicolas waved him to, but came straight to the point. 'Nicolas, I'm afraid I don't want to buy into your treatment centre. But are you prepared to sell your lease on the premises? I think this place would be brilliant for something else I'd like to do.'

Slowly, Nicolas's face turned purple. 'Sell *what*?'

It took five minutes. Dominic timed it on the wall clock. Five minutes for Nicolas to scroll through leaning-across-the-desk anger, 'Who the hell do you think you are, strolling in here and trying to end my business?' dull, hopeless sorrow, 'I had a lot of dreams,' slumped-into-a-chair self-pity, 'It's always the little guy that gets squeezed out,' and hand-to-head regret, 'I should have taken more advice before I took the place on.'

Dominic let Nicolas vent until finally reaching sour pragmatism. 'I suppose we could talk about it.'

Then he stirred. 'How long does the lease have to run?'

'More than twenty years.'

'OK, I'm still interested. I'm sorry if my proposal isn't what you wanted to hear. But, if you're prepared to consider it, I suggest you get some figures together. Maybe you'd like to have the lease valued? While you do that, I'll make further enquiries about whether my idea's likely to float. Then we could talk again.'

Nicolas wiped his glum face on his palm, hair lank, skin pink and stretched shiny. 'We can talk now.'

But Dominic shook his head. 'I need to speak to the hotel. I only want this place if I can rent some of the grounds, too. Without it, my idea will come to nothing.'

The word 'nothing' caused Nicolas's colour to drain. 'The lease is a valuable asset—'

'Only if somebody wants it,' Dominic said, with some sympathy. 'I'll understand if you want me to drop the idea. You could advertise the lease, if you can afford to wait ...?'

'What you don't seem to realise is that I've got a thriving concern, here.'

'If it's a thriving concern, I'm wasting your time.'

Nicolas halted, blinking rapidly. His chest heaved. 'You're a chancer,' he managed, tightly. 'You think that me looking for investors means I'm in trouble and that you can get something for nothing.'

Anger flared suddenly in Dominic, but he clenched his teeth against the impulse to fire back a sarcastic reply that, in fact, he knew precisely how it felt to lose a dream and understood Nicolas's distress – but that that didn't alter the fact that Nicolas's business was about to go belly up. Instead, he made his voice calm and reasonable. 'What I think is that I might be able to get the lease at a fair market value. It's a depressed market, but that's not my fault. I've had a cursory look at your business and the lease is the only asset to interest me.'

Nicolas dropped his head back into his hands, staring at the desk. 'Let me think.'

Waiting for Nicolas to chew the situation over, the heat of the room began to press its heavy hand across Dominic's face and, with a sinking heart, he recognised a coming sleep attack. He opened the door in search of fresh air, wishing he'd put ProPlus in his jacket. He could use some caffeine.

'I don't know where it all went wrong,' Nicolas muttered.

Dominic yawned, wanting to drop into a chair but not wanting to, because he knew that if he did, he'd be gone. He strove to stay in the moment. But he answered, unguardedly, 'Sometimes we all need to be open to new ideas.'

The area around Nicolas's lips whitened as he slowly raised his gaze. 'Liza?'

Dominic was jolted back to wakefulness by the unhappy sliding sensation that went with saying the wrong thing to the wrong person. 'What?'

'Liza's "new ideas",' Nicolas clarified. 'It sounds to me as if you've fallen for her line that we could make megabucks, here, if we just turned complementary medicine into a circus.'

'As I don't want a treatment centre, Liza's views are irrelevant.'

But Nicolas wasn't going to let a logical argument cheat him of an opportunity to vent about Liza. 'Bloody woman,' he spat. 'For years therapists have been battling for respectability, and now Liza's trying to drag us into gimmickry, for reasons best known to herself.'

'Survival?'

Sweat popped on Nicolas's forehead like liquid anger. 'If that's what it takes for complementary medicine to survive then I don't want anything to do with it!'

Dominic made a huge effort not to allow himself to be deflected from his purpose, despite the urge to make Nicolas see the speciousness of that argument. The greater need was to get the meeting over before sleep jumped on him again with both its heavy feet. 'Which brings us back to where we started. Are you interested in selling your lease?'

The walk home was an ordeal. Dominic fought falling asleep on his feet, heaving one eyelid open then the other, knowing that October wasn't the time to find a patch of grass for an emergency nap, but the cold hardly registering. Crosswind stayed close to his ankles, his nose touching the back of Dominic legs rather like Ethan's little hand patting for the attention of a grown up. By the time Dominic finally regained Miranda's house, his face was a leaden mask and darkness filtered into where his brain ought to be. He managed, 'Hi,' for Miranda, as he shut the door.

In the kitchen, folding clothes as she kept an eye on Ethan through the window to the back garden, she glanced around. 'How did it go?'

'Later,' he said. Or thought he said.

Upstairs, heavy, using the handrail to drag himself up, legs like weights, banister, door to his room. Yellow-orange walls combining oddly with his navy quilt cover. Heavy colour, made the box room press in on him. With the last vestige of energy he fumbled his phone timer to thirty minutes and dropped down onto his bed, still wearing his boots.

Fallingggggggg ....

He was trying to implement the unusual circumstances and events process with a watch of seriously mute controllers and an air traffic monitor that was completely blank. Through the window, the aerodrome was operating without any control. Kenny stared at him from the left-hand seat and—

Bee-beep, bee-beep. Thirty minutes had passed in an instant. The phone's alarm dragged him awake. His eyelids fluttered and he began to swim through the final flickering images of the Stansted control tower.

He listened to the piercing, unrelenting alarm, giving himself time to orientate, to feel secure, waiting to welcome the approaching clean feeling of being awake and alert from the miracle midday-sleep fix. Slowly, he swung his legs around so he could sit on the edge of the bed, *bee-beep, bee-beep,* reaching for his phone, *bee-beep,* and taking three attempts to drag along the arrow that would clear the alarm.

He blinked in the daylight. Rubbed his eyes, his mouth, ran his fingers through his hair.

Finally, he pushed himself upright and headed for the bathroom. By the time he'd taken his second white pill of the day, brushed his teeth and washed with cold water, he was in gear. He could hear Ethan downstairs, indulging in the joys of yelling, and remembered his promise. Walking a lively three-year-old to the swings behind the village hall would be an OK thing to do on an autumn afternoon, until he got busy with real life again.

But first, he woke up his iPad, clicked on the *contact us* tab on the Port Manor Hotel website and took the number for Isabel Jones: finance and premises. Picked up his phone and moved into phase two of his life: getting Isabel Jones's direct line, introducing himself and pitching straight in. 'I'd like to speak to you about the lease that Nicolas Notten currently holds on The Stables Treatment Centre. I'm interested in taking it over.' He knew from earlier internet research that Isabel Jones, having worked for the hotel for years, had married one of the two Pattinson brothers who owned Port Manor. He liked the fact that she still used her maiden name. It suggested that she wished to be seen as an independent force.

'I see.' A note of surprise in her pleasant, assured voice. A pause for thought. 'Do you have some reason to feel Mr Notten might be agreeable to that?'

'I've approached him and he's prepared to talk. But my interest depends upon whether the hotel will consider leasing or renting me the land on that side of the park, too – from the treatment centre down to the lake, that whole area.'

Now she did sound surprised. 'The big slope? It's not an area we have plans for ... would you like to come in and tell us yours?'

Chapter Ten

Liza's thoughts had whirled for days. And the more they whirled, the more her new idea – her new, new one; not her old, new one – filled her imagination with bursts of bright-future colours: if Imogen and Fenella didn't want to go into partnership with her then she would take over the centre's lease herself. Fen and Immi would pay their rent to her, she would be rid of the Nicolas encumbrance and she could run The Stables exactly as she wanted.

After wakeful nights and distracted days, she'd confided in Cleo and Justin, who were not only happy to help her create a back-of-an-envelope business plan but gratifyingly confident in her ability to force the centre into profitability. 'Without Nicolas to hold you back, the centre will take on your personality,' Cleo enthused.

'Dippy?' grinned Justin.

'Innovative.' Cleo had frowned him down. 'Sparky. Different. Fun.'

With her self-image as a whacky young entrepreneur enshrined, Liza fairly skipped into work on Friday morning. Nicolas's office door was shut. She frowned at it. It had been shut all day yesterday, too. Until recently, Nicolas had generally been visible, listening through his half-open door to what went on in the centre's daily business, trundling forth occasionally to chat with the clients, though Liza doubted that a rotund sweaty guy being a phoney was an effective way to encourage repeat business.

Her hand hovered to knock.

But, 'Liza, phone!' Pippa called, and she had to backtrack to the front desk to explain reflexology to a prospective client.

Call over, Liza glanced down her client list for the day. And halted. 'Dominic Christy's made another appointment.'

'He rang and booked your last slot.' Pippa didn't pause in clicking her computer mouse, but gave a little smile. 'He's nice, isn't he?'

'Mm.' Liza was non-committal. 'I hadn't picked up a returning-client vibe from him.' Though, on examining the idea, she had no objection to seeing him again ... 'I need to do some reading before he arrives. I'll do it at lunch time.'

The morning slid by. After her last client, Liza took out her sandwich, opened her laptop and typed 'Narcolepsy' into the search engine, selecting a nationally recognised site from the page of suggestions. Her eyes flicked down the information, skimming *neurological disorder ... chronic sleep disorder,* until she reached a succinct explanation. *Narcolepsy is characterised by Excessive Daytime Sleepiness (EDS), whether or not night-time sleep is adequate. A person with narcolepsy is likely to be drowsy or fall asleep or suffer fatigue throughout the day, including at times and in places that might be inappropriate and inconvenient. EDS may occur several times a day, with almost no warning, and be irresistible. Typically, naps refresh the sufferer for a few hours. Sudden involuntary sleep and microsleeps are common. Drowsiness may persist for prolonged periods.*

Night-time sleep may be fragmented, with frequent awakenings ... Much about narcolepsy is yet to be understood ... Narcolepsy is a spectrum disorder ... Narcolepsy cannot, presently, be cured ... Other sites repeated similar clinical yet superficial information and several linked her to a message board called PWNsleep – PWN standing for 'people with narcolepsy' – which obviously told it as it really was.

Tenzeds: I hate the cataplexy. It's OK if I laugh and take

a light hit, everything just goes a bit sparkly and maybe I slur my words. But I had one really bad episode and hit the floor in front of unsympathetic spectators. Made me feel vulnerable.

Sleepingmatt: Yeah, you might need new meds. Or stay away from unsympathetic people ...

And:

Nightjack: N much worse, at the moment. Falling asleep in meetings.

Tenzeds: I didn't know it could get worse!!! Depressing. ☹

Then:

Brainwave: Terrifying dream about a monster on my chest. Couldn't make myself move so I could wake up and breathe. Hate this shit.

Inthebatcave: Always right on top of you, aren't they? I think—

'Liza, your two o'clock appointment.'

Liza jumped, jolted back into her workaday world. She managed a smile for the client, lovely old Jeanie Rose, who lived in Port-le-bain and had reflexology whenever she fancied a treat. 'Hello, Jeanie, come in.' She shut her computer, brain jangling with what she'd read. Information, speculation, but few absolutes. 'Take a seat. How are you?' She listened, automatically making notes. Dominic's life must be a battle against the soup of daytime sleep attacks, night-time wakefulness and terrifyingly lucid dreams.

He didn't really show it, much. How hard was that?

Liza had a break before Dominic's appointment and found herself gazing at Nicolas's closed door with a growing need for action. Nicolas was lurking in there. She'd heard the rise and fall of his voice on the telephone. The door was an obstacle between her and her goal of making the treatment centre a wowie place that attracted flocks of clients.

She crossed the corridor and knocked.

'What?'

Not encouraging, but, obeying her impulse to act, she entered anyway. Nicolas was at his computer, documents scattered as if they'd been flung on the desk around him.

Slowly, he transferred his gaze to her. 'Can this wait?' he asked, tonelessly. 'I've got a lot on.'

She hesitated. He looked hollowed out with fatigue, his hair hanging, shirt collar wilting, and her instinct was to apologise and withdraw. But what if the reason he'd hidden himself away was that he was staring bankruptcy in the face? Her wanting to buy the lease might avert disaster. She would be the cavalry, galloping to the rescue! Pinning in place her most winning smile, she sat down. 'Can we talk about the centre?'

A twist of the lips. 'What is it that's going to make our fortunes this time? Pet pampers? Moon therapy for werewolves?'

Liza abandoned the winning smile. 'I've come up with a solution that will mean I can do my thing and you can do yours.'

Interest warred with distrust in his eyes. 'Go on.'

She breathed in through her nose and allowed it out very slowly, to combat a nervy suspicion that what had seemed so sensible moments before would sound ridiculous, now. She lifted her chin. 'As things don't seem to be going well for you, I was wondering whether you'd like me to take over the lease? I think that with only therapists here and a few new ideas I could make it work—'

And then Nicolas was on his feet, hank of hair quivering

over his forehead and spittle gathering unattractively at the corners of his mouth. 'You! Buy my lease? *Buy*. Don't say "take over", as if it has no value! What with?'

Liza scrambled up, feeling safer if she wasn't being yelled down at. She swallowed, heart hammering. 'A loan, I expect. I'd need to know what the costs would be so I could talk to my bank manager.' She had no idea who her bank manager was, but was sure she must have one. She had bank accounts, ergo she must have a bank manager.

He sneered. 'Suddenly you're the big business woman, are you? What the fuck do you know about running a business?'

She blinked. 'I already run—'

His eyes narrowed. 'Don't call being a self-employed reflexologist "running a business". How the fuck do you think you could make a success of this place, when I can't?'

Fury flamed through her. 'Because you're the problem! You're deadwood, Nicolas – you put nothing in but you want to take plenty out! A child could see what's wrong.'

'A child?' he spat. 'So you do qualify. Fluffy, airheaded, pie-in-the-sky, too-big-for-her-boots little blonde with big ideas. An overactive imagination doesn't pay the bills, Liza.'

'Evidently,' she returned, sweetly, 'neither does the total lack of one.'

Dominic sat in Miranda's passenger seat, trying not to feel like a spare part as she drove him to The Stables, Ethan singing gustily from his red child seat in the back. 'Freddy frog, Freddy frog, what on earf you finkin' of?'

Dominic grinned in admiration. 'Great song, Ethan.' Then, to his cousin. 'Thanks, yet again, Miranda. I'll walk back.' Miranda never complained but he hated having to inconvenience her, hated having to plan ahead rather than hop into his car and drive wherever whim took him. The loss of his driving licence was a steaming frustration.

'Will you be in for dinner?' She turned the car in the stable yard.

'Freddy Frog, Freddy Frog,' yelled Ethan.

'I think I might leave you guys to have a family evening together and call in at the pub for a steak.'

'Time for a meat fix?' She rolled her eyes, but grinned.

'Something like that.' He hopped out, 'Bye, Ethan!' He shut the door on another less-than-tuneful request to know what on earf Freddy Frog was finkin' of, and headed for the black door in the corner of the yard.

This time, when Pippa showed him into Liza's treatment room, Liza was already in it, her back to the door as she arranged the contents of her small, square, white trolley. Her hair was twisted up at the back, only the finest of blonde strands lying softly against her neck. Although she'd decreed the dark green uniform 'gross', he'd developed quite a fondness for it, not just because it had featured in a better-than-usual dream, but because it followed her particularly neat little hourglass figure so well. 'Hello, Dominic,' she said, without looking around. 'Take a seat. We'll talk about your last treatment.'

He hesitated. 'What's the matter?'

'Nothing.' She was rubbing sanitising gel into her hands, over and over, until every germ must surely be lying on its back with its feet in the air.

Slowly, he sat. 'Either you've got hay fever, a cold, or you're crying.'

'I'm not crying.' She turned slowly, eyes and nose pink. 'I've *been* crying. But now I'm fine and we can begin your treatment. Did you have any effects after I saw you last time?'

'Why have you been crying?'

'I had a row with Nicolas.' She took her seat and picked up a pen. 'But I can recover while I give the treatment –

women can multitask.' Her smile was watery. 'Did you notice anything at all after your last treatment?'

Blotches showed through her make-up, but she obviously wanted to ignore little things like that, so he went along with it. 'I had a good night, after my treatment, which always helps me the next day.' He knew it was what she wanted to hear and, coincidentally, it had the added bonus of being true.

Her smile flickered into warmth. 'Really? Is that what's made you decide to proceed with further treatments?'

He shrugged. 'You recommended a course of at least six treatments so assessing the benefits after only one would be irrational.' He hoped *and your hands + my feet = incredible* didn't show on his face.

'Great. I've done some reading on narcolepsy.' Then she paused, uncertainly.

'It's pretty crap,' he supplied. 'But I don't let it beat me. Or even beat me up.' No need to go back over how it had felt to know that he, a brilliant, decisive controller, might not be able to process simultaneous inputs. How the impossibility of rotating through morning, afternoon and night shifts filled him with despair. His anxiety that his life was happening without him.

'It's no wonder you want to take control of things.' Liza glanced at her notes, but added nothing to them. 'If you'd like to take your shoes and socks off and make yourself comfortable on the couch, I'll begin your treatment.' And, finally, they were where he wanted to be, with her cool smooth hands on his feet as he watched her through slitted lids. Her blotches were fading and her eyes bore only a hint of pink, but he felt a wave of anger at Nicolas.

Then the side of her palm smoothing his instep melted him into a pool of bliss and the pads of her fingers along the base of his toes etched a beatific smile across his face. He closed his eyes. How many treatments had she suggested? Six? He could manage six thousand.

At the end of the treatment, Liza had to give Dominic a little shake, the bones of his shoulder hard beneath her fingers. She kept herself busy for several moments, while he widened his eyes and rubbed his face, before giving him a tall drink of cold water and relating the reflexes she'd picked up – pretty much the same as last time. He listened as he sipped, dark blond hair tumbling above his eyes.

Then he put down the glass and moved off the couch and went to the chair to slide back into his shoes and socks. 'I'm your last appointment, aren't I?'

'Yes, I'm not working this evening.'

He tied his laces and propped his elbows on his knees. 'I'm going to The Three Fishes for a steak. Why don't you come along, and tell me what happened to make you cry?'

She darted him a glance. His grey eyes gleamed and she felt a lick of heat. 'I'm fine now. And you shouldn't drink alcohol after a treatment.'

He smiled. 'I won't, if you'll be there to keep an eye on me. Thing is, I think I've dropped you in it, with Nicolas. If I did, then I need to understand what happened so that I can put it right.'

'How could you drop me in it?' But then she glanced at the treatment room door, close enough to Nicolas's office that conversation might be overheard. 'OK, let's talk in the pub. But I have things to do, first.'

'I can wait.'

It took her only half an hour to prepare her treatment room for the morning – she and Fenella were working this Saturday. Dominic did stuff on his phone as she moved towels from the washer to the dryer and put more in to wash, wiped her dispensers, laid out fresh towels on the couch, folded the rest into her cupboard and fetched her coat, ready to drive him back to Middledip.

Outside, he shoehorned himself into her Smart car with exaggerated difficulty. 'Nice golf buggy.'

She sighed as she strapped herself in. 'When I can pop into spaces other cars can't, the smartarse remarks tend to stop.'

He grinned. 'Sorry, didn't mean to hit a nerve. It's, um, compact. But don't let Ethan see it or he might put it in his toy box.'

Even if she'd been driving a stretch limousine, space in the car park beside The Three Fishes wasn't an issue so early in the evening. The bar was more than half-empty and Dominic led the way through it, under the arch of rust-coloured stone to the dining area, where it was even quieter. Just one other couple looked up from their menus to say hello. Liza noticed the woman's eyes on Dominic as he shrugged off his jacket and hung it on the back of his seat.

Tubb, whose mouth turned down at the corners when he smiled, not that he smiled much, brought the menus and took their order, and Liza waited until he'd delivered tall glasses of water to the table before demanding, 'How do you think you've dropped me in it?'

Dominic's eyebrow curled in a frown. 'A sleep attack was trying to get me and I somehow repeated what you'd said about him needing new ideas. He pounced on it, and said that I'd obviously been talking to you. Which was true. I didn't come up with a way to deny it and he ... vented a little.'

'Oh.' She absorbed the information. 'He did seem unjustifiably angry today.'

'Sorry. Again.' He smiled. 'I seem to have the knack for making things awkward for you. Would it help if I talked to him?'

Sinking down in her seat, Liza made a face. 'Relations between Nicolas and I have been deteriorating. I think he's a stick-in-the-mud, he thinks I'm ridiculous. And, today, I thought he was a sweaty, annoying little tit and he thought I was a fluffy, airheaded, pie-in-the-sky, too-big-for-her-boots little blonde with big ideas.'

Laughter shook its way slowly up his body, making his eyes dance. 'Nobody held back?'

'Not much.' She smiled, reluctantly.

'Can you continue to work together?'

'Immediate short term, we'll have to.' She hesitated, wondering how much to tell him and, still sore from Nicolas's scorn, half-suspecting her plans *were* pie in the sky. 'I'm not sure how things are going to work out.' She nodded at his drink: water, slices of lemon and lime bobbing at the top with the ice, like hers. 'Good choice. Water will help you detox.'

He pulled a face. 'That's only because you're breathing down my neck. What's your excuse? I would have thought that after a bad day in the treatment room you would've been glad of a drink.'

She picked up her spoon and checked how she looked upside down. 'I'm driving.' And then, truthfully, 'I stopped.'

'You're really that much of a health-freak?'

'Not at all. It's a control issue.'

'Oh?' Curiosity laced his voice. But then his steak arrived and he addressed himself to the business of disposing of ten ounces of beef and a potato-field worth of chips, so she allowed herself to relax as he chatted about Miranda's admirable whole-food, wholemeal, additive-free dietary philosophies and his corresponding yearning for meat, fat and sugar, preferably with a side order of salt.

'I'm not vegetarian but basic healthy eating is good for you and for your energy levels,' Liza observed. 'Your steak's good protein, and so would the roast veg be, if you weren't just leaving it on your plate. But look at that mound of chips! Carbs unlimited. After the initial glucose peak, your blood sugar will plummet and that's when you might feel sleepy.'

He looked amused. 'So I should eat my veg, like my mum always told me?'

She shrugged. 'All the veg and about one-quarter of the potatoes would contribute to a stable blood sugar and, therefore, energy level.'

But, by the time she'd drunk jasmine tea and he'd drunk more water with the long-suffering air of the beer-deprived, it was she who was smothering yawns. 'I've had it. Want a lift home?'

'But—' he began. Then, after a beat, 'OK, thanks.' Laughter lurked in his eyes. Probably coming up with a new miniature car joke, she thought, pulling her jacket on crossly.

They hurried across the dark car park, wind buffeting and icy rain prickling. But it wasn't until they'd gained the safety of her car and she was clicking herself into her seatbelt, saying, 'You'll have to remind me where Miranda lives,' that she discovered what he thought was so funny.

'Great End.'

She halted. Spearing him with a glare, she twisted the key in the ignition and flipped on the wipers, dropped the clutch and shoved the car in gear. 'Great End ... *there*?' She nodded at the long, narrow cul-de-sac diagonally across the road.

He made a show of peering through the windscreen into the windy darkness. 'That's it.' He threw back his head to laugh at her exasperation. 'It's the kind of distance that golf buggies are designed for, right?'

Fury buzzed suddenly through her veins, shorting the circuit to common sense and reason. 'What *is* this? National Treat Liza Like a Stupid Blonde Day?' Boiling blood floored her accelerator and his reply was shoved back down his throat with a satisfying, 'Oof!' as the 'golf buggy' rocketed to the exit, engine protesting. Slamming on the brakes, she performed a scant one-second check each way for traffic, stamped again on the accelerator, catapulted across the road to two-wheel it into Great End – and found herself facing a Range Rover in the middle of the road. 'Oh *fuck!*'

Hands clenching around the steering wheel, she mashed the brake pedal, yanking the wheel violently to the left towards a shrinking gap that she feared was too skinny even for a Smart car.

She screamed.

The car jerked and stalled.

With an angry *blaaaaaah* of its horn, the Range Rover wheeled slowly past, its doors almost touching Liza's window.

Sudden silence.

Liza felt herself begin to shake as the adrenaline that had flash-flooded her system gurgled away in disgrace.

Slowly, Dominic unpeeled himself from the dashboard, his expression unreadable in the darkness. 'You OK?'

'Of course,' she began, hoping that the thundering of her heart would soon stop making her feel sick. Then she noticed him rubbing his forearms. 'You weren't wearing your seat belt!' she said, horrified. 'I'm *so* sorry. I can't believe I did anything that childish.'

He laughed, albeit breathlessly. 'I suppose I ought to be complaining bitterly about being thrown against the dash, the door and the seat in a five-second journey. And that I saw my life flash before me when we were careering head on towards that Range Rover. But it was fun.'

'Fun?' She'd never felt more mortified. 'It was a stupid overreaction to your stupid jokes.'

He was still rubbing his arms, so they must really be stinging. 'But at least I know I'm awake.' His grin glinted in the light from Great End's only streetlamp. 'I ought to apologise for pissing you off but I'm actually tempted to go for a goodnight kiss, just to see whether I can handle the flame-breathing, demonic goddess of passion it might unleash.'

She giggled. But her heart was still bouncing off the walls of her chest and, somehow, the giggle broke. And became a sob. Appalled, she clapped a hand across her mouth.

Dominic pulled back. 'Wow, it was a joke. I'm not going to try anything. I don't hit on a woman when she's down.'

She swallowed. 'It's not—' But post-adrenaline-rush tears prickled her eyes.

Dominic slid one arm cautiously about her shoulders. 'You're shivering. Come indoors, I'll make you a hot drink.'

She shook her head. In fact, she shook all over. 'I can't go in like this. Miranda will think something awful has happened and insist on ringing my sister.'

'That's true. Miranda's been in mother-hen mode over me, since narcolepsy came into my life, so she'll cluck all over you, too, given half the chance.' He hesitated. '*Has* something awful happened? You seem on an emotional hair trigger.'

She half-laughed. 'Not recently.' She shook harder, all the tension and guilt of the past year apparently awoken by her stupid mad dash.

'Shall I drive you home?'

She wanted to chirp, 'I'll be fine!' But she was vibrating as if her muscles would soon shake from her bones. 'I'm not usually a wuss.' She shivered. 'But I've turned to jelly.' Jellyfish. Blindly stinging, uncaring at inflicting hurt. And she'd just almost got both of them hurt. Badly. Sickness swam over her in waves as she unfastened her seatbelt and he jumped out and ran around the little car, opened the door and waited as she slid over to the passenger seat, taking her seat belt and clicking it into place for her. Then he dropped the driver's seat down and back before taking her place.

Then she remembered. 'But you're not supposed to be driving!'

'Nope.' He put the car into first, nosed into a nearby drive that she supposed must be Miranda's, reversed around and drove to the mouth of Great End. 'My licence has been suspended. Where do I go?'

'But won't you get in trouble?'

'We both will, if we're caught. Left or right?'

'Left.' She directed him down Main Road and right into The Cross. It took only three minutes. They drew up outside number 7 and she didn't object when he eased her out of the car as if she were ill, took her key and opened her front door. Still absurdly gripped by post-meltdown shakes, she let him deposit her on her sofa. He draped his coat over her, and she huddled and trembled while he clattered around in her kitchen and presently returned with two steaming mugs. 'I couldn't find proper tea or coffee, so it's that jasmine stuff.'

She nodded. Her eyes felt squinched half-shut and gritty. 'I don't do much caffeine. I'm sorry. I'm never like this.'

Dominic frowned as he slid the mugs onto the table. 'What's wrong with caffeine? You're still shivering.' He dropped down onto the sofa beside her and slowly, delicately, as if giving her plenty of opportunity to object, put his arm around her.

Gratefully, Liza shared his body heat. 'Dull skin, high blood pressure, headaches. I'm *honestly* never like this.'

'It also keeps you alert. Want me to get your sister or one of your friends?'

'Cleo's got enough on her hands with the kids. And my friends live in Peterborough.'

'I can't leave you on your own like this. Are you ill?'

'No, it's emotional.' Her teeth chattered.

'You don't get emotional for no reason.' He waited, as if leaving a blank for her to fill in. But she remained silent. His voice dropped. 'I'm a good listener. Sometimes crap has to come out.'

He was warm and comforting and she let her head fall onto his shoulder, her arms sliding naturally around him. It seemed a long time since she'd nestled against the bulk of a man's body. 'Sometimes it stays hidden because it's really ugly.'

'True.' He paused. 'How about I tell you mine? It might be uglier than yours.'

'Bet it's not.'

'Oh, I don't know.' His arm tensed. 'I left my girlfriend the day she phoned and told me she'd had a miscarriage.'

Chapter Eleven

PWNsleep message board:

Tenzeds: N was diagnosed at a really bad time for me. It changed everything.

Nightjack: There's a good time? *Ironic laugh*

Sleepingmatt: I think he's got a point. If other things in your life are good and you have support, it's got to be easier than if not.

Tenzeds: 'Supportive' my partner was not.

Girlwithdreams: That's harsh. I hate it that a person would be like that.

Dominic's chest rose and fell on a sigh. 'Natalie's career in marketing was going well and we didn't mean to start a baby – in fact, we were both shocked to find ourselves the creators of living proof that no contraception's foolproof. She actually tried to hide the pregnancy, but morning sickness gave her away. Once I got over the shock, I was pleased about the baby, but it threw her for a loop.'

'Oh no.' His sweatshirt was soft beneath her skin but, under it, she could feel his muscles working against her temple as he swallowed.

'It came after we'd been through a patch so sticky we could walk on ceilings.' He smiled, crookedly. 'I guess we kissed and made up too thoroughly.' His voice became husky. 'Natalie wouldn't have been a stay-at-home mum, not like Miranda, but other couples seem to combine family and careers. I didn't know it was narcolepsy at that point and was still trying to get well enough to return to work but we could have afforded a nanny after Natalie's maternity leave … Anyway, she was all over the place. Said she felt invaded, a host to a parasite, and how was I going to do my share with a baby? I might fall asleep if I was in charge, or be impossible to wake when the baby cried during the night. And I couldn't reassure her, because she might have been right.' She felt him wince. 'She'd never wanted to get married but I suggested it again, anyway. It didn't help. Things were causing arguments that never had before – suddenly she had issues with Kenny, who I've been mates with since school. I know Kenny's a bit of a one-off but she'd always seemed fine with him. And she'd say things like, "Dominic, please get better," as if I just wasn't trying. When I dozed off during cosy activities like watching a DVD on a rainy Sunday she said I must find her boring. I asked her to just wake me but she kept letting me sleep, then being upset about it.' Thoughtfully, he added, 'It's difficult to explain, but her not waking me felt like a kind of betrayal. She knew that I was massively frustrated about wasting my life on unscheduled sleep, but she not only let me do that, she made me feel guilty about it. Normally a reasonable and articulate person, she became irrational, and unwilling to talk about why.

'But I tried. Really focused on her. She calmed down a bit and I began to hope that she was over the shock of the pregnancy.'

'Like it had been denial hormones, or something?'

He hesitated. 'I don't know. Is there such a thing?'

'I don't know, either. But my sister managed to deny her first pregnancy for months, so I suppose there must be.'

'Maybe, because she did begin to say that she wanted to find a way to work things out. Then she went off to a conference in Manchester – and rang to tell me that she'd miscarried. I felt sick.' His shoulder rose and fell on a sigh. 'I was concerned for her, especially as she sounded really odd. I assumed she was feeling terrible, maybe out of guilt for not wanting the baby. But she brushed away any suggestion that she should have stayed in hospital, or that I should go up there. "It's not as if you can drive, is it?" she said. But I got on a train.' He wiped his forehead with his sleeve. 'I found her at the Marriott in Deansgate, exactly where she'd told me she would be – but the conference facilities were all listed as in use by other organisations, not hers, and I didn't see any of her colleagues around.

'Her best friend, Virginia, was with her in a room with two double beds, though. And it's *so* not Natalie, sharing a room. Virginia said that "the hospital" had told Natalie not to be alone for a night or two. But when I asked the name of the hospital they just looked at each other.' His voice hardened. 'I got curious about why Virginia was so conveniently in Manchester, as she's a vet who lives in Islington, and Natalie hid behind wounded dignity, saying that I obviously didn't trust her and so there was no point talking about it.'

He took a long, deep breath, making Liza's head lift. 'It was a nightmare; Natalie stuttering and stammering and Virginia trying to head me off really obviously with exclude-the-man remarks like, "Do you really think you ought to be badgering a woman who's just been through something so major?" and refusing to leave, even when I swore at her. Then a nasty suspicion began to dawn on me and I asked Natalie if she'd got rid of our baby. She was like a statue. Just wouldn't answer. Or couldn't, I suppose, if she hadn't expected me to turn up and thought she still had time to get her story straight. I saw panic in her eyes, and my knees … I don't know if you're clear about how cataplexy works? It comes with emotion. It had only been a sort of fuzzy weakness in my legs before when I laughed or got angry, but this time I felt as if my knees had disappeared. My head tipped back off my neck and I hit the deck. That was when I cracked my shoulder.

'Natalie and Virginia were *watching*. They just stood there, Natalie crying and Virginia wringing her hands. I couldn't speak, I had to stay down and wait for my strength to wash back in.

'When I was operative again, I rang a guy on Natalie's team in Hertford. I knew him pretty well and so I asked if Natalie was at the conference. He started to say, "What conference?" then got all flustered as he realised that there probably was a reason that I was asking him, not Natalie, and did a last minute, inadequate, job of trying to cover for her.' He laughed, humourlessly. 'I ended the call and asked Natalie to explain and—' he cleared his throat – 'she just carried on crying, and Virginia stared out of the window as if waiting politely for me to leave. So that's what I did. My knees had come back and my head was on straight and I got back on the train and went home to pack. I moved into a motel for a while then, as Kenny was starting a contract in the States, I sublet his place in Royston. Natalie did ask a few times if we could meet and talk, but I couldn't see much point, if she'd aborted my baby.

'Ironically, it was the scene with Natalie that allowed the consultant neurologist to confidently diagnose the narcolepsy, because not all narcoleptics have cataplexy but all cataplexy sufferers are narcoleptics. So then I had to cope with the shock and what narcolepsy meant. No more career as a controller. Driving licence not coming back for a while. Parents bewildered. On top of that, there was no more baby.' He swallowed. 'Losing Natalie became only a part of it.'

Liza tightened her arms around him. 'I'm so sorry.'

'Yeah. It sucked.'

His body heat had chased away most of her shivers but she wriggled her arms through the sleeves of his coat so that she was wearing it back to front, and passed him one of the cups of jasmine tea. He sniffed it cautiously, before sipping, and made a not-as-horrible-as-I-thought-it-would-be face. She settled back between an arm of Dominic and an arm of sofa. 'Is there any feeling left between you?'

He shrugged. 'When she realised I'd really left her she seemed totally shocked. Said that splitting up wasn't what she wanted and she knew that she'd handled my illness and her pregnancy badly. But she had to admit that she'd had an abortion, so there was no going back, for me. And I doubt she would've stuck around when I got my diagnosis, anyway. Not once she knew it isn't the kind of thing you get over.' He sipped, pensively. 'How would she have hacked having a boyfriend who had gone from normal to disabled, a good job to no job? She was more about what it meant for her than what it meant for me. At work, there are laws to protect you, but there's no legislation to say your partner's got to deal with your bad diagnosis.'

'Ouch,' said Liza, sympathetically.

'Our house was sold. I got on with learning about living with narcolepsy, developing my sleep hygiene routine, taking drugs, being a zombie most mornings and folding up under sleep attacks during the day. If it wasn't such a bad joke, I'd say it was a nightmare. And I get those, too.' He glanced down at her as she pulled his coat away to let some air in, the tea warming her from the inside. 'You OK in there? I can move into a chair if you want.'

She discovered that she didn't want. 'Not unless you do. It's sort of comforting to share the sofa, to be honest. A break from relationships isn't so much about no sex but about no physical contact, except cuddles from Cleo and the kids. Which are not so much reassuring as consolatory,' she added, honestly.

Gently, he looped his arm back around her. 'So would this be OK?'

'If you don't mind?' she answered, politely.

'Not at all. You could even move onto my lap, for a more complete cuddle experience?'

'Don't spoil it!' She frowned in mock reproof. Her voice sounded odd in her head with her ear squashed against him. She closed her eyes, listening to the comforting beat of his body. And suddenly she was talking. Telling him what had happened to her. 'I was in a relationship with a man called Adam. He was a really good guy. A good boyfriend. Or he would have been for someone else. Not me.'

'Why not for you?'

A sigh began in the arches of her feet and heaved out through her chest. 'I'm just a crap girlfriend. Adam did everything right. He loved me and made me feel special. He put me first, he bought me presents, he was thoughtful in bed. He was everything I felt as if I ought to want. Cleo had this awesome relationship – in her own peculiar way – with Justin, and I wanted to feel that way about Adam, too.'

'But you didn't?'

'I tried.'

'You shouldn't have to try.'

'No,' she agreed, despondently. 'But I thought that if I could make myself into the kind of woman who would be happy with Adam, then I *would* be happy with Adam. But there were a lot of differences between us. I'm not close to my parents because they're very much absorbed in their own little world, but he has this huge family: three brothers, two sisters, at least five-hundred-and-forty grandparents, aunts, uncles and cousins. It meant a superabundance of family occasions.'

'Don't all families have gatherings of the clan? I don't have siblings but I do have a load of cousins, aunts and uncles, and I regularly have to put on a tie and turn up at a wedding or christening.'

She struggled to express the scale of the issue. 'But Adam's mum, Ursula, and all of Ursula's sisters, throw every one of their children a proper birthday party, every year. Not just when they're twenty-one or something. *Every* year – and that's before they even get started on engagements, weddings and christenings. Ursula Überhostess is a vicious competitor. A fortune goes on balloons and streamers, work-of-art handmade cakes and enough homemade food to save a starving nation.'

'Sounds a bit full on,' he admitted.

'I began to feel like the Queen, obliged to dress up, turn up and smile for hours, whether I liked the company or not. So I generally drank my way through it. And Ursula would take it upon herself to "have a little word with me" about how "bubbly" I was getting. The more little words she had with me, the more I'd bubble. Every time a party invitation arrived, I'd say to Adam, "Why don't you go to this one without me?" and he'd be so hurt and dismayed that I'd go through the whole torture again.'

'Definitely girlfriend abuse.'

She laughed, unwillingly. 'I suppose it sounds as if I'm making a lot out of nothing? But I felt I was being stuffed into a straightjacket of other people's expectations, and that Adam never saw the real me – just what he thought his girlfriend should be. Anyway, along comes Adam's thirtieth birthday party. Because it was a "special" birthday, Ursula rented a hall and planned a big bash, mostly populated by Adam's enormous family, and I really tried to conform. But while Adam got deep into doing the rellies thing, I got—'

'"Bubbly?"'

'So bubbly I could hardly stagger about.' Trying not to let her voice waver, she told him about the helium balloons and how the duck voice had seemed so hilarious. Until Adam's proposal. And her brutal refusal. '… and the whole room went deathly quiet. Then some people began to laugh, as if they knew I could only be joking.

'But I wasn't. They realised the depths of Adam's humiliation and there was this horrible shocked silence, instead.'

Liza closed her eyes against the images of Adam lurching to his feet, death-white, eyes enormous with pain. Stumbling down the steps, blundering through his party guests. The old familiar cold corkscrew of misery twisted her insides.

Dominic held her a little tighter. 'Public proposals are manipulative because they're difficult to refuse.'

'But, unfortunately for him, I didn't find refusal difficult,' she pointed out, sadly. 'He ran off. Rochelle and Angie got me home and I rang him ...' Tears began to slide down her face. 'I told him how sorry I was and then, well it seemed like the right thing – I said that I thought we were probably over.' She was drowning in boiling tears, now, choking, sniffing, forcing the words out. 'Then Adam slashed his wrist.'

Chapter Twelve

Liza blotted her face and blew her nose. She had a pulsing whole-head headache, the table was sprinkled with a confetti of disgusting damp kitchen roll, a wet patch was dark on Dominic's sweatshirt and her throat felt as if she'd been crying razor blades. Dominic simply held her.

Finally, she took a rasping breath. 'Most people ask whether he died.'

'Did he?'

She shook her head, dislodging a late, lone tear. 'And then they want to know whether it was a real attempt or a cry for help.'

'Which was it?'

'I've never dared to ask.'

'You poor woman.' He gathered her up and onto his lap, just as he'd joked about doing. It really was a complete cuddle experience. Non-threatening, non-sexual; he was just offering her the shelter of his Dominicness. She felt surrounded, enveloped in his warmth. He'd be a good man for cold winter nights. She clung on, closing her sore eyes, allowing herself the heat, the feel, the heartbeat of another body.

'I'm glad he lived.' His voice was soft. 'Not just for him, poor guy, but because you're staggering around under enough guilt.'

'Not according to Ursula. The next day, I answered my flat door – I lived in Peterborough, then – to find Ursula screaming, "Heartless bitch!" right into my hangover. I nearly threw up over her.' Liza shuddered at the memory of the plummeting sense of horror. 'She told me that Adam had slit his wrist and it was all down to me. Then she jumped back on her broomstick and bansheed off, leaving me terrified, not knowing whether Adam was even alive. So I rang one of his brothers, Ben, and he told me that Adam had cut one wrist in the shower and then come to his senses and called an ambulance. He was in hospital, in no danger but had tendon and nerve damage.' She scrubbed at her eyes. 'He had to have counselling, later, and operations to repair the damage. Apparently, it's pretty agonising to mess up slitting your wrists.'

'Poor guy,' Dominic repeated. 'I think he might have chosen a pretty inefficient way to end things. I've read that you have to know how to do a good job and if you take time to research it the moment of blind despair would probably be past. That's why so many people do a bad job.'

'Oh.' She digested this. 'Are you saying it wasn't a serious attempt?'

'I'm not qualified to judge.' His voice reverberated through his chest wall and into her ear pressed against his shoulder. 'But he obviously came pretty smartly out of the despair, if he called his own ambulance. How is he now?'

'I don't really know.' Her voice was small. 'Ben got me in to see him in hospital when Ursula wasn't around and Adam was so sad. I felt terrible. But I felt ... relieved, too, that I hadn't said yes to him and tied myself up in something I didn't want.'

She steeled herself for her final confession. 'When he came out of hospital he kept calling round or phoning. So when I moved here, even though I'm terrified he'll hurt himself again and it will be my fault, I made it a clean break. I didn't give him my address at home or work and I changed my phone number.' She took a shaky breath in. 'Am I a horrible bitch?'

He stroked her shoulder. 'No, and I don't think you need to feel so guilty. Pretty shitty of his mother to blame you for what he did. You're perfectly entitled to reject a proposal. The circumstances were particularly crap and public for him but, helium and Donald Duck aside, he orchestrated it.'

'Oh,' she said again. That was what Cleo, Rochelle and Angie all said, too. 'But can you imagine how devastating it was for his family?'

'Of course.' He was stroking her back, now, over and over, over and over, warm and soothing. 'I can see more clearly that nobody thought of how devastating it was for you.'

She was just feeling reassured and validated by his view of things when he added, 'And I can even understand why you'd think erasing men and alcohol from your life would stop bad things happening.'

She stopped short, absorbing the arrangement of words, the hint that her thought process was flawed. At last, she muttered, defensively, 'Well, it worked.' And in case she got to like the feel of his body against hers, she slid off his lap.

He stayed for another hour, until she was dry-eyed and had drunk more jasmine tea and insisted several times that she was fine. Eventually, she pushed his coat back at him. 'I could use some time on my own.'

'OK, I know how it feels not to want fussing over – although don't tell Miranda I said that. I'll shoot off.'

She managed a smile, though her face was so tight from tears that she felt as if the skin might split. 'I probably sound incredibly ungrateful—'

'I know how it feels to be guiltily ungrateful, too – ditto, about telling Miranda.' He cut her off with a quick kiss to the temple. She could imagine him giving the same kind of kiss to an aunt. 'You just want some you time. You've had a bad day.'

She rubbed at where a headache pressed with a gnarly hand. 'And tomorrow's not likely to be good, either. I have to talk to Nicolas some more. We might not have left much unsaid, today, but we did leave things unfinished because he never actually said that he didn't want to sell me the lease of The Stables. If he will, then I have to see if I can get the finance. If not, I'll have to decide when to relocate.' Then she caught sight of his expression – shock with a generous dash of horror. 'What?'

'Shit.'

'What?'

He blew out his cheeks. 'I didn't know that that's what you were arguing about, that you were hoping to buy the lease. I've approached him about it, too. And the hotel – I'm just waiting on Nicolas naming his price before setting up a meeting with them.'

Slowly, Liza slumped back onto the sofa. 'Oh.' She held her head harder. 'But you don't want anything to do with therapy.'

'No.' His eyes were rueful.

'So … what's your angle?'

His expression darkened at the edge to her voice. Slowly, he put his coat down and sat down again. On a chair this time. Carefully distant. 'It all depends on me being able to lease or rent the land beside the centre, going down to the lake. I have an idea for an action-and-challenge centre – paintballing, kayaking, zip ropes, a climbing wall; that kind of thing. My mate Kenny's an instructor and he's finishing a contract in America so he might be interested in being a part of it.'

She struggled to make sense of his words at the same time as fighting fresh, self-pitying tears. *But I want it!* she wanted to cry. 'They're outdoor things. I don't see why you need The Stables.'

'For changing rooms, team room, showers, kitchen.' His eyes were compassionate. 'Sorry. I did ask several times if you were still going to relocate. You said yes. I'm not trying to put you out of business.'

Suddenly, she was on her feet, fighting a feeling of being incredibly, irrationally let down. 'But that's exactly what you're doing.'

He rose, too, warily. 'But the centre doesn't work, you told me yourself.'

'Not with Nicolas in charge – but with me!' She found herself thumping theatrically on her chest. 'I can make it work. I'm going to put a beautician in Nicolas's room and do pampers and parties. And find some way to exploit the wasted space that's reception. All that's wrong with The Stables is Nicolas and his dozy ideas.'

Dominic looked uncomfortable, regretful. 'I'm sorry to spoil your plans. But couldn't you do all this somewhere else?'

She folded her arms. 'Couldn't you put your stupid outdoor games somewhere else? I was at the centre before you came up with your bright idea.'

'And I made my offer to buy the lease before you made yours.'

They stared at one another.

Liza felt ridiculous. Here she was cuddling this man – *taking up all his evening whilst you wailed all over him,* a little voice inside her argued – and all the time he was after Nicolas's lease. *Her* lease. Anger flickered. She drew herself up. 'So?'

'So ...?'

'So what are you going to do, now that you know the situation?'

His gaze narrowed. 'I'm guessing you have an opinion on what I should do?'

'Bale out,' she said, promptly. 'Because otherwise you'll put me, Fenella and Imogen out of business.'

'Or you could pull out? Because otherwise my business won't get off the ground.'

'But it's not your ground!'

His expression softened. His hair was falling in his eyes. Suddenly he looked once again the nice – and smoking hot – guy she'd known till now. 'So, convince me it ought to be yours. What do you have in place? A plan?'

'Yes!'

'Agreement from Nicolas that he'll sell you his lease?'

'Not yet.'

'Do you have the finance to pay the premium, the deposit and the initial rent? The solicitor's fee? The accountant?'

'Not *yet*!'

'OK, let's suppose for a moment that you try hard to get the finance, and you can't.'

'I'll keep trying.'

'For how long?'

'As long as it takes.' She matched him stare for stare.

His expression wasn't soft any more. 'So you want me to give up all my plans, *just in case* yours come off? Even though I already know I won't have trouble with the finance?'

'Why? Are you rich?'

'No,' he retorted. 'But I have my half of the proceeds from my old home in Hertfordshire plus a sizeable chunk of loss of licence compensation from the insurance I carried as an air traffic controller. I have agreement in principle from my bank for the rest, if the figures turn out to be more or less what I've forecast.'

'Oh.' She watched him slip back into his coat, her mind working feverishly on potential holes in his clever-clever plan. 'But you don't have collateral. I have this house.'

He glanced around, not trying to hide his smile. 'I should

think the mortgage is bigger than the house. It goes well with your car.' He leaned forward as if to pop another of those annoying little kisses on her forehead.

She swatted him away. 'Don't diss my house. It's *my house*. It means I don't have to go and plonk myself on relatives.' That was mean. That was below the belt. But she'd spent the evening curled up on his lap and now—

'Point to you,' he nodded, annoyingly not getting pissed off at her low blow. And he turned for the door, which was a pity because it pre-empted her relieving her feelings by ordering him to leave. 'Sleeping in my cousin's spare room sucks and she has a tendency to try and rescue me – that's another thing I feel ungrateful about. I need my own place. So you can see why it's important to me to get my business plans on the go. Then I can find a flat and stop my life being so crap.'

'But my life sucks, too,' Liza protested at the closing door. 'My life sucks *more*.' Which sounded really childish.

And made him laugh. She heard him, just as the door clicked shut. Bastard.

Chapter Thirteen

It was that day again, Diagnosis Day, when he'd discovered the truth about what he'd fought not to accept. He was locked in.

Dominic could see the huge black padlock on the door of the doctor's office as he turned away from the big, grey doctorly desk, desperate not to have to see Dr Meadows's sympathetic expression or hear the confirmation that there truly was something wrong with Dominic's brain. That regular sleep was necessary to normal human function and, for the rest of his life, he was going to need drugs to even attempt that normality.

Despite the futility he lunged for the door but suddenly Natalie was leaning against it, blocking his escape, her eyes filled with accusation – perhaps now he could see why she couldn't have had the baby? How was she supposed to have coped?

Anger and guilt flooded through him.

They would have found a way.

Other people coped with worse. Much.

But Natalie was turning away—

Dominic surged for the surface of consciousness, trying to fight his way out from under the sleep monster, to burst out of the dream consultant's room of unhappiness and anxiety.

He lay still, heart pounding, still tasting the sourness of a particularly realistic unreality as he tried to wrestle the negative emotions back into their compartments. Anger. Worry. Resentment. Those emotions weren't productive. They weren't even accurate in the context of real life – on Diagnosis Day he'd felt *relief*, in a massive wave, to learn that there was a physical reason for the horrible sleep attacks and lack of concentration. Something that wasn't his fault. The enemy had shown its ugly face and so he could learn what to expect and where best to place his defences.

It was almost time to get up, and though his bed's seductive arms were trying to tempt him back, he needed to get away from the bad dream. He pushed against the mattress, getting himself up onto the side of the bed. Across the room, Crosswind opened one eye then resettled himself on his beanbag. Dominic shoved himself up to his feet, felt on the shelf for his meds, took the white pill, the yellow.

He wasn't crap – the narcolepsy was. All he had to do was learn to live with it.

And then his first alarm clock went off. He turned on it on a flame of rage, 'Fuck off!', slapping at the big blue button so hard that he swiped the clock from the bedside, against the wall and onto the floor.

Crosswind launched out of sleep, bounding to the floor and barking himself round in a furious circle. Then he skittered over to Dominic, whining, ears back anxiously, tail beating at a low, unhappy angle. *There's nothing here, boss. What's up?* Slowly, Dominic sank back onto the bed. 'Sorry, mate. It's just me.' He patted his lap and the little dog sprang up, tail wagging properly now but eyes still worried. Ashamed of letting anger gain control, Dominic smoothed Crosswind's hairy, intelligent little head. 'Shh, it's fine. Don't fret. I'll get through it, OK?'

Miranda's voice came through the door. 'Dom? What happened? Are you all right?'

He took a slow, deep breath. He would cope. He really would. 'Yeah, sorry, Mi. Had a bad dream and knocked my clock off and it frightened Crosswind. Give me a few minutes.'

'OK, if you're sure,' she agreed, hesitantly. After a moment, he heard her move off down the landing.

He sat still, stroking Crosswind, still trying to orientate himself in a new day, taking comfort from the warm furry body snuggled trustingly against him. 'I hope that she didn't feel vindicated about the abortion, when I was finally diagnosed.' Crosswind pricked up his ears and the ruff above his eyes lifted like surprised eyebrows. 'We would have had to think things through, but we would have worked it out.' Crosswind cocked his head, brown eyes thoughtful. Dominic sighed. 'Guess we'll never know. But it's behind us, now. I can't change history. I have to get myself a new life, get the adventure centre going.' Crosswind pulled away and jumped down, running to the door to scratch and whine.

Dominic reached for his sweatshirt. This was reality. He had to let the dog out to pee.

Chapter Fourteen

PWNsleep message board:

Tenzeds: Conundrum: always want more energy. Never want more meds.

Girlwithdreams: Avoiding high GI foods and keeping hydrated helps energy levels.

Tenzeds: *Whispers* Wtf's GI food? Something to do with American soldiers?

Girlwithdreams: *Sighs but ☺* The glycemic index is a measure of how carbohydrates affect blood sugar levels. Eat low or mid GI foods for energy.

Tenzeds: Just as long as I don't have to eat nettles and lentils ...

Girlwithdreams: No! *exasperated face* Exercise should help, too.

Tenzeds: Happily, I like exercise.

Crosswind circled expectantly, tail quivering, eyes glowing with canine intelligence, as Dominic tramped across the village playing field beside Miranda's husband, gentle, dreamy Jos. Jos had seemed happy enough to leave Miranda watching a rerun of *Ground Force* while he and Dominic braved the raw October afternoon, but being happy was Jos's thing. He was colossally happy with Miranda and Ethan, judging by the undisguised worship in his dark brown eyes when he looked at either one. He was content to restore old cars at the village garage, and satisfied any need for variety in his life via his facial hair experiments, presently a goatee that ended in a tiny plait, echoing the thick plait that snaked down his back.

'Hope you don't mind coming to meet Ethe from this party at the village hall,' Jos remarked. 'He really wants you to show the other children Crosswind doing tricks.'

'Crosswind likes playing, that's all,' Dominic reminded him, just as he had reminded Ethan. But Ethan had brushed such purism aside with joyful pleas for 'tricks' and Dominic, having helped Jos sandpaper and paint a window frame and Miranda to rake up leaves, had had a sad absence of better plans.

Helping to dispel any lingering bad feeling from his dream, this morning he'd received an e-mail from Kenny.

Doc, finished this coarse and im heading home how are your plans going because i need a job lol.

Heart soaring, Dominic had sent back: *My plans aren't finalised but they're looking good. Can you come up and have a look at the premises I'm trying to get? I'll get Miranda to let you crash on her sofa.*

The reply: *Cool ill ring you*

The exchange had made him restless, raring to go but spinning his wheels. He shifted the diagonal strap of his long narrow black backpack to a more comfortable position and Crosswind danced closer, tail a blur, eyes eager. 'In a minute,' Dominic promised.

Kicking through the grass, as if reading his thoughts Jos turned the conversation to Dominic's business plans. 'So, who goes to action-and-challenge centres?'

'Weekend Rambos. Weekday corporate teambuilding – you know the stuff, when CEOs think that their staff will soar to new heights if they learn how to build a raft together.'

Jos looked vaguely surprised. 'Do they? Why would it?' The closest he ever got to the corporate world was driving past business parks around the edges of Peterborough.

'Teamwork,' explained Dominic. 'Problem solving, conceptualising solutions, planning, communicating. Or, sometimes, they send their staff out to have fun at a kart track.'

Jos's eyes gleamed eagerly. 'Are you going to have a kart track?'

'No, it would be a bit hairy, considering the slope. Mountain biking would be possible ... I'm still working on my ideas. But I'm going around in circles until I can get permission from the hotel to buy the lease – if Nicolas hasn't decided not to sell, meantime. Or to sell to someone else.'

They reached the car park that ran around two sides of the village hall, presently more occupied by adults rocking buggies and keeping beady eyes on children racing around the tarmac than by parked cars. Dominic called Crosswind to sit by his feet so no parent would be nervous that he might turn out to be a frothing pitbull dressed up in curls and a square-faced doggy grin.

One of the adults was a woman almost hidden by a yellow bear-ears hat and a dark green coat that ended around her ankles. She was wearing something that looked like a backpack worn on her front, as if she were a London tourist wary of pickpockets. As Dominic watched, she dropped her face to the backpack and went, 'Nom nom nom! Nom nom nom nom *nom!*'

For a startled instant, he wondered whether it was a nose bag, not a backpack. But then Jos laughed and the girl lifted her head and turned, the plaited woollen ties of the ridiculous hat swinging in time with the pom-poms on her suede boots. The 'backpack' had a baby in it, and the baby's downy head was what she'd been pretending to eat. Judging by his gummy smiles and crinkled eyes, it had sent the recipient to baby utopia. He kicked and laughed, one tiny arm looped neatly around Liza's left breast, the mittened hand resting on the flesh visible in the V of her coat. Dominic was reflecting that he'd smile, too, if his hand were so fortunate, when he realised that he was being glared at, reminding him of his new place in Liza's life as The Competition.

'Lucky little chap,' he said, gravely, ignoring the glare. Then, 'Lovely little chap,' with exactly the same inflection, as if that's what he'd said the first time. He took the baby's hand – the one that was flailing loose, not the one that had possession of the smooth foothill of Liza's breast – and shook it solemnly. 'Good afternoon. I'm Dominic Christy.'

Liza defrosted enough to reply on the baby's behalf. 'He's Gus, my nephew. Hello, Jos.'

Jos gave her his shy smile. 'You on auntie duty?' They fell into conversation about children that Dominic didn't know, although it became apparent that one was another Sunday afternoon partygoer, Shona, Liza's niece. Dominic unhooked his arms from his backpack and Crosswind immediately bounced, barked, and began to whirl on the spot. 'Sit, Crosswind,' Dominic murmured, and Crosswind did the excited-dog thing of pseudo-sitting, bum not quite touching the ground because his tail had become a propeller. His gaze was fixed on Dominic as he unzipped the sides of the pack to ease out a green-and-red, double-kick skateboard, battered graphics and pitted wheels bearing testimony to much use.

A sharp bark: *Get on with it, boss!* and Crosswind shuffled on his bottom.

'Won't be long.' Dominic spun the wheels with his palms, then put down the skateboard. He straightened, and saw Liza watching, eyes full of questions, which was better than her glaring knives at him. Giving her his sweetest smile, he went back to examining his skateboard.

Then the double doors at the front of the village hall banged open and children spilled into the grey light, half into coats and clutching clown-strewn goodie bags, smiles outlined in chocolate and blackcurrant. A small partygoer in a black-and-red dress raced over to Liza, windmilling her arms. 'Aunt-ee Lie-zah!'

Dominic watched Liza crouch down and scoop the excited child against her. 'Hiy-ah, Sho-nah!' And carefully present the baby's head to be kissed.

Then Ethan came charging through the pack. 'Dommynic! Did you bring ...? *Yeah*! Maff-yoo, Maff-yoo, Dommynic brought it! Show Maff-yoo, Dommynic!' People turned to watch the excitement as 'Maff-yoo' evaded an expectant parental hand to run behind Ethan.

Crosswind, forgetting his doggie manners, shot off to round up Ethan and escort him to Dominic with shrill barks of joy.

'Stand still, then,' said Dominic, quietly to Ethan. And, more sharply, 'Crosswind! Quiet!' He picked up the skateboard and, selecting a smooth and empty section of the car park, bowled it across the surface with a practised underarm. Yapping with glee, Crosswind raced in pursuit and sprang into the air, landing with three paws on the board, 'scooting' manically with the other, whilst the parents laughed and the children clapped, goodie bags spilling onto the damp ground. 'The dog skateboarded! Mummy! Daddy! That dog skateboarded!'

Dominic ran after the slowing board, scooping it up as Crosswind jumped off and raced a circle, tongue out, eyes alight and tail an almost invisible indicator of waggy doggy joy. Dominic launched the board once more. Two sharp barks and a nail-clicking scurry from his bandy legs and Crosswind hurled himself back onto the deck, scooting furiously. 'Yeah, yeah, see the doggie!' squealed the children, while the adults laughed and clapped.

It generally took about a year for Crosswind to get tired of the skateboard and Dominic jogged relentlessly from one end of the car park to the other to retrieve and relaunch the board. He probably would have called it a day much sooner if it hadn't been for Liza holding hands with the golden-haired little girl, dancing and laughing, clutching her bear-ears hat and baby Gus joggling like a doll.

Finally, parents began to turn children for home and Dominic paused, breathing hard, to rub Crosswind's ears. 'That's enough, fluff face.' Crosswind laughed up at him, panting, but obviously game for hours more fun.

Jos had fallen into conversation with a man with twin girls and Ethan, eyes beginning to puff with fatigue, had opted for a perch on his daddy's shoulders. As Dominic prepared to slide the board back inside its carrier, a pair of black suede boots appeared beside him, pom-poms swinging, with a niece-sized pair of party shoes alongside. 'Shona wants to know if she's allowed to stroke your dog.'

Dominic smiled down at Shona. 'You bet. His name's Crosswind. Put your hand out for him to sniff, first.' Opportunistic when it came to jelly and cake residue, Crosswind licked Shona's fingers, making Shona giggle, and Liza crouched down to stroke his curls back from his eyes. Crosswind flattened his ears and half-closed his eyes in tongue-lolling rapture.

Liza glanced at Dominic. 'Can you ride the board, too?'

'A bit.' He pulled the lead from the front pocket of his backpack and snicked it onto Crosswind's collar, earning him a canine dirty look, and offered Liza the human end. 'He'll pull, so hold tight.' Then he gave the nose of the board an expert nudge with the toe of his trainers to point it towards a clear area of asphalt, planted his left foot over the front axle and launched with his back foot, enjoying hearing the familiar *whizzzzzzzzzuzzzuzzz*, got both feet on deck, adjusting his stance with a tiny bunny hop. Then he put his back foot on the tail and popped it, keeping his front foot just behind the front axle to snap the nose from side to side. Dropping down, he got back to speed then, back foot on the tail, popped up into an ollie, caught the deck, ollied one-eighty frontside, popped it again and, using the side of his front foot, kickflipped and landed it several times, once with a double rotation.

'Look at Dommynic!' he heard Ethan roar. Crosswind yapped, *Why can't I play?* One-eightying, Dominic raced back through a series of ollies and kickflips, until he popped it hard with his front foot, nollie flipped, and landed it in front of Liza.

Shona was clapping. Liza was laughing. She cocked one eyebrow at him in the last of the autumn light. 'Not bad.' She reached up, pulled his head down so that she could put her lips against his ear, her words no more than a breath, making the pit of his stomach judder. 'OK, I'm impressed. But that lease is still mine.' Then she produced a small pink bear-ears hat from her pocket and plopped it on Shona's head. 'Come on, let's take Gus-Gus home and see what Mum's made for tea.'

And she slapped on her own stupid hat and turned to march away across the playing field.

He watched her go, wondering whether he'd just met the real Liza Reece for the first time. She'd been fun. Dancing eyes and cocky comments, joggling the baby while she poked fun at him. No temper. No ungraciousness. No pain on her face, or strain. On the other hand, she hadn't cuddled up and rolled her head on his shoulder, exposing the soft curve of her neck and making him burn to swoop on it, either ...

He watched the swing of her coat, the turn of her head as she looked down to talk to Shona and cuddled that lucky baby to her breasts. It was a damned waste that a woman with such an obvious capacity to care should have thrown up so many walls between herself and men.

Jos, still wearing Ethan on his shoulders, grinned and clapped him on the arm. 'Put your tongue away, skateboy. You showed off all your best tricks but it got you nowhere. It's a serious bummer but let's go home for tea.'

Chapter Fifteen

PWNsleep message board:

Brainwave: I need to change something. My office is so quiet and stuffy ... even the normals are getting sleep attacks! I'm thinking I need a new job.

Tenzeds: I've got similar plans. Have hopes they'll work out.

Girlwithdreams: I wish mine would.

Dominic claimed his spot at the kitchen table with his phone, iPad and notepad, as Miranda baked and talked and listened to the radio and Ethan eeked, whooped and eeeee-owwwwed his way through a game of 'parachuting' off a chair with a tea towel.

Dominic rang Nicolas and got straight to the point. 'Now you've had a few days to consider, what are your thoughts about me taking over your lease? Do you have a figure for me?'

A hesitation. 'I'm still talking numbers with my advisor, because there's someone else interested.'

'Liza Reece?'

Nicolas was clearly taken aback either by Dominic's knowledge or his willingness to share it. 'That's right,' he agreed, cautiously. 'And in many ways, I'd prefer the place to go to her and to continue, however approximately, to be a treatment centre.'

It was a transparent attempt to play Liza off against Dominic but, though Dominic's dream was fresh and compelling, he wasn't about to be negotiated into paying unfeasible sums to make it real. He made his voice polite but bored. 'Would you like me to withdraw my offer? If

I need to start looking elsewhere, then I'd like to get that underway.' Through the window, he watched the trees in the garden stretching their black arms to the clouds, summer's green-leaf clothes turned to brown autumn rags.

Nicolas answered stiffly. 'I'll get back to you soon.'

Dominic ended the call with a casual acknowledgement, as if not fizzing with frustration at Nicolas's indecisive, clumsy parrying.

'Cheee-arge!' Ethan bowled across the kitchen, ricocheting off Dominic's chair. 'Dommynic, can you play with me?'

For an instant, Dominic yearned for the calm atmosphere of the control tower and the relatively stress-free task of stacking inbound air traffic before clearing them to land, thousands of airline passenger lives in his hands. 'A bit later, Ethan, OK?'

'OK. Cheee-arge!' Ethan screamed off down the hall.

Dominic picked up his notebook and pen. He was fairly certain that he could outbid Liza but he tried never to be careless when reacting to situations. He wrote *Liza* in the middle of his page. Her image flashed across his brain, blue eyes gleaming, blonde hair flying.

'Cheee-arge!' Ethan raced back in and paused beside Dominic's chair, breathing heavily. 'Got a sword, Dommynic?'

'Sorry, I'm afraid I haven't.' Dominic ruffled Ethan's fair hair, hoping Ethan wasn't going to try too hard to drag him into a game, because he would really rather think about Liza Reece. In fact, though he didn't want to injure Ethan's feelings by pointing it out, there were quite a lot of things he'd rather do than race around yelling 'Cheee-arge!'

Miranda came to the rescue. 'Dominic doesn't have a sword because they're not nice things, Ethan, because they hurt people. But if you wash your hands, you can paint the egg on the pastry for me. Then we can put the pie in the oven, ready for lunch.'

Ethan shouted, 'Yeah!' and began screeching a kitchen chair over to the sink.

Dominic turned back to his pad. When Liza laughed, all trouble vanished from her face. Her laughter was like musical notes tumbling from her lips, spangling her eyes, flushing her skin a perfect, palest pink. He enjoyed making her laugh. He began a spider plan around her name. *How big a loan can she get?* And, *Is there family money?* She'd said she wasn't close to her parents, but it would be unsafe to assume they wouldn't help her. And, for all he knew, her sister could be a closet millionaire. *Does Nicolas want her to get the lease? Does Nicolas not want her to get the lease?* There was definitely antipathy. *Is she likely to chicken out? (Prob not.) Is she capable of running the centre? (Probably.)* With more thought, he added, *Probably capable of anything.* And grinned, remembering her trying to face him down about the lease, as if she were big and scary. As if he hadn't just held her whilst she broke her heart about Adam, her body against his, boneless with sorrow, her tears soaking through his sweatshirt. To his skin, making it hot and damp.

What a mixture she was: wary, sad, angry, funny, quirky, bright. Grief stricken. Radiating 'don't touch' signals that he was sure were self-defence, not froideur. But she was like an air traffic controller who'd been in radio contact with an aircraft when it fell from the sky. She hadn't made the decision that led to disaster, but she hadn't reacted in a way that would avert it. She was tormented by guilt.

He must be crazy for being so attracted to her.

Potentially, she stood between himself and his goal.

And he was a goal-oriented man. Had been. Would be again. Was. But when she'd demanded that he leave The Stables to her, fight written all over her tearstained face, he'd been within a breath of saying, 'OK.' Which was stupid. Unless, on some level, he'd hoped that capitulation would prompt her to haul him off to bed. Not that he would have taken much hauling … In his imagination, he let his arms slide around that waist that looked as if he could wrap himself around it twice, and waft her smoothly up her stairs.

Will her bid drive the premium up? How can you prevent that?

He could prevent the premium being driven up – for her – if he dropped out. He stared at his plan. Getting the lease represented a giant stride towards his dream. But it had never occurred to him that realising his dream might mean trampling on someone else's.

His phone rang, vibrating against the table top like a giant bee. *Kenny* said the screen. He answered with a lift to his heart. 'Ken!'

Kenny's voice hadn't changed since the days of school detention, loud and brash. 'Hey, Doc, there's a big black Jag been left in my garage. I'm thinking of putting it on eBay.'

Dominic laughed. 'You leave my Jag alone. So you're back in England?'

'Got in yesterday. All ready to join you on your great adventure.'

'I'm still in the working-towards-adventure phase.'

'Have you asked your wonderful cousin if I can surf her sofa? Remind her how much she loves me.'

Dominic laughed and glanced at Miranda. 'Kenny wants to know if you love him enough to let him sleep on your sofa.'

Miranda grinned over her specs, cutting surplus pastry from the edge of a pie with efficient little chops. 'Always,' she declared. And, with the wisdom of long acquaintance, 'But he has to behave.'

Dominic relayed the information. 'How about you drive up in the Jag? Then we'll have transport up here.' After Kenny had hooted with glee at the idea and the call ended,

Dominic realised that he'd been phone doodling, making the L of Liza heavier and more ornate, going over and over that one letter.

Ignoring it, he worked at his plan for a bit longer, making to do lists and contingency lists and every other kind of list that seemed useful.

His eyes began to get heavy.

His mind began to slow. Ethan's shrill commentary on how to paint a pie with egg became pleasantly soporific. He sighed. Looked at his watch. Nearly midday. 'Time for some zeds.'

'OK, lunch will be ready not long after you wake up.' Miranda had flour on her chin and her smile was fond and understanding enough to make him slightly uncomfortable with it. Pity Natalie hadn't been half so accommodating. About half would be a reasonable level.

Upstairs, he set a phone alert for thirty minutes, then, grudging the time and resenting the necessity, dropped onto the single bed and let the darkness have him.

Then there were stars in the darkness, dancing with shadows, flickering, glimmering as he rushed towards them or they rushed towards him, fast and flying and exciting—

He woke with the alarm and pushed himself up to sit on the side of the bed, feeling giddy but strangely at peace. There were definitely times when the weirdness of narcolepsy was fantastical enough to be enjoyed. The vision of stars had been amazing.

Not as good as the vision of Liza Reece making love to him, of course. He wished for that one to return every time he shut his eyes.

Liza enjoyed the quiet that normally came before her first client. She looked over her Monday appointments, checked supplies and generally centred herself.

So she was irritated when Nicolas strolled into her room.

He smiled.

She raised her left eyebrow. Being able to move her eyebrows independently was surprisingly useful – the left made her look quizzical, and the right confused.

'Good weekend? Nice rest? Calmed down a bit?'

She took a deep breath and squelched the desire to spit fire at him. 'Sorry?'

'From your tantrum. On Friday.'

She changed eyebrows. 'What I remember about Friday is you being a shit.' Turning to her filing cabinet, she picked up her appointment list.

Behind her, Nicolas's laugh sounded forced. 'Come on, Liza! You provoked me.'

She would not erupt. That's what he wanted, to make her look like a hysterical babe. 'How?'

A pained pause. 'You know how you've been.'

'No? Tell me.' Her fingers walked over the alphabetical tabs, pausing to pick out Yvette Elmoor and Enid Round.

'Just, you know. Difficult. Unreasonable.'

'I wasn't remotely. I asked you a civil question and you threw a giant strop.' Wow, serenity was satisfying.

Nicolas fell silent.

Extracting the notes for the last two on her list, Marcie Yeo and Abby Andrew, she closed the drawer and carried her neat pile of notes to her desk. Silence grew thick and prickly. Nicolas stared at the ceiling, as if the secret to conversing with women might be written there. Or maybe he was praying. Finally, he sighed, and sat down. Liza neatened the notes, took her seat and looked him in the eye, controlling the conversation by speaking before he could. 'If you'd been my employer, I would be taking you to a tribunal about your unacceptable behaviour. If you don't want to sell your lease then say so, and I'll look elsewhere. Don't yell insults and try to intimidate me.'

'I think you're exaggerating.' But Nicolas looked down at his hands. Even this early in the day, his shirt collar was curling.

Liza checked the time. 'Pippa will be bringing my first client in.'

He climbed to his feet. At the door, he hesitated. 'So, when I get a valuation on the lease, we'll talk again?'

Absently, she nodded. 'Let me know the figure and I'll decide whether I want to go any further.'

The door clicked shut behind him. She counted to ten, to give him time to get into his own office.

Then she leaped out of her chair, punching the air and swinging her hips to a whispered, '*Yes! Yes! Yes!*' She was one step closer to her goal. Only a teeny step. But a step.

As she was scheduled to work until eight, Rochelle and Angie had agreed to meet her in The Three Fishes.

Her optimistic mood had carried her through the day and she fairly danced up to the table and plumped down beside her friends. 'I'm going to try and buy Nicolas's lease off him and run The Stables myself,' she announced, breathlessly.

But almost before Rochelle and Angie could arrange their expressions into surprise or pleasure or wonder, Dominic turned from the bar and said, 'That's funny. So am I.'

Angie and Rochelle's attention flipped from Liza to Dominic.

Liza glared at his grin, his hair flopping back from his eyes, aggravated that she hadn't noticed him standing nearby, gilded by the lights over the bar, before she went into broadcast mode.

He picked up his beer and sauntered to their table. 'Hello, Liza.' He dropped another of those annoying kisses on her temple – not even a proper kissy-cheek thing. 'Hi, I'm Dominic Christy.' He extended his hand first to Rochelle and then to Angie. 'As this seems to be the blonde table, do you mind if I join you?'

Rochelle and Angie predictably – if traitorously – chorused, 'That would be lovely!' and Liza cursed under her breath. All day she'd looked forward to springing her plans to revolutionise the treatment centre on her friends, enlisting their help to brainstorm funky treatments until clients burst The Stables at its seams. But not in front of Dominic, as his own plans would work out if hers didn't. And hers would work out if his didn't. Dominic reached a stool from another table and settled in to chat Rochelle and Angie up quite blatantly while Liza went to buy herself a drink, as she was the only one without.

Janice, the barmaid, was alone behind the bar and Liza had to wait, breathing in the beery smell, while Janice pulled foaming pints in her smiling, unhurried way. In fact, it took so long that Rochelle called over, 'Get me and Angie another spritzer, Lize!'

And Liza was forced, by good manners, to ask, 'Dominic?'

Amusement flickered in his eyes as he glanced at his emptying glass and smiled lazily. 'A pint of Guinness would be great. Thanks.' Evidently, he wasn't above accepting offers made through gritted teeth

By the time she'd got her order, Dominic, Rochelle and Angie were chatting like old friends. Liza slid the tray onto the table, bumping Dominic's elbow and not saying sorry. 'So,' he said, passing the spritzers to Angie and Rochelle with a smile, which meant they both said thank you to him, instead of to Liza. 'You and Nicolas sorted out your differences?'

'Some,' she said, briefly. 'Great shoes, Ange.'

Angie lifted a foot to display tan leather flatties with

extravagant tooling and thick yellow overstitching. 'I got a bonus last week. So, what's going on, Liza? How come you and Dominic both think you're going to run The Stables?'

Dominic got his answer in first. 'Unfortunately, I'd already expressed interest in the lease before Liza mentioned that she had her own plans.'

'But, unfortunately, Dominic didn't realise that if Nicolas couldn't make the treatment centre pay, I was willing and able to step up.'

Rochelle's eyes shone with mischief. 'So, you two are going into partnership?'

'No!' they said, together. And Liza wondered whether Dominic's reaction was mirrored in her face – aghast eyebrows flying up over unflatteringly horrified eyes.

Dominic made a smooth recovery. 'It wouldn't work. My idea of teamwork is for everyone in my team to do as I say.'

Liza snorted. 'That doesn't surprise me. And I'm not a do-as-you-say woman.'

'And that doesn't surprise me.'

'I'll take that as a compliment.'

Dominic pulled a face of extravagant amazement. 'Seriously?'

Rochelle laughed. 'Dominic, why don't you come to our Halloween party at my flat in Peterborough? The thirty-first is on a Monday, unfortunately, but a party's a party and I always give one at Halloween. Liza can give you a lift because she's boring about drink so she's bound to be driving both ways. Aren't you, Liza?'

Liza's jaundiced response was lost in Angie's enthusiastic, 'Good idea! The guest list's a bit light on men.'

Dominic gave Rochelle the benefit of his slow smile. 'In that case, do you have room for another? My mate Kenny will be here for a few days.'

Liza jumped in smugly. 'Then I can't give you a lift because

I'm not going to get two of you in my little Smart car, am I?'

But he just grinned. 'Kenny's bringing my car up, as it's been stored in his garage. He's happy to do a bit of chauffeuring, because, if my plans come off, he's going to work for me as an instructor.'

'So, he can drive you to the party.'

He gave her a pitying look. 'Kenny won't go to a party and not drink. No, I'll get the insurance sorted and you can drive mine. Thank you.'

Chapter Sixteen

PWNsleep message board:

GuiltyGeorge: Awww no, my GP's treating me like a kid and sending me to bed at the same time every night!

Tenzeds: Sleep hygiene? ☺ To be positive, it does provide you with a form of taking charge of your life. Taking charge makes me feel better. Sometimes.

In preparation for joining the ranks of business owners, Dominic looked for ways to feel positive and productive.

Building on his fitness, he took Crosswind on longer walks and ran or took his board and skated in the late afternoons.

He had long exciting phone-planning sessions with Kenny and shorter calls to finance and insurance providers over the boring bits. He had a preliminary meeting with an accountant in Bettsbrough.

As a smooth changeover was essential, prescription-wise, if he was to avoid becoming inoperative, he got his GP in Hertford to put him in touch with a suitable one in Peterborough, ready for if he moved into the area.

And, to make such a move possible, asked local estate agents for rental property listings, discovering there were several available actually in Middledip, all in an area called Bankside. 'The new village,' Miranda explained, with an expression that suggested only the old village was cool. 'Jos calls it Little Dallas. It's all porticoes and pillars.'

Office hours had never applied to him, but now that he needed to be functional at the same time as the ordinary working world, he began concentrating on his sleep hygiene, setting his morning alarms for seven and keeping busy until his noon sleep. In the evenings, he entertained Ethan, building Duplo castles and squidging Play-Doh, then played poker with Jos, which prevented evening-television-induced torpor. At ten, he retired to his room to read, sitting with his back against the cool of the wall. When he got into bed at eleven he was ready for sleep, rather than sleep being ready for him. He stuck to the regime religiously all week.

By Saturday, he was sick to death of it.

Even though he hadn't experienced any of the groggy days when the sleep monster wouldn't let him out from under him, he decided that nobody could live so unnaturally cleanly forever.

He texted Kenny: What's your ETA? Kenny returned: 2pm put beer in frij. Dominic walked Crosswind early and took his second white pill late, anticipating that the evening would be stimulating, with Kenny around, but bedtime would be delayed. When Kenny drew up, Dominic was so glad to see his childhood buddy that he went outside to greet him, though it wrenched his guts to see Kenny climbing out of the smooth black lines of Dominic's S Type.

'Hey, Doc!' Kenny did the cool-but-manly clasp-hands-bump-shoulders thing. Tanned and lean, his brown eyes were bright and his hair fell as if he'd had it styled that morning. Kenny might have trodden the wilderness trails but his look was anything but Grizzly Adams. 'So what's it like giving up the control tower for village life?'

'I'm getting into it.' Dominic ran a hand over the hot shiny bonnet of his Jag in a silent but loving greeting. 'Say hi to Miranda and co, then we need to go into Peterborough and hire Halloween costumes for a party on Monday.'

'Awesome.' Kenny hopped the hedge and jogged indoors for just long enough to dump his gear, get Miranda and Jos laughing, Ethan shouting and Crosswind barking. Then they were strapping themselves into the car's black leather interior, Dominic, in the passenger seat, pricked with a thousand needles of jealousy as Kenny shifted from park to reverse, turned the car and hummed forward in the smooth glide that Dominic ached to have back under his control.

He forced himself to switch focus. 'Turn right and you'll pick up the signs to Peterborough as soon as you leave the village.'

Kenny drove one-handed into Main Road, past The Three Fishes and the turning for Great Hill Road. 'Impressed that you've lined up a party on a weeknight.' He accelerated as they left the village, between leafless hedges and ploughed fields. 'And tonight, how about we take Miranda and her clan out to dinner, as they're letting us crash at their place? They'll have to disappear early because of little Ethan, then you can show me the clubbing in Peterborough.'

'I've been so taken up with getting my life back on track, I haven't done any clubbing.'

Kenny glanced over sharply, making the car jink towards the verge and Dominic clutch the sides of his seat in an effort not to protest. 'You're kidding me.'

Dominic shrugged. 'It would mean a taxi in and out of Peterborough and I wouldn't know anyone once I got there.'

Kenny shook his head despairingly. 'That's why you go to clubs, Doc, to "get to know" women. Never mind, we'll get Jos to drop us off in the city and see what we find. You're not hiding away in the sticks because you're still hung up on Natalie, are you?'

'No.' Dominic didn't elaborate. Somewhere in the corners of his mind he was aware of the reason that he hadn't looked outside Middledip for entertainment. Liza Reece. Pulling him like a magnet.

Kenny let the car slow as he approached a junction, checking both ways. 'You in touch with Natalie? I know she didn't deal with it when you … got ill.'

Kenny's tone was artificially casual and Dominic suppressed a sigh. Natalie hadn't been the only one not to deal with his narcolepsy. Kenny had been just as all-too-obviously uncomfortable with it. His heart dipped in disappointment. 'Once the house and finances were settled there wasn't much need for us to communicate but she sent me an e-card on my birthday and she e-mails now and then. She went to New York for a while, with her company, but it wasn't permanent.'

Another few minutes and they had reached the ring road around Peterborough, Kenny glancing from mirror to mirror as he slotted into the circulating traffic and straight into the fast lane until he reached the slip road marked City centre. 'She could spring some surprises, couldn't she? Natalie.'

Rocking in his seat as the car whizzed around the roundabout, Dominic sighed. 'And she got no more predictable as our relationship stalled. You know what she did with … with the baby.'

Kenny sucked in a big breath. 'Yeah. Totally shocked.' Left at the next roundabout, then right, following the flowing traffic over an old-fashioned bridge of blue-painted iron to the rising hulk of the shopping centre and the satellite multi-storey blocks, a contrast to the graceful spires of the cathedral to their right. Kenny aimed the car towards the entrance of a car park as if flying a spaceship on a video game.

Chapter Seventeen

PWNsleep message board:

Tenzeds: It's hard when N affects my mates. But then when they're tactless ...! Grr.

Sleepingmatt: Some people are *rses, mate. They can't help it.

Girlwithdreams: Is it sympathy or empathy that's the prob?

Tenzeds: Empathy, lack of. Sympathy, if there's too much! ☺

Dominic tried not to feel pissed off that, last night, Kenny had abandoned the heat and noise of the nightclub for the delights of a drunken, giggly, high-hemline, low-neckline woman with short black hair and smudged black eyeliner, leaving Dominic to queue on his own at the rank for a taxi back to Middledip.

Now it was Sunday afternoon, just when he'd planned to take Kenny to Port Manor and show him the location for his dream, and Kenny still hadn't made it back to Miranda's house. His phone was off, as if Dominic didn't already have enough frustrations.

So, here he was, staring out of Miranda's sitting room window at the scudding clouds and bending trees, on his feet because last night he'd drunk too much and slept too little and he knew that if he sat down he'd be gone. Despite his lunchtime nap, his head was shadowy and he was already full to the brim with coffee.

Negativity washed over him like dirty water. Maybe this was all just too hard. Taking Crosswind out after lunch had been the only time he'd felt alert today, and now the little dog slept on the rug before the fire, twitching with dreams. Perhaps he should start a dog-walking service. Or maybe he should forget his dreams and look for an employer to set goals and make allowances for him.

He searched inside himself for strength. Determination. Motivation. For even the minor kind of energy that had Miranda singing to herself in the kitchen and Jos doing something under the bonnet of the family car. Nope.

Slowly, he turned away from the window. Giving up, giving in, he let himself drop into a fat floral armchair and his eyes rest on the flickering flames behind the fireguard.

'Read to me, Dommynic?'

Dominic turned, blinking. He'd missed Ethan coming into the room but now the little boy was leaning over the chair arm, candid blue eyes hopeful. ''Kay,' Dominic managed, heavily.

Weight on his lap. Ethan's chatter, distant. Distance. Falling. Head tipping. He snapped it back. Sounds. Front door? Someone coming … Head tipping …

Then Dominic was trying to read a huge book, though the words meant nothing. The book was the one that Miranda's mum, Aunt Louise, used to read to him and Miranda, about dogs with eyes like saucers and toy soldiers with one leg. *Three dogs, their eyes growing larger and larger and Kenny, wanting Dominic to read to him. 'You know I can't read, Doc—'*

Ethan, whining. 'Dommynic isn't reading—'

Miranda's voice—

Dogs and soldiers—

A bell, loud and tinny. Dominic opened his eyes. Adjusted his head so that his neck stopped hurting. The bell rang on. He gazed around, trying to work out what was happening – did his phone make that sound?

On the table beside the armchair was a white device like a big bottle top with numbers all round it and the noise seemed to be emanating from that. He wiped his face, rubbed his eyes. Picked up the white device and pressed a button marked 'off'. The ringing stopped.

Crosswind had pushed himself up to a sitting position on the fireside rug, blinking away sleep, one ear folded back. He yawned and shook his head, looking as bleary as Dominic felt.

In the other fat floral armchair sat Kenny, staring. 'Fucksake, Doc,' he said, quietly.

Dominic felt a hot flush of mortification. 'Yeah.'

'I mean, fucksake. I walked in and just watched you flake out. It's like you have no control. You just, like, fall unconscious.'

'Welcome to my world. But next time, wake me, OK? Don't just ...' *Don't just watch, you freak,* he stopped himself from snapping. He glanced down self-consciously, checking for morning glory or disarranged clothing, waiting for the weight of a sleep attack to slither off him, for the prickling anger to disperse. Knowing that it soon would, that he only felt like that in the first horrible minute of waking and discovering he'd shown weakness in public. Waiting for it to be safe to stand up, he let his mind admit his surroundings: Ethan's high piping and Miranda's voice coming down the hall.

Then they were there, Miranda holding Ethan on her hip. 'Now Dominic's woken up, look.'

Ethan frowned accusingly at Dominic, finger and thumb hooked damply into his mouth. 'You went to sleep.'

Dominic managed a smile. 'Sorry, Ethe, I think you asked me to read to you just as I was dropping off. Do you want me to read your story, now?'

Ethan shook his head, fingers still in his mouth. 'Mummy readed it to me, anyway.' Then he laid his head on Miranda's shoulder and screwed his eyes shut. 'I'm 'sleep, now.'

144

Miranda grinned at Ethan's elaborately unrealistic 'nap', but her eyes were shadowed. 'I gave you about twenty minutes, because you'd already had thirty at lunchtime, was that OK? I set the oven timer.'

'Resourceful.' He felt strength return and rose to his feet, moving away from the chair, the scene of his embarrassment. He'd talk to Miranda alone, later, explain that, although he was grateful, it would have been better to rouse him and give him the chance to get himself some privacy. 'Thanks.' He yawned and stretched.

Then he was feeling OK. Everything was becoming bright and clear. He grinned at Kenny. 'So you finally found your way back? The light will soon be gone today so I'll take you to Port Manor tomorrow. How about we take Ethan and Crosswind over to the playing fields, now, to make up for my failure in the storybook department?'

'Yeah!' shouted Ethan.

Crosswind jumped to his feet, shook himself hard, collar and identity disc tinkling, and was eyes-bright awake.

Good trick. Dominic wished he knew it.

It was one of way too many lulls in the week's bookings. Liza kept finding reasons to pass through reception so she could check whether the big black car was still parked in the stable yard. An hour ago, Dominic Christy and another man had climbed out of it; she happened to have been at Pippa's desk and had watched them. The other man had gazed around at the buildings, nodding while Dominic talked, pointed, explained.

Zipped into jackets, hair blowing, both men looked alive and purposeful. Occasionally, Dominic said something that made the other man laugh. Then they turned their backs on the buildings and walked to the crest of the slope down to the lake. Dominic indicated the vista, portioning off part of the landscape possessively with his arms. Then they stepped onto the grass, disappearing in horizontal slices as they strode down the steep incline.

Huh.

Back in her treatment room, which looked out in the opposite direction, towards the hotel, Liza looked at the grey flags of clouds the sky was flying and wondered whether rain dances worked. And if there was a dance for particularly torrential rain to make Dominic and his friend race back to the car, preventing Dominic from showing off what he obviously saw as his new kingdom. Or maybe the grassy slope could cave in under the torrent and he'd shrug and move his planned outdoorsy centre to ... somewhere else. A really good somewhere else, she thought, generously, where he would be happy and fulfilled and make lots of dosh.

And then Liza would have no competition for the lease and Nicolas would have to let it go – to her – for some affordable sum. She could make a huge success of her new venture. And also lots of dosh.

Sorted.

Except, it wasn't raining. There was no landslip. He probably wouldn't even get mud on his shoes.

She looked across at Nicolas's door. Shut again. Some suit had gone in first thing this morning, armed with laptop and briefcase. Nicolas had given the same suit a tour of the centre three days ago, without introducing him to anyone. Liza suspected he was valuing the lease and had returned today to help Nicolas decide on an asking price.

Or he could be another person interested in taking the lease. The idea collided uncomfortably with the walls of her stomach. Her hands clenched and she wanted to shake Nicolas until he spat out how much he wanted for his precious lease, so that she could make an appointment with the bank and set the ball rolling.

When Pippa appeared, tall and leggy, 'Here's your eleven o'clock, Liza,' for an instant Liza wanted to tell the client to go to hell. Her head was whirling too hard for her to feel like giving, accommodating. But dragging her thoughts from Nicolas's office and Dominic striding the grassy slope, she pinned on a smile. 'Hi! Come in – I'm Liza Reece.' The client was new, in her twenties, hair, nails, make-up and clothes good, exactly the core area that Liza saw providing the additional clients she would need for her treatment centre.

New clients would be crucial, if she was successful in buying the lease.

She closed her mind to the spectre of failure while she talked to the client and treated feet that spoke to her of migraine and eye issues.

And when her client had left, enthusing about how amazingly relaxed she felt and clutching a handful of cards to pass out to her friends, Nicolas finally shouted across the corridor, 'Liza! Can you come in a minute? I've got a number for you.'

Anticipation trembled up from the soles of her feet.

Chapter Eighteen

Liza opened her door to find a shivering blond devil wrapped tightly in a red shiny cloak on her doorstep. 'Bit old for trick or treating, aren't you?'

The devil clutched his wired and padded red-satin tail against a sudden gust of raw October wind that caught his cloak to allow her a glimpse of a bare chest beneath. He glared from under knobbly black horns affixed somehow in his hair. 'You're wearing jeans! Are we going to be the only morons to turn up in fancy dress?'

If the devil on her doorstep had never expressed interest in The Stables, she would probably have got the lease for a song – rather than the figure Nicolas had come up with, more the price of an entire music shop – so Liza toyed with letting him think that, yes, he was going to be that moron. But as Rochelle would have a hissy fit if Dominic turned red satin tail and ran from her Halloween party, she shrugged into her cosy ski jacket and swallowed her malice. 'My costume's at Rochelle's. We're going as the three witches of Macbeth.' She stepped out of her house and halted, staring in dismay at the black hulk drawn up to the kerb. 'That's not your car, is it? It's a tank!'

Dominic opened the rear car door. 'Kenny will drive there and the roads will be empty by the time you drive us home. Just get in, Liza. I'm freezing my horns off.'

Slowly, Liza slid into the black interior. 'Wow. It's huge.'

'Music to the ears of any man,' declared a voice, and Liza saw that there was another devil in the driver's seat, a devil with hair the golden brown of muscovado sugar, twisting in his seatbelt to gaze at her. 'Hi, I'm Kenny. Dominic didn't mention that you're a supermodel.'

Diverted from rising panic over the prospect of driving what seemed to her a stretch limo, Liza grinned. 'I think they're taller. But thanks.'

Dominic groaned theatrically as he leapt into the front passenger seat and slammed the door. 'Just drive, Captain Bullshit.'

Kenny didn't shift his smouldering gaze from Liza. 'Know what, Doc? If Liza's driving back later, I think she ought to sit in the front, so she can get a better feel for the car.'

Aggravation burning over the lease, Liza agreed sweetly. 'That's a good idea.'

'No, it's not,' growled Dominic. 'Drive.'

Calmly, Kenny turned off the ignition and folded his arms. 'Move to the back, Doc, or we're going nowhere.'

By the time they arrived at Rochelle's, Liza felt a smidgeon more cheerful. Dominic had glowered through all of Kenny's jokes, making her feel that by pinching the front seat she'd made him pay, in some petty way, for his inconvenient desire for The Stables. They climbed out of the car and music thrummed down to the street.

Kenny executed a few hip-hop steps on the pavement. 'I hear a party.'

Dominic just wrapped his cloak and tail around himself silently whilst Liza, who knew the code, got them through the main entrance door.

At the top of the stairs, Rochelle's front door was propped open by a vampire distributing glasses of red wine. 'Bat's blood?' he offered, thickly, around his fangs, raising his voice against the racket emanating from behind him. Then to Liza, severely, 'You don't get any until you're properly dressed. Only people in cool Halloween costumes are entitled.'

Behind the fangs, Liza recognised Jack, one of Rochelle's workmates, young and biddable, which was probably how he'd ended up manning the door. She kissed his cheek, careful of his make-up, which smelled of cold cream and powder. 'Make sure these guys get a drink, then.' Dominic and Kenny had certainly earned their bat's blood, red Lycra-covered legs and black boots showing below their cloaks, tridents in their hands and pointy tails bobbing behind them. 'Where's Rochelle? She's got my— Whoa! Cool witchy costume, Rochelle.' Her friend, appropriately magically, appeared from the crowd. Her madly tousled blonde hair, short black dress and star-spattered pointed hat was teamed with a shimmering black cloak, silver-tipped wand and spike-heeled, lace-back PVC thigh boots. 'I suppose you know that Macbeth's witches are meant to be ugly?'

Rochelle assumed her prettiest pout. 'I'm sure Shakespeare would be the first to grant poetic licence. But, erm, Liza – there was a problem with your costume. You have got one,' she added, quickly. 'You just can't be a witch, because the dress we'd reserved came in needing repair. But I've got you something so cool. You'll look so hot. It's in my bedroom, on the hanger behind the door.'

Dominic followed Kenny into the party, turning his shoulders to ease between werewolves and wizards, welcoming the warm fug of crowded bodies after the dismal chill of outdoors, letting his eardrums relax against the clamour of voices raised over loud music. Angie, wearing the twin to Rochelle's cutie-sexy witch costume but with ankle boots, paused in handing out a plate of chocolate witch hats. 'You made it!'

'Just got here. This is Kenny,' Dominic shouted.

Angie batted her eyelashes at Kenny when he kissed her cheek, and introduced the nearest partygoers: two skeletons, a heavily bandaged invisible man, a few zombies, vampires of both genders, a pretty woman dressed as a bat and having trouble with her oversized wings, Sick Superman, Undead

Barbie and Willie Wonka's evil twin. Undead Barbie, with blood-matted blonde hair, sultry blue lips and a push-up black bra that was doing a heroic job with her major assets, made an instant hit with Kenny. Dominic looked around, not really listening to Kenny's enthusiastic launch into tales of white-water rafting and abseiling, all the more impressive for being true.

Evidently, Rochelle took Halloween seriously. Pumpkin lanterns burned on tables, hairy spiders descended from light fittings, a noose dangled in the hall-slash-alcove that housed doors to other rooms. So many people were sardined together that he had to hook up his tail to prevent it being stepped on. Now he knew why Crosswind carried his straight up in the air.

Angie fought her way back, this time with white marshmallow ghosts and dough witches' fingers, complete with flaked almond fingernails. 'Where's Liza?' she shouted over the music.

'Think she went off to change,' he shouted back.

She nodded. 'Have you finished your bat's blood? There's wizard's brew in the kitchen.'

'What's in it?'

'Vodka, lime and apple juice. Or there's dragon's puke, if you prefer. It's mainly advocaat, with chopped up jalapeño peppers in it.' She wrinkled her nose. 'It's a bit ick, to be honest, but Rochelle thought it would be funny. Last year we did dragon's diarrhoea, with Tia Maria and chocolate Angel Delight, but nobody would touch it.'

'No?' He pulled a face of mock astonishment, and Angie giggled as she turned to offer others the ghosts and witches' fingers. She threaded her way through the throng and Dominic accepted a mission to secure wizard's brew for himself, Kenny and Undead Barbie. Liza still hadn't reappeared when he returned, drinks held high to avoid the worst of the jostling. He'd left off his watch as it didn't really go with Lycra leggings and a cloak, but it seemed as if she'd been gone a long time. He'd planned to grab a quiet word with her but, at this rate, the party would be over before he managed it.

Suddenly, Rochelle was in front of him. 'Love the devil costume. You wear it well.'

The room was getting warm and he'd pushed his cloak back over his shoulders, finally feeling the benefit of an outfit that bared his chest. 'Glad you recognised the devilishness. My cousin's three-year-old said I look like red Batman.' He let his gaze drop. 'Love your costume, too.' Her dress was tighter and shorter than Angie's and she filled it more ... well, just more.

'Good,' she said, complacently, 'that's the idea.' And she began to ask about his nascent business project, drawing her head close to hear his answers, taking his arm, skin on skin, so they wouldn't be parted by people buffeting past. He liked Rochelle; she looked great and was funny and direct. Her bright eyes were emitting a primary radar signal of interest and appreciation and there was no reason that he shouldn't bounce it right back at her. He could forget Liza Reece, refuse to be sucked in by her blue eyes and curvy little body, and enjoy being with someone who wasn't afraid to show interest in him.

Breathing in the mixed scents of woman, apple juice and vodka, he tilted his head to dodge the brim of her hat and catch Rochelle's artfully artless suggestion that they should meet up for dinner some time so he could tell her more about his plans. She produced her phone from the belt of her dress. 'Put your number into my mobile, then I'll ring you and you'll have mine.'

But, as he reached for her phone, he glanced over her shoulder. And a ton of hot lead hit him in the chest.

Liza was stalking towards them looking totally, murderously pissed off. But, also, absolutely mouth-watering in a tight black-and-gold striped fuzzy strapless dress with some kind of voluptuous black bulbous thing around her behind, and stiff transparent wings. Dominic heard himself make a noise in the back of his throat. Behind him, Kenny went, 'Wow!'

Liza glared people out of her way, eyes of ice daring anyone to comment. 'Rochelle!' she hissed, when she reached them. 'What the fucking hell am I supposed to be? Some kind of insect slut?'

Rochelle gurgled. 'You're a hornet! Isn't it amazing? I knew only you'd be small enough to get into it. And if you knew how hot you look, you'd be sending me a thank-you card. Doesn't she look hot?' she appealed to Dominic and Kenny.

'Yes,' they croaked.

Dominic cleared his throat. 'So what's with the thing at the back?'

Liza half-turned to exhibit the black rubber bulb around her buttocks. 'I think that's my abdomen and stinger. This dress takes short to a new level, Rochelle! It's so tight and rubbery, it's like wearing an innertube. And about as comfortable.'

Rochelle gave a bewildered shrug. 'But, Liza. You. Look. Hot.'

'Let's get you a drink, and then you'll get in the party spirit.' Kenny offered Liza his arm. 'Wizard's brew, bat's blood or dragon's puke?'

'Water.'

Kenny looked horrified. 'What's that?'

She grinned, reluctantly. 'Comes out of a tap. It's what I drink. That's how come you can drink wizard's brew and I can drive Dominic's tank home.'

'Actually, that works for me.' He pulled her hand through his arm and steered her off towards the kitchen, leaving Dominic to be mesmerised as her abdomen and stinger wiggled away. He flicked his cloak back around himself. Men in tights had to be discreet.

The room just got fuller and fuller. Noisier and noisier. Hotter and hotter.

Liza, though hardly able to breathe, got used to allowing room for the wings and stinger that formed the least comfortable parts of the clinging costume. Kenny was intent on impressing her with his American adventures. Nearby, Dominic cast her the occasional unreadable look, trident resting negligently on his shoulder, tail hooked fetchingly over one arm. She tried not to look at his chest, luminous, naked and sculptured in the light produced by the dozens of candles and lamps that Rochelle deemed suitable to the occasion. His cloak fell red and sinuous down his back and she was getting the full effect of the Lycra skimming his hips and ... things, before it disappeared into knee-high black boots. People accepted making fools of themselves as part of the Halloween fancy dress fun. But Dominic didn't look foolish. 'Awesome' was the word that kept flashing across her mind.

Kenny was dressed almost exactly like Dominic. He was good-looking, with his outdoor tan, told fantastic stories about his time in the States and even demonstrated his social graces by remembering to ask her about herself. But he didn't look awesome. 'So,' she asked, idly, 'why do you call Dominic "Doc"?'

Kenny leaned closer so that she caught the sweet/sour smell of wizard's brew on his breath. 'When we were kids, we had to have our initials on school stuff and he's Dominic Osborne Christy. But, also, 'cos he's just too fucking clever.'

He beamed, as if he expected to be congratulated on drawing the conclusion. 'He always was clever, right through school. Much cleverer than me.' And he began on a stream of memories and anecdotes of the days when young Dominic, Kenny and Miranda had scuffed along to school together, 'Although Miranda was the year above, and bossy,' and how he and Dominic had vied for the school sports prizes. 'Dominic, he's good for a sprint. But I can stay the distance.' A big, lascivious wink.

Liza didn't react. 'And did you know Natalie?' It was only polite to keep the conversational ball rolling. It wasn't that she was curious about Dominic's ex ...

He threw back his cloak and staggered slightly. 'Natalie? She was always going to let him down. But how do you tell someone something like that?' And he steered the conversation back to his experiences on North Carolina wilderness trails, eyes blurring as he sucked down wizard's brew.

Liza let her attention wander. Candles were guttering, now, their growing and shrinking shadows emphasising the wobbliness of some of the drinkers. She came back to herself with a jolt when Kenny hooked his hand around her waist, causing the stupid wire of the wings to bite into her flesh.

'Ow!' She grabbed the fabric to counter the weight.

Kenny moved in, dipping his head. Over the noise, she caught the end of a sentence: '—as sexy as you.'

Oh ... don't think so! On full unwanted-kiss-alert, she jammed her free hand against his chest and pushed, but met the human wall of shoulders behind her, making the wings jab her from a new angle. '*Ow*! Kenny—'

'Would now be a good time to talk?'

Her head whipped around. Like a ninja in Lycra, Dominic had appeared beside her. Thankfully, she pried off Kenny's arm. 'Yes, now would be great.'

'Doc! Dom!' protested Kenny, swaying chummily up against Liza.

But Dominic somehow turned himself into a barrier with Liza one side and Kenny the other, allowing her to make a getaway. Once in the tiny hall alcove, where the temperature was a degree cooler and the noise a decibel less, she paused to let him catch up. The doors to the kitchen and bathroom stood open, the one to Rochelle's bedroom was shut, a stern notice declaring the room *Strictly out of bounds. Trespassers will be sent home.*

He stooped to put his mouth close to her ear, and his breath stirred her hair. 'OK?'

'Yes. Thanks. You arrived at a good time.'

'I guessed that by your expression. Ken can get a bit enthusiastic.'

She grinned, reluctantly. 'Just a bit.' Dominic's naked chest was inches from her face so she fidgeted at the shrink-wrapped dress to avoid looking at his musculature, checking that her – not especially substantial – underwear was covered, thinking dark thoughts in Rochelle's direction. She'd never worn anything less comfortable in her life, especially with that stupid bustle making her feel as if she had an inflatable bum.

'I got "the call" from Nicolas this afternoon. With what he wants for the lease.'

She nodded glumly, her gratitude at his rescue disappearing, *phht*.

He stepped aside to let a skeleton into the bathroom. 'Shall we compare notes? I think he's come in way too high.'

'Me, too.'

He sighed, pulling the end of his tail out of the path of a vampire making for the kitchen. 'Now you've shown interest, he thinks he has leverage and I don't know if I can get him down.'

She glared indignantly, which might at least disguise how much Nicolas's figure had shocked and scared her. 'And if you hadn't shown interest he would never have come up with such a stupid number.'

Slowly, he closed his eyes, and leaned back against the wall.

Oh crap. Liza felt sudden compunction. She laid reassuring fingers on his arm. Warm. 'Do you need to sleep? I can drive you home straight away. Or Rochelle will probably let you rest in her room.'

His eyes flipped opened. 'I'm not sleepy, I'm counting to ten, you bloody annoying woman.'

She snatched her fingers away. 'You turn up out of the blue and expect me to disappear my business out of your way, and *I'm* annoying?'

He took a long, slow breath. 'OK,' he said, neutrally. 'Let's just accept that we both want the other to back off.'

'And neither of us is going to. But,' she couldn't resist adding, 'morally, you should, because I'm the one already *in situ*, who'll lose money during the process of relocation. Whereas all you have to do is find somewhere else to set up. You've invested no dosh.' She folded her arms. Then quickly unfolded them, because pulling the elastic sheath tight threatened to catapult her boobs into the middle of the argument.

'All I have to do? Like spaces suitable for action-and-challenge centres are ten a penny and an investment of time is of no consequence? That costume is totally distracting, by the way.' His gaze, more pewter than silver in the dim light, flickered south for a moment.

'How do you think I feel?' Then she blushed because she didn't really want to admit that she found his costume distracting, too. 'About investing time, I mean.' She tried to take a deep, calming breath, but couldn't because of the dress. It was making her feel smothered, her skin moistening under its rubbery embrace, her heart pulsing as if it were trying to find room to beat. Unless that was Dominic—

A line of people began to filter past into the kitchen, and one was Rochelle, swaying on her spike heels, ducking the noose that hung from the ceiling. 'Dominic!' She settled her silver-taloned hand on his bicep. 'Weren't we talking about dinner?'

And then Kenny was there, too, clutching an empty glass. 'We could make it a foursome, Liza.'

Liza's eyes flicked to Dominic. He was frowning. And, this time, he didn't rescue her from Kenny. Instead, he shrugged. 'Sounds OK.'

So she shrugged, too. 'Could be fun.' Deliberately, she turned away, drifting into the main room to talk to an insane clown.

Midnight. Rochelle and Angie were trying to organise some witching-hour game involving blindfolds, wet rubber gloves and peeled grapes; Kenny had stumbled off somewhere. Dominic had been watching Liza mingling with vampires and mummies until she'd disappeared into the kitchen and re-emerged with a steaming mug of something. He watched her body move on an enormous sigh and obeyed the pull he'd been trying to resist since she'd proved so unreasonable about the lease.

'We can leave any time you want,' he said, joining her in the doorway.

Her eyebrows rose. 'Lightweight.' Then, 'Oh … yes, we can leave if—'

'I'm fine,' he stressed. 'It's you who's making with the huge sighs.'

'I'm fine, too.'

'Good.'

'Yes.'

He hesitated. 'I need to tell you something about Kenny.'

Her grin flashed. 'I would have thought Kenny's told me pretty much everything there is to tell.'

He gave her a rueful look. 'Annoyingly enough, he doesn't tell lies. He really does the white-water rafting, potholing, skydiving, running and everything else. It's impressive. I just feel I need to warn you – he's probably after no-strings sex.'

She pulled a stricken face. 'Now I feel I have to warn you – so's Rochelle!'

The ludicrousness of the conversation suddenly struck him. He laughed. 'Oh, OK. I didn't mean to—'

But Liza's attention had flicked away from him like a whip. Her eyes had become round and apprehensive and were fixed on a point behind him.

And then she removed herself from the room. Stepping backwards as if over landmines, silently feeling behind her for the handle to Rochelle's bedroom door. Turning it. Back, back, through. Door closed. Gone.

Dominic blinked. Then turned to identify what had sent her to ground.

A lanky figure stood some yards behind him, dark eyes staring from the hood of an artistically ragged black cloak. Rochelle and Angie were gazing across the room in horror, exchanging urgent whispers. Rochelle switched her gaze to Dominic. 'Where's Liza?' she mouthed.

Minutely, Dominic indicated the bedroom. Rochelle mimed heart-clutching relief, then pointed at the newcomer, mouthing, 'That's Adam.'

Nodding his understanding, Dominic shifted so that he was leaning against the door that Liza had shut behind her, watching as the hooded figure drifted around the room like a Ringwraith, body loose but eyes sharp and searching, peering into corners. Long hands emerged from the cloak and pushed back the hood, revealing a sensitive, intelligent face and a mop of fair, collar-length hair. A few people greeted him but he just smiled and prowled on. Closer, closer.

Then he was hovering only a couple of feet away, glancing into the kitchen and the bathroom. His eyes settled on Dominic. Then shifted to the closed bedroom door.

Dominic waved his devil's trident. 'Sorry, mate. Someone's getting changed.'

Adam nodded and turned to push the kitchen door more fully open, then a laughing group clutching full glasses barrelled out, sweeping him briefly back into the main room.

Dominic opened the bedroom door and slid through. 'It's Dominic.'

The whole room seemed to relax on an exhale. He moved in the direction it had come from, picking out Liza's shape in front of the window. 'Was Adam invited?' He kept his voice low.

'No! He knows that Rochelle has a Halloween party every year, though. I suppose he invited himself.'

Now he could see the gleam of her eyes in the city light that filtered through the curtains. 'Are you … scared of him?'

'Not scared of him. Of course not. I just don't want—' Her voice broke.

'—your nose rubbing in his problems?'

'—his pain. I'm scared of his pain and what it might make him do. It's already made him do … what he did. To his wrist.'

'Pain's a part of life,' he said, sombrely. 'We all suffer it, learn to live with it. You can't let his pain control you.'

Silence. Then, bleakly, 'Some people learn to live with things. But others obsess. Destructively. Unpredictably. He's in a bad place and I'm struggling with the knowledge that I could change that, if I just let things slide back to how they were before.'

'That's no answer! He needs real help.' For the first time, he realised how petal-soft a heart was encased in that fiery little body. She hid it well. He put a comforting hand on her arm, gently, barely touching. 'And so do you. You need support in refusing to take responsibility for him. Do you want me to help?'

Chapter Nineteen

'How?' It was a ridiculous idea that he could. But they were in a ridiculous situation, huddling together in the dark in Rochelle's strictly out-of-bounds bedroom whilst Adam haunted the party.

He shrugged, and his warm naked chest brushed her arm. 'We go out there and act like a couple. Let him see that you've moved on.'

She inched back in case the naked flesh touched her again. But she couldn't bring herself to step completely out of the warm cell of air that seemed to surround him, the scents of alcohol and shower gel mingling. 'How?'

He sighed with exaggerated patience. 'I put my arms around you, kiss you, whisper in your ear—'

'Don't be an idiot!' She did step away. Right away. Into a cool space where Dominic wasn't overheating everything, sucking her in.

'It's pragmatic. A clear signal, an opportunity for him to back off with no loss of face. Or you could cower in here indefinitely.' A pause. His voice softened. 'Or just greet him like an old friend then move on to chat with others. Won't he get the message?'

'It sounds reasonable when you say it.'

'Because it is. Give the guy a chance to get over you, Liza. Hiding away from him might be feeding his fantasies that you have a future. He's probably reasoning that if only he could talk to you, he could undo all the bad that happened.'

She stood in the darkness, heart thudding uneasily. Trying to 'visualise what success would look like', as Cleo would say. Adam, maybe looking sad, but accepting they had no future. Perhaps being bitter or angry but *going away*. Leaving her to a life not controlled by guilt. She took in a long, slow breath. 'You're right.' She began to cross the room, aware that he was moving through the darkness beside her. 'It'll be OK. Adam is an intelligent guy and —' Dominic reached around her to open the door and Liza let out a yip of surprise.

Adam lurked in the hallway like a servant of the Dark Lord, flickering candlelight illuminating the folds of his cloak. Behind him, Rochelle and Angie were in the centre of a huddle of people passing around objects from a black bin liner amidst shrieks and laughter. 'Hello,' Adam said, smiling painfully. His eyes rested for several long seconds on Dominic, then returned to Liza. 'I've been looking for you, Lize. To talk.'

She swallowed. Misery and guilt swooshed over her as she met his brown eyes and saw hurt a mile deep. Hurt she'd caused. When he lifted his hand to push back his hair, his left sleeve fell back. Two pink scars lay on his arm like accusations: the self-inflicted one across the wrist, the other, the repair, bisecting it. Ugly shiny pink worms. Tears ached in her throat.

Adam glanced at Dominic. 'Me and Lize are going to talk.'

Dominic ignored the hint that he should leave. 'Really?'

Liza licked her lips. 'There's nothing we need to say that we can't say in front of other people, Adam.'

Adam didn't get angry. He didn't really do angry. He just got sadder. 'There's loads. We need to get our relationship back on track.'

Dismay fluttered into her throat. 'We can't.'

His lines in his face grew deeper, longer; his mouth set itself to *stubborn*. 'We can. I'm not involved with anyone else and neither are you.'

Liza's vision of reason and rationale bringing success dissolved and she grasped instantly at Dominic's stupid, half-baked, crappy, simplistic, but possibly effective, idea. 'I am involved. With Dominic.' She slid her arm around Dominic's waist.

Adam's eyes turned down in panic. 'You're not!'

Lazily, Dominic scooped Liza up against his side, snuggling her there as if he knew how their bodies fitted together. Which was pretty well, actually, her shoulder under his arm, her breast pressed against the rack of his ribs. His hand hot on her hip. 'I'm afraid we are, mate. When a couple rendezvous in a bedroom, it's not usually about meaningful conversation.'

A still, silent moment.

Liza watched emotions war in Adam's face, willing the longed-for acceptance to appear. Or even bitterness and anger. Instead, what she saw was grief. Black, swamping grief, deadening his eyes. Then he whirled and blundered through the rubber gloves and grapes game, and out of the door.

Horror-movie possibilities blazed into Liza's mind. Her feet twitched, as if they wanted to run after him. She felt Dominic's arm tighten. 'You're not responsible,' he reminded her, softly.

She turned and flattened her palms against his chest, ready to thrust him away. 'But he needs help.'

His grey eyes were steady. 'You're the wrong one to give it to him.'

She swallowed. 'But what if he tries to commit suicide again?'

Slowly, he covered one of her hands with his, thumb moving absently on the underside of her wrist. He breathed a sigh. 'That would be terrible. But running after him still isn't the right thing to do. The only thing you can do to make him happy is carry through a phoney change of heart, live with a man you don't want, give up your whole life to a lie. Take the expected place within his family. Are you that good at faking? It would make you miserable and, in the end, him, too.'

Liza almost staggered under a wave of clammy dismay. Endless relatives calling, Ursula interfering, Adam being gently manipulative until he got his own way in everything. 'I can't do that,' she agreed, hopelessly. 'But there must be something I can do. It's my—'

'If you say it's your fault,' he snapped, hand tightening uncomfortably, 'I'm going to tell your sister you need help and she'll check up on you eight times a day.'

'She would, too,' she agreed, gloomily. Somehow, instead of pushing him away she'd sunk against him. Again. Taking strength from him. Again. Listening to the regular thud of his heart, feeling secure. Maybe it was habit-forming and she'd need a stronger and stronger fix – last time she'd been wearing two coats, this time he was half-naked and she had on the stupidest tiny dress. So next time …

He shifted, and she realised that he was easing his hips away. Oh …! Hastily, she straightened, so that the embrace slackened, gave him the distance he evidently needed for comfort. 'There must be something I can do,' she repeated, to get her mind off the likely reason for Dominic not wanting her to be aware of what was going on in his pelvic area. Fighting the – at this moment inappropriate – instinct to check it out.

'What about his brother, the one who took you to hospital?'

'Ben.' She ran through Ben's probable reaction without much pleasure. He'd been a condemnatory supercilious snot when Adam had hurt himself. But, 'Better than ringing his mother,' she acknowledged. 'I've left my bag in your car and my phone's in it.'

'I've got my phone.'

'Really?' Once again, she fought the urge to let her gaze

skim over him. There didn't seem many places to put a phone in his costume. She forced herself to deal with the crisis of the moment. 'But I need Ben's number. It's in my contacts.'

'Let's call him from the Jag, then.' He fished around behind himself and produced the key fob for his car.

'Where was *that*?'

He laughed. 'There's a pocket inside the waistband, like you get in cycling shorts. Come on, let's get this over with.' In a minute he'd bundled up her clothes from Rochelle's room, draped her coat over her as best he could for her wings, checked out the Kenny situation and discovered he'd already left, probably with Undead Barbie, although Angie wasn't sure, reassured her and Rochelle that the Adam situation was under control, then towed Liza to the door.

Outside, the wind pounced on them like an ice demon, making them gasp as its icy fingers fastened gleefully on their exposed flesh. Liza grabbed fruitlessly at the two sides of her coat. 'I can't believe I came downstairs dressed like this. It's f-freezing!'

Dominic huddled himself into his thin and inadequate cloak, bleeping the car open as they scurried across the pavement. The driver's door was closest so Liza had it open before Dominic had run around to the passenger side, but then discovered the challenges in entering a car in wings and a stinger. She finally managed to perch uncomfortably on the padded hornet's abdomen with the stinger sticking out coquettishly beside the gear stick. Which wasn't a proper gear stick, because Dominic's great tanky car was an automatic. The wire frame of her wings dug viciously into her shoulder blades so that she had to lean forward whilst she fished her phone out of the side pocket of her bag, wincing.

The screen lit up, and in moments she had selected *Ben* from her contacts list and could hear the ringtone in her ear.

'Yes?' Ben's voice.

'It's Liza.'

'Yes.'

She hesitated. He didn't sound surprised and he didn't sound encouraging. A terror of saying the wrong thing, of doing something to invoke disaster, engulfed her. She swallowed hard, twice, trying to force sound past the stiffness of her throat.

Ben sounded bored. 'Are you still there?'

On a gasp, she managed, 'I'm worried about Adam.'

His voice hardened. 'Bit late for that.'

Liza flinched. 'I saw him tonight and he—he got upset.'

'Shit! What did you do this time?'

She gripped the phone harder, reliving the grief in Adam's eyes. She blurted, wretchedly, 'He was at this party and wanted to talk, but I couldn't see any point because nothing's changed. He ran out—'

'—and now you want me to talk him down from the ledge,' he finished for her, voice vibrating with anger.

Then Dominic twitched the phone away from her fingers and began speaking in unemotional, clear sentences. 'Look, mate, your brother obviously needs help. Liza's not responsible for him but is worried he might self-harm. She's been good enough to notify you of the unusual situation. Whether you act on the information is up to you.' And ended the call.

Liza sat, numbly. 'His family all hate me.'

He turned in his seat, the scarlet of his cloak washing out to a strange orange under the streetlights, the horns still poking roguishly through his hair, his eyes glittering. 'They're projecting their fears for Adam onto you. It's not fair, but it is understandable. When people are scared, they lash out. They blame. And if they can't find someone to blame with just cause, they find a scapegoat.'

'Oh.' She sniffed, wondering if he was right.

He still held the car remote and he flicked the key part out and, reaching across her as if perfectly familiar with her personal space, located the ignition by feel, turned the key one click, watched the dash readout, then turned it again and the engine burbled into life. Huddling into his cloak, he stabbed the red buttons of the climate control unit. 'This outfit isn't designed for an English October night.'

'Neither's mine.' Her bare legs glowed ghostily in the dashboard light and she briefly considered whether she could get back into the jeans and coat she'd arrived in, but an excursion into the biting wind back to Rochelle's bedroom didn't appeal. Sighing, she dragged on the seatbelt, wincing as the wings dug deeper into her shoulders. 'So, how do you drive an automatic, then?'

'You seriously never have? And here was me trying to console myself with the thought that if I have to be driven around, at least I get a slutty hornet chauffeur, tonight.'

'The slutty hornet only passed her test a couple of years ago. And has never driven an auto, nor anything bigger than a Corsa, so she needs to be told how.' Cautiously, she blipped the accelerator, listening as the car went from a whispered, *rrrrummmm,* to a throaty, *RRRUMMMMMMMMMM.* Actually ... quite nice. *RRRRAAAOWWWWMMMM.*

His breath caught, as if in pain, but his voice remained even and reassuring. 'It's straightforward. There's no clutch and you don't have the bother of changing gears, once you've put the car in drive. Put your foot on the brake, and move the shift to where it says *D*.'

She did that. The stick shifted, as if through greased ball bearings, sinuous and satisfying.

'And when you're ready, let the brake off and do everything but change gear.'

Checking behind her and indicating, she moved cautiously out from the kerb, took the first left and left again, checking her mirrors, creeping through the near-empty streets. She felt somehow lost inside such a big vehicle, as if it had swallowed her. But once she'd glided onto the dual carriageway and found the car responsive to her foot on the accelerator, began to enjoy flying through the night. 'This is easy,' she marvelled. 'Like steering a giant leather armchair.'

He laughed. 'My poor Jag. Emasculation in one sentence.'

'But I thought it would be difficult.'

'A big car isn't any harder to drive than a little car. It might be trickier to park, though. We'll leave it outside your house. I'll run back to Miranda's and Kenny can pick it up tomorrow. Or whenever he reappears.' He raised his hands against her argument that she could drop him at Miranda's or change to the Smart and drive him back there. 'Liza, I used to move hundreds of aircraft in and out of a busy London airport every week. Trust me to supervise the parking of my car.'

They took to the dark country roads towards Middledip. The car's interior had warmed nicely and a half moon was edging the breaks in the ragged clouds with silver in a satisfyingly spooky way. 'I love your car. Even driving in possibly the least comfortable Halloween costume in the world.'

Dominic stared through the windscreen. 'I hate being chauffeured.'

She bristled. 'By me?'

'By anyone. You. Kenny. Jenson Button. Angelina Jolie. I just want my licence back.'

'Oh.' That was OK, then. 'When will that be?'

'When my consultant and the DVLA agree that I'm fit for it. Then I'll probably never let anybody else in the driving seat ever again, so enjoy it while you can.' In her peripheral vision, she saw his horns illuminated for a moment by passing headlights.

She changed the subject. 'Tell me about you and Kenny. You seem an unlikely pairing.'

'We are.' He stretched and yawned. 'At school, I was good at academic stuff and Ken thought it was torture. He was unpredictable and anti-authority, probably because he learns differently, being severely dyslexic. If he wants to know something he treats you like a live reference book – questions, questions, questions, committing your answers to memory, in the same way you or I might learn a poem. In a huge comprehensive school, that need couldn't always be met.

'He comes from a big family with not much money, whereas I'm an only child and both my parents are in reasonably well-paid professions. I think we each envied the other what he had. I wanted siblings, he wanted privacy and clothes that were new.

'Our common interest was sport. We kept ending up on the same teams for athletics, footie and rugby. Then Mr Pryor arrived, a sports teacher who was interested in adventurous stuff like kayaking and climbing, and Ken suddenly found a use for school. We built our own kayak on a project Mr Pryor masterminded and he encouraged Kenny to do the stuff he excelled at. He also persuaded him to take a couple of exams and I helped him as much as I could. We were brothers-in-arms in everything except girls, because we liked the same ones. We adopted the "All's fair in love and war" code. He took Tanya Rowlands off me, I stole Melanie Smith from him.' He laughed. 'Ken's always so alive. It's going to be great to have him around. You didn't see him at his best, getting drunk and hitting on you.'

She guided the Jag around a long curve. 'And now I've kind of been cornered into dinner with him and you and Rochelle. I was hoping you'd object.'

He made a balancing-the-scales movement with his hands.

'I thought a foursome left us all with the most options. It's light and non-committal. If I'd headed Kenny's foursome idea off he would have pushed to take you out alone.'

'Good point.' Checking her mirror and slowing as the lanes delivered them to the lights of Middledip, Liza took Main Road then Ladies Lane to Port Road, passing Cleo and Justin's house with all its windows dark, to The Cross. She managed to position the Jag tolerably close to the pavement without scraping the wheels. There was just about room for it without overlapping the Gatehouse frontage. Mrs Snelling had put a note through her door when Rochelle had dared to intrude her car bonnet into what Mrs Snelling saw as her air space. 'There.' She was surprised at her own satisfaction. Cars, usually, were just cars, but driving Dominic's Jag had aroused her latent girlracer.

Dominic gazed out as garden shrubs tossed their wild hairdos in a surly autumn wind and spatters of rain crackled against the windows. The flimsy satiny fabric wrapped around his body didn't look weatherproof. He grimaced. 'I can't believe I didn't think of stashing a jumper or a coat in the car. That's a criminal lack of forward planning.'

She shifted around uncomfortably on the rubber abdomen to face him. 'Are you literally going to run back to Miranda's? What if you meet someone? The village will seethe with tales of the devil riding out on Halloween. Babies born to Middledip women next July will be suspiciously examined for horns, tails and cloven hoofs.

'I don't have any clothes to fit you but I could lend you something to wrap up in, as I haven't thanked you for helping me out, tonight. With Adam. I mean.' She hesitated. 'I'm conscious of the fact that, twice, when I've been upset, you've been a good friend. Even though we're in direct competition for The Stables. And we've argued a bit. You helped me with Ben, too. You always seem to be there at the right time, for some reason.'

He turned his head her way. The streetlamps threw half his face in shadow, emphasising the line of his jaw and set of his mouth. He let several heartbeats pass.

'C'mon, Liza. You really don't know how much I want you?'

Chapter Twenty

'Oh!' Liza felt as if his words were warm honey, pouring slowly down her body. Every nerve ending awoke and the old her, the pre-Adam Liza, was suddenly bursting to supply a smooth and reciprocally interested response – designed to get her into bed with Dominic. Soon.

But New Liza *had completely forgotten the script*. Too scary! Too sudden! Too much potential for disaster. She couldn't vanquish New Liza's demon of guilt that had possessed her for over a year. 'I … um.'

Silently, he waited.

New Liza busied herself with her bag, flipped off her seatbelt and fumbled to open the unfamiliar door. Then, '*OW!*', came to a sudden stop.

Dominic was holding on to her stinger.

'Forget I said that, if it makes you uncomfortable.' His voice was low, non-threatening. He kept to his own side of the car, apart from the hand that had the stinger. 'But you're not going to let Adam guilt you into never making love again, are you? Run away from sex for the rest of your life?'

'Let go!' She yanked the stinger resentfully from his hand. But she let the wind slam the door, closing them back in again, safe from the rain. 'Making "love"?' She tried to laugh but it was an angry sound. 'Love. The L word's a weapon, supposed to make you forget what you want. Make you want what they want. And if you don't, well then "love" makes a handy lever.'

Gently, he took her hand, his expression intent in the harsh relief of lamplight. His skin was smooth, warm, his voice husky. 'Love's not the only route to great sex. It might not even be the best route. Sex is something other. An intimacy all to itself. Something fantastic. I think sex between us would be the best. If you're letting what Adam did stop you enjoying a healthy physical life, you really are letting "love" be used against you. Make the "L" word "lust" instead.'

It seemed to sizzle through the air. *Lussssst ...* She looked down at their hands. His was warm. Scalding. Old Liza prickled with heat. *Awarenessssss. Promisssssse.*

Perhapssssss ...

'The thought of going back to trying to be what a man wants me to be makes my throat close up,' she said, stubbornly.

'You don't need to be anyone but Liza. Reality check: I'm a man. I don't need to love you to want you. I'm interested in sex.'

She laughed, unwillingly. 'That's an unusual seduction technique.'

'Yeah, well. Call me Mr Truthful. Your self-imposed baggage and the whole Liza's-the-only-person-on-the-planet-to-find-love-painful thing is crazy.'

'Self-imposed!'

'Totally. What happens between you and me, happens between you and me. What happened between you and Adam, happened between you and Adam. It was a terrible experience, but you don't have to suffer pointless self-discipline to atone.'

She snatched her hand from under his. 'Sorry if I'm being boring.'

He threw back his head and laughed, the sound loud in the confines of the car. 'That's one thing you never are.' He took her hand back, lacing her fingers through the spaces between his. 'It's about time you started trusting your instincts.'

'What? The ones that made me think I could be what

Adam wanted? That he'd be good for me? Or the ones that made me say "no" when he proposed?'

'Yes, those. That made you run from something that was obviously wrong for you.

'You're giving him the power, letting him make you miserable and take your sex life off you. You're eaten up by your guilt and he's using that. He probably doesn't even realise it. He's a poor, lovesick guy who's having trouble moving on. And you,' there was a note of apology in his voice, 'you're making it possible. You're playing his game.'

Outrage began to bubble up behind her breastbone. 'So, by going to bed with you for this "best ever" sex, I prove to myself that I'm not controlled by Adam? Another original seduction technique.'

He kissed her fingers and then let them drop. 'It's not as cynical as seduction.'

'So if I suggested we go up to my bedroom now, you'd refuse?'

'No way.' He laughed softly, a rich, dark sound that trickled over her skin. 'I'd sprint up there. But even if that's not going to happen it doesn't mean I'm wrong about Adam controlling you.'

'When *I* resume *my* sex life, it's going to be *my* decision, *my* call, and in *my* control, OK?' she snapped.

'OK.' There was laughter in his voice. 'Can I give you my number and hope it's me you call?'

She snorted as she dragged her coat around her wings and stinger as best she could and flung open the driver's door. 'I'll get you the sofa throw so you don't get hypothermia.'

He still sounded amused. 'I appreciate it. Though it doesn't rate high as a consolation prize.'

She could feel him behind her as she hurried through the rain and into the house. Snapping on the sitting-room light, she grabbed the faux-fur throw from the back of the sofa, shaking it out as a barrier between them.

The teddy bear gold of it was like his hair. She glanced at him. He hovered just inside the door, watching her hands, twirling his trident pensively. His cloak hung not quite closed, so that she could see the crease in the centre of his chest. His eyes lifted to hers, full of light. *Silver and gold*, she found herself thinking. Eyes, hair. He smiled. Slowly, lazily.

Whoah ... fire ripped through her. Old Liza wondered suddenly what the hell she was holding out against. It didn't matter how many times he butted heads with her over the lease, how much of his plain speaking she didn't want to hear, she'd spent the last year circling in an emotional desert and he was the only man who'd made her notice that she was thirsty. And she'd really noticed. Now he was offering to slake her thirst. And he was single. And she was single. And he was hot and wanted her. *You really don't know how much I want you?* he'd said. And the right kind of flirtatious answer suddenly floated into her mind. *The same way I want you?*

What she was feeling wasn't the wispy threads of desire. It was full-on, getting-painful lust, the kind Old Liza used to feel, only to be satisfied by hot banging sex.

Old Liza let the throw slide slowly through her fingers and pool on the sofa back. 'Shall we go up to my bedroom?' The words hung on the air for several moments.

And felt suddenly clumsy, badly timed. Before she knew it, damn, New Liza had jumped back in, glancing down nervously, smoothing the throw back into place.

He cleared his throat. 'All of a sudden, I find I'm in no condition to sprint.'

She laughed, but it was shaky. Why had she just blurted the words out when they hadn't even kissed properly? Panic prickled. She gazed at the yards of carpet between them. She should have offered him coffee. Offering coffee was a ritual with a purpose. It got rid of yawning spaces. They would have been seated together on the sofa – after she'd done something with her stinger and wings – and wafting closer.

'Um, I'm—'

'Out of practice?' His voice reached across the room like a helping hand.

Flushing, she nodded, shooting him a glance under her lashes. He was crossing slowly towards her, bringing the hunger in his eyes. He ought to look ridiculous in horns and a tail, but he didn't. He looked purposeful. Intent. She stood absolutely still, watching his face, uncertainty fading as she read his desire and felt the power that came with knowing that she'd put it there.

By the time his body was close, her face was tilted up to his.

Then his lips were soft on hers. Moving on to her cheekbones, her eyelids, questing, questioning, checking that she was OK with him. With them. With what was happening. Was going to happen. Long kisses. Approaching the green light with caution in case he screamed up to it and she switched it suddenly to red.

The air left her gently, out, out, like a yogic breath, emptying her of everything that was stale and bad. And it was Old Liza who took the next, joyous inhalation, blood roaring in her veins. She reached up to slide her arms around his neck and make their bodies touch.

He pulled her up against his hardness, up onto her tiptoes, his cloak tangling between them. He scrabbled for the fastening at his throat, yanking, thrusting aside the yards of material so that overheating flesh met overheating flesh, his kisses hot and hard and hungry.

He was breathing like a bull. 'I need to get you out of this costume. One of the places I most want to touch you is

177

shielded by this damned abdomen, your wings are scratchy and trying to stick me in the eye, and that elastic looks like it's just waiting to cut off my circulation. How does it come off?'

'I wriggled into it, so I suppose I have to wriggle out. It's incredibly tight.'

'I defy it to defeat me.' He ran his palms slowly, soooo slooooowly, up from her waist, over her breasts, until he could hook his fingers in the banding at the top. 'Wow, it *is* tight.'

The fabric stretched just enough for him to break her breasts free but she had to waste her first deep breath for hours on, 'Ow-ow-ouch! Something's digging in my back.' She began to turn, which, as Dominic had goals of his own, meant her wings dragging across his face, making him swear. 'Sorry, but it's really hurting!'

She held still, while he, muttering darkly about delayed gratification being severely overrated, eased what felt like a small dagger from just right of her spine and coaxed her costume to her waist, his warm hands guarding her flesh from the spiteful wire that attached the wings to the fabric.

'You're scarlet. It's been scratching you all evening.' He kissed her neck, drifting on down to the sore places, licking them to make her first hotter then cooler, as his hands gripped and eased the fearsome elastic tube of a dress over the curve in of her waist, the curve out of her hips. She let her head tip back and breathed deeply in relief at having enough space for her lungs to function.

He bunched and inched the recalcitrant folds that just wanted to ping back into place. 'I loved this outfit, earlier, now I hate it. It's like trying to squeeze you out of a tube of toothpaste.' Finally, he grabbed and hauled, almost pulling Liza off her feet as the elasticated sheath sucked its way past her bottom and snapped down around her knees, taking her knickers with it. 'Phew.' She kicked free, catching herself a parting slap from the stinger. Then hesitated.

Suddenly, she was scared to turn around to face him. It was so long since she'd had a first time.

She was naked and he still was half-dressed, though Lycra leggings and a tail didn't leave a whole lot to the imagination. And nor did his hardness, pressing against the small of her back.

He froze, too, and it was as if the White Witch of Narnia had turned them into statues. Then he cleared his throat and squeezed her waist. 'Yes.'

She found she had to clear her throat, too. 'Yes ...?'

'Yes, I do have condoms.'

'Oh!' She laughed, relief hitting because, although he'd picked upon the wrong anxiety, he'd known she needed reassurance. Mentally passing his outfit under review, she found herself diverted. 'Where?'

'Wallet,' as if she'd asked a stupid question. 'You didn't think I'd be wearing one just in case, did you?' Having allayed what he obviously saw as her anxiety, he slipped his hands around to her breasts, *mmm*ing deep in his chest when his smooth hands made contact and she jumped. Pressing against her, he set his teeth gently against her neck.

Her breath skipped and hopped as he brushed over her with his fingertips, but her mind wouldn't quite let go of the logistics. 'So you seriously have a wallet and a phone on you?'

His laugh was a breath that collided hotly with her nape. His teasing hands trailed down, over hips and waist, up, back to her breasts. 'You can search me, if you want.'

Old Liza knew that kind of game well, and being good at it involved taking her opponent by surprise. Reaching one hand back, she slid it up his thigh, over the smoothness of the Lycra. And cupped him. 'Is it here?'

'Jeez!' He bucked against her. 'How the fuck am I supposed to hide anything there?'

She pressed her back against his chest, liking his heartbeat pounding against her. 'I remembered that film, *The Dreamers*, when the guy carries a photo of a woman between …'

'A photo I can just about believe. But a wallet and a phone?'

She let her hand drop with a sigh of mock-disappointment. 'Then you'd better show me.'

'It's boring in comparison.' He turned her around, stooped, delved in the cuffs of his boots, and emerged with his phone in one hand and his wallet in the other, like a conjurer.

She laughed as he balanced both on the back of the sofa, released straps on the boots and kicked them off. 'Boy scout.'

'Am prepared as hell, right now. And getting more prepared by the moment,' he admitted, battling his way out of his costume, evidently unabashed by nakedness or first times.

Liza hardly had time to feel more than a gush of heat at the glimpse of hard flesh and downy hair before he swooped her up and balanced her on the back of the sofa beside his wallet and phone. Open against him. '*Whooh*,' she breathed, clinging on to the breadth of his shoulders as the scalding heat of his erection sent shockwaves through her. 'That's prepared.'

His lips moved in a butterfly dance across her face. 'Getting there.'

She tilted her hips, hearing his long groan of pleasure as she moved against him. Celibacy was enticingly near its end and she was beginning to want urgency. She'd explore him at her leisure, later. 'We need more?'

'Lots.' His mouth made a hot trail of butterfly kisses across her face, then he settled his hands behind her shoulder blades, kissed her hard on the lips, licked her throat and tilted her back so that his mouth could find her breasts. The room wasn't warm and the draught from under the front door trickled across her body like invisible fingers. But the places where Dominic touched made her blood boil beneath the skin.

A colossal case of goosebumps whooshed up from her toes and she arched to meet him, excited by the sensation of empty air behind her. The sofa rocked alarmingly but she wound her legs around his waist, hanging from him as he explored her with his lips, his tongue, his teeth. The latex devil's horns were still stuck in his hair, giving her the sudden wild sensation of auditioning for *Rosemary's Baby*. She forgot to breathe. Her entire body was about wanting, wanting him inside, wanting to touch what she'd been watching across the room all evening.

'How many condoms do you have?' She squirmed and shuddered, leaning back further, harder against him. If he let go of her now, she'd probably get whiplash.

He adjusted his stance to balance her out. 'Two in my wallet, three in the car.' One arm was looped securely around her waist, the other hand was stroking high, higher as his mouth sucked harder.

She clutched at his arms, digging her fingers into the muscle and sinew that had corded to support her weight. 'Let's sacrifice the first. Now.'

He lifted his head to smile, heaven in his eyes, hooded and heavy with sex. 'Let's make it worth the wait.' And he dipped his head to lick her stomach.

She rolled her head back and let the wanting build, moving against his hand, his mouth, prevented from taking the initiative by her position in mid-air while he strung her out to whimpering point.

But then he straightened. 'Got to ... Where's my damned wallet gone?' searching urgently between the sofa cushions, until, finally, she had to cling onto him as he found what he wanted. She heard the tearing of the packet as his hands worked behind her back. Then he was smoothing the condom on and, suddenly – inside her. Hard. Harder. *Harder.*

Then he got control. Kept it, rocking her on helpless waves of pleasure, lovely and lean and fluid, supporting her, holding her from falling. 'Good for you?' His voice was raw.

'Good!' she gasped. Then was flung beyond conversation as she rose up on a switchback of pleasure. Intense. Teetering on the edge of more.

She knew what the more was and that she needed it *right now*. 'Dominic!' She ground urgently against him so that he groaned and gasped and kicked up several gears, giving her what she craved, hotter, stormier, until the waves were crashing and wild.

And carried her away.

It seemed a while before she floated dizzily back to shore. Catching her breath. Savouring the final ripples of pleasure.

Slowly, he pulled her upright so that they could prop each other up, damp skin against damp skin, as they remembered how to breathe. She was almost surprised to find herself still perched on the back of the sofa because there had been a distinct sensation of plunging, flying, whirling through space. She ran her lips lazily along his jaw line: firm, lean, just asking to be tasted.

Dominic pulled her close, as if trying to absorb her, rumbling against her neck. 'Wow. That was hot. Best ever.'

And whilst she didn't actually disagree … she wondered how he could be so undisguised.

'Air Berlin bravo echo romeo three five three five, please monitor tower one two three decimal eight … Topswiss echo zulu sierra five zero seven, pushback and start-up approved to the bravo east line …'

Liza hadn't checked the time that they'd finally gone to sleep, but it had been late. They had been exhausted, sated, plastered nakedly together, Dominic's horns and trident discarded on the bedside table alongside his wallet and phone. She'd plummeted into oblivion, rather than drifted.

So she'd definitely had *some* sleep.

But now she was wide awake because Dominic was talking to the darkness. 'Jetset Foxtrot Charlie Alpha four three two seven, Stansted delivery, slot time fourteen-thirty, cleared to … Clacton8romeo departure, squawk six four two two … Topswiss echo zulu sierra five zero seven, taxi via charlie holding point sierra one runway two two.'

In the pauses, she imagined dream pilots answering a Dominic once again seated in the light, high above Stansted Airport, the runway rolled out below the air traffic control tower. She wondered how it had felt to be up there, to understand the phrases streaming into her ears, to know how to work the equipment, to leave no room for error. To live in a world where sleek metal monsters roared up into the sky only when you said they could, like a giant child dictating some complex game of who could and could not play with his toys.

And how it felt to have lost that.

She wriggled onto her side, sliding her arm across to stroke his neck and the silky skin just below his ear. 'Air Berlin—' The stream of words faltered. She fitted herself to his side and let her hand drift over his chest. It was delicious to have a warm, pulsing, breathing body in bed with her again.

He sighed and shifted. Drowsily, he freed an arm to loop around her and settle her head against his shoulder. 'I often don't sleep well in an unfamiliar bed.' He was mumbling, almost slurring, but there was a note of apology, as if aware he'd probably been doing something that would keep her awake. He kissed her hair.

'I thought that you'd sleep the kind of sleep that nothing could wake you from.'

He yawned, began to move his hands over her, gradually wakening. 'Mostly. Not always.'

'So will you suffer for this, tomorrow?'

He shook with laughter. 'Suffer? I might feel sleepier, but to hell with that.' He stroked her buttock, following the smooth curve from back to thigh. 'What about you? Do you have to work tomorrow? Today?'

She groaned. 'Yes. I've got a nine o'clock start so I'll need to get up in about four hours. But now I'm awake.' Her hand traced the ridge of his collarbone, over the plates of his chest to the softer flesh of his abdomen, testing the wiry hair with her fingertips. Man. She'd almost forgotten how to enjoy the shape of a man. 'I do know a great way to get back to sleep, though.' She twisted and slid her body over his until she was on top, skin tingling as it pressed against his.

He groaned; a deep, contented thrum. 'The rest of the condoms are in the car.'

'Don't need them.' She began to kiss down his body, flicking with her tongue, down and down.

And she took a refresher on all the softness and the hardness, the silkiness and the coarseness that was a man's body. And then they slept.

Chapter Twenty-One

PWNsleep message board:

Tenzeds: Amazing what a difference it makes to energy levels when I have purpose in my life.

Girlwithdreams: I've just read about a diet high in protein and amino acids helping with energy. Alcohol might have a detrimental effect on energy, too ... Loading with water might help.

Tenzeds: Give me a break! N is bad enough without giving up *everything* good. Wtf really wants to drink water instead of beer? Not even any caffeine involved! I live with someone who only eats healthy. (Sorry. Frustration talking. I know you're right.)

Finding himself in an unfamiliar bed made waking easier and also reassured him that making love to Liza hadn't been a dream. He fought to stay at the surface, to orientate himself. The other side of the bed was empty and cool. From the bathroom, he could hear the splashing of the shower.

It was still dark but his phone told him it was after six. Way early. But if Liza was up already ...

He heaved himself around so that he was sitting on the side of the bed, waited for a bit more clarity, located his wallet and, from the zipped pocket now empty of condoms, fumbled for his emergency stash of one yellow tablet, one white. Then he got his legs under him and made it to his feet, checking for balance.

In a moment he was opening the door into the tiny bathroom, stepping over the side of the bath and insinuating himself into the warmth and steam behind Liza. He tilted the showerhead so that the water slapped him in the face for a few seconds, then turned the stream back on her.

Eyes closed, she tipped her head to rinse her hair. 'You're up.'

'Naked soapy women tend to have that affect on me.' He pressed against the back of her. Her shower gel was lime, sharp on the moist air, and he put his lips to her shoulder as if to taste it, smoothing his hands over her skin.

'I'll take you back to Miranda's before I get ready for work.'

'That's a big hint that I should stop touching you, is it?' He didn't stop touching her.

'We do need to get going.' But she rubbed her behind against him, which did a great job of getting him going, but not in the way she'd meant. 'I'm going to spare you the walk of shame.'

He laughed. But he got it. She wanted to drive out the devil under cover of darkness.

Twenty minutes later he was creeping into Miranda and Jos's house. He clicked the front door slowly, carefully – but, from upstairs, Crosswind burst into a volley of '*Welcome home, boss!*' barks. Cursing, Dominic ran lightly up the stairs to reach him before the racket woke up the household.

But as he swung around the newel post at the head of the narrow staircase Miranda emerged from her room in a dark blue dressing gown and, from the room beside her, Ethan erupted into the day in yellow Buzz Lightyear pyjamas, beaming a joyous, early morning, creased and crumpled smile. 'Hello, Dommynic! You still look like red Batman!'

Dominic ruffled Ethan's bedhead hair and tried to keep moving. 'Hiya, Ethan! Yes, suppose I do.' On the other side of his bedroom door, Crosswind's barking and scrabbling rose a pitch past frantic. Miranda reached for the door handle and let loose the hound.

Trapped, Dominic had to brace against the banisters while Crosswind leaped a frantic welcome at his legs.

'Long party?' Miranda's eyes brimmed with laughter.

'Um.' He grimaced as Ethan joined Crosswind in bouncing and yapping. 'Quiet, Crosswind! Down, good boy.' Crosswind, at least, he could tell to shut up.

Ethan went from shrill to deafening. 'Dommynic, can I play with your cloak, please? And your fork? Where have your horns gone? Has Kenny still got his horns on? Is he still wearing his cloak?'

As the least said to Ethan about Kenny's current whereabouts, the better, Dominic swooped Ethan up so that they were nose-to-nose. 'Tell you what, let's have a getting dressed race. You go in your room and get dressed and I'll go in mine, and whoever is the winner can let Crosswind out in the garden and,' he paused impressively, 'wear the cloak.'

'Yeah!' screamed Ethan, wriggling down and grabbing Miranda's hand. 'C'mon, Mummy, help me beat Dommynic in a gedding dressed race!'

'OK, Ethan.' Miranda allowed herself to be dragged into his room, still raising her eyebrows at Dominic over her shoulder. 'Then Dominic can tell us all about his party last night.'

'Yeah!' yelled Ethan, as he disappeared.

Dominic dressed – jeans felt comfortably secure after Lycra – but kept his sweater in his hand for when Ethan came banging at his door.

His reward was a scream of joy. 'I won, Dommynic's not ready, Mummy!'

Heaving a theatrical good loser's sigh, Dominic shucked into the sweater before securing the cloak loosely around Ethan's soft little neck. 'Let's let Crosswind out, then.' He held the ends of the cloak and Ethan's hand to navigate the stairs.

But Ethan's interest in letting Crosswind out shrank to turning the key and throwing open the door once he realised he wouldn't be allowed to run around the garden in the cloak, as the hire shop would take a sour view of it having been dragged around a damp garden. Dominic, keeping him in view, wandered out into the freshness of the morning while Crosswind peed on the statue of the green man.

Ethan ran circuits around the kitchen table, cloak flying. 'Red Batma-an! Can I wear the tail?' he shouted.

Dominic raised his voice. ''Fraid not, mate. It's attached to the trousers and they're too big for you.'

''Kay!' Ethan resumed racing around the table. Miranda appeared, dressed and available to look after Ethan, so Dominic eased the back door shut to avoid more of the cousinly knowing looks. And reflect on the night before.

It had been incredible. He'd told Liza that, in the car, and she'd laughed, blue eyes wide and hair yet to be dried. 'I bet you say that to all the girls.'

Which had given him pause. But, no, usually he said 'great', which was nowhere near 'incredible'. He wasn't sure that he'd ever reached 'incredible' before. What he hadn't said was that being inside her had made his world make sense for the first time in a year. The feeling of being alien to himself had glugged away. Peace. A sense of rightness in armfuls and handfuls of Liza Reece.

But then her smile had changed, become something just for him, and she'd agreed, softly, 'Yes, it was incredible.' She'd shuddered, turning him on like an acetylene torch. Then checked her watch apologetically. 'But I really need to do my hair and get ready for work.' And, dismissed with a light kiss, he'd found himself out of the car and watching her do a three-point turn in the steeliness of what passes for dawn on a dank first of November, watching her drive away. Liza driving. Driving him nuts. Him driving into her—

He shook his mind out of her bed. The shower, dress and car journey period had been so brisk that he hadn't felt it provided adequate opportunity for exploring what the deal was regarding their ... whatever it was. Seeing each other. Non-relationship. Night of amazing sex. One-all-too-short-night stand. Mr Truthful, he'd fibbed about not being up for a relationship. He was pretty much up for whatever it was that had happened, though.

But neither had they returned to the delicate subject of their conflicting interests in the treatment centre, and that could be tricky.

He yawned and jammed his hands into his pockets against the chill. The rain had stopped but the moist air made the garden smell of cabbages. By no stretch of the imagination had he practised sleep hygiene last night, and he sighed in anticipation of how much of today would be lost to catch-up sleep and general zombieism, flopping from untired to mega exhausted at no notice. He yawned again, then smiled. Worth it, though. He thought of her beautiful hands on him. Beautiful mouth. He shivered. Beautiful everything. Nights like that were worth zombieism.

He forced his thoughts into business mode. What should he do regarding the lease? He had every intention of asking to see the valuation, or getting his own, but valuations could be meaningless. His business courses had taught him that an asset was worth what somebody would pay for it. And, despite the steepness of the premium, his first action after getting the call from Nicolas had been to ring Isabel Jones and set up the meeting to talk about renting the land beside the centre. Today, at three. But that had been before he'd spent the night making love to the competition. Should he and Liza talk first? Or should he have his meeting, and talk later?

The price Nicolas was asking ... Should he and Liza be looking for a way to work in cahoots? Together, they might be able to control Nicolas, make him revise his price, by acting as if they weren't both in the hunt.

But they were both in the hunt.

If they negotiated Nicolas down by manipulation, which of them would take up the lease?

It might be gentlemanly for him to bale out, but not pragmatic. Even if Liza could get the money together, the Pattinson family were likely to favour his offer because it would mean an income stream from land that had previously not produced one. He wasn't gentleman enough to throw away his dreams in a futile gesture.

An early nap helped negate some of the follow-on effects of a short and broken night, but he anticipated mainlining coffee in an effort to keep the sleep monster at bay. He took a second shower and put on a good shirt, ready for his meeting with Isabel Jones, then ran down to the kitchen, Crosswind weaving around his feet.

'Dommynic!' shouted Ethan, from his vantage point on his booster seat, facing the door. 'Shona and Gus are here for lunch. Look!' He gestured with a wedge of Miranda's homemade seedy brown bread.

'Wow,' said Dominic, his usual adult-pretending-to-listen-and-be-impressed response. Then an alert shrilled inside his head. Shona and Gus were the names of Liza's niece and nephew. And they were unlikely to have arrived at Miranda's house alone.

But, by the time his brain had processed the thought, he'd reached the doorway. From next to Ethan the attentive little face of Shona stared. And beside her sat a dark-haired, dark-eyed woman, cradling a sleepy baby Gus in one arm. She was staring, too.

Miranda grinned across a table full of chopped vegetables, dips and salad, her oval glasses catching the light. 'Sit down,

Dom, this is my friend, Cleo. Liza's sister. Ethan and Shona were due a playdate, so I suggested lunch.'

Dominic said his hellos to the children and, suppressing a sudden desire to claim a lunch appointment elsewhere, shook Cleo's hand, the one that wasn't hooked around the baby. Cleo smiled, but her dark eyes were assessing. Surreally, although Liza was blonde and blue-eyed where Cleo was dark, rounder, taller, their wide-open, unafraid expressions were identical. It made him smile. 'Liza didn't mention you'd be visiting Miranda today.'

'She wouldn't know. I haven't seen her for a week.'

'Dommynic, can Crosswind—?' Ethan began to clamber from his booster seat.

'Make the dog skateboard!' Shona threw her legs off her seat, too.

'Sit down, please!' chorused Cleo and Miranda, in an identical Mother Voice.

'Awwww ...'

'Anyway, Crosswind has to run around the garden because I can't take him out till later and he'll have to stay in my room whilst I'm out.' Dominic chivvied Crosswind outside and shut the door on his injured look before the children got into trouble for not eating their lunch.

'Awwww ...' But the children settled back into their seats and, with much the same feeling of accepting the inevitable, Dominic took the remaining place at the table, glad that he'd slept so there would be no risk of falling into stupor before Liza's sister's eyes. He helped himself to salad and cheese.

Ethan and Shona fell into some game involving ordering the contents of their plates according to colour preferences, leaving their mothers free to focus on Dominic.

'So, Miranda says you're moving into the area?' Cleo joggled Gus gently as she ate a cherry tomato.

'Hopefully.' He helped himself to homemade chutney. He'd have to gargle before he met Isabel Jones but Miranda's caramelised onion chutney was beyond his powers to resist. 'Liza's probably told you that there's an issue.'

Cleo nodded. 'She told me about you wanting her Stables.'

Dominic smiled neutrally, and didn't point out that The Stables was no more Liza's than it was his. Cleo was being protective. The light in her eyes made him suspect that she might be capable of casual decapitation if a threat to Liza made it necessary.

But, as he didn't plan on hurting Liza – although them both wanting the same business premises was unfortunate – he felt no need to be defensive. Instead, when Cleo asked him about what he was doing in Middledip, he provided a precis of how he'd left Stansted and a relationship at around the same time, directly or indirectly because of his narcolepsy. She'd probably had all that from Miranda, anyway. And it got it out of the way.

The baby stretched and mewed and Cleo patted his nappied bottom. 'So all you need to do is find somewhere to site your new business, and you're on the way to reinventing yourself?'

He nodded as he buttered more bread, not reacting to her implication that he hadn't already found a site for his business. It was great bread, though he preferred the white kind. Without bits in.

Cleo didn't press her question. Instead, she blindsided him. 'I'm getting married, soon.'

His brows flicked up. 'Congratulations.' Had Liza mentioned a wedding? No, he would have remembered.

'It's the budget wedding of the year. Registry office and village hall. Justin took it into his head that we have to be married, so we're throwing it together as we go along. The only night the village hall was free was the fifth of

November, probably because the bonfire party will be on the playing fields and nobody but us is mad enough to want to have a function at the same time. But Justin said we'll treat it as part of the celebrations and he's had the invites done at work.' She picked up an already-opened envelope from beside Miranda's plate, extricating a pearly white card deftly with the non-baby hand. 'Here's the invitation, for the reception.'

Dominic saw *Miranda, Jos, Ethan, Dominic and Crosswind* in fat, sloped handwriting. 'Oh no, I don't expect—' he began, quickly.

'I included you because I'm hoping you'll do me a favour and bring your performing dog. Shona went on and on about Crosswind skateboarding. We're really on a shoestring, we can't afford a conjuror or clown, and the place will be swarming with kids. They'd love him.'

'But if there are fireworks—'

'They'll be in the evening. I'm talking about something for the kids in the afternoon.'

'Crosswind isn't really an act—'

'No, Miranda tells me that he's just a natural superstar who loves an audience. I'm hoping that, you know, you could let the kids have something to watch for twenty minutes or so.' Having cut across his every sentence with smooth precision, her eyes had softened, now, cajoling, hopeful.

Incredibly difficult to resist.

Especially when Miranda chimed in, 'And you know how Crosswind loves to show off, Dom.'

Damn. He sighed. 'I'll bring Crosswind for a quick visit. But you don't have to invite me to your wedding.'

'It's more of a party. The actual wedding ceremony is at noon, just us, the kids, and close family. And I wouldn't be so rude as to exclude you. Miranda tells me that you're probably going to rent a flat in Little Dallas, so you're already a villager. I know it's short notice, but that's Justin for you. No sooner does he decide to do something then he acts.' Cleo shifted Gus up onto her shoulder, where he lay as still as a doll, whilst she rubbed circles on his back. Her eyes smiled coaxingly. 'We'd love you to be there.'

He was in no doubt that Cleo meant, *I want to see how Liza is with you,* and decided to leave it to Liza to head her sister off, if she wanted to. He could always make a later excuse. An urgent nap, or something. 'OK. Thanks.'

'Miranda says you have a friend staying. You can bring him along.'

'Mummy, can I get down?' bellowed Ethan.

'Mummy, can I get down?' yelled Shona.

'I'm not sure if he'll still be here. But thanks.' Dominic helped himself to more cheese and chutney and grinned at the idea of dragging Kenny along to a stranger's wedding swarming with kids. It would be so not his thing.

'*Mummy*—' Ethan and Shona shouted together.

In the racket of the children being allowed to abandon the table for the sitting room and the delights of Ethan's toy chest, Dominic excused himself. He'd barely made the hall when the doorbell ding-donged and Kenny let himself in wearing new-looking jeans and shirt. Probably Undead Barbie had been despatched to shop for him. A swathe of shiny red Lycra hung over his shoulder and his trident was tucked under his arm.

Ethan and Shona tumbled over each other to greet the newcomer in the hall. 'Kenny!' yelled Ethan, bouncing on the spot. 'You're not dressed like red Batman any more. I saw Dommynic dressed like red Batman, this morning, and I beat him in a gedding dressed race, and he had to let me wear the *cloak*!'

Kenny looked at Dominic over Ethan's head. 'Still dressed like red batman this morning, was he?' And, as the children yelled their way back to the toy chest, 'Stay at Rochelle's place, Doc?'

From the kitchen, Miranda giggled. 'Guess again, Kenny.'

Dominic tried to frown down first Miranda and then Kenny. Everyone was showing way too much interest in where he'd chosen to spend last night. And with Liza's sister listening ... 'I've got this meeting with Isabel Jones in an hour. Any chance you could take my car and drop our costumes back in Peterborough? They have to be handed back by five or we forfeit the deposit.'

'OK,' Kenny said, slowly. 'I'm not needed in this meeting?'

Dominic felt suddenly awkward. He'd asked Kenny up to give his opinion on the site for his project, but today's meeting was about money, not where to build the kayak shed. 'Not this one, Ken.' He glanced at his watch and started for the stairs.

But Kenny didn't step aside to give Dominic room. Instead, he dropped his voice. 'Liza, presumably?'

Dominic stared at his friend, surprised to detect ice in the words. 'No reason why not, is there?'

'Because you know I'm taking her out to dinner? With *you and Rochelle*?' Anger was tightening the skin around Kenny's eyes.

'Rochelle kind of put me on the spot about dinner,' Dominic pointed out, reasonably, wishing he'd pulled the kitchen door shut behind him so that their conversation was no more public than it had to be. 'I didn't exactly say yes – just that it sounded OK. No arrangement was made.'

'An arrangement *was* made – between me and Liza.'

Dominic sighed. 'Kenny, I don't have time for this. I have a meeting. Anyway, Liza said "Could be fun." That's not an arrangement.' Then, as Kenny's eyes blazed, he felt his own anger kindling. 'Sorry if I stepped on your toes, mate, but you didn't bother to check out the position with me and

Liza before you barged in, so no complaints, eh?' He tried to diffuse the situation with a grin. 'And you went home with Undead Barbie, didn't you?'

'Only,' said Kenny, stiffly, 'after I saw you coming out of a bedroom with Liza. What was your chat up line? "I have a rare sleep disorder, please will you take me to bed?"'

Fury burst like fire deep in Dominic's guts, clenching his fists. But he smothered it, shoving his hands in his pockets. Mindful of the kids – and, for that matter, Cleo – listening, he contented himself with deadly emphasis. 'Yeah, right, Kenny, I always wanted a disability, just to give me a cheesy chat up line.' He clapped Kenny on the shoulder harder than was necessary. 'I see you'll use any weapon. All's fair in love and war, eh?'

After a moment, Kenny gave a crooked smile. 'Yeah, Doc. All's fair in love and war.'

As Dominic brushed past and up the stairs, he heard Cleo remarking drily, 'Men snapping at each other over my sister. Quite like old times.'

Well, why settle for awkward when you could have total cringing embarrassment? In the safety of his room, he dialled the number Rochelle had lodged in his phone last night as he grabbed his jacket, wallet and keys. And ProPlus, in case nobody offered him coffee and he needed a caffeine hit.

'Hi,' said Rochelle, in his ear.

Dominic thanked her for the party, then decided that there was no way of saying what he had to say other than directly. 'Rochelle, I feel a bit awkward about this, but I'm not sure that the dinner we talked about is going to come off.'

Rochelle laughed. 'Did it help?'

'Sorry?'

'I'm not stupid, Dominic. I did notice that you blanked out of our conversation once Liza walked back into the room. I just said it to give Liza something to think about.'

Cautiously, sheepishly, he admitted, 'It might have helped.'

'I don't mind if it did,' she said, generously. And, honestly, 'But I wouldn't have minded if it hadn't, either.' Then, more seriously, 'Give Liza a bit of slack, though, won't you? She was never that great at relationships, even before Adam.'

He laughed, shortly. 'She's made it pretty clear that we're not in a relationship, so slack is kind of a given.'

Chapter Twenty-Two

Despite the bench in Peterborough's Cathedral Square feeling as if it wouldn't be out of place in an igloo, as the departing sun drained the colour from the day, Liza had had to sit down and gather her thoughts.

She'd heard on the news that banks were being stingy with their lending, but she hadn't anticipated quite what it meant until Emily, a suited young banker, had taken Liza, burdened with the two awkward drawstring bags that held the hornet costume she must return this afternoon, into a claustrophobic little office behind a wall of ATMs. She examined Liza's proposal at the speed of light, enquired about things Liza didn't have, then broke the bad news with a regretful smile. 'I'm afraid that without adequate security, this proposition isn't going to fall within our parameters.'

Liza had made the appointment more in optimism than expectation, but the words still burst open a crevasse of disappointment at her feet. 'I suppose that if I'd made a couple of decades' worth of mortgage payments rather than a couple of years, there would have been enough money in my house to make it worth the bank's while to repossess it if I failed on the loan payments?'

Emily smiled sympathetically. 'We usually speak in terms of whether there's sufficient equity, but that's more or less it, yes. You've demonstrated that you can meet the rent; it's the loan for the premium that's the problem – putting it simply, you're asking for too much money. There's no way for me to know whether you'll make enough profit to service such large repayments. Another option would be that someone in your family give us a guarantee for the loan, with enough equity for a second mortgage to support it.'

Liza thought about her parents' reaction if she suggested they put their home at risk for her, and snorted. 'That's not going to happen.'

'Then, I'm sorry but ...' Emily refreshed her sympathetic expression. She probably got a lot of practice. 'Is there anything else I can do for you, today?'

Liza bit back the impulse to say, 'No, just give me the bloody loan!' And, gathering her bags of slutty hornet, left.

It was Dominic's interest in The Stables that had caused the lease premium to become stupidly inflated. And her conscience, which had been jabbing her about spending last night naked and sweaty with him but not mentioning her appointment at the bank, could be quiet. The field was now clear for him to take her Stables and make a huge success of his business – while she slaved through the process of locating new premises, keeping client numbers up and relocation costs down.

If he hadn't arrived on the scene—

He wouldn't have melted her bones. She shivered at the memory of last night. The ways he had touched her. The velvet of his tongue. Temptation had been fierce, but giving in to it had tangled together business and pleasure.

She sighed. She almost felt down enough to excuse a chocolate Brazil nut flapjack. But loss of the slutty hornet hire deposit loomed large in her mind and, a sigh hanging white in the crisp air in front of her, she persuaded frozen legs to propel her stiffly in the direction of the hire shop.

The shop windows were full of pink fairy and yellow chicken costumes, punctuated by an exceptionally sincere Barack Obama mask. Pushing open the glass door, she nearly collided with Kenny King coming the other way. 'Hey, Liza!' He gave her a kiss on the cheek, and then a hug. 'Bringing your hot costume back?'

Liza stepped aside to let him out. 'I guess you're doing the same?'

He stayed exactly where he was. 'Yeah, Doc was bleating about getting it back so we didn't lose our deposit.'

'I don't want to lose mine, either.' But Liza didn't intend to shimmy between him and the wall to reach the counter and the lady hovering behind it. 'Excuse me.'

He gave way, but only to move back into the shop along with her. 'So, we still on for dinner?'

'Um …' Liza hoisted her bags up onto the wooden counter, where the silver-haired lady assistant wore a waiting smile, opening the drawstrings so that the costume could be inspected: the hated wings of wire in one and the dress-of-uncomfortability in the other. 'I need to return this, please, and get my friend's deposit back for her.'

'Receipt, dear?'

'She still has it.'

'Oh.' The silver-haired lady's voice dropped to a whisper. 'I can't really go giving you someone else's deposit, dear.'

Liza could see perfectly well that it was dodgy to give her Rochelle's money, but elected to embroil herself in a long discussion about it in the hopes that Kenny would become bored or remember that his parking ticket was about to expire or something. But, no. All through a phone call to Rochelle, who was perfectly willing to call in with the receipt and collect the deposit herself, Kenny waited, hands tucked comfortably into the front pockets of a navy hoodie with *Wilderness trail tramp* stitched up one sleeve.

The receipt/deposit crisis over, Liza punched more buttons on her phone, paused as if reading a message and went, 'Oops!' Then she swung on Kenny and brushed a kiss vaguely in the vicinity of his cheek, an unmistakeable dismissal. 'Got to run.' And ran, the dinner question successfully avoided.

The meeting with Isabel Jones went well.

Until it didn't.

Isabel was exactly the type Dominic liked to deal with – cool, calm, controlled, commonsensical and with the power to make her own decisions, getting the conversation on-topic even as she showed him to a tubular metal-and-cream leather chair. 'Prior to this meeting, I spoke to Nicolas Notten to check he's willing to sell the lease, and shared views with relevant others in our organisation.' She seated herself in the power chair behind the desk, big, black, padded and swivelling. 'So there's nothing to stop me listening to your plans.' She smiled. Her royal blue suit would have looked over bright and unbiz on anyone with less confidence. But confidence didn't seem to be an Isabel Jones issue. Thirty-something, her glossy dark hair swept down to her shoulders and her spike heels made her almost as tall as Dominic. He might have thought her hot if he wasn't currently into quirky, snippy little blondes.

Following her lead, he moved straight into his pitch. 'I want to open an adventure and challenge centre. The lake's ideal for paddle sports, the slope for mountain biking, all-terrain skateboarding and an assault course. And there's enough flat ground by the lake for archery, if I put up screens.' His iPad, containing his notes, lay on the desk, but his plan was as clear in his mind as the holding points on Stansted's taxiways.

Isabel made rapid notes in black pen on ruled white paper. 'So, who do you see as your customers? Corporate teambuilders?'

He nodded. 'They've got to be core because it's such big business. But also school groups, youth organisations and weekend Rambos.'

She nodded. 'The corporate groups and weekenders would certainly benefit us in terms of reciprocality.'

'How do you see that working?' A useful phrase taught on one of his courses for when he wanted the other party to fill in blanks in his knowledge.

'In the most fundamental terms – your customers becoming our guests. Weekend Rambos might book rooms or dine with us, possibly bringing partners along. Corporate customers might also do those things, plus hire conferencing facilities.'

'Plus, you'll get the rental income.'

'Which has to be considered,' she agreed. 'So tell me how you see your project.'

The floor was his. He talked about finance, insurance, advertising, Kenny managing the instructor side, mentally ticking boxes as every point was covered. He felt clear-headed and focused, relishing the sensation of doing something instead of hanging around Miranda's place, making plans.

Isabel nodded and noted and he was just congratulating himself on getting her on board, when she said, 'So how do you envisage tying the adventure centre in to The Stables?'

He paused, wondering how that could not be obvious. 'The building will house the team room, changing rooms, equipment storage, and, of course, the kitchens and toilets.'

But Isabel was frowning. 'How are you going to shoehorn that lot in with the treatment centre?'

A snake of doubt wriggled in the pit of his stomach and coiled itself up like a threat. He wasn't sure why it was there but it seemed that the obvious must, indeed, be stated. 'The adventure centre will replace the treatment centre. I've no intention of running the two together.'

Slowly, Isabel Jones capped her pen, laid it down on her high-gloss desk and leaned back. 'Then we can't do business.'

They stared at each other. Dominic tried to read what was going on behind her dramatically made-up eyes whilst his mind cast around for where the meeting had derailed. 'Shall we back up a step?' he began.

Smoothly, she overrode him. 'I'm sorry, this isn't negotiable. The treatment centre must be part of The Stables. It's in our brochures.'

Chapter Twenty-Three

As he digested her words, Isabel expanded. 'Port Manor Hotel has its brochure content decided one to two seasons in advance. The same content goes on our website, and on the websites and apps of tourism organisations and strategic partners. If the treatment centre were to cease to be, it would be a planned change, the result of conclusions drawn from analysis and assessment. Forward preparation would be lengthy. A major redesign of all promotional and publicity material would be incurred, at significant expense.

'Going forward, we're not undertaking that analysis, we're not planning that move, because we view The Stables as a benefit to our guests with few, if any, direct costs to us.' She smiled, faintly. 'The treatment centre stays.'

Mentally, Dominic cursed himself with foul obscenities. How had he overlooked something so obvious as the hotel wanting to keep the fucking treatment centre? He'd been told that they'd invited tenders for it – hadn't that been a big enough clue?

He drew a deep breath, fighting to keep shock from registering on his face. Bad. This was bad, but he had been trained to think fast and react decisively in a developing situation. 'OK,' he said, as if Isabel Jones didn't hold all the power and that the world of free enterprise wasn't new to him. 'Convince me that the treatment centre is profitable.'

Isabel looked amused. 'I don't need to.'

'You'll need to convince *someone* that it's profitable, if you want them to buy the lease and trade from the premises. It's not just a case of Nicolas Notten not wanting to run the treatment centre any more, and you saying, "OK, Nicolas, just find someone else who will." Nicolas Notten *can't* run the treatment centre any more, because he's losing money. Any interested party will see, as I have done, that the treatment centre isn't making a profit. And they'll pootle off and find something better to sink their money into.'

Just for an instant, Isabel's gaze wavered. But she said, 'There's another interested party already, I believe.'

Rolling his inner dice, Dominic closed the case of his iPad. 'Liza Reece? Yes, she's got great ideas for the centre.' He shifted forward on his chair, as if preparing to rise. His heart was thumping and he felt awake and alert and alive, as he had in his previous life in Stansted Air Traffic Control Tower. Ms Jones was underestimating him. Always a mistake. He smiled. 'All she needs, I suppose, is the appropriate finance.' He shrugged. 'But now it's apparent that the only business acceptable to the landlord is exactly the business that's failing ... Finance is going to be a challenge, isn't it?'

Isabel Jones sat very still.

Dominic rose, reached out as if to shake her hand. And then hesitated. Frowned. 'Of course, we might be able to come up with something that works for all of us.' And, coincidentally, provide him with a beautifully neat way through the Liza Reece minefield. His heart congratulated him with a happy little skip.

Her brows quirked. 'Let's hear it.'

'OK.' He resumed his seat. 'But if the treatment centre aspect is non-negotiable then I'm going to need a concession on the rent.'

She laughed, incredulously. 'OK, let's not hear it. If the beautiful vista of the big slope is to be besmirched by ugly equipment, there needs to be something in it for us.'

Dominic recognised a blag when he heard one. 'There's loads in it for you – a new stream of income from the big slope, potentially bringing in guests, someone who could yet keep the treatment centre viable and in your brochures, with the necessary finance already in place. The adventure and challenge centre will be an attraction, not an ugly wart. We can go reciprocal on promo so far as websites are concerned and by the time you're planning your next brochure, I'll be up and running and we can talk about including it there, too.

'It all looks better, to me, than a tenant who's going to go belly up at any moment, leaving empty the treatment centre you're so keen on keeping open. Or did I miss something?'

When Liza drove into The Cross she saw two things. Or, rather two people: Dominic lounging on her garden wall under the street light, his feet propped on his skateboard, and Mrs Snelling talking at him, arms like mug handles as she planted her hands on her hips.

Slowly, Liza pulled her car up at the kerb. Driving home, numb with misery, she'd faced what the bank's response to her precious plan meant. She was going to have to leave The Stables.

And there was Dominic giving her his killer smile over Mrs Snelling's shoulder as if all was well with his world. It would have been pretty bad mannered of him not to smile, after last night, but it was as welcome as a wasp in her bra, as he personified what had gone wrong with her delicious plan.

Mrs Snelling swung on her as Liza pushed open the car door. 'I was just telling this man not to sit on the wall.'

'It's my wall,' Liza pointed out.

'That's what I said.' Dominic smiled again. Right into her eyes, as if Mrs Snelling wasn't there.

Mrs Snelling's mouth flattened into a disagreeable line. 'But I can see him from my sitting room.'

'Shut your curtains! It's dark, anyway.' Brushing Mrs

Snelling's pudgy shoulder aside, Liza grabbed Dominic's jacket. 'Come inside. You're obviously making the place look untidy and I've got something to tell you.'

Dominic scooped up his board as he let himself be pulled to his feet. 'Funny. I've got something to tell you, too.'

Realising that she'd towed him right up to her front door, Liza hastily released his sleeve. 'Sorry.'

'I don't mind hot women being unable to keep their hands off me.'

Behind them, Mrs Snelling gave an audible snort as Liza turned the key and pushed open the door. 'You've just given my infuriatingly nosy and judgemental neighbour a new bad thing to think of me.' On her way to the kitchen she dumped her coat over the back of the sitting-room sofa, as if to disguise what had happened there. Now wasn't the time to face it. There were issues in more urgent need of resolution. Like how she was going to earn her living. 'Sit down. I'm making coffee.' She took the block of freeze-dried coffee out of her bag and clunked it onto the worktop, dragging out a chrome cafetière from the back of a cupboard.

He stowed his skateboard in a corner of the kitchen floor, folded himself into a chair and leaned back, legs crossed comfortably at the ankle, showing no sign of feeling awkward. 'Caffeine, eh?'

She filled the kettle with a rush of water. 'I've had a bad day.'

His thoughtful gaze followed her as she filled the cafetière with scoops of coffee and steaming water and set it on the table with mugs and milk, then delved into her bag again for a bar of Bourneville chocolate.

'Wow. Sugar, too. *That* bad a day?'

'Worse.' She took a seat at the other side of the table, so that he'd get the message that this was a business meeting. Not that he'd tried to kiss her hello or anything, so maybe he was perfectly happy that last night remain a when-it's-over-it's-over hook up.

Such a lack of expectation would uncomplicate things beautifully.

And now definitely wasn't the moment to examine how she'd feel if delicious sweaty sex and passing out in a heap of entwined limbs turned out not to mean a damned thing. And it was stupid to be aggravated by his not showing any reaction to her obvious grumpiness.

Ripping the chocolate wrapper, she broke off four squares for herself, then spun the pack across the table in his direction. 'The bank says I haven't a hope of getting the finance for the lease at the stupid numbers that Nicolas is talking. So, lucky you.'

His dark eyebrows lifted fractionally. 'Oh. Crap for you, though.'

'Crap with disaster icing on.' She slid two squares of chocolate into her mouth, adding, thickly, 'I hope you have better luck,' in the tone that meant she didn't.

'I think I already have.' He did, at least, sound apologetic. 'I met Ms Jones, the finance bod from Port Manor Hotel, today, and, after a bit of a scare when I thought I'd screwed up, it went well.'

She took a long pull from her coffee, letting it melt the chocolate in her mouth. No way should she feel aggrieved that he'd had his business meeting, just like she'd had hers. Just because they'd made love. Just because she'd opened up to him in the most intimate way. Just because they'd talked and laughed and he hadn't sulked when she'd turfed him out without morning sex. She dragged her mind away from the sex. His nakedness against hers. Hard. Hot. And it wasn't his fault that his meeting had gone well and hers had gone badly. 'Congratulations.'

'It's a bit early for that.' He broke some squares from the

chocolate and returned the rest. The table was small, so it didn't create much distance. He was close enough that she had to avoid his legs under the table, could smell the frosty tang of outdoors on his clothes and see every glint of gold in his hair. 'Thing is, the hotel wants the treatment centre at The Stables. It's in their brochures. I've tried everything I can to avoid taking it on but Isabel Jones says that if I want the big slope area, I have to take on the treatment centre.'

Liza grabbed another four squares of chocolate and gave a disparaging snort. 'What do you know about running a treatment centre?'

'Nothing,' he admitted, cheerfully, his gaze on her mouth. 'So how about we work something out where you run the treatment centre for me? You put into action your ideas for making the centre profitable, on whatever business model you think will work best with the other therapists, and we work out a fair rent for you to pay to me – obviously, I'm not looking to make a loss. But I don't have to take a salary out of the treatment centre, like Nicolas did. My profits are going to come from working in the adventure and challenge side. I've negotiated with the hotel so that I can rent the big slope and the part of The Stables that's currently empty, plus take over Nicolas's lease for your bit. We have to do the sums, but I'm guessing we'll find your rent to me to be only a little more than the total of what you three therapists have been paying to Nicolas.'

Her heart somersaulted. But she frowned and continued to let the dark delicious bitterness of Bourneville seep over her tongue, because if she let her smile muscles take charge, then her face would become one jolly grin of joy that he was unexpectedly offering her a route forward in a way that she could afford. Galloping to her rescue; making her forget that his scenario wasn't what she wanted to achieve. Distracting her from how dashed her hopes were.

She needed to explore his proposition up, down and inside out, inspect the ointment for flies before she didn't look the gift horse in its mouth. If something looked too good to be true, it usually was. 'If that's the case, and if Imogen and Fenella were to pay me the rent they pay Nicolas, plus I let out his office as another treatment room and maybe utilise part of reception, too, there's a way for me to keep Pippa on and still make quite a bit.' She allowed disbelief to fill her voice, as if giving him the chance to realise that he must have got something wrong.

But he didn't backtrack. 'Go for it. You make it as big a success as you can and leave me free to concentrate on my own stuff. Isabel showed me a plan of the other leg of The Stables and it has everything I need except the toilets and kitchen, so both business would have to share the ones the treatment centre currently uses.' He smiled, slowly, conspiratorially, joyfully. As if the deal was done. 'Other than that, well, you know I'm not interested in the holistic stuff.'

'You should be,' she retorted, picking up her coffee cup and staring over the rim. 'Stags and hens.'

'What?'

'You know that one of my ideas for The Stables is to have pamper sessions for hen nights? We could cross promote. The basic idea would be for the hens to come for treatments and the stags to crash around on adventures, but there are bound to be hen parties just as keen to be adventurous and stags who'd go for the treatments. Stag and hen parties are huge business. People are always looking for new and different.'

Fresh excitement blazed in his eyes. 'Wow, your ideas are great. And we should be able to get stags and hens concessionary rates at the hotel. Isabel's keen on reciprocality.'

'She'd be stupid not to be. Think about the bar bills stags and hens would run up. But I don't see how you can afford not to put my rent up, now you know how much that greedy bastard Nicolas wants as a premium on his precious lease.'

Dominic's eyes half-closed in satisfaction – reminding her suddenly of last night. 'But I'm not going to have to pay his greedy bastard premium, am I? Not now. When you tell him you're out of the running, I'll, um, renegotiate.'

'And if I don't drop out you can afford his greedy bastard premium anyway, so you'll just outbid me.' She refilled both coffee cups from the cafetière and divided the last of the chocolate equally. 'You just get luckier and luckier,' she said, slowly. But, still, a little bird of excitement fluttered behind her breastbone. Could his proposal work out? She could stay at The Stables, make more money, get rid of Nicolas, implement all the ideas her head had been bursting with. And Dominic would stay—

And Dominic would stay … The bird fluttered harder, flapping, as it sensed a trap. 'We'd be in this together,' she realised.

He planted his elbows on the table; leaned closer. A stillness stole over his face. 'And?'

'*And* …' He was so close that she could see flecks of blue and silver in his eyes, and every one of his thick dark lashes. 'Isn't what you're suggesting a lot like a relationship?' There. Right there. Ointment. Big fat fly.

A black frown snapped down above his eyes. 'A business relationship. You'd be managing the treatment centre for me.'

'So now you're saying I'd be your *employee*? After having my own biz?'

The gift horse set its mouth in a grim line. His eyes narrowed. '"For me" was probably the wrong phrase. You'd simply be running the treatment centre so that we can both get what we want. You'd still be self-employed, you'd have a "biz", but with a wider scope and more income, and would be paying rent to me, not Nicolas.'

His gaze never wavered. But he was looking wary and tense. And, as if to fulfil his every apprehension, Liza felt her heart deflate into a pancake of disappointment. 'My disastrous relationship with Nicolas proves that I'm not good at being answerable to anyone.' She paused. 'I can't give you an answer just now. I need to consider my position.'

Silence. His gaze bored into her. Eyes flat, excitement gone. 'I get it,' he said, finally, slowly. He looked suddenly fatigued. Disappointed. Grim. Unhurriedly, he reached inside his jacket, took out a blister pack of white pills and washed two down with a swill of coffee. 'Last night's getting in the way.'

She flushed. 'I want to believe it's a good thing that you're offering me. But, yes, it would mean us spending a lot of time together, which could get messy if we're—'

Slowly, he pushed back his chair. Waited a beat and then climbed to his feet. 'If we're having sex.'

Swallowing an unexpected ache in her throat at the non-compatibility of business and that particularly sweet pleasure, she nodded. 'It would be a screaming nightmare if things go wrong.'

He drained his coffee mug and slapped it down, the noise loud in the quiet of the kitchen. 'Just got that from findafeebleexcuse.com? How convenient for someone who thinks they're rubbish at relationships.'

'It's not convenient. It's a valid consideration. Because I am rubbish at relationships.'

He zipped up his jacket and rammed his hands into his pockets. 'If forgetting one night of sex will put everything on a business footing, then consider it forgotten.'

211

Taken aback at this slamming of his cards on the table, she breathed, 'Oh!'

He strode past her, face constructed of flinty hard lines in the harsh kitchen light. 'Don't look so affronted. I'm trained in problem solving. You told me the problem, I've solved it. To be honest, Liza, if you don't take this opportunity, I'm going to have to offer it to Fenella or Imogen or find someone else. I need the centre.'

He swiped up his skateboard from where he'd left it, tossing back over his shoulder, 'It's you that's optional.'

He skated hard up the pavement of Main Road, past the garage where Jos worked, its doors shut for the night, fuelled by anger adrenaline – not just anger at Liza, for trashing his fine bloody dream. He was cursing himself.

He was supposed to be able to deal with changing scenarios. Observe. Assess. Plan. Formulate strategies and have contingencies in place. And wasn't he supposed to be the fucking bloody perceptive one? He'd known that Liza was wary and edgy and stubborn and suspicious and focused on her own goal.

But he'd disregarded all of that knowledge.

He hopped the board off the kerb to allow two middle-aged women by, before bunny hopping back onto the path again.

In the euphoria of his meeting with Isabel Jones, he'd seen only what he wanted to see – attaining his personal goal in such a way as not to rob Liza of The Stables. He'd wilfully ignored the fact that his solution would involve a big compromise for her.

Where had he left his brain?

He slowed as the lights from The Three Fishes came into view, curved around the pillar box on the corner of Great End in a rush of wheels, then stepped off the deck and kicked the board up into his hand. Legs suddenly heavy. Adrenaline ebbing.

His position was stronger than hers, his proposal more attractive to the hotel. But he shouldn't have been so pleased with himself. For fuck's sake, he was meant to be a people person. He trudged across the road towards Miranda and Jos's warm, safe little house. All he'd had to do was make sure Liza had some control. No wonder, in her disappointment, that she'd seized on their history as an excuse to refuse. He edited and reran his opening in his mind: *I have an idea, but I don't know if you want to hear it, when the bank's just knocked you back.*

And if she hadn't wanted to hear it right then, her natural curiosity and cussedness would have made her want to hear it tomorrow or the next day, when the rawness of defeat had begun to heal. That's how you dealt with awkward situations. You managed and finessed them.

You didn't ignore someone's setback and try and palm them off with a consolation prize. Especially one that so admirably suited your own purpose, your own grand plan, that happened to be going exceedingly well.

And then you really, really, *really* didn't lose your temper and stalk out when that someone failed to fall to their knees in gratitude. That was just throwing petrol on the fire.

He let himself into the light of Miranda's hallway, dragging off his jacket in the sudden warmth. Crosswind frisked out of the sitting room, all propeller tail and welcoming woofs. 'Hiya, Crosswind.' Tiredly, Dominic opened his arms and, in an instant, they were full of warm, fluffy, wriggling dog, his face under assault from a cold nose and a hot tongue. He listened, and heard Jos on the phone in the kitchen and the splashing and singing from the bathroom that signified Miranda supervising Ethan's bath time.

Good. He didn't have to talk to anybody just yet. He

yawned, turning his head away so that Crosswind wouldn't use it as an invitation for some tongue action. 'Five minutes,' he muttered. 'Or ten.' He headed for the sofa, set the alert on his phone, and crashed out, the comforting weight of Crosswind still in his arms.

Chapter Twenty-Four

From the sitting-room window, she watched him launch his skateboard into the middle of The Cross with three mighty pushes of his right foot and no apparent regard for the likelihood of approaching traffic, settle both feet on the deck, hop the board onto the pavement, lean left, and vanish around the corner of Crowther's shop.

Douchebag. Smug, smartarse, up himself douchebag.

She wished she hadn't let him share her chocolate.

In fact, she was tempted to run over to the shop to invest in one of those huge slabs of Dairy Milk and then send Dominic bloody Christy the empty wrapper. She had only a hazy idea of how that would express her displeasure, or even exactly what form her displeasure took or whether she had any right to feel it. But. Anyway. Something was bubbling in her anger cauldron.

But before she could decide on a better bitter revenge, she received a text from Cleo's Justin. *Can u talk to Cleo about the wedding for me? She's being difficult.*

Welcoming the distraction, she responded, *OK, after dinner*, decided it was too cold to go to the shop just for Dairy Milk, and flung some chicken and a rainbow of chopped veg into her wok. Dominic Douchebag wasn't worth the bad karma that came with revenge and she refused to sully her brain with the notion that she'd all-but-dismissed his offer with stupendous imprudence – not mature caution.

She arrived at Cleo's house two minutes after eight and Shona promptly thundered downstairs to launch herself at Liza from the fourth step. 'Aun-tee Lie-zah!'

Liza fielded the pyjama-clad missile in mid air. 'Sho-nah!' But then Cleo, hair sticking out as if she'd been tearing at it, sent her a silent scream of frustration, and Liza turned a stern look on her niece. 'Were you in bed?'

Shona flicked her mother a glance from under long lashes. 'I wasn't asleep.'

Liza smothered a grin as Cleo mimed banging her head against the wall. 'You're not supposed to get up, though, are you? I'll tuck you back in and read you a story.' Shona was a great sleeper, once she gave into it, but the older she got, the less giving in seemed to appeal. Between her bed-evasion tactics, Gus's colic, Gus waking Shona and Shona waking Gus, Cleo sometimes seemed close to gibbering with sleep deprivation.

Liza had better have Shona and Gus after the wedding, she decided, guiltily, as she trod upstairs, Shona hanging around her neck like an orang-utan baby. Cleo was Liza's go-to person during trials and tribulations, but rarely asked for anything in return.

'Right.' Tumbling her niece, angelic in lemon-yellow pyjamas, back into her white wooden bed, Liza composed her face into decisive lines. 'One story. If you get up again tonight, I won't ask Mummy if I can look after you at the weekend.'

'I don't want you to look after me,' retorted Shona, grinning like the Joker as she wrapped her little arms around Liza and dragged her down to snuggle.

'Oh. Right.' Liza sighed, obligingly snuggling. The four-year-old was getting too clever for mere grown-ups to manipulate. 'Well, don't get up again, anyway.' She settled Shona, who smelled of shampoo and baby talc, against the hollow of her shoulder, and picked up a book of dog stories from the bedside table, choosing the one she knew to be the longest in the hopes that Cleo might grab a few minutes of feet-up time. 'Fluffy was a fox terrier,' she began.

Shona stabbed the picture of a fox terrier with a dimpled finger. 'I saw that dog that skate boarded, today.'

Liza paused. 'Crosswind? Did you?'

'Me and Mummy and Gus went, and I played with Ethan, and we had bread and carrots for lunch, even though I don't like carrots, but the man called Dominic put Crosswind in the garden.'

'Went where? Ethan's mummy's house?' Liza tried not to let indignation enter her voice.

Shona nodded, pretending to stroke the pictured fox terrier with one finger. 'But he got the dog out of the garden before he went out and he rolled over on the carpet and he walked on his back legs.'

'Dominic rolled on the carpet?'

Shona erupted like a giggle fountain. 'Crosswind, the dog!' And demonstrated, by kicking off the duvet and waggling her legs and arms whilst making breathy, 'Rrrrh, rrrrh' noises.

'OK, let's stop being a dog, now.' Liza flipped the duvet back into place and flattened Shona into human form.

'Rrrrh,' persisted Shona. But by the time that Liza had read the story she did finally look soft and drowsy, accepting a last cuddle preparatory to the turning out of the light. She halted Liza just as the door shut. 'I do want you to look after me, really.'

Liza grinned as she crept away. 'OK. I'll ask Mummy.'

Downstairs, Cleo and Justin half-lay at opposite ends of the sofa, managing, by dextrous entwining of limbs, to massage each other's feet as they watched TV. Liza shifted a yellow changing mat, a pot of baby wipes and a fluffy orange goggle-eyed duck from a chair, so that she could sit down.

Justin withdrew his attention from the sci-fi film exploding all over the TV. 'Liza, tell your sister that she has to have a wedding dress.'

Liza raised aghast eyebrows at Cleo. 'You have to have a wedding dress!'

Cleo smiled serenely. 'No, I don't. At least, nothing new. I have that ivory-coloured suit I only wore once.'

'Wow.' Liza was impressed. 'Can you get back in that so soon after having Gus?'

Justin glared at Cleo. 'It's our wedding day and I want you to have a new dress.'

'We can use the money better in other ways. And I can't bear the idea of trudging around shops with Gus and Shona in tow.' Cleo heaved a huge, downtrodden, martyred sigh. 'You haven't bought a new dress, have you, Liza?'

Liza had fully intended to suffer wearing a past-season dress in the interests of her personal economy drive, but when Justin's glare turned meaningfully in her direction, she executed a hasty rewriting of plans. 'Tomorrow's Wednesday and I'm not working till three, so I'm going to hit the shops in the morning.' As she wasn't going to be paying Nicolas his greedy-bastard premium, now, she could kind of afford it, if she steered clear of designer labels. 'Let's go together and I'll look after the kids while you try things on.'

Cleo groaned. Justin lifted her right foot and kissed the instep. 'I've got the money from the extra work I took on. Go with Liza and get a dress that I'll love.' His voice softened. 'Maybe a red one ...'

Cleo opened her eyes to slits and smiled, slowly.

Wistfully, Liza envied their ability to communicate without words. And Justin had kissed Cleo's foot when she wasn't fresh out of the shower. It made her feel, just a tiny bit, the way she used to when Cleo got something that Liza didn't get on a long-ago Christmas. She fought down the feeling that Cleo's relationship was a good example whereas Liza's had proved to be more of a horrible warning. 'So, where are you guys going for your wedding night?'

'Here,' said Cleo. 'It's not worth the effort to do anything else, with the kids.' Justin grimaced, but didn't disagree.

But Liza had had time to get her plan together. 'I'll have the kids. You can put Gus on the bottle for the night. In fact, I'm working afternoon and evening on Monday, so you can stay away two nights, so long as you're back to take the kids by late Monday morning.'

'I don't know—' Cleo hesitated.

Justin turned on her a face of yearning. 'Two. Nights'. Sleep. We could book a hotel somewhere. Anywhere.'

'Mm-mmm.' Cleo gave a blissful shiver and gave Justin another of those special telepathic smiles. 'Sis, I love you. There's almost no one else in the world I could put on to have Gus while he's being such a monster.'

'So long ...' Liza stipulated, meanly, 'as you tell me what you were doing at Miranda's house, today?'

Dark eyes widened – Cleo's customary expression of innocence. 'Miranda invited us for lunch, so the children could play.' Then the eyes began to sparkle. 'I like your new guy, by the way.'

'He's not my new guy.'

'I like the guy you spent the night with.'

Liza glared. 'Don't tell me that he told you!'

Yawning, Cleo wriggled herself more deeply into the sofa. 'Not as such. Miranda seemed to think that's what had gone down. Then Dominic looked so incredibly uncomfortable to meet me that I thought she must be right. And then the other guy, Kenny, arrived and started accusing Dominic of cutting him out ...'

From upstairs, Gus, as if sensing that Cleo was getting too relaxed, set up a rising wail.

Groaning, Justin rolled to his feet. 'I'll get him.'

It was obviously time for Liza to leave the family to do family stuff. 'I don't know why everyone should be so bloody interested in my love life,' she grumbled, climbing to her feet.

Cleo hauled herself from the depths of the cushions to grab Liza for a warm, soft hug. 'Because everyone wants you to have one. It'll be good for you. I was thrilled to hear two men arguing over you! And Dominic is single. And hot. And nice. And Miranda says you'd be good for Dominic—'

Liza pulled away. 'I wasn't good for Adam, was I? And I don't need to be set up by the Mummies of Middledip. That's just sad. I'm the one who decides what's good for me. And if I'm not happy single, why should I be happy in a relationship?'

Cleo dragged her back into the hug with big-sisterly determination. 'Nobody set you up, Liza. You jumped the guy all by yourself, and it's nothing to be ashamed of. In fact, I'd love it if you jumped him again. And got drunk at my wedding on Saturday, too.'

'But then I wouldn't be able to have the kids.'

'Ah.' Cleo released her as Gus's crying drew nearer. 'Then a couple of glasses of cava will have to be enough.' And, as Justin returned with a small mass of angry arms and legs that turned out to be Gus, 'I've invited Dominic on Saturday, by the way. He's going to bring his dog to entertain the kids.'

Liza halted in the act of grabbing her coat. 'You haven't!'

Cleo lifted her eyebrows. 'Why shouldn't I? I like him. And you seem to like him enough to drag him into your bed. He's going to bring his dog to entertain the kids for a few minutes in the afternoon, before the bonfire and fireworks.' She took Gus from Justin and Gus's screams raised a few decibels, in case Cleo had somehow missed the point he was trying to make.

Liza had to complain over him. 'But we've just had a row!'

Cleo exploded with laughter, making Gus throw his arms wide in panic. 'Excellent. The real Liza has stepped forward.'

In between bursts of uncomfortably dreamy sleep, Liza's thoughts whirled. Dominic had caught her off-guard with his business offer.

Should she have snatched off his arm rather than snapping off his head? Or was it asking for pain to get into a business relationship with a man who'd just comprehensively blown her out of the strange half-life she'd occupied since Adam?

Staring into the darkness, she wondered whether Dominic slept well when he was angry – which he had so obviously been. Narcolepsy didn't guarantee sleep; he could be as restless as she, flipping his pillow, fighting his duvet, beyond irritated that she hadn't fallen in with his plans. Or, in the grip of REM sleep, perhaps enjoying vivid dreams of throttling her.

She grinned. Most likely, having made the decision to replace her in his business plan, he'd exhaled gustily and sunk into instant heavy sleep … just as he had in her bed. Before he'd surprised her by emerging from his dreams to make love again.

Could sex filter into his dreams? That might be wild.

Annoyed to be kept awake thinking about sex with Dominic, about The Stables, and what to do about Dominic's offer – if it still existed – she dragged her laptop off her bedside table. A little mindless surfing would, eventually, make her brain calm and her eyelids grow heavy.

In the morning, light-headed with lack of sleep, Liza rocked Gus's buggy and tried to keep Shona entertained as Cleo, from not wanting a wedding dress, became Bride on a Mission, flying through shops and fitting rooms until Liza would have cheerfully minced her up and stuffed her into the only-worn-once ivory suit if it had brought wedding dress hell to an end.

Happily, it took mere hours to locate the perfect dress of brocade and satin in a little boho shop in one of Peterborough's vaulted arcades, extravagant enough to please Justin but with no designer label price tag to make Cleo come over all cheap. In the same shop, they found a dress for Liza that complemented Cleo's choice but said 'entourage' rather than 'bride', and failed to resist a lace number for Shona and velvet waistcoat and bow tie for Gus. Courtesy of McDonalds and Mothercare's mother-and-baby room, they scrambled to feed both kids and themselves, then rushed to get Liza to work.

In the car, Gus sleeping and Shona drowsily watching the whizzing scenery, Liza managed to do what she'd failed to, last night – tell Cleo about Dominic's offer regarding The Stables. And her doubts about it.

Cleo listened as she drove. 'What would you like Dominic to do? Absolutely ideally? What would success look like?'

Mentally, Liza sighed at Cleo's training and coaching phraseology. It was so difficult to fudge replies. '"Absolutely ideally", which means I don't consider his feelings at all, I suppose I'd like him to start his business somewhere else, so that, with no competition, I can force Nicolas to drop his price for the premium.'

'Is that the only possible outcome of Dominic withdrawing?'

'No,' Liza admitted, sighing. 'Nicolas could stay, though he'd probably have to modify his ideas to avoid bankruptcy. Or he could sell the lease to someone else. Both of which could leave me back at square one: forced to relocate. Which,' she brightened, 'is why I'd *have* to convince him to drop his figure and sell it to me.' Drop his figure a canyon deep. But she didn't say that.

Cleo indicated to leave the dual carriageway and approached a roundabout where traffic swarmed like killer bees. 'Which do you think would be the bigger success?'

Watching the buildings give way to hedges and fields as they left the parkway behind, Liza thought hard. 'I don't know,' she admitted, slowly. 'Financially, there's a lot to be said for working with Dominic. There would be the stags and hens angle contributing to a higher turnover. But, emotionally ... is it a good idea to be involved with him business-wise, when we've—'

'Tricky.' Cleo slowed the car to pass a tractor and muck spreader. 'If the worst-case scenario would be that you accept his offer and things don't work out, what happens next?'

'I suppose I relocate.'

'So you need to assess whether it's better to relocate now, or hang on to see what happens between all the other parties in case you can salvage something, or give Dominic a try. Which option gives you the greatest opportunity for reward?'

Liza groaned aloud. 'Cleo, plain English! What reward?'

Cleo took a hand from the steering wheel to enumerate with her fingers. 'Which option will make the most money? What provides the opportunity to run your business as you want to and create your own success? Emotional reward – well, who the hell knows what shape that would take? Not you, apparently. But, at the very least, you show signs of liking Dominic.' She glanced sideways at her sister with a wink.

Unwillingly, Liza laughed. 'Probably accepting Dominic's offer. But I could, conceivably, achieve it all if he would back off and leave The Stables to me.'

Cleo checked her mirrors and steered the car into Main Road. 'Liza, that boat has sailed.'

Although Liza's schedule said she'd begin work at three, it turned out that her first appointment wasn't until four. Wishing she'd thought to ring Pippa before bursting a vessel to get to work, she washed and dried the glasses used for after-treatment drinks of water, tidied her desk and checked her appointment list, ready to get out notes for any returning clients. She paused. Damn. Her eight p.m. client was Dominic.

She'd planned to keep out of his way until she'd decided how to feel about all kinds of things. Including him. And his offer, which was both too good to be true and too good to refuse. Yet she hadn't accepted it.

Because she was being sensible. Or a scaredy cat. Or a moron.

She grabbed her towels and fleece blankets from the dryer in the kitchen to fold them neatly into the treatment room cupboard. Deep ruby red, for the towels, had been a mistake. It wasn't a peaceful colour and it wasn't a Liza colour. Cleo was reds and oranges; Liza was blues and blacks and purples. She'd order blackberry or hyacinth, next time. Her hands halted and she stared sightlessly at the fluffy fabric. When and what would 'next time' be? Would she still be at The Stables? She loved its peaceful, leafy, dramatic location in Port Manor's great park. She'd hate to relocate to soulless, ugly brick-box premises in Bettsbrough or Peterborough. And not all her clients would migrate with her. Once again she'd have to grind through relentlessly enthusiastic promotion to rebuild her list and hope she could pay the mortgage, meanwhile. She wouldn't have the back up of being able to sell her car to tide her over because the new premises, unless she moved house, too, would no doubt be a car ride away.

And she didn't want to move out of Middledip.

Which brought her back to Dominic's offer … and there she was, thinking about him all over again.

And she was shattered. Really, truthfully, shattered. She yawned until her eyes watered. The rest of the day was going to be horrible if she couldn't shake off this dragging lethargy. She checked her watch. Still half an hour until her four o'clock client. Taking out her phone, she set an alert for twenty minutes, grabbed one of the freshly laundered blue fleece blankets and hopped up onto her treatment couch. Closing her eyes, she stretched and yawned, took a few yogic breaths and let herself soak into the couch as if she were made of syrup. Sink. Ooze. Her yoga classes were about the only thing she really missed about Peterborough. Pity there wasn't room at The Stables to get instructors in to take classes ...

When her phone buzzed and beeped twenty minutes later, she could have thrown it across the room in frustration. Not fair! She'd only slept for about two minutes, hadn't she? Although she did also feel sufficiently grit-eyed and fuzzy-headed to have slept for a thousand years.

It seemed as if daytime napping worked better than that for Dominic—

Damn. Thinking about him again.

In fact, she thought about him, indirectly, throughout her next two appointments, gradually acknowledging the sad fact that he had access to more cash than she did. That made him more attractive to the hotel, as well as to Nicolas, and her shoestring plans didn't stand up well against his big, properly financed ideas.

Did Dominic seem likely to get The Stables?

Yes.

Was he really a douchebag?

Not much. OK, no.

Then she'd rather that he didn't have to line Nicolas's pockets any more than was reasonable.

During her break, she approached Nicolas's office,

reflecting that only a matter of weeks ago his door would have been wide open rather than barely ajar and she would have bounded in with whatever was on her mind.

She knocked and pushed the door open. 'Hello,' Nicolas greeted her, unenthusiastically. He didn't wave her to a chair or smile.

She took a breath. 'I'm not going to pursue the idea of renting The Stables, Nicolas.'

'Oh?' His frown was sudden and startled. 'Why's that?'

Obviously, she couldn't say, 'I'm pulling out so Dominic can knock you down on the price.' So, improvising the sort of vocabulary she thought that Cleo might use, she said, 'I've run a variety of scenarios with my business adviser' – Cleo had advised about the business, right? – 'and with the bank, and have concluded that there are probably better options for me.' She turned back towards her own room.

'Liza!' Was that a note of alarm in his voice? His frown had certainly deepened into furrows. 'I'm sure you'll appreciate ... Business being ...' He cleared the hesitations from his throat and produced a whole sentence. 'May I ask you not to speak about your decision, for now?'

'Actually, I can't commit to that.'

An instant's fury blazed across his face, but he replaced it with a wistful smile. 'Why don't you sit down for a moment, and I'll get Pippa to bring us coffee? It's really quite important that I can rely on your discretion.'

'Important to you,' she agreed, not sitting down. 'But I have to look after my own interests. Got to go – I've clients booked in right up until nine.'

'Yes, but Liza—!'

She left his words on the air behind her.

It was exactly eight when Dominic arrived. Pippa, Nicolas and Fenella had gone home and Liza and Imogen were showing in their own clients. 'Hi,' he said, casually, shaking drizzle from his hair and unzipping a black hiking jacket beaded with moisture. He followed her to her room. Quietly courteous, he behaved as if there had been no sizzling sex between them, no roaring row.

But he didn't sleep whilst she did his feet.

Liza was conscious of his half-open eyes and that he didn't let go completely. When the session was over, she'd held the warmth of his feet in her hands for the last time and he'd drunk his water and they'd talked about whether he'd slept well after his last treatment – he said that he had – he replaced his socks and shoes and slid into his jacket.

She waited, sure he'd made the appointment for a reason, either to repeat his business offer or to reverse gracefully out of it. But he just smiled a smile that barely reached his eyes, nodded, and made to leave, and it was her own voice that she heard. 'I told Nicolas that I'm no longer interested in the lease.'

He paused in the doorway, checked Nicolas's office was empty, then returned. 'Oh?' His eyes looked particularly bright when his attention was caught.

'I just thought it would be useful information for you.'

Slowly, he nodded. 'You're right.' His expression gave little away. She'd become used to the slow smiles that echoed in his eyes. 'How about you tell me on Saturday whether you're in or out on my project?' And he stepped forward, pressed a brief, impersonal kiss on her forehead, and left without waiting for her reply. Evidently, he wasn't angry now. He didn't look stressed or depressed or fatigued. He might have made the appointment to mess with her head or just because he liked having his feet done.

But she saw that what he'd snapped at her last night was true – whatever happened at The Stables, Liza was optional.

He was focused on his project. His dream.

Chapter Twenty-Five

PWNsleep message board:

Tenzeds: I think the sleep hygiene's making a difference. I've got loads on, but I cope if I stick to my sleep schedule.

Inthebatcave: Yeah, definitely a balancing act, sleep-v-activity. Even stuff you want to do can get to you if you don't get your rest.

Girlwithdreams: Do other forms of relaxation help? Like deep relaxation, yoga style? It helps you deal with stress.

Tenzeds: Lying down relaxation? It kinda turns into a nap. ☺

Natalie smiled but Kenny just stared. Dominic could see a shadow behind Natalie and fear rocketed through him. He didn't know what that shadow was but he knew it was bad and it was threatening Natalie. And Kenny wasn't trying to help her. Dominic tried to shout, to move his arms … and couldn't. Natalie began to cry as the shadow came closer and he tried to shout to Ken, 'Get her, get her, get— '

Dominic woke, heart pounding. Natalie wasn't there. Kenny wasn't there. There was no shadow. In fact, the room was dark. The reason he couldn't move his arms was that Crosswind was standing on him, whining. Not Natalie crying.

He dragged his hand from the quilt and sleepily ruffled Crosswind's furry flank. ''S'OK.' Probably he'd been thrashing in his dreams, catapulting Crosswind into doggie worry.

He didn't let himself fall back to sleep. The dream was too near the surface, waiting to drag him back. He'd suffered from nightmares long enough to recognise them for what they were: unpleasant, scary at the time but, ultimately, just another dream in a long list of dreams. But he didn't want to see Natalie cry.

It was six thirty so the alarm would go off in half-an-hour, anyway; he was only that amount short of a perfect eight hours. He swallowed his meds, showered himself completely conscious, dressed, and took Crosswind for a dawn walk across the playing fields, down Port Road, through The Cross. The morning was blustery and wet and he turned his face into the rain, letting it wash away the stupid nightmare and bring him properly into the day. Liza's house showed a light upstairs, as he strode past, Crosswind running, nose down and tail up, beside him.

Turning back up Main Road, Dominic wondered whether Liza, Ms Unpredictability, would, ultimately, turn down his offer because of the sex. If so ... had it been worth it? That night had been amazing, but if he'd been able to get her on side first, he might have still had the amazing night (maybe more), at a later date.

On the other hand, if she had persisted in her unreasonable philosophy that working and sleeping with him were mutually exclusive, he might never have had the amazing night at all.

So, it had been worth it. Bliss had no price. Heaviness settled in his groin when he thought of those sensitive hands trickling over his body, her lips soft, white skin flushing pink with desire, her body filling the spaces his didn't. That kind of connection was much more than sex.

Yesterday evening's reflexology treatment had been a fishing expedition. Lying on her couch, his mind had at first worked furiously as he tried to assess whether her emotions were still high and irrational, or whether she'd be receptive to him saying, 'OK, I know what I suggested is definitely a Plan B, for you. But it's a good one. I'm not Nicolas, all negativity and interference. The treatment centre will be your baby but the financial risk will be mine.' But he knew that she'd wanted it all, risk included; her professional persona had made her mood difficult to assess … and her hands on his feet had exploded his concentration. He'd felt himself sliding sideways into that place where 'alert' didn't figure. Asking for her to opt in or out of the project by Saturday had been about his limit of functionality before he wandered back to his bed in Middledip and dropped into the blackness.

And now, as Liza definitely came under the heading of things he couldn't control – in fact, half the time she made him forget who he was and what he was doing – he might as well turn his mind to compiling a mental 'to do' list of things he could.

At nine he rang Stuart, an estate agent who was still e-mailing him copious property details. 'I need a place in Middledip, now, possibly very short term. I want to be in within days.'

Stuart sucked in his breath in traditional estate agent doubt. 'Well, I don't know—'

'It can be done,' Dominic inserted, gently. 'It just needs you to identify a property that the owner is desperate to let because it's been on the market for ages. Tell him or her that I'll pay double the deposit if the rent's right but I'm not committing to more than a month at a time until my affairs become more settled, and to think of me as a stopgap that might turn longer term.'

Stuart laughed. 'Mr Christy, it's not as easy as you make it sound.'

'No problem. I'll ring an agency that can make it easy.' Dominic pressed 'end call'. He grinned at Miranda who was preparing apples for the freezer and trying not to trip over the ball of fluff at her feet begging for apple peel. 'How long do you think it'll take him to ring back?'

Miranda pushed her glasses up her nose with her wrist. 'Three minutes.'

'I say two.'

'You know you're welcome to stay here as long as you want.' She held up a big S shaped piece of peel and Crosswind rose on his hind legs in ingratiating showmanship, ready to swipe it out of midair.

'I know.' Dominic leaned back and linked his fingers behind his head. 'You and Jos have been fantastic.'

'I teased you too much about Liza, didn't I? Sorry. You don't have to go, Dom, I'll butt out.' Miranda looked apologetic.

'That'll be the day.' He grinned. 'But I do want my own space. It's way past time.' The phone began to ring. He checked the screen. 'See? Two minutes.' On the sixth ring, just before the call could go to voicemail, he picked up.

'It's a bit unorthodox, but if you give me an hour to collect some information, there might be a couple of clients I can talk to.' Stuart had evidently realised that he had to act in order to earn his commission, but chose to save face by making it sound as if he was doing Dominic a massive favour.

'Sure,' Dominic agreed, affably. 'Ten o'clock, mate.'

Dominic rang off as Kenny shuffled in, bent at the knees so that Ethan, clinging in monkey mode to his back, wouldn't be concussed by the doorframe. 'What's happening at ten?'

Dominic explained. Then, 'If I can get sorted with a place, will you drive me back to yours to get the rest of my stuff? I can ring for the furniture in storage to be delivered.'

Kenny yawned. In the past days, he'd demonstrated an awesome ability to lie-in on Miranda's sofa, through Jos getting ready for work and playing games with Ethan, Miranda preparing breakfast and Dominic taking Crosswind out, his excuse being that he was last in the bathroom queue, anyway.

Morning pressure on the bathroom was yet another reason for Dominic to move out. Maybe he'd been spoilt, but he valued staggering straight to the shower when he got out of bed without allowing for the small-child-means-small-bladder equation and Ethan's screams of distress if the bathroom was occupied when the small bladder reached capacity. And, although he'd dismissed with a joke Miranda's guilty conclusion that she should butt out, he was tired of living under her well-meaning gaze.

Kenny swung Ethan down onto the floor. 'Fantastic. I can crash with you for a bit until we see what's what with the adventure centre and I get moved up here.'

Trying to ignore an unexpected sinking sensation, Dominic managed a smile. 'What else?' What else? He'd used Kenny's place when it had suited him; he'd asked Ken to come up to Cambridgeshire to look at the adventure centre. He could hardly refuse him a bed. It kind of crossed any one-bedroom properties off the 'possibles' list, though, because damned if he was going to trip over Kenny on the sofa for the next few months – if he got The Stables lease. Mentally, he crossed his fingers. If he didn't get the lease, Kenny would disappear to find another job and when Dominic next heard of him he'd be in Tasmania or Timbuktu.

He'd give Nicolas until Monday to stew, and then put in a cheeky counter-offer.

Getting the lease was looking more likely now that Liza had told Nicolas that she was out. Typical of Liza to make up her mind what to do, do it, and tell him when it was done. In fact, there had almost been a challenge in her voice. *OK, it's yours. Put your money where your mouth is.*

Putting Liza and his mouth together in one thought created a dizzy rush of desire. Once she'd made up her mind to have sex with him, she'd really gone for it. Hot, urgent, focused—

'Dommynic, you got a sword, yet?'

Dominic jumped from his reverie to see Ethan standing before him, a black pirate's patch affixed drunkenly over his left eye. 'Afraid not,' he said, apologetically.

With a great grin of joy, Ethan whisked two plastic daggers from behind his back. 'I got some! Now we can play pirates—'

'Ethan!' Miranda dropped two slices of apple in horror, and Crosswind's teeth came together with a satisfied click as he made them disappear. 'Where did you get weapons?'

The smile slithering from his face, Ethan retreated a step from the wrath of Mummy. 'They're not weapons, they're swords. Maff-yoo's mummy said I could bring them home to play.'

Miranda made a visible effort towards calm. 'Swords are weapons, Ethe. You didn't have them with you when I picked you up from Mathew's house.'

Ethan stuck out his bottom lip. 'They was in my packpack.'

Dominic smothered a grin at Miranda's outrage, feeling sorry for Maff-yoo's hapless mummy who, evidently, was not aware of Miranda's pacifist philosophies. But probably soon would be.

'I've explained why I don't like you to play with toys like that.'

'But Mummeeeee—'

'Ethan, hurting people is wrong, so it's not nice to pretend to.'

'Aw, MummEEEEEEEEEEEEEEE—'

Over Ethan's head, Dominic watched Kenny melting out of the kitchen, down the hall and through the front door, pausing only to swoop up his walking boots. Kenny wasn't big on Ethan at full wail. Which left only Dominic to offer distraction. 'Would you like to watch Crosswind skateboard, Ethan? Just until I get the phone call I'm waiting for?'

Two cross faces cleared miraculously and Ethan reached Dominic's side in two Tigger-like bounds. 'Yeah!'

'Yes, please,' Miranda corrected, automatically. Dominic sent her a 'give him a break' look and she turned back to her apples with, 'Thanks, Dom.'

'Thanks, Dom,' echoed Ethan.

So Dominic spent the next half hour in the road outside, bowling his skateboard along the asphalt whilst Crosswind hurled himself onto the deck with ecstatic barks, and a dancing Ethan roared encouragement from the pavement.

By the time it was time to go indoors, Crosswind was panting, Dominic's legs were feeling the burn, but at least Ethan had forgotten his earlier disappointment sufficiently to race through the kitchen screaming, 'Chee-arge!'

Then Dominic's phone rang and Stuart told him he had two flats for him to look at in Bankside. He needed only a little nudging to agree to meet Dominic at eleven, leaving time for a cup of strong coffee first.

One of the flats proved to be little more than a studio, a lounge with a cramped corner that passed for a kitchen adjoining a bedroom via an open archway. 'No,' said Dominic, definitely.

'The other one's in that nice new development, Copse Corner Court on Great Hill Road, but it's fifty pounds a month above budget,' warned Stuart. He wore the estate agent uniform of sharp blue suit and neat brown hair as if it was made for someone smarter, shifting his trendy glasses uneasily on and off his nose.

'Let's look.'

Bankside – or the new village or Little Dallas – wasn't large, so the second flat was a two-minute ride away in Stuart's blue Ford Focus. But even though it was in Copse Corner Court, an attractive two-storey complex of flats nestling under artistically arranged pitched roofs and gables, Dominic could see why the flat at the far end of the development had never found a tenant.

Bad design.

Really bad. To reach the first floor flat involved a staircase so twisted that it almost amounted to a spiral, but with none of the grace. The landing was surprisingly large but there was no window, just a skylight in the sloping roof, which made the landing bright and airy but left the stairwell dim.

Inside, an OK sitting room overlooked the car park and shrubby garden and was divided by a breakfast bar from an equally OK kitchen. The main bedroom, with a view over a few roof tops and a brown-and-green carpet of farmland, was disproportionately large and had a generous en suite, leaving the second bedroom as a long, narrow cell that even a single bed would overcrowd. Its mean little window was high in its narrow wall. When Dominic hooked his elbows on the sill to pull himself up, he saw that this was to accommodate the pitch of another, lower, brown-tiled roof. Beside the second bedroom lurked a cupboard of a shower room.

Kenny would have to manage.

'Yes,' Dominic said. 'If you can get fifty pounds off the rent.' And, as Stuart began to ease his collar and splutter, 'You seem to me the kind of guy who can make things happen. Phone the landlord and tell them three months' money will be in their account this afternoon if they can give me possession by Saturday. But I need an answer in case I have to look again with a different agency.'

Stuart's expression became almost pleading. 'But what about—?'

'You can make it happen,' Dominic repeated, encouragingly. He wiped thick dust from a light switch. 'Look at this place. It's never been occupied because it's the space left after designing the rest of the complex, and it's awkward. The landlord should be glad to finally get some return on it.'

Stuart looked as if he didn't know whether to be pleased that Dominic thought he could be an ace negotiator, or anxious at the idea of having to ask for fifty pounds off the rent. 'I'll see what I can do.'

Feeling the encroaching weight of the heavy fuzzies, Dominic let Stuart deliver him back to Miranda's house.

''Lo, Dommynic!' bellowed Ethan, racing out of the sitting room on the heels of Crosswind. The house still smelled of apples. 'Can we play—?'

Crouching down to receive Ethan in his arms and simultaneously rub Crosswind's wriggly back, Dominic gave the little boy a consolatory squeeze. 'Sorry, Ethe. Got to sleep now.' Crosswind stood up on his hind legs, resting a paw on Ethan's shoulder.

Ethan tutted and slid an arm around Crosswind, like a little playmate. 'Aw. You always got to sleep.'

'Tedious, isn't it? But I'll only be half an hour.' He gave dog and boy a combined hug then pushed himself upright, waved a hand through the kitchen door at Miranda and made for the stairs, knowing that he'd function better after a few zeds, even if frustrated by the necessity. Over seven days, his catnaps added up to at least three and a half hours, and that didn't include coming round time. That was the equivalent of an entire morning wiped from his life, each week. He shoved through the door to his room, everything slipping out of focus as he heeled his shoes off, set his phone alert for thirty minutes and rolled down onto the bed.

It was a damned—

Chapter Twenty-Six

PWNsleep message board:

Tenzeds: OK, family can cope with my narcolepsy. But one friend ... Not so much.

Brainwave: My mates tend to ignore it, which is OK.

Nightjack: Mine, too, except they elaborately avoid the word 'sleep'!

Girlwithdreams: Tenzeds, if your friend is struggling with your narcolepsy, and you're struggling with his struggling, how cool is this friend, really?

Tenzeds: He's my oldest.

Girlwithdreams: You'd like him to be more concerned?

Tenzeds: I don't want anyone to cluck over me! But accept what I have to do to manage the narcolepsy? Yes. Is that too much to expect?

By Saturday, as Kenny drove them back up the A14 from Royston, the Jag stuffed with their possessions, Dominic felt as if he'd spent a couple of days in a washing machine on spin.

On Thursday afternoon, he'd signed up for the flat at Stuart's office in Peterborough, then, as Miranda had agreed to dogsit, he and Ken had driven straight to Royston. Camping out in Ken's place, which looked like a luggage hall hit by a hurricane, as it was littered with stuff belonging to both Dominic and Kenny, they'd sat up until the early hours making lists and diagrams on a big pad and compiling Internet browser bookmarks for suppliers of kayaks, assault course builders, and ideas for how to construct an all-terrain skateboarding slope.

On Friday, he'd collected fresh meds. He hadn't quite got used to the fact that drugs for narcoleptics were too strong and strictly controlled for him to have been able to create a stockpile, and had come dangerously close to running out. By next month, he should have safely transferred to a surgery in Bettsbrough.

He arranged for a man with a box van to visit the self-storage place he'd used, collect his half of his and Natalie's furniture and deliver it to the new flat. He got his suit cleaned, as he supposed he couldn't avoid Cleo's wedding and the trousers had picked up a strange mark on the leg. He finished packing everything that he'd left in Kenny's flat.

He was glad Kenny had a second bedroom, even if its bed was an inflatable, because, though he was wired with elation, he was exhausted enough by a late night and busy days to need two naps on Friday. It was more comfortable to be able to put a closed door between him and Kenny's obvious uneasiness while he plunged into the short period of oblivion that made all the difference to his operating efficiency.

Apart from that, Kenny seemed as excited as Dominic, and had become a machine gun of incessant questions. 'So, you really think you can save money on the assault course by utilising some of the trees in the coppice?' And, 'So you think that setting up the archery should be a doddle compared to the rest?' Or, 'What Health & Safety information have you got, so far?'

Dominic felt warmed that Kenny was so engaged. It was like old times, Kenny's absorption of information depending on Dominic's patience in articulating what he'd read. But coaching was tiring. Especially when the demands came at the same time as he and Kenny were thundering up and down stairs to load the car.

And now they were actually in the car, heading back to

Middledip in time for Dominic to join Miranda, Jos and Ethan for Cleo's wedding reception.

Joy.

At least nobody had suggested he bring a date. He'd hated attending weddings with Natalie, the feeling of being on the defensive, ready for the 'When will it be your turn?' comments that had always made Natalie embarrassingly evangelical on behalf of those who chose to live without the paperwork.

And he'd never been able to imagine himself doing the 'Will you marry me?' thing and waiting for the response. A strange ritual, with unpredictable results ... as Adam had proved.

Liza – who would probably come out in boils if he ever attempted to put a ring on her finger – was supposed to be giving Dominic her answer about whether to throw in her lot with his at The Stables today, and even waiting for that made him feel antsy, in view of her unexpectedly pissy reaction to the idea of working for him. *With* him. If he'd got that right, he might have already achieved his goal. Now, she was probably going to resist out of sheer obstinacy. And although he'd talked the talk about her being optional, fulfilling his new dream would be more fun with her on board. He imagined having all that energy around to feed from. Imogen and Fenella were probably perfectly nice women, but they weren't the ones with the chutzpah to try to oust Nicolas and stamp their own style on The Stables.

And he had no real idea where to look for someone else to run it.

Liza would have to be persuaded.

'Tell me again why we can't have the fan descender?' demanded Kenny, jerking Dominic from his thoughts.

Dominic slid down in his seat. 'Too much money for what is, basically, a tower housing a vertical jet of air for people to hurl themselves into. Slow motion freefall can't be satisfying or exciting enough to justify the outlay.'

'I'd still have it.' Kenny swerved the Jag into the outside lane. 'The punters would love it.'

'They'll love everything. It's going to be brilliant.'

The bride wore red.

Nothing seemed traditional about the Reece sisters so Dominic shouldn't have been even passingly surprised that Cleo would get married in a ruby dress that snuggled around the top half of her and flowed around the bottom.

Liza's dress was of similar fabrics but in a smoky blue, short, clinging to the roundness of her behind, snug at her waist and baring her shoulders. Teamed with snappy, strappy purple ankle boots it made her look … edible. He wanted to nibble his way along the sexy line of her collar bone to the whiteness of her throat. And down—

Liza looked up and noticed him as he followed Miranda, Jos and Ethan across the wooden floor of Middledip village hall. He sent her his blandest smile and she returned one just as neutral, then she gave her attention to her niece who, wearing a dress that looked as if it was made from froth, swung from Liza's hands. Noisy, excited, red-faced kids frolicked around them like a pack of puppies. A DJ did his stuff up on a small stage and the guests piled cards and presents in an empty corner, then arranged themselves about the tables in an everybody-knows-everybody-else straggle.

'Shona! Chee-arge!' bellowed Ethan, racing off and leaving the grown ups to deal with the boring business of finding seats and buying drinks.

'Chee-arge!' howled Shona, abandoning Auntie Liza and thundering to meet Ethan like a mini medieval jouster.

Jos, taking a seat beside Dominic on the end of a table of friends, stretched and sighed contentedly. 'This is great.

240

We can drink beer while the kids entertain each other.' Jos hadn't quite made it into a suit, but the blackness of his leather trousers, cowboy boots and embroidered shirt gave him a style all of his own.

Miranda looked equally chilled, eating salted peanuts, which she'd never countenance on her table at home, and nursing a giant glass of red wine. And, apart from a casual enquiry about where Kenny was – he'd remembered an urgent appointment with his walking boots – she'd apparently turned over a new leaf so far as sticking her beak into Dominic's doings was concerned, chatting with her friends and not even mentioning Liza's presence. Dominic was free to look around at the hall, with its pitched ceiling and run of French doors at the side.

And notice Liza. Some sort of feather thing nodded in her hair as she scooped her sister's baby out of his buggy and carried him off to a quiet corner by the gifts to give him a bottle. Dominic looked away.

He looked back. Baby Gus wrapped plump fingers in Liza's hair as she settled him in the crook of one arm and Dominic was shocked by a sudden clenching of his heart. His baby would have been a little person, like Gus. Dominic would have been watching him grow, getting his head around how narcoleptic dads coped. Wondering if the genetic marker had been passed on. His knowledge of infant development was hazy but he thought that his baby ought to be sitting up and banging toys and laughing, by now. If Natalie hadn't ...

The baby could never have been a person, to her. Just a medical condition to be attended to, like a mole on her collar bone, removed because it got in the way.

And then he realised that Liza was meeting his stare questioningly. He sent her another of those bland smiles, and turned to talk to Jos. It would do Liza good to wonder what was going through his mind.

He'd spent enough time trying to work out what the hell was going through hers.

The buffet looked as if it had been attacked by a plague of locusts. The children were still screaming around the dance floor. The adults lounged on chairs now adorned with discarded jackets and ties. The only 'speech' had been from Justin, Cleo's new husband, who had removed his arm from around his wife only long enough to climb on the stage to say, 'Thanks for joining us. Have a great time.' So far as weddings went, it was a great arrangement; the bride and groom doing the ceremony thing and their friends just turning up for the party. But, sitting still for so long, Dominic became aware of the creeping onset of slow-motion heaviness. The change of pace and routine in the last few days had caught up with him; he'd risked a daytime glass of champagne and hadn't been able to get any coffee to counteract it. Sleep was creeping up on him, ready to clamp its chloroform pad to his face.

He tapped Miranda's shoulder. 'I'm going to catch a few extra zeds and fetch Crosswind.'

She nodded and smiled and didn't, for once, say, 'Will you be OK?' He made the five-minute walk back to Great End and Crosswind greeted him with the hysterical yapping joy of a dog who'd feared itself abandoned by humankind. 'Hello, mate.' Dominic held onto consciousness long enough to open the back door so that Crosswind could frisk into the garden, then, close to dropping, selected the fifteen minute alert on his phone and crawled onto the sofa. On Sunday, he'd go shopping for a bed and, once it was delivered, the flat would be more or less habitable and he'd be back in his own space—

The phone was beeping. It had reached its crescendo, which explained why Crosswind was whining and panting meaty

242

dog breath in Dominic's face, giving him the incentive to heave against the sofa arm until he was, roughly, sitting up, and could fumble with the phone until it shut up. Crosswind hopped down onto the carpet and looked expectant.

Dominic gazed at him, letting his head clear. 'You've got potential as an alarm clock but we're going to have to make some changes to your approach.'

Crosswind laid back his ears and beat his tail.

'I'm supposed to be taking you back to this wedding to entertain the kids. Fancy it?'

Crosswind whirled in a circle and yapped. Dominic yawned through washing his face and collecting a few items in a small red-and-yellow bucket from Ethan's toy chest, ready for the Great Crosswind Wedding Show. He changed into a more casual jacket. A suit never looked its best when it'd been slept in.

So that Cleo and Justin could enjoy a carefree wedding day, Liza had taken responsibility for their children. Gus, apart from feeding and changing, seemed shocked into unusual docility by the noise and the number of laps he was passed to, until, finally, he fell asleep and could be snuggled carefully into his buggy.

But Shona was poised to take up any slack in auntie capacity, twirling her sash and demanding that Liza be included in every jump and hop of the games she devised for the mass of children. So it was with relief that Liza saw Dominic stroll in, a kiddies' bucket in his hand and his fluffy dog trotting obediently on a lead.

'Crosswind! Dommynic!' Shona and Ethan screamed off towards the new attraction, a posse of kids on their heels.

Dominic clicked his fingers and opened his arms. 'Hup!' Crosswind sprang into the air to be caught against Dominic's shoulder, safe from the seething mass.

Smoothing her hair, Liza followed the children. She'd kicked off her boots for one of Shona's games and the worn stone floor was cold beneath her feet. 'Thank you for not forgetting,' she said, politely.

'No problem.' He looked relaxed and more familiar now he'd ditched the jacket to his suit – although he'd looked as hot as a jalapeño in it. A smile lurked in his spooky eyes as he met her gaze over Crosswind's folded ears and the late afternoon winter sun shone in through one of the tall windows, colouring him gold.

Liza felt as if something unseen vibrated through her, cutting them off from everyone else in the hall. She wanted to ask why he'd stared at her, earlier, his expression so strange. Why he'd been absent for over an hour.

But that would tell him that she'd noticed.

She took refuge in rubbing Crosswind's ears, making him go soft eyed in bliss. 'Shall I make the kids sit down, so Crosswind doesn't get stressed?'

He raised his eyebrows at the screaming horde milling around his legs. 'I'll be impressed if you can.'

Raising her voice over the music, she assumed her grown-up-in-charge voice. 'Kids, if you want to see the dog do tricks, you have to sit down.' In three seconds, every child was seated on the dusty village hall floor.

'OK, I'm impressed.' Dominic stepped back, the sun still making a halo of his hair. Setting Crosswind on his four bandy legs and unclipping his lead, he scooped a lime green ball from the bucket. 'Want to play, Crosswind?' Crosswind launched into a happy dance, bright eyes fixed on Dominic, and barked.

'He said "yes",' Ethan translated importantly, surging to his knees.

'Everyone needs to sit down,' Liza reminded him, softly.

Dominic turned and ricocheted the ball from floor to wall; Crosswind soared up to intercept it in mid-air as if he, too, was made from rubber. The children shouted, 'He's jumping! He's catching!'

'Good lad.' Dominic gave Crosswind plenty of approving fuss and a dog treat from a pack in his pocket. Then, 'Skirmish!' Crosswind dropped his belly to the floor and crawled. 'Poor Crosswind. Poor, poor Crosswind,' and Crosswind adopted a pitiful limp, hanging his head as if in misery. The children screamed with laughter.

Liza grinned. Crosswind was so obviously enjoying himself, eyes alight, tail a blur, ears up, patently anticipating fuss and dog treats as his reward for every moment of obedience, gazing at his master with adoration.

'Watch out!' shouted Dominic, pointing behind Crosswind, and Crosswind whipped around to look, snarling fiercely enough to see off the scariest of street gangs. Just as quickly, he whipped back to face his master, tongue lolling in a big doggy grin. 'Feeling itchy?' Crosswind rubbed his face on the floor. Laughter swelled from the row of adults who'd come to watch from behind the children. Ethan jumped to his feet, but Miranda was there to take his hand and keep him from ruining the show.

'Gimme five!' Dominic held his palm out in front of him. With a yip of glee, Crosswind leaped up and touched it with his paw.

Then Dominic uncoiled a rope from the bucket and began to skip. Crosswind jumped in, bounding into the air like a puppet dog on strings, ears flapping, face almost level with Dominic's.

'Yeah! The doggie can skip!'

Letting the rope go limp, Dominic dropped to his knees. 'Wow, that made me hot. I'm hot, Crosswind.' He held out an arm.

Propelled by his ever-wagging tail, Crosswind gripped the cuff of Dominic's jacket delicately in his teeth and backed up, pulling the sleeve right off Dominic's arm. Dominic turned and Crosswind repeated the feat with the other sleeve.

As the children clapped, Dominic folded his jacket into a tight square and put it on the ground. 'Time for bed.' Crosswind lay down with his head on the jacket like a pillow, bounding to his paws after a 'sleep' that lasted only a scant second.

Crouching, Dominic suddenly levelled a two-fingered 'gun' at his dog, brow curling sternly. 'Freeze!'

Crosswind froze, quivering.

'Spread 'em!' Dominic slapped the wall. Crosswind stood up on his hind legs and propped his front paws on the white emulsion, waiting for Dominic to pat him down before he moved. But it seemed that he moved too soon. Dominic extended his hand-pistol again and shouted, *'Bang!'* And Crosswind dropped instantly to his side on the floor, the image of a mortally wounded dog. Except for the tail, rotating wildly enough almost to move him along the floor and the eyes waiting eagerly for the next game.

The children screamed with laughter, and Liza found herself laughing with them.

Ethan broke free from Miranda's restraining hand, yelling, as usual, at the top of his voice. 'Dommynic, Mummy thinks you're dickless!'

Dominic paused. His blazing gaze flicked to Miranda, who, eyes round in mortification, was shaking her head wildly, a horrified hand across her mouth. 'She may do,' he said, gravely, 'but, hopefully, the word she used was "ridiculous".' And he began to laugh. He tipped backwards from a crouch, until he was somehow lodged up against the wall. And became silent, whilst around him the adult portion of the audience enjoyed the joke.

It wasn't until Crosswind bounded over to stare fixedly into his human's face, one paw on Dominic's leg, that Liza realised what was happening. Quieting, a few of the adults began to look askance at tableau of man and dog.

Uncertainly, she took a step.

Miranda did the same.

The knowledge that he'd probably choose Liza's brand of concern over Miranda's made up Liza's mind. She strolled over and dropped down beside him, as if taking a break on the village hall floor was completely natural. Miranda gave Liza a quick smile and turned away.

Dominic's face was still. After several seconds he blinked, his eyelids somehow not quite in sync. He blinked again, and they were.

'Your dog's a lot of fun. The kids have really enjoyed it.'

He blinked again, stirring.

'Thanks a lot for bringing him,' she continued, chattily, watching the audience lose interest and disperse now that the entertainment seemed over.

He managed a nod. Obviously recognising the return of normal behaviour, Crosswind jumped to his paws, tail blurring, and Dominic lifted his hand to the dog's furry head. ''M all right,' he said.

Liza tapped her fingers absently along to Bjork, mulling over the way that Dominic accepted his condition without whinging, even though, in a succession of kicks in the guts, he'd lost his career and his girlfriend and his home. In response, he'd adapted, reinvented. Accepted what he could and couldn't have. Refused to let the latter screw with the former.

And she saw that her best option was to do the same. It was time to stop mourning an opportunity that had probably never quite been there. She breathed in the last of her regrets, and expelled them. The next breath brought acceptance. 'If you still want me to manage the treatment centre, if you think that we can work together, I'm in.'

Slowly, one corner of his mouth lifted, and his eyes gleamed. 'Good. I was hoping you'd try to seduce me into withdrawing my offer for the lease, but OK.'

She laughed. 'I might have done, if I hadn't thought you'd cheerfully co-operate up to the point where you had to give up The Stables.'

'You're really getting to understand me.' His smile faded. 'But, to be serious – that night? It's forgotten.'

'Of course,' she agreed. Of course.

Then Ethan raced up and skidded to a halt against Dominic's legs. 'Please will you get me a drink, Dommynic? I'm thirsty-thirsty-thirsty! Mummy and Daddy are *talking* all the time.'

'Let's go to the bar, then. Here, Crosswind.' Dominic pulled the lead from his pocket, snicked it onto Crosswind's collar and climbed to his feet, saying, to Liza, 'Let's have a planning session. When's your next day off?'

'Tuesday.' The space beside her felt suddenly cold.

'Wanna drink, Dommynic!' Ethan swung Dominic's arm, face screwed up in an expression of wretched neglect.

Dominic let himself be dragged a step nearer the bar. 'Great. My side of things will be taking most of my attention, but the sooner we do some preliminary joint promo, the better. If we can start a buzz about what's coming, it'll make it easier to hit the ground running. I'll try and make contact with local media before our meeting. Midday in the pub?'

'Fine.'

'Wanna drink! I'm *thirsteeee* …'

And Liza was left on the floor, trying not to notice that he hadn't offered to buy her a drink. Then she told herself that there was no reason in hell for her to be hurt that he was totally willing to forget 'that night' if he thought that

248

remembering it would prevent him from getting what he wanted. The Stables. His lovemaking had satisfied some part of her soul and several parts of her body, but that memory lapse was what she'd demanded.

She'd just thought he'd have put up more of a fight.

Chapter Twenty-Seven

Excessive daytime sleepiness was a central symptom of narcolepsy. After two nights with a baby who wouldn't sleep for more than two hours at a stretch, no matter how often he was fed, changed, rocked or had his feet done, and run ragged during the day by an endlessly energetic four-year-old, Liza was beginning to experience some excessive daytime sleepiness of her own. Eyelids of lead, legs of water, she found herself pretty much living upstairs where it was handy for clean clothes and the toilet.

For what seemed like the hundredth time, she sat on the bathroom floor and changed Gus's nappy.

Shona crouched companionably beside her. 'Gus doesn't have a front bottom.'

'Because he's a boy.' Liza struggled with baby wipes that refused to emerge from the pack singly. Finally triumphing, she fought to clean Gus up, and he fought to kick her away.

'I'm allowed to wipe my own front bottom,' observed Shona.

'Well done.'

As Liza and the baby wipe won the battle, Gus began to cry.

'But I'm not allowed to wipe my back bottom because I get poo everywhere.'

'It's tricky stuff,' Liza acknowledged, gravely.

'So Mummy has to do it. Mummy says she gets all the best jobs.'

'I know how she feels.' Liza fastened Gus into his nappy, into his vest, into his suit-thingy, washed her hands and scooped him up. 'How about I read you a story?' Gus turned puce with the effort of howling.

Shona bounded to her feet, almost tripping Liza over. 'No! I want to play "snakes slide downstairs".' Shona flopped down at the top of the stairs and balanced on her little round belly.

'*Waaaaah!*' bellowed Gus.

'Whoa, Shona! You'll fall.' Cheeks aching with yawns and head ringing with baby screams, Liza clutched Gus against her shoulder and lunged, abortively, for Shona's legs.

'No, I won't,' contradicted Shona, breathlessly, bum joggling as she snaked down the first two steps.

'*Waaaaah!*' bellowed Gus.

'I'm sure Mummy doesn't let you—'

'She does!' Gathering speed, Shona bumped down steps three to eight.

'*Waaaaah!*'

'Shona, I'm sure she doesn't!'

'She do-oe-oe-OES!' Shona jolted down the last few steps to land in a triumphant heap in the hall. The doorbell rang. Gus threw up hotly down Liza's neck. And stopped crying.

Feeling put upon – and sicked upon – Liza muttered, 'Hell-hell-*hell*.' Clutching the handrail with one hand and the baby with the other, she trod rapidly down the staircase.

'Bad word,' Shona pointed out. 'My tummy hurts.'

'Not surprised.' Clinging on to her patience, Cleo guided Shona to one side and reached around her to open the door.

Cleo and Justin beamed from the doorstep, wearing the glossy, languorous, loved-up look of a couple who had just spent two days in bed, a civilised amount of it sleeping, and had risen late and showered in peace. 'Mummy! Daddy!' shrieked Shona, hurling herself at her parents' legs. 'My tummy hurts.'

'About time!' Liza grumped. 'I hope you had a scrumptious time, I'm late for work and there's baby sick in my bra.' She thrust Gus, gurgling and grinning now, at Justin.

'Lucky you.' Justin went to kiss his baby son but drew back at the unmistakeable whiff of vomit.

Cleo turned Liza around and propelled her towards the stairs, much as Liza had steered Shona a few seconds ago. 'We'll pack up the kids' stuff while you jump into the shower. At least he didn't get your hair.'

'Big comfort.' Liza trudged back the way she'd come, way too tired to take the stairs at a run.

'My tummy *hurts*.' Shona began to wail. 'Ow, Mummy, my tummy!'

Behind Liza, Cleo tutted. 'I suppose you've been playing "snakes slide downstairs"? How many times have you promised not to? You get carpet burns on your tummy and … No, don't cry, sweetie. Mmm, poor Shona. I've got cream in my bag that'll soon make the nasty burn go away.' Cleo's comforting maternal coos faded as Liza shut herself thankfully in her bathroom and dragged off her jeans and top, threw the top in a basin full of water and gave herself a two-minute scrub under the steaming needles of water, then hurried, towel-wrapped, into her room for fresh clothes. Cleo's and Justin's voices floating up the stairwell, cosy and warm as they talked to their children. Most of the time, she envied them their family life. But, right now, they could keep it. It was exhausting and smelly.

From the bathroom, her phone began to ring. Swearing, she shifted into reverse and went back to fling up the lid on the wash basket and delve for it in the pocket of her jeans. 'Yes?' breathlessly.

'It's Dominic. Change of plan – BBC Radio Cambridgeshire has a cancellation and can get us on Morning with Rebeccah Stillwater tomorrow, which works really well as it's your day off, so we need to be in the Cambridge studio by eleven. Which means we need to have our first planning meeting tonight.'

'Isn't it a bit previous, to get on the radio? We'll jinx ourselves if we do it before you've signed the lease. And I'm sleeping tonight,' she added, firmly, stifling yawns as she whizzed back to her room, opened a drawer and grabbed clean underwear.

'It's never too early. I'm creating buzz. There's no such thing as a jinx.' A pause. 'I meant the evening.'

'So did I,' she agreed, quickly, glad he couldn't see her face heat up at the idea of him being involved with her night. 'But I'm out on my feet and – um, OK, I suppose you know how that feels.' She pulled fresh jeans off a hanger, awkwardly, with one hand, glancing at her watch. *Eek!* If she didn't get dressed and leave *now*, her first client would be waiting for her. That was a discourtesy she never allowed to happen. The fastest way to get to her client was to get Dominic off the phone and the fastest way to get Dominic off the phone was to agree with him. 'I finish at nine. Meet you at The Three Fishes.' Ending the call and dressing as fast as a fireman, she sniffed down her top to check for parfum de sick and ran for the front door, calling to Cleo and Justin, 'Glad you had a great time, give the kids my kisses, some of their clothes are up in the spare room, just shut the door when you go and it'll lock.'

'Kids, mess, and my sister rushing off,' she heard her sister observe, before the door slammed. 'Back to Earth.'

By nine, Liza's eyes felt as if they'd been dipped in egg and rolled in crushed biscuit. She hadn't had a break from clients all day, which would normally be a cause for celebration. But, *ohhh*, she was *tired*.

The last to leave, she set the alarm and locked the door to The Stables by the light from the security lamp, hunching against the wind, and blearily drove her little car to The Three Fishes. Inside, she spotted Dominic lounging at a corner table with a pad, a pen and a pint of dark beer, and dropped into the empty chair. She waved to Janice, behind the bar. 'I need coffee or I'll pass out.'

'Poor thing.' Janice pushed a tall white mug into the front of the coffee machine.

Dominic frowned. 'What's up?'

Folding her arms on the table, Liza propped her chin on them and tried to keep her eyelids up. 'Tired. Beyond tired. I looked after Shona and Gus. Gus thinks sleep's a waste of time.'

He smiled, faintly. 'I agree with him.'

'Suppose,' she sighed. 'You often feel that if you don't get sleep in the next few minutes you'll just fall down, don't you? I'm beginning to empathise.'

'I do fall down, occasionally. Here's your coffee.'

With a groan, Liza levered herself up and folded her hands around the hot mug that Janice deposited before her. Fixing her eyes owlishly on Dominic, she made herself concentrate as he began to talk about The Stables, tapping his pad and making little ticks as he covered each subject, rent first. 'This is the figure I suggest, if I can get Nicolas down to something halfway between what I want to pay and what he wants me to.'

She knew the total of what the therapists currently paid Nicolas, and what Dominic needed from her was a shade less. 'I can make that,' she said, half-surprised that his earlier forecasts hadn't proved to be ridiculously optimistic. She tried to listen as she sipped coffee and he rattled on about radio, local press, free press, newsletters, website, Facebook, Twitter, and when he hoped to take over the lease. 'I've asked Nicolas for a meeting to renegotiate the premium, but he hasn't got back to me yet. Then it should be all systems go.'

She nodded.

His eyes were on her. 'You're exhausted.'

She nodded again.

'You're not concentrating.'

She shook her head. Then nodded, unsure which was appropriate.

He drained his glass. 'Come on. I'll see you home.'

'Got my car.'

'You drive, I'll pinch you to make sure you stay awake.'

'But then you'll have to—'

'—walk home to my new flat! For all of ten minutes, yes.'

'So where's—?' She had to break off to yawn.

'I've rented a place in Bankside.' He hooked his arm under hers and steered her out to her car. In a few minutes they were drawing up outside number 7, Liza still yawning.

Once he'd checked she could steer her key safely into the lock of her front door, he made arrangements for the radio interview. 'Kenny will be there, too, to show everyone that we have all the expertise we need. He can drive us in the Jag.'

She yawned. ''Kay.'

He kissed her lightly on her forehead. 'Go to bed.'

And her fatigue fled for a second as she got a flash image of her bed – him in it, hair tousled, hard, naked body gleaming as he moved against her, inside her. His hands. Tongue. Heat flickered.

As if she were transmitting her thoughts, he paused. His palm brushed her cheek, gentle as breath. Then he kissed the corner of her mouth. And, for an instant, caught her lower lip gently between his teeth.

'We're going to be able to do this, aren't we?' she asked, hoarsely.

'What?'

She swallowed. 'Work together. Without … stuff getting in the way.'

Slowly, he withdrew. 'We both have dreams to make come

true, remember? We're adults. We can cope with "stuff".
"Stuff" happens and—'

'And goes wrong.'

'If you say so.' He retreated another step. 'Let's keep the focus on realising dreams. See you tomorrow.'

The village was still as Dominic strode towards Bankside past the eclectic mix of houses that had grown up in Port Road over a couple of centuries.

The new flat was in chaos, but as soon as the beds had been delivered Dominic had moved into the capacious master bedroom, Kenny into the cell-like spare, though Ethan had cried because Dommynic wasn't to live at his house any more. It was good to be in his own place again, but to reassure Ethan that Dommynic wasn't dropping out of his life, he'd call in tomorrow when he walked Crosswind before the radio interview.

With Liza.

He tried to concentrate. Promotion, organisation, administration. Nearing his goal was energising him, driving him, making it easier to accept the infuriating need to take naps and keep to his routines. And, most of the time, that Liza was out of bounds even though, minutes ago, her nearness had grabbed him by the groin and demanded that he kiss her mouth, dizzy from wanting it so much.

He crossed the road, passing houses in darkness or lit only upstairs, and turned into Ladies Lane. A dog barked, a car rumbled, its headlights sweeping over him. Liza. Smelling of coffee. Eyes fatigued, blonde hair flipping as she moved her head. He'd been on the brink of kissing her deeply, his carefully evolving business plans vanishing from his mind at the need to feel his body wrap around hers. Her shape was so right. Just right. For a lustful moment, he'd let himself think about them climbing the stairs to her bed.

But, even in exhaustion, her lust radar had bleeped, as if triggered by a sensor on the front of his boxers, and she'd warned him off.

He turned left, between the last two stone houses and into the modern brick, appropriately named, New Road that opened into Bankside. It was like stepping into a different world, a Narnia of symmetry and tidy blocks of houses all of the same design.

Well, OK. Liza obviously needed absolute reassurance that their relationship was going to be a working one, unsullied by blazing attraction or red-hot sex.

Turning into Great Hill Road, he hopped the wall into the Copse Corner Court car park, passing the dark hulk of the Jag, fishing out his new keys.

So, obviously, the only way forward was to keep everything strictly business.

Strictly.

Business.

For now.

Chapter Twenty-Eight

Liza had never been in a radio studio and it was much more laid-back than she'd imagined. A smiley, calm broadcast assistant, Beth, escorted them from reception through a succession of doors opened via passes, introduced them to Harriet, the golden-skinned producer, and showed them into Studio 1 where Rebeccah Stillwater beamed from behind a bank of monitors, keyboards, and panels of fader controls, amber hair pushed behind black earphones. Behind her, a green *on air* sign was illuminated but a red *mic live* was dim. At the guests' side of the desk a colourful array of microphones sprouted, yellow, blue, green, red. The walls were red and one enormous window gave a view into the next studio, where a squat older guy could be seen apparently talking to himself, and another to where Harriet and Beth were seated, in the main office.

'Hi!' Rebeccah beamed, pulling her earphones away from one ear. 'Thanks for coming in. If you can take the blue, green and yellow mikes ...?' They sat in a silent row facing her, Liza in front of the blue microphone, Dominic on her right. 'Great. Is this your first time on radio? Nothing to worry about – hang on.' Rebbecah brought up the music that had been playing in the background, voice mellow as she moved closer to the large black mike that hung before her face and the red *mic live* light lit. 'Isn't that a fantastic song? One of my favourites. So, let's see what the traffic's doing today. With the travel news, here's Callum.'

'Thank you, Rebeccah. The A14 seems to be OK, but I'm afraid those of you heading for Cambridge city centre from the A10 might be in a queue—' The unseen traffic announcer's voice faded as Rebeccah moved a control, paid attention to her monitors and clicked her mouse.

Rebeccah took over again from Callum. 'And my guests in the studio today are going to be Liza, Dominic and Kenny, who're here to tell us about their exciting new venture, right here in Cambridgeshire.' Apprehension shivered suddenly up Liza's spine. She often listened to BBC Radio Cambridgeshire and it was weird to think she would be the one speaking in other people's cars and kitchens. She swallowed a need to cough, assailed by a sudden panicky conviction that her voice would roll itself into a ball of dust in her throat. Rebeccah moved sliders, clicked her mouse and watched her monitors. 'After this ...' Then the music swelled, sank to background again, *mic live* dimmed, and Rebeccah dropped her earphones around her neck and became a normal person, instead of a radio presenter. 'Great to have you in the studio, your venture sounds wonderful.' She spent the next few minutes getting them to relax, making sure she was putting the right name to the right person, asking about The Stables and sounding really, really interested.

Dominic, on the green microphone, seemed comfortable. Liza let her butterflies be tranquilised by his steady body language and the way he talked to Rebeccah as if the mike wasn't there. Maybe all those years of talking to unseen pilots over the airwaves made this a familiar environment for him. She swallowed some of the water that Beth had provided and found that she could answer naturally when Rebeccah asked her off air about the treatment centre. Now she just had to do the same thing when *mic live* applied to the blue microphone.

In fact, once on air, Liza began to enjoy herself. Some of the questions that had been asked off air were asked again, giving her a comfortable feeling of familiarity, but Rebeccah bowled the interview along with fresh material, too, drawing Kenny, on the yellow mike, into the conversation, 'So, Kenny, you're the guy who'll be showing folks how to paddle their own canoes?'

But giving the lead to Dominic, who remained chatty and chilled. 'We're going to be a great venue for team builders, weekend adventurers, and even stags and hens. That was Liza's idea.'

'You're going to be doing all the holistic stuff, Liza – for the hens?'

'For everybody,' she answered, firmly. 'My team will do everything from single or series treatments to pamper evenings or even pamper weekends.' Then they paused for Rebeccah to feed in the weather report and play another record. A buzz of fresh questions, and then Liza was shocked to realise that almost twenty-five minutes had passed and Rebeccah was winding up their segment.

'So that's The Stables, at Port-le-bain, in the grounds of Port Manor Hotel. From December, if you feel like having an adventure or a treatment, a hen night, stag party or birthday treat, The Stables will be the place to go!' Rebeccah moved on to her next segment, waving goodbye, as Beth waited to show them out past Harriet, through the office, through the door to reception, and into the car park outside.

Suddenly, they were grouped in the winter sunshine, grinning at each other. 'Well, that seemed to go OK,' observed Dominic, zipping up his jacket.

'It was easy,' Liza agreed, almost sorry that the fizz of being live on air had to be left behind. 'I can't believe how well it went. I woke up this morning petrified that I would dry up.'

'Me, too.' Kenny wiped his forehead. 'You were the star, Doc, as always. The man who gets everything he wants.' His eyes flickered to Liza. She flushed, and, for the first time, wondered whether the friendly rivalry between Dominic and Kenny was completely friendly.

Well, there was no room now for that macho-pride bloody nonsense! The three of them had bound their immediate futures together and the only way it was going to work was if sexual tension and egos were set aside. Wasn't that why she and Dominic were busy forgetting 'that night'?

'Shall we stop for lunch?' she suggested. They needed to establish trust, Cleo would say, whisk away vestiges of wanting or jealousy from the dark corners of everybody's minds and overlay them with cordial co-worker relations.

And, perhaps because Dominic was enthusiastic about the ideas and expertise that Kenny brought to the business, there was no clashing of horns during their pub lunch and celebratory glass of wine, though Kenny's brow did darken when he declared, 'But we do need that fan descender, Doc,' and Dominic just grinned and said, 'Sorry, Kenny. Not right away, anyway.' Which emphasised Dominic's role as the man with the money, who made the decisions. Liza could see from Kenny's eyes that he still had to get used to that. She might even have a few similar moments herself. Working with people could be—

She jerked up, checking her watch. 'Whoops. We've announced to the whole of Cambridgeshire that things are going to change at The Stables, but I've just realised that I haven't told Imogen and Fenella.'

Dominic cocked an eyebrow. 'Are you worried about how they'll react?'

She shrugged. 'Neither of them were interested in sharing the management of The Stables, so I hope they'll react well, but I don't want them miffed because everyone else knows before them.'

'OK, let's head to The Stables. I'll give Nicolas a nudge about our meeting.'

'I might just tilt my chauffeur's hat over my eyes and wait outside. Leave the business stuff to the business people,'

Kenny said, idly, his gaze following the curvy young waitress who had just brought their bill.

For a moment, Liza thought it was a barbed comment. But Dominic only nodded, and she remembered what he'd told her about Kenny's strengths being in action. And Kenny seemed perfectly at ease on the half-hour journey back, chatting to Liza in the front of the big black missile of a car, as Dominic headed for the back seat and almost instantly became silent.

Kenny peered into the rear view mirror and shook his head. 'It's weird to see him like this,' he whispered. 'Going off to sleep everywhere.'

Liza spoke at normal volume. 'It's just a medical need.'

Kenny agreed too quickly. ''Course. He always enjoyed his sleep, did Doc. But all kids get drowsy sometimes and all teenagers don't want to get up in the morning, students would rather sleep than work. We've all been through it. I just don't know how he let this thing get a grip.'

She laughed, to cover up a lancing irritation. 'It's not an addiction, Kenny, a craving for alcohol or drugs that he's let get the better of him! It's just that his hypothalamus has stopped producing enough orexin to regulate his sleep. If he'd stopped producing insulin and become diabetic it wouldn't be weird, would it?' And she changed the subject, asking Kenny about his time in the States, until Dominic's phone alert went off and, after a couple of minutes, he joined in the conversation.

When Kenny parked the car in the yard beside a red VW at The Stables, the day was fading to grey. Liza opened the passenger door and hopped out as Dominic climbed from the back. 'I suddenly feel nervous,' she confessed. 'I hope they're OK about it.'

'They should be, you're going to help them get more clients.' Dominic gave a reassuring smile, then halted, brows clanging down into a straight line over his eyes. 'Oh crap, here's—'

'Hello, Liza,' said a soft voice.

Liza's heart lurched as she swung around to stare at a gangly figure that had materialised from beside the red car in the winter afternoon gloom. 'Adam!' Never more than wiry, now Adam was thin. Gaunt, even. His eyes looked too big and heavy for their sockets and his coat, a long dark grey one that Liza remembered shopping for, hung off his shoulders. Even his teeth seemed too big for his mouth. 'I was driving out of Bettsbrough when you came on the radio. It was so good to hear your voice. I thought I'd stop in and say hi.'

Dumbstruck, she swallowed. She'd chosen not to tell him where she was living or working, then … Mentally, she smote her forehead. She'd gaily let Rebeccah Stillwater broadcast the location of The Stables to the entire county.

'So, what I was just thinking—' He cleared his throat. 'I could take you out to dinner or something? So we can catch up? Just for old times' sake,' he added, swiftly, while Liza felt the old guilt rising as she saw in Adam's eyes the soul-crushing grief she'd put there. He managed another smile. 'I feel as if—'

He glanced at Dominic. Kenny was no longer in the car but had turned his back, as if to give Adam privacy. Dominic stood his ground, as if not to. Adam stooped closer. 'There's so much stuff we didn't say, Lize. That I didn't say, anyway. I need to talk things out.'

She hesitated, wondering, wretchedly, whether he was right. Everything in her protested against the idea of cosying up to Adam over the dinner table. But was that a selfish wish to avoid confronting sadness at close quarters? Or did she owe it to him, to give him a chance to draw a line under 'them' and move on? Closure, it was called. She'd attained it in that awful moment on stage when her instinctive reaction to Adam's proposal had been revulsion and the relationship, for her, had crashed and burned. But Adam, he'd never understood why his fabulous gesture had gone horribly wrong.

'Well ...'

Instantly, Adam added, 'At least one more time.'

She felt the tug of Adam trying to make her a thread in his life tapestry, fastening her in with family gatherings, work parties, shared friends. The intensity of his love. And his need. Meeting him might be a sop to her conscience, but his expectations would be raised. Look how he'd subtly repositioned his request when she'd uttered just one *Well* ... instead of an instant refusal.

She took a step away. 'Sorry,' she muttered. 'Adam, I'm so sorry.' Then she whirled blindly for the door to the treatment centre, aware of Dominic falling in beside her and working the door handle for her when she fumbled it. And of nothing else but the crashing of her panicked heart, making her dizzy, hot, unable to get her breath, air hitting an obstruction in her chest, hurting, suffocating, frightening.

Indoors, she homed in on her treatment room and its carefully cultivated serenity. But when she tried to snap the door shut behind her, she found Dominic in the way.

'I need—'

'I know.' He smiled, crookedly. 'You need to be left alone. But I need to be happy that you're not going to faint or hyperventilate. Sit down and I'll go to the kitchen and make you some of that calming jasmine stuff, and if you're breathing normally by the time I get back, that's when I'll go.'

Slowly, she lowered herself into her chair, willing her heart steady, forcing her breathing to come from her abdomen, resenting Dominic's refusal to be shut out but also glad of it.

Breathe. Breathe. Let the abdomen rise. Fall. By the time he returned and she took the steaming mug, she was thinking normally. 'Thanks. But it's camomile tea that's calming, not jasmine.'

He quirked a brow. 'If you've recovered enough to be ungracious, I'll leave you to whatever the hell jasmine tea is meant to do for you while I try and grab Nicolas. Will you be OK?'

'Fine,' she muttered. She watched him leave as steam rose over her face. Her eyes burned. It was probably the tea.

Dominic knocked on Nicolas's half-open door and stuck in his head, aware of the slight body odour that hung around wherever Nicolas did. 'Sorry to wander in unannounced, but do you think we could arrange this meeting?'

Nicolas was leaning over his desk, pen in hand. His face shone. It was impossible to tell whether it was fresh sweat caused by Dominic's unscheduled appearance, or a constant coating resulting from keeping his office like a sauna. 'Sorry. I don't know when I'll have time.'

Dominic remained in the doorway, itching to reach around and throw open the window. 'How about we arrange it now?'

Nicolas glanced at his watch. 'Sorry.' He put the top on his pen and laid it on the desk. 'I have plans.'

Dominic chose not to take the hint. 'It would only take a moment. Or don't you want to sell the lease any more?'

'I do.' Nicolas at least sounded positive about that. A long pause. 'But you want me to drop my price and I need to think about that. Ring me in a couple of days.'

Reluctantly, Dominic accepted that there was a point past which there was nothing to be gained by pressing. He let himself back into Liza's treatment room, trying not to feel uneasy at Nicolas's froideur. 'Come on. We'll drop you off.'

She was sitting exactly where he'd left her, frowning at her cup, now empty. She didn't look up. 'Is that an order? Give a man an inch and he turns into a ruler.'

He swung on his heel, infuriated that the happy, enthusiastic Liza he'd spent the day with had morphed back into the snarky, spiky Liza he'd met in this very spot a month ago. 'Fine. Stay here. I thought you might want a lift in case Adam might be hanging around outside.'

A long, trembling sigh made him hesitate and glance back. She looked delicate and vulnerable, in her treatment room all alone. She placed her mug on the desk, and smiled, slowly, apologetically. 'I meant: thank you, Dominic, that's really thoughtful and a lift would be great.'

'Don't confuse me by being pleasant.' Waiting as she switched off the lights and shut the door, his hands ached to reach out to her.

Whether to hug her or shake her, he hadn't decided.

Liza reached up to close her bedroom curtains.

And froze.

On the traffic island in the middle of The Cross stood the figure of a man, completely still. Tall and thin, his gaze seemed to be fixed on her front door.

Adam.

Glad she hadn't yet turned the lights on, heart thumping, she pulled the curtains slowly shut, as if he might hear the rings moving along the curtain poles. Then she made a tiny gap and peeped out. He was still there.

She shut them tightly. She wouldn't let him get to her. She wouldn't think about the sadness in the depths of his eyes or the droop to his shoulders. Not wanting the brilliance of the overhead light to alert him to her location in the house, she switched on the television, glad the curtains were thick enough to disguise its lesser illumination. Flicking around until she found an episode of *Friends* she concentrated on the voices of Ross and Rachel as they stumbled through some excruciating convolution in their relationship, welcoming the sound of other humans. She turned up the volume to let the audience's laughter fill the room, lying on her bed, trying not to think about Adam and feel guilt. Remorse. Anxiety. Horrible wormy feeling of culpability. So down. So trapped in her own house by the Spirit of Bad Stuff Past.

When she peeked out after two more episodes – Adam was still there.

Chapter Twenty-Nine

Dominic frowned at his iPad, trying to make sense of an e-mail that had just pinged into his inbox from Smiths, the consultants and suppliers for some of the equipment he was poised to buy as soon as the lease was signed. *Re the message your Kenny King left on my voicemail, we need to do an on-site survey before quoting for the fan descender,* Wayne Smith (Director) had written. *Does this mean you're ready to proceed? We can do the entire site survey at once, if so.* Dominic looked up at Kenny, who was standing at the front window to Dominic's new flat, glaring at rain that blew in slanting sheets across the car park. 'Kenny, why would you leave a message on Wayne Smith's voicemail asking for a quote on a fan descender?'

Kenny's shoulders tensed. He didn't turn around.

'Look.' Dominic rubbed a hand over his face. 'I know the ballpark figure for the fan descender and I know I can't afford it yet, OK? I'm not sure it's ever going to be worth its price tag.'

Muttering something that might have been, 'For fuck's sake,' Kenny hunched his shoulders. 'What you ought to be worrying about, Doc, is whether you can rely on Liza. You need to rethink. Find someone else to run the therapy stuff.'

Dominic dug deep for patience. He felt torpid and dull with inaction, fighting off the craving for a second nap of the day. Sleep hadn't yet become insistent but it was probably only Kenny's restless tension that was keeping him awake. When Kenny didn't have enough to do he became a caged chimp – rattling his bars and ripe for trouble.

They'd had a week of waiting for Nicolas to resume negotiations, or even return phone calls. Now, the flat was sorted, furniture set out, possessions stowed, shopping done; they'd walked what felt like most of the countryside around, swum at the pool in Bettsbrough and tried a couple of gyms, but Kenny had been bored to boorishness so often that Dominic had begun to be pleased whenever Ken wanted to walk or run alone.

And, although blatantly bringing up Liza to deflect Dominic's attention from his interference over the fan descender, Kenny was voicing Dominic's own anxiety. Because, since Adam had showed up, Liza had yanked her head into her shell. Dominic had been for a treatment, called at her house, and taken her out for a drink. She'd been pleasant but quiet and had sidestepped any attempts to talk business.

Kenny didn't seem able to leave the subject alone since Dominic had told him the bare bones of Liza's history with Adam. It had seemed only fair, as Kenny, like Dominic, was looking for employment and income from the adventure centre and hadn't bargained for its fruition being annoyingly dependent on the treatment centre running alongside – and, therefore, the person who ran it.

'You saw the effect that Adam had on Liza,' Kenny grumbled, spiking up his tawny brown hair in his reflection in the window. 'I'll bet she's thinking about pulling out, now he's hanging around like a fart in a car, not letting her conveniently forget what she did.' He swung away from the glass and snatched up a pair of black weights that he'd left crossed on top of the bookcase, exhaling hard before beginning a series of bicep curls.

'It's a developing situation,' Dominic agreed, stifling a yawn. With everything about the adventure centre whirling in his brain, he'd been lying awake too much. Narcolepsy really pissed him off, the way it could flip from an inability to wake to an inability to sleep. 'I'm looking for a way of helping it develop in my favour. Team-building experience is telling me that I need positive engagement with Liza. You know the stuff. Break down barriers. Foster links. Offer trust. Communicate. Share a fun activity.'

'Just junk her.' Kenny breathed in between words as he worked his muscles.

It looked as if Kenny and Liza could use a little bonding, too. But Dominic needed to get one-on-one with Liza first, to cut out distraction. Or give her nowhere to hide. Or have an excuse to spend time with her. 'I'm not going to junk her,' he said, mildly. 'I'm going to show her the benefits of being on my team.'

Kenny snorted, breathed, curled. 'Admire your philosophy. But a team's only as strong as its weakest member, so pick the best team while you still can.'

Dominic heaved himself to his feet, feeling sleep retreat just an inch, as soon as he was up. 'Why don't you put your wet-weather gear on and go out?'

Kenny began pumping the weights faster. 'Because there's – nowhere to – dry it in – this fucking flat.'

Leaving his friend to take out his frustrations on his weights, Dominic went to his bedroom to phone Liza. He really liked the room; bright and airy even when the rain was spattering on the window in fistfuls, and there was plenty of space for his new king-sized bed. He sat with his back against the coolness of the wooden headboard because he knew the sleep monster was waiting for him if he let himself get too comfortable. Then, tonight, it would be easy for it to play its current favourite joke – he could buy a bed but couldn't buy sleep. The bed made him think of sex and sex made him think about Liza and he wondered, fleetingly, whether, if he could just get her under him, he could love the sadness out of her. That was a thought to stop his eyes from closing. If he suggested they met—

But then he realised that Kenny had followed him and was standing at the door. He hesitated. Should he put off the phone call? Mentally, he shrugged. Ken had invested a lot of time in the action-and-challenge centre and if it made him feel in the loop to listen while Dominic set up a bit of bonding with Liza, it couldn't do any harm. It was surprising and worrying how quickly he and Kenny had got on each other's nerves, over the past few days. They were to work together, so tension couldn't be allowed to develop.

Ringing Liza could be frustrating, her availability depending upon clients and her whim but, this time, Pippa was able to get her to the phone.

'What are your plans for the weekend?'

Her voice was flat. 'Taking Saturday off because I'm doing a pamper thing on Sunday for a WI in Bettsbrough.'

'So Saturday afternoon would be the best time.' He waited.

A note of interest crept in. 'For …?'

'To promote better understanding of one another's areas of operation.'

'How?' One wary word, but at least he'd piqued her curiosity.

'I'm going to give you a taste of action and challenge. Wear jeans, sensible boots that keep your feet dry, and an outdoor coat.'

Silence. He crossed his fingers. Whether it was for the good of his nascent business or just for his soul, he had to shake Liza out of her Adam-remoteness.

'OK,' she agreed, sounding interested. 'As long as I can give you a taste of something treatmenty in return. You don't have any open wounds on your feet, do you?'

His heart hopped at this glimmer of the real Liza. If she wanted to give him a reflexology treatment, he was fine with that. In fact, he was tingling just at the thought. 'My feet are in perfect order. What time do you want me?'

By ten on Saturday morning, having dropped Crosswind at Miranda's, he was wishing he'd developed athlete's foot or a nice big verruca, because, it turned out, the treatment on offer wasn't reflexology.

'We're having a what?' he demanded, following Liza's behind through the glass door painted with the word 'Nibbletastic'.

'Fish pedicure.' She smiled at a redhead in daffodil yellow behind the reception desk. 'Hello, Dana. I've booked two for ten o'clock. But be careful with my friend, here. He's fresh meat.'

Dana gave Dominic a sparkling smile. 'Let's get you initiated, then.' She led them up a few steps into another room, where padded chairs stood behind rectangular tanks full of bubbling water. And darting little fish.

He stood back, warily. 'This is a joke, right?'

'Why should it be a joke?' Liza took one of the cream leather seats and bent to the laces of her blue boots. 'I want to screen off part of reception for a fish spa, at The Stables. Pippa should be able to look after the fish spa as well as run front desk, which would mean I could keep her on. Set up and running costs are reasonable. Garra rufa fish pedicures are becoming incredibly popular.' Her feet were bare now, and she took some wipes from the redhead and began running them over her feet. 'I think four tanks would really bring people into The Stables.'

Gingerly, Dominic took a seat. 'So what do I do?' The sound of the oxygen feed to the tanks bubbled through the room.

Dana took over. 'Put your feet in the tank – the fish will do the rest. Fish pedicures originate in Thailand, where people realised that the garra rufa fish eat dead skin. At the end of the half-hour, your feet will feel smooth. And most people feel relaxed, too, because it's such a pleasant sensation.'

'Half an hour?' Dominic watched Liza slip her high-arched feet into the water in front of her, and dozens of fish shot from all corners of the tank to swarm – could fish swarm? – all over them. Each fish was dark greeny-brown and about three inches long, pulsing with delight at attaching its mouth to Liza's feet. His toes curled in his shoes.

Dana held out a handful of wipes. 'Ready?'

Slowly, he removed his shoes and socks, wiped his feet and rolled up his jeans. His feet were inspected and passed fit to fish with. Unfortunately. He'd been hoping that it would be against Fish Rights.

'Put both in together,' Dana advised, 'so you get an even number of fish on each foot.'

Resisting the temptation to screw up his eyes, Dominic slid his feet into the cool water. And then needed every morsel of his willpower to resist the urge to snatch them out again as the garra rufa latched onto him with unsettling enthusiasm. It was like a fizzing, wriggling electric shock, as if the water was alive. His toes twitched convulsively. He wasn't worried by the fish, of course; he'd been an enthusiastic scuba diver.

But it tickled. Ooo-oooh, it tick-led.

Liza didn't seem to be having a problem, so he clenched his fingers around the arms of the chair as a fish worked its way industriously up his instep.

Her eyes began to dance. 'You're supposed to relax.'

'Right,' through gritted teeth. Another fish whisked along his sole and began munching between his toes. He fought the urge to kick clear. He had to do this. It was teambuilding. Bonding. And his sweating discomfort was at least amusing Liza out of the remote place she'd inhabited recently.

'Just chill,' she cooed. 'Put back your head, close your eyes. Listen to the music and the rhythm of the bubbles.'

He tried, and the tickling grew marginally more tolerable. At least there was no possibility of his falling asleep. He tried to distract himself from the nibbling that was progressing with excruciating thoroughness across the sensitive centre of his arch. 'So how has your week been?' *Is Adam still a problem?*

'Not very interesting. Except a woman came to The Stables, asking for Kenny.' Her voice was soft and slow, definitely relaxed, but it said: *I'm not ready to talk about Adam.*

He opened his eyes. 'Who was she?'

She shrugged. 'She didn't give a name. She sounded a bit surprised that he wasn't there and that Pippa had no idea who he was.'

'Odd.' He shot a glance at his watch. Only five minutes had passed. Hell. His instep twitched. 'Kenny has been known to be economical in giving his contact details to women. Could she have been Undead Barbie, without undead makeup?'

'Too tall. Very striking, kind of upmarket.'

He laughed. 'Kenny does have a weakness for "a posh bird". Expect he talked about working at The Stables to one of his clubbing adventures and she tracked him down.' He looked at his watch again. This was torture. Even with Liza in the next seat, blonde hair swishing every time she turned her head to regard him with those pretty blue eyes, he couldn't wait for the session to end.

An hour after leaving Nibbletastic, they were standing on the breezy bank of a river. Liza gazed at the great white hulk in front of her. 'It's a boat.'

'It's a Viking 28 fibreglass river cruiser,' he agreed, as he unpopped the navy blue canopy at one side. 'I've hired her for the day. Jump on.'

She stayed where she was, gazing about at the ranks of boats bobbing in the sunshine where the river widened beside an old mill. 'Can you drive it?'

'Yes.' He swung one leg and a blue coolbox aboard, then held out a hand. 'Hold on here – no, not to the canopy rib, to the hand hold. Put your foot next to mine and shift your weight forward. There.' He guided her smoothly into the cockpit. 'Welcome aboard the *Dreaming Desdemona*.'

She laughed, sandwiched between him and a tall chair in front of a steering wheel and knobs and dials. He'd forgotten to let go of her hand, but it felt warm and secure as she got used to the sensation of the boat moving beneath her. 'Dreaming?'

'Yes, how could I resist her? The clue is probably in "cruiser". Cruisers cruise, they don't go very fast. Let's explore.' He brought his other leg on board and guided her past the tall seat and down two steps to unlock a low wooden door.

The inside – the cabin, Dominic called it – held sofa things upholstered in pink, facing each other with a table between, and then a little oven, hob and sink, and a cupboard that turned out to house a chemical loo and a wash basin. In the pointy end was a separate space with two converging sofas. 'These will make up into a bed, and so will those,' he said, indicating each set of sofas. 'And, look behind you, there's a double berth under the cockpit.'

She stooped to look. 'It's only about two feet tall!'

'It's for lying down in. You make use of all the space, on a boat.'

She was pleased with the compactness and cleanliness of everything and, outside the windows, the lazy sliding of the khaki water. 'I've always thought boats would be bare boards, dampness and oil. But it's just like a Wendy house.'

He looked pained. 'I'll turn the gas on in the cockpit so that you can play house and make the coffee. I'll get the engine warmed up.'

'Where are we going?' she shouted, as the engine huh-huh-huh-chug-chugged into life before steadying to a loud grumble.

He shouted something that sounded like, 'To the pond,' which made no sense to her, so she set about opening cupboards until she located mugs and coffee for him and jasmine tea, which he'd thoughtfully provided, for her, and waited for the kettle to boil. By the time the drinks were made and drunk and Dominic had turned the bottled gas back off, Liza had found her river legs and adjusted to the sensation of standing on the back of some rolling, ponderous creature, so she joined him in the cockpit, zipping up her ski jacket and sniffing the fresh air.

The day being cold but fine, they folded the boat's blue canopy back like a giant pram hood. The engine had warmed up and they cast off, *Dreaming Desdemona* drifting away from the bank as Dominic settled himself behind the steering wheel. 'Room for a little one up here.' He patted the space beside him, as if she were Crosswind.

Being up on the seat turned out to be the warmest place in the cockpit because the windshield pushed the breeze above them. And Dominic always seemed to radiate heat. 'This is really good. I can see over the banks to the fields.'

Pushing a long lever to his left slowly forward to increase the engine note, Dominic turned the chrome steering wheel and eased the boat into the centre of the river. They moved slowly through the scenery, reeds and weeds stirring, cows looking up from their grazing, Canada geese not taking any notice of them at all. Liza breathed in the smells of diesel fumes and nettles. Occasionally, a boat would come from the other direction and they'd move to the right-hand side, slowing so as not to create too much of a wake, waving and calling hello as the other boat thrummed by.

'Why are we doing this?' she asked, idly. 'You can't put anything this size on the lake at Port Manor.'

He tweaked the steering wheel. 'No, that would be like keeping a whale in a swimming pool. I'm going to have paddle sports on the lake, but I couldn't see you taking to kayaking in this weather so I took the gin palace option, which isn't very adventurous or challenging, but is fun.'

'And I can just sit and relax.' A church steeple drifted by, beyond the hedgerows with the final few orange leaves clinging.

'Except you're going to learn to drive it. I put my feet in with those bloody fish.'

Excitement shot up her back. Take control of this shining white, benevolent river creature? 'You've got a deal. Swap seats.'

'So why are you not intimidated by this when the size of my Jag freaked you out?' Dominic shifted the long lever so that it clicked into a central position and the engine note dropped and, while they slid off the seat and threaded themselves back on in reverse order, *Desdemona* floated gently.

'It's slower and there's not much traffic.' But once she was behind the wheel it seemed much bigger than it had a moment ago – she wasn't going to wimp out now, though.

'Twenty-eight feet long, but she's narrow beam.' As if that was some kind of comfort. 'This lever's the throttle. Just push it forward a bit. A bit! Now steer her like a car, but with tiny movements. Think ahead, because she won't respond straight away – straighten slightly – and she doesn't have brakes. Though you can give her some reverse thrust and slow up, if you have to.'

Being in charge of *Dreaming Desdemona* felt unreal.

It was like trying to steer a huge marble on a small tray, in slow motion. Except for when she realised they were heading for the bank or, once, for an oncoming boat, and *Desdemona* proved Dominic right about her response to the wheel – then it felt as if they were moving way too fast. She squeaked and swore and cheered and zigzagged Desdemona down the river, somehow keeping out of trouble, though Dominic, laughing, once had to reach his arm around her and shove the throttle lever into reverse, winding the wheel swiftly in the opposite direction from the way she'd been turning it, until they were straight again.

When they reached the pond, which proved to be a place where the river slowed and widened into a kind of big round lay-by, he taught her to steer the boat in a figure of eight around two buoys, his voice patient and steady even when she mowed the buoys down instead of pivoting the boat around them. 'It was too much boat to get through at that angle, anyway,' was all he said, his leg warm against hers in the confines of the seat. 'Throttle back. Start turning hard now … good! Straighten, straighten … There you go.'

'I did one!'

'But you're supposed to be doing an eight.'

She laughed, feeling his warmth leaning with her as she made *Desdemona* turn again. It was companionable. That's what she told herself, suppressing an urge to melt against him and reach up and nip his ear with her teeth, imagining him making that growl deep in his throat that he had when she'd pleased him in bed, maybe scooping her onto his lap. They turned and leaned the other way, and she left his lap alone.

Eventually, they took the cut out of the pond, back into the river, moored, and lit the little oven to heat ready-meals he produced from the coolbox. Eating pasta together was

278

companionable, too, although she couldn't help pointing out, 'You could have bought wholemeal because the energy is more slow release.'

After lunch, he rolled himself into the double berth to 'catch zeds' while she washed up the few things they'd used and heated the kettle again for when he woke.

In the silence, she had time to think, to sink into the hollow horribleness that kept sucking out her insides whenever Adam appeared. As well as lurking outside her house, he'd turned up in the stable yard several times. Seeming to know exactly when to catch her leaving or arriving, he was scarred in so many ways and his big, soulful, accusing, pleading eyes pierced her heart and enraged her in almost equal measures. She hadn't told anyone about how he was making her life a misery because it was her problem, and everyone would say tell the police and what if that pushed him over the edge to some new act of self-harm? Adam was turning her days as sad and grey as he was, the personification of her guilty conscience. At least a hundred times a week she wished that she'd handled things differently a year ago, had realised earlier that loved-up and settled was so not her. That relationships seemed to be for other people.

And, fervently, she wished that she hadn't got drunk at Adam's birthday party, because she might have been able to handle things more kindly and not humiliated him so brutally, if she'd been sober.

She was tempted to crawl in beside Dominic to catch a few zeds of her own because he was big and solid and comforting and being haunted by the Spirit of Bad Stuff Past had left her short of sleep.

But going to bed together wasn't what Liza and Dominic were about any more and once she was beside him desire for sleep would vanish and desire alone remain, hot and pulsing. It was biological, she told herself. Women were programmed to react to good-looking men. There were chemicals in her body; chemicals with a function.

But it was something else when a man could hook you with his gaze and make your breath catch. It was dangerous.

So she just watched the lazy khaki water, and the coots bobbing by.

When she heard Dominic's phone alert, she listened to him move, wait, move, yawn. Then he rolled out of the berth and sat up on the floor. Putting the kettle back on to boil gave him another half-minute to bring himself around before she glanced his way. He must have been pretty deep. His cheek held a pink sleep crease, his eyes were bleary.

Her impulse was to ask if he was OK, but she was pretty sure he wouldn't appreciate it. So she said, 'You were really tense about those fish. They weren't piranhas, you know.' The kettle whistled and she created a cloud of steam pouring the water into two mugs.

Pulling himself up, he dropped down onto the other sofa, half-smiling, half-yawning. 'OK, I might as well admit it. It was torture. I'm ticklish.' He looked sheepish at the admission.

She beamed. 'Yeah. I know. Miranda told me, after your first treatment.'

Later, when they were taking the boat back in the last of the daylight, Dominic driving and Liza watching yellow pinpricks of light decorating the villages in the misty dusk, he took her hand from where it lay on the seat between them. 'Are you still cool about running the treatment centre?'

A moment passed. 'I think so. I told Fen and Immi our plans and they were enthusiastic. It's probably the best of all worlds for them – getting rid of Nicolas but not having to run the place themselves, and freedom to be a bit more inventive with what they offer clients.'

He sounded pleased. 'On the principle that keeping people informed keeps them happy, I suggest the four of us have a meeting, soon.'

She stared out of the window. 'I suppose we could.'

Gently, his hand squeezed hers. 'Why the doubt? Adam?'

'He's ... making me uneasy.' Understatement. He was making her feel as if she were tiptoeing in stilettos on ice, expecting any moment to crash on her face. Despite the comforting warmth of Dominic's hand, her throat suddenly felt tight.

The boat chugged on. Dominic pulled her close, companionably, comfortingly. 'You're not responsible for him.'

Despite his warmth, she shivered. 'That's irrelevant if he does something stupid because of me.'

He sighed. 'It's difficult,' he acknowledged. 'But you can't give up your life to his problems.'

The hollow horribleness came creeping back. She slid herself out of the circle of his arm. 'I'm cold. I'm going inside.'

But the cabin didn't seem so welcoming, now. She turned on the light and the heating – this Wendy house had all mod cons – but still shivered. It was obvious that Dominic had been disappointed with her responses, and she wanted to bounce with enthusiasm, had been trying all week to rekindle the buzz she'd felt at the radio station. But it wasn't happening.

It was dark by the time Liza and Dominic reached Middledip. They'd bickered not-quite-amicably for most of the forty-minute journey home, because Dominic had the stupid outmoded idea that he ought to see her home, as if she wasn't capable of dropping him off at his new flat in Bankside and then driving across the village to The Cross. And now he was getting his own way by the simple expedient of refusing to tell her his new address.

'Then I'll just drop you somewhere on the Bankside estate,' she argued.

'How? By lifting me out of the car?'

'By kicking you up your awkward, stupid arse,' she snapped, frustrated into turning down Port Road to The Cross. 'Control freak.'

'I prefer "controller",' he corrected, with mock dignity.

Liza indicated and began to slow as she reached number 7.

And then saw a thin figure waiting in the halo of a streetlight. Her stomach lurched.

'Shit!' She stamped on the accelerator, swerving awkwardly across the triangle of The Cross and swinging up Main Road. Heart thumping, she straightened the car until she was driving on the correct side again.

'Your neighbour seems to be letting Adam sit on your wall,' Dominic observed.

'Yes. Shit. Fuck. Why can't she come out and be horrible to him and scare him off?' She slowed to a crawl up Main Road as she steadied her breathing, trying to form a plan of action.

'I thought he's not supposed to know where you live.'

'It won't have been hard to work out where to look, once he knew where I was working. He knows that Cleo lives in Middledip. He probably just asked at the shop or the pub.' Liza pulled to the side of the road to wipe her sweating palms down her jeans.

He watched her closely. 'You don't seem completely surprised.'

She groaned, letting her head tip forward to bang on the steering wheel. 'He's been hanging around outside. I suppose now you feel vindicated in your insistence on seeing me home?' She twisted round to glare at him, as if it was somehow his fault.

His face was impassive in the light from the dashboard and the streetlight outside. 'I do, but, don't worry. I don't expect a sudden onset of graciousness, just because I tried to do the right thing. I won't even mention that your ex is stalking you.'

Her laugh was almost a sob. 'Sorry. Adam's freaking me out. It's not quite so bad when he just skulks around The Stables, but now he's started hanging around outside my house. I feel as if I ought to just drive up and walk straight past him … but I don't want to. I don't want another horrible conversation about getting back together. It's not that I'm scared of Adam …' She squeezed her eyes tight shut, hating the feelings of helplessness and fear that were hurting her chest.

'You're worried about what he might do – and whether it would be your fault. I'm beginning to see what's making you so jumpy. His actions aren't exactly those of a balanced man.' He rubbed his chin thoughtfully. 'How about I invite you to my new flat for supper, to give him time to get fed up and go?'

Relief surged through her, and she thrust from her mind the thought that she was letting Dominic rescue her again. Opening her eyes, she wiped her palms on her jeans and put the car in first gear. 'Thank you,' she said, as graciously as the Queen. 'I appreciate your kind invitation and am delighted to accept.'

Dominic enjoyed giving Liza a tour of his flat. Especially the bedroom. He waited for her to go pink and avert her gaze from his bed, and grinned when she did exactly that. 'Blondes are such fun with their blushes,' he commented, making her scowl and blush more fiercely. But winding her up at least distracted her from Adam's stalking.

'Wow,' she said, gazing at everything other than the bed. 'Your room is huge and Kenny's is—'

'A cell. But I'm sure he's slept in worse places.'

Heading back towards the lounge – and, yes, her eyes flickered back to the bed as she left, he was satisfied to note – Liza asked, 'Kenny not here?'

Dominic let his eyes slide down to his favourite part of her rear aspect as he followed her. 'Now the rain's stopped he's walking or running all the time to stop him going stir crazy while we wait for Nicolas to stop dithering.'

'What are you feeding me for supper?' She tucked his favourite part under herself on one of the tall stools at the breakfast bar, hiding it from his view. Shame.

He took up station on the other side of the bar, which gave him a view of the front of her, instead, which was no bad bargain. 'Chicken and pasta in cheese sauce.' He began taking out pans and chopping boards.

She raised one of her silky little eyebrows. 'I'm impressed.'

'Good.' He might have stuck the chicken in the oven with oven chips, if he'd been alone, but her presence was sufficient motivation to get busy chopping onions and mushrooms. It wouldn't matter that the sauce came out of a jar. And Liza seemed quite content to watch him as he worked, doing a good job of hiding any remnants of Adam-anxiety she might be feeling.

When his phone rang, he almost let it go to voicemail. But then he spotted the caller's name on the screen and wiped his hands before picking up his phone. 'It's Nicolas! Maybe we're going to get some progress. Hello, Nicolas. This is Dominic.'

Nicolas's voice was loud in his ear. 'I'm upping my price.'

Dominic froze. 'You're *what*?'

'Upping the premium on the lease. Someone new has come into the picture and he's already offered more than the figure I gave you. As your aim is to negotiate me down, rather than accept that figure, I'm keen to pursue the new guy. But I'm giving you the opportunity to counter offer, of course.' Triumph was thick in his voice.

Dominic maintained his calm, although his heart was banging in his ears. 'Have you talked to Isabel at the hotel? She's not likely to give up renting the big slope out, too—'

'Isabel has already met and approved the prospective tenant,' Nicolas put in, smugly. 'He wants the big slope, and he can ensure the treatment centre continues. And he's offered the hotel a higher rent, too.'

'But it's not worth more. So the offer may well fall through.' Logic was always his strongest weapon.

'We'll just see, shall we? I can give you forty-eight hours to consider a counter offer.'

'Right.' Ending the call, Dominic managed to string about seven swearwords together without repetition. 'Fucking Nicolas has pulled a flanker,' he added. 'He's got someone interested in the lease on even better terms than he offered me.'

Liza said, faintly, 'Wow.'

He nodded slowly, staring at the strips of chicken glistening on the chopping board, revolting him now. 'Alarms are ringing in my brain. I would have suspected him of trying to get the price up with a fictitious bid if he hadn't sounded so sure of himself. He even had the answers ready about the other party being able to keep the treatment centre on.'

He looked up. Her face had paled, her blue eyes were enormous. Compunction hit him like a truck. 'Crap. I didn't exactly break that gently, did I? I hadn't even got as far as thinking how this affects you.' Remorsefully, he scrambled for positives. 'The new person might still want you to manage it. Or might have loads of ways of bringing in clients, all the things that Nicolas set his greasy face against.'

'Or might be bringing in a complete staff,' she completed, quietly. 'I might still find myself looking for new premises. If only you'd been able to get things moving before this new person—' Her hand flew to her mouth. 'Oh no,' she breathed. 'Have they been able to nip in with their offer because of me dragging my feet?

'No point worrying about that,' he protested, automatically. But he knew she'd probably read the thought in his eyes.

Chapter Thirty

PWNsleep message board:

GuiltyGeorge: I got into a conflict and my body passed out whilst my mind stayed with the action. Wtf?

Brainwave: Probably cataplexy. I get hit at all levels from a wishy washy wave to crashing to the deck.

Tenzeds: Me, too. Like everything with N, the intensity is random. Bet you don't have a diet tip for cataplexy, Girlwithdreams! :-)

Girlwithdreams: You're right. Meditation might help on a general level, I suppose. Or not.

Monday morning. Her first client was at eleven, so she had plenty of time to change into her tunic, the hated green. If she'd taken over the treatment centre, she'd been going to order something funky: black or darkest purple.

Someone had bundled towels she'd left in the drier onto her couch. She began folding them slowly, lethargically, almost queasy with the certainty that she'd let this thing happen, a new purchaser for the lease popping onto the scene, no matter how much Dominic insisted it wasn't her fault; that Nicolas being elusive suggested he'd probably been in talks with the other party all along. It didn't alter facts: Liza's plans were up in the air. And Dominic's dreams were in the toilet.

After Nicolas's phone call, they'd picked at their food gloomily, searching for ways forward. Dominic had tried to telephone Isabel Jones and had been told to call back on Monday, which had filled his grey eyes with a storm of frustration.

He'd insisted on riding shotgun when she drove home under a dark starry sky and she hadn't demurred, even though it meant Dominic had to traipse back home to Bankside, but there had been no sign of Adam loitering and she hadn't known whether to be glad because she didn't want any more aggro, or sorry there was no one for them to take out their lousy moods on. But, then, glad again, because who could predict the waywardness of Adam's reaction if two clouds of disappointment rained down on him?

This morning Nicolas had people in his office, voices rising and falling on the other side of the door, measured, amicable. A woman's voice, difficult to catch, and a man's. Laughter. Liza frowned. Her hands stilled. She glided nearer to the corridor. The man's voice became more assured, rising to a fast trot of enthusiasm. Louder.

'… ideas,' he said. 'I've done loads of research and I know exactly where I'm going to take The Stables. But what you need to know is that we've got the finance and I want to move quickly. Isabel's already instructed her guy to get the lease for the big slope drawn up. Once your paperwork's in order, too, we'll sign on the dotted line. The sooner the better.'

Then Nicolas's voice, approaching his office door: 'The forty-eight hours will be up this evening, so if the original party hasn't come back to me, I'll get onto it tomorrow.'

Liza hopped smartly to one side, out of sight, as the office door opened for Nicolas to shout, 'Pippa, three white coffees, please!' Then she leapt back into the doorway to crane over his shoulder, making him pull back like a startled tortoise. She smiled blandly. 'Morning, Nicolas.' Then backed casually away, shutting her treatment room door.

But her heart was thundering. Scrabbling for her bag, she whipped out her phone. She might be able to put things right.

Please be there, please be there … 'Dominic,' she hissed, when he answered on the sixth ring, 'I think it's Kenny.'

He sounded puzzled. 'You think what's Kenny?'

'I think it's Kenny who's outbid you. He's here, in Nicolas's office, talking about the lease, about moving quickly and signing on the dotted line. And he's with that woman, the tall, upmarket one. It's definitely them.'

A long silence. Then, warily, 'I'm awake, right?'

'Yes, you bloody are!' She recapped in a kind of whispered shout. 'Kenny is in Nicolas's office, with Nicolas, with that woman who was here asking for Kenny, and I think they're on the verge of agreeing terms for Kenny to take over The Stables!'

Then she was listening to silence. Her phone screen said *call ended*.

Dominic arrived in ten minutes.

Liza was hovering in reception, hoping that her eleven o'clock client wouldn't be too prompt, and with some vague idea of finding a way to detain Kenny and his lady friend if they tried to leave before Dominic got there. But then the gleaming black Jaguar stormed into the stable yard, Dominic bursting out of the driver's seat, hair streaming like liquid gold in the wintry sunshine.

Throwing open the door, she hustled him up the corridor and into her treatment room. 'You're not supposed to be driving!'

'Don't give a fuck.' Dominic wore all the signs of a man in a towering rage, eyes blazing, mouth like granite. 'Are they still in the office?'

'Yes—'

He spun on his heel. Then he whirled back and dragged her up against him on her toes, hard, kissing her mouth, hard. 'Thanks for ringing me.' He put her back on her feet and launched like a missile at Nicolas's office door, banging it open. 'So, Kenny—!'

His sentence strangled in his throat.

Liza followed, worried that cataplexy had slapped him, in the emotion of the moment. But he had turned to rock while Kenny, suddenly on his feet, glared. And the willowy woman with chestnut hair gazed at Dominic.

Dominic sagged against the door jamb and said in a quite different voice, 'Natalie?'

Natalie? Liza's heart gave a great thump. Dominic's ex. Here. With Kenny. And Dominic's gaze was fixed to hers like a tractor beam.

The woman smiled, tremulously. 'I'm back in England.' Then, as Dominic remained silent, 'It's so good to see you.' Her voice wavered uncertainly as she pressed on. 'Kenny told me what was happening, and how difficult things are for you, so that's why we've put together this rescue package. I'm glad we could come up with something that worked.' She glanced at Liza, uncertainly, then back at Dominic, a tiny crease on her brow. 'Are you all right?'

Liza was clamping her lips together in an effort not to ask the same thing, torn between leaving to give Dominic privacy, and staying in case he needed backup.

A long moment. Two. Three. Then Dominic pulled himself upright, switching his gaze to Kenny. 'You're the guy who's outbid me.'

And Liza decided she had to stay. Whatever was happening, if it concerned The Stables then it concerned her. It was her damned livelihood – for the moment – too.

Nicolas, however, took the opposite view, scrambling out from behind his desk. 'Um, you obviously don't need me here. I'll, um …' He dithered like an anxious mouse until Liza moved aside. Profound relief slackening his face, he scurried out.

Kenny's voice was hard. 'Sorry, Doc. I just got so pissed off with you never taking my advice, I began to wonder why you should be the head man. I know that's how you like to see yourself, the clever one, the one in charge.' His lips twisted. 'But why should I work for you? Why shouldn't I work for myself?'

'*What*?' demanded Natalie, swinging on him, eyes huge.

Dominic ignored her, his gaze boring into Kenny. 'So that's why the endless questions? While I thought you were throwing yourself into the adventure centre, you were actually letting me coach you into ripping off all my ideas? Except with added fan descender, because you think you're right about that and I'm wrong?'

'You're not always right.' Kenny looked mutinous.

Several heartbeats, then Dominic returned his gaze to Natalie. 'Tell me what you're doing here.' His voice was calm, low, the sound of one who knew the other intimately, could exclude everyone else in the room with a change of tone.

Kenny put a hand on Natalie's shoulder, but she brushed him aside and rose. Even white to her lips, she was stunning. Liza had time to envy her height and her poise, the river of hair running over her shoulders. She looked bewildered, frightened. 'But you and Kenny have negotiated this between you, haven't you?'

'He must have forgotten to include me in the negotiation. Why don't you explain?' he said, silkily.

A tear formed on Natalie's lashes, and trembled. 'Kenny told me how ill you are. How you got yourself into a jam, starting up a business you couldn't possibly carry through. That you'd obviously bitten off more than you could chew, but with his contract ending he could take over your project, get you out of the jam, but he needed more money.' She glanced at Kenny, who had stuck out his jaw and shoved his hands into his pockets, like a naughty child he knew he was about to be found out.

'And you're involved because ...?'

Natalie licked her lips. 'I'm putting the rest of the money in,' she said, with only the hint of a quaver.

'And the money's coming from ..?'

Natalie's eyes were pleading. 'The house, Dom. My half.'

Silence. 'And you didn't think to ask me whether I wanted this arrangement? You didn't think I'd want to be involved at all? Not even as a *sleeping* partner?' he added ironically. 'For fuck's sake, when have you ever known me to go into something half-arsed, without logic or research or system? Get myself in a jam?'

'Kenny was so worried about you! He said that you simply couldn't be relied upon to run a business or look after clients, that you were either asleep or half-asleep most of the time.'

Dominic's breath hissed between his teeth. '*Couldn't be relied upon?*' He took a moment to gather control. 'Even if you couldn't see that he might be playing on my disability and your doubts about my competence, why didn't you just pick up the phone and ask me?'

'I thought—' Her gaze flickered uncertainly. 'Kenny said it was better if I stayed in the background while he sorted things out with you; that it was a male pride thing. Everything in your life was a climb down, now, and you were having trouble adjusting. When I analysed my behaviour over your narcolepsy, I saw I hadn't been supportive of your illness.'

'I'm not ill. I'm narcoleptic. I manage it.'

'I wanted to help. I never wanted us to split up, Dominic.' Miserably, she whispered, 'I thought we might get close again, if I helped.'

Slowly, Dominic shook his head. 'We didn't split up

because you thought my narcolepsy was more about you than about me. We split up because you aborted my baby.'

Instantly, Kenny bristled past Natalie like a belligerent dog. 'It was my baby.'

Dominic recoiled, as if a giant hand had slapped his face. In the silence, Natalie began to cry.

Impulsively, Liza slid her hand into Dominic's, squeezing it, feeling his fingers shut around hers, even as he transferred his attention from Natalie to Kenny and found his voice. 'Yours?'

Kenny's eyes glittered triumphantly. 'The good guy doesn't always get the gal, Doc. Your sleep thing wasn't just about you. Nattie was struggling and you weren't noticing. She turned to me. And I was there for her.' His mouth turned down. 'I wanted us to be together, but when she'd done the deed she went all horrified, all, "Ooh, what have I done? Dominic mustn't know." And she got rid of my baby. *My* baby. Because of you.'

But Natalie's hands were over her mouth, tears easing from horrified eyes that were fixed on Dominic. 'No, no, it wasn't like that! I was feeling sorry for myself and I got drunk, Dominic, I swear. I wouldn't have cheated on you if I hadn't been drunk. I love you!'

Dominic seemed turned to stone. 'How do you know it was his?'

Natalie dropped her wavering gaze. Finally, she admitted, 'I fudged the dates, Dom. You know there were those few weeks—'

He sighed. 'When you moved into the spare room?'

Miserably, she nodded. 'It happened then,' she whispered. 'I was drunk and didn't think about condoms.'

Dominic sent a look of disgust Kenny's way, before turning back to Natalie. 'So when you wanted to make up it was just so that all you had to do was lie about the dates?'

'Not just!' she cried. She swung on Kenny, fury lighting her eyes. 'Why did you have to tell him? He never needed to know! Why hurt him? And all that bullshit about him wanting to pull out of the adventure centre, that he was too ill.' And to Dominic, tears rolling down her high cheekbones, 'None of it's true, is it? I'm so sorry, Dom.' She started towards Dominic, her hands outstretched.

But Kenny yanked her back. 'You went to bed with me and he was too sleepy to notice! Don't apologise to him.'

And then Dominic was lunging for Kenny, roaring 'Bastard!', trying simultaneously to put Natalie behind himself and swing a savage punch at Kenny.

'Stop!' burst out Liza. 'Stop it, now. Or I'll phone the police.'

Three bodies stilled. Three heads turned towards her.

She took a deep breath over the thundering of her heart. 'You can't use someone's office, our place of business,' she emphasised, 'for a brawl. You need to take this somewhere else. Our clients expect to have their treatments in peace and quiet.' She made her voice severe and sensible and hoped nobody could see how much she was shaking.

And she tried not to wonder if she was breaking things up because Dominic going for Kenny's throat the instant he'd laid a hand on Natalie had made her feel deeply sick. Though her heart ached for him.

The three subsided. Exchanged glances. Natalie picked up a black leather handbag and Kenny unhitched his jacket from the back of his chair. Dominic sent Liza an unreadable look.

'It was meant to be a rescue package,' Natalie insisted, piteously.

Liza couldn't help herself. 'But Dominic doesn't like being rescued!' Then she glanced at Dominic's face. 'Oh. Sorry. Now I'm butting in.'

From the corridor, Pippa said, in a small voice, 'Um, Liza, your eleven o'clock's waiting.'

'Sorry, Pips. I'm coming now.' But Liza didn't go into her treatment room until she'd watched Dominic, Kenny and Natalie follow one another down the corridor, across reception, and out. That was fair enough, she told herself, blinking. It was about them.

Not her.

Chapter Thirty-One

Liza stared at Cleo. 'That can't be true!'

Cleo, lounging on the sofa, helping Shona practise her S's in scarlet gel pen on pink paper, smiled smugly. 'It is. Seven hours last night and eight the night before.'

'But Gus has never slept more than two or three hours at one time.' Liza looked down at her nephew, sitting up in her lap, blowing bubbles and kicking his legs.

'It's bliss.' Cleo dropped a kiss on Shona's head. 'No more colic. Goodbye whingey baby, hello sleepy baby. It just happened overnight.' She sighed in pleasure. 'Sleep affects everything.'

Liza kept her gaze on Gus, who rewarded her with a gummy grin, probably feeling great because he was getting so much sleep, but thought about Dominic, whose life had fractured and reformed in a crazy pattern, because of sleep. 'True.'

'How's everything with you?'

Liza put on her bright voice. 'Fine. I'm meeting Angie and Rochelle at a wine bar, later.'

'Any news about what's going on with the treatment centre, since the bust up?'

Liza shrugged, and tickled Gus's nose to make him smile again. 'Nicolas hasn't been in for two days. Me, Fen, Imo and Pippa are just carrying on regardless, waiting to see what happens.'

'What about your man? Hasn't he told you what's going on?'

'Who's Auntie Liza's man?' demanded Shona, golden hair dancing as she swung her gaze between her mother and her aunt.

'I haven't seen him since Monday. And he's not my man, there's no such person.' She stroked Gus's downy head. Glaring daggers at her sister's dark smiling eyes, she mouthed, 'Bugger off!'

'Bad word,' declared Shona, with four-year-old righteousness. 'You only make words without saying them when they're bad words, Mummy told me.'

Cleo shot Liza a mischievous grin. But then her expression softened. 'But we love Aunt Liza a lot, don't we? Because she does nice things like taking Shona and Gus to the play park.'

Gus reached out a slobbery hand to grab a fistful of Liza's hair and Shona nodded emphatically. 'Yes, we love you a very lot, Auntie Liza. A very lot.'

'And we want her to be happy.'

'Yes, we want her to be happy a very lot. I think Gus has done a poo.'

Liza, who had just come to the same conclusion, was glad of a reason to end the conversation before the threatening prickling in her eyes at being loved 'a very lot' turned into tears. But at least familial love was a love she seemed able to return. She dumped her noisome nephew in her sister's lap. 'Sounds like my cue to go. I'm meeting Rochelle and Angie. Kiss, Shona. Kiss-kiss, Gus-Gus.'

Shona turned her cheek up for her kiss, holding her nose. 'Phew. Poo.'

Cleo slung her arm around Liza's neck. 'Say hi to Angie and Rochelle for me and have a great time. You look hot in that dress, by the way. Is Dominic going to be there?'

'No.' Liza searched through her bag for her car keys.

'Oh. Well, anyway. Have fun.'

Outside, the air was sweeter, but cold. Liza's little purple car waited at the kerb and she whacked the heating up full blast for the drive into Peterborough, wishing Cleo wasn't so obviously keen that Liza have a good life. Because, sometimes, life wasn't particularly good and all you could do to distract yourself from that hard fact was climb into a little black dress with a flirty hem and meet your fun friends in a wine bar, and hope that things would get better.

The wine bar was right in the city; a cellar, furnished, bizarrely, with old school desks and stools like barrels. With red light flooding the walls from downlights, it looked like a cross between a classroom and a troll's cave.

Rochelle and Angie leaned on the bar, large glasses of white wine gleaming. Rochelle rolled her eyes when Liza bought a bottle of sparkling water.

'I'm dri-ving ...' sang Liza, returning eye roll for eye roll.

'Get a ta-xi ho-me,' Rochelle sang back.

Liza looked at the bottles of wine gleaming seductively behind the bar. She thought about Adam who, thankfully, because she didn't think she could have borne any more shit in her shitty week, had been conspicuous by his absence since his vigil on her wall last Saturday. But he could turn up, him and his wounded eyes, any time, and then she'd require a clear head to inch over the thin ice that was Adam. 'Not tonight.'

Angie and Rochelle shared a sigh.

Angie announced, 'We've decided to get you fixed up.'

'I don't want you to fix me up.'

Rochelle threaded a hopeful arm around Liza's neck. 'Because you're hooking up with the luscious Dominic?'

'No,' Liza responded, shortly.

'So being fixed up will be good for you. Oh, Liza! Don't you remember how much fun we used to have before you let what Adam did turn you into an angel of purity? Talking to men in wine bars? The kiss-a-stranger game? A few drinks?'

'I liked the kiss-a-stranger game,' observed Angie, moistening her lips.

Sighing, Liza gave ground. 'I'm here, aren't I? I've made an effort. And,' she pointed at her feet with both index fingers, 'I've bought new shoes.' They were perfect: hyacinth blue, with silver pin heels.

'Seriously cool,' Rochelle admitted.

'But I'm not going to kiss strangers.'

'Lol! You haven't said you won't talk to men,' beamed Angie.

'Right.' Rochelle's face was full of determination. 'Let's find some.'

For the next hour the wine bar filled up and Liza allowed herself to be drawn into conversation after conversation as Rochelle and Angie burst their bras to get her fixed up, manipulating people so that Liza always ended up standing next to some man. The room grew warm and the conversation louder and she tried to relax and just enjoy the evening, but felt her friends' expectations pressing her down. Her bottle of water was renewed by a nice guy who introduced himself as Marcus, really attentive, good hair, tall, looked great in black jeans, and he didn't query her not drinking anything stronger, so he'd obviously been briefed in advance.

Marcus was superseded by Shaun, who took the alternative approach, declaring he'd just landed a great new job and wouldn't she join him in a glass of champagne?

Then Richie, who—

Liza pre-empted his pitch with a polite smile. 'I'm just going to ...' She waved in the general direction of the Ladies. He smiled in a 'Yeah, right, I've heard that one before,' sort of way, and Liza hit the stairs.

Once up in the street, she caught her breath, sent mental apologies to Rochelle and Angie, and headed for her car.

Chapter Thirty-Two

PWNsleep message board:

Sleepingmatt: Struggling with depression, recently. Bad event kicked it off and it's hard to shake.

Tenzeds: With you re bad event, mate.

Nightjack: My GP gives me antidepressants, if I ask. I don't often ask. ☺

Sleepingmatt: I know it's not just me. Loads of people with N struggle with it. When one of you guys doesn't post for a while, I think, 'Bet they're down with the black dog ...'

Dominic slumped on the sofa and stared at the television. He had a documentary channel on. Something about Concorde. He felt like crap. His watch was in the bedroom and he couldn't be bothered to press the button on the TV remote that would flash the clock, so he didn't know the time. The window was a dark square, but November days were short. Crosswind slept twitchily on his doggie beanbag. Dominic had managed to take him for a walk, earlier, fighting sleep as he trudged, his face a leaden mask, prising one eyelid up and then the other until he could stagger home. Crosswind hadn't asked to be taken out since, so probably his circadian rhythm was telling him that it was night.

He could go to bed.

He could switch the TV channel to something he actually wanted to watch.

He'd slept a lot in the last couple of days. He thought, anyway. Heavy face. Forehead dragging. He'd tried to focus on his pain, because focusing on something was better than focusing on nothing. Kenny and Natalie. Behind his back. Together. The thought made him feel sick.

He hadn't taken his meds, which was bad, and he vaguely regretted it. But he couldn't be bothered to work out when to take them and sleeping blocked out black, bruising truths. Giving in to dark moods was bad, he knew, but the temptation to float into a limbo where dreams eclipsed reality … Natalie's voice floated through his head, *I'm sorry … I didn't mean to … I got drunk … I couldn't cope with you not coping. I didn't know it was going to turn out to be narcolepsy …* Fucking narcolepsy. *I'm so sorry, Dominic. Try to understand. I still loved you, but …*

That's not how love works, he'd said. *I'm over you, but you can't expect me not to care about you screwing around. With someone I thought was a friend.*

Her face had crumpled. *But I'm not over you … let's talk … please!*

Kenny's *it was my baby* had boomed between them. Natalie had stopped. Covered her eyes.

The weirdness of REM sleep flipped his consciousness and he saw Natalie with a snake, a knife, a baby.

He felt like an idiot about the baby.

And then he felt disloyal, because it wasn't the baby's fault.

Then he felt like an idiot again, because loyalty didn't come into it when it wasn't his baby. It had been Kenny's baby. He felt like an idiot about Kenny. About Natalie. Mess. Not the baby's fault. Felt bad about the baby. Poor baby.

His eyelids drooped. *Natalie cradled the baby. She didn't speak. Then the baby became Gus. The woman became Liza. Liza turned and stared and Natalie appeared beside her. She spread her empty arms. The baby was gone.*

He pried his eyelids up. Natalie wasn't real. The baby

wasn't. No Liza. No Gus. Eyelids so heavy. *Voices, whispering voices, lots of voices, talking about him. Telling him about Natalie. Why hadn't they told him before? Then Natalie, Natalie was in the flat, he could hear her.* He lurched to his feet, half-waking, half-sleeping, stumbling around, checking each room.

Natalie wasn't there. Idiot.

Collapsing back onto the sofa, he stared at the television, something about space probes, now, until his eyes began to close.

Kenny with Natalie, arms and legs wound around—

A loud noise. His eyes broke open. The TV was still on, bright, blaring. The noise came again. Not the TV. Crosswind uncurled himself, shook, barked and leaped up on Dominic. He was real because Dominic could feel the scrape of claws on his chest.

Noise. He knew what it was, if he could only think—

Again. Long, this time, repetitive, *beeeeeeeeeeee beeeeeeeeeeee beeeeeeeee.*

The intercom.

Somebody was standing at the outside door, pressing the intercom button. Somebody wanted to talk to him.

He didn't want to talk to them. Anyway, he was made of concrete. Beeeeeeeeeeeeeeeeee … Crosswind scratched at his leg. Kenny flickered into his head, trying to give him a headset. *He was in the control tower. An Airbus 320 was sliding along the runway, stretching longer and longer, and he reached for the headset. There was an alarm going off, the aircraft was in trouble, the pilot was trying to contact him for information. He must respond! The alarm, beeeeeeeeeeee …*

'Dominic!'

Crosswind barked right in his face. Dominic opened his eyes.

'I know you're up there because I can see your telly's on!'

Liza.

Kenny, Natalie, and the aircraft, faded away. He moved his eyes to the window. The curtains were open. The window was open. The TV flickered on an ad for shaving cream, the On Screen Man looking as if smoothing the creamy white peak over his jaw line was about to give him an orgasm.

'Dominic!' Liza's voice snaked through the open window.

Crosswind barked louder, tail whirring. *Come on, boss! Get with the programme.* Dominic felt shards of wakefulness. Liza. His heart rate picked up. But he didn't know what to say to her about The Stables and … He'd talk to her tomorrow, when he hadn't been in the same clothes for so long. Put his alarm on and start a new day. Take his meds. Call her.

'Dominic, I know you're there and I'm going to stand here and shout until you let me in. I'll wake up your neighbours.'

But they'd go to sleep again. He stretched, feeling some of the numbness of the last couple of days retreating as the stimulus of Liza's voice needled through his head. He suddenly realised that he was cold.

'I'll call the police! I'll tell them that I'm worried you're not answering the door and your phone's on voicemail!'

He pulled it out of his pocket. Screen blank. Must have run out of charge.

Silence. She'd probably gone. But Crosswind was still whining and wagging, plainly wanting Dominic to return to normal. He would, tomorrow, he promised himself.

Then Liza's voice came again, louder, deliberately threatening. 'Dominic, if you don't let me in, *I'll fetch Miranda.*'

Crap. Miranda had a key and would burst in and start looking after him, tutting and clucking. He pushed himself to the edge of the sofa and to his feet. He staggered slightly, but he'd shaken out of it.

He was back.

Crosswind clicking at his heels, he crossed to the intercom box beside the front door and pressed the red button that would release the lock downstairs. Opened the upstairs door. 'Wait, Crosswind.' The little dog took up station on the threshold, ears up, tail a blur, as Dominic retreated, switching on lights, turning off the television.

Then Liza was in the doorway, blue eyes big, rubbing Crosswind's head as he bounced for attention, but her gaze on Dominic. Her coat was open over a dress that hugged her body, completing his journey to alertness. Wow, she was a hot package. Relief washed across her face and she started towards him, nearly tripping over Crosswind. 'Why are you shivering?'

Lifting his hand to halt her before she got too close, he turned away to close the windows. 'Bit cold. I'm going to shower and shave.'

The ghost of a smile. 'Good. You look like hell.'

'Thanks.' Funny, because he was feeling better all the time. 'Um … Crosswind probably needs a quick visit to the outside world.'

'I'll take him.' She clicked her tongue and Crosswind, the tart, scurried off happily down the stairs, a flash of white woolly tail beside her spiky blue shoes.

Into his room, stripping off his clothes, turning the shower on high, letting the hot needles warm him, washing away the last rags of dream Natalie, Kenny and baby.

Everything was clear. Vivid. Real.

From his bedroom he heard Liza return, talking to Crosswind, moving around, the sound of water rushing from a tap. He shaved, not getting the absurd amount of pleasure On Screen Guy had seemed to, but feeling better, brighter. Back. Clean boxers, jeans, sweater. Clock. Twenty past ten. Presumably at night. OK. He could deal with that.

Liza looked up as Dominic reappeared. Apart from a hint of strain around his eyes and a lingering pallor, he looked normal. A different man to the one who had regarded her so warily, blearily, disconnectedly, when she'd burst in on him fifteen minutes ago. She gave him a smile. 'I'm making coffee.'

He hesitated. 'OK.'

Her turn to pause. 'Is that wrong?'

'I don't usually take caffeine in the evening, because it affects my night. But I've slept so much it'll probably be OK.'

She tipped both mugs of coffee down the sink. 'I have jasmine tea in my bag.'

Alarm flickered across his face. 'Better idea.' From the fridge he took a bottle of wine, peeling off the dark green foil and rattling through a drawer for a corkscrew, extracting the cork with a moist pop. 'Alcohol isn't ideal, but it's better than coffee.' He took two wine glasses from a cupboard and half-filled each with pale gold liquid. He came closer and put one in her hand and clinked it with his.

She felt really strange, holding it as if she was doing something wrong – that smoking-behind-the-bike-sheds feeling. 'Why?'

He guided her to the sofa with a warm hand between her shoulders. 'It's symbolic. If you drink it, you're refusing to be controlled by Adam.' He pulled her down beside him. 'You're not an alcoholic so one drink won't hurt you, and you never need to drink again.'

She tried to negotiate. 'I'll drink it, if you tell me what's going on with The Stables. The therapists are restless.'

He sipped. The wine shimmered. His eyes challenged.

'Start with what you've been doing for the last couple of days,' she prompted.

The wine lay on his lips. He licked it off.

Slowly she lifted her own glass. The wine tasted weird. Metallic. It slid down her throat, chilled yet with that alcoholic warmth.

Immediately, he rewarded her with information. 'We went to Port Manor Hotel, where Natalie's staying, and talked. The edited highlights are that they had a drunken one-night stand whilst I was trying to recover from pneumonia and reeling from what turned out to be narcolepsy, because Natalie wasn't coping with the new Dominic. When she realised she was pregnant, she panicked, because she knew it must be Kenny's. Didn't want to be a mother, didn't want a lifetime of passing the baby off as mine and, maybe belatedly, realised she didn't want our relationship to end. Then I found out about the abortion and ended things anyway.' He shook his head in disgust. 'I can't believe that I didn't pick up the real reason Natalie suddenly took against Kenny. It's no wonder Kenny thought that I was too sleepy to notice. In fact, I noticed everything, but misinterpreted one fundamental element – the reason that Natalie didn't want to be pregnant.'

He stopped. Looked expectantly at the glass of wine. Liza took another sip. It tasted more familiar this time.

He continued. 'Kenny was devastated about the abortion, but he'd always had a thing for Natalie and despite it, and her being desperate to brush the one-night stand under the carpet, he still wanted to get together with her when we broke up. When she didn't want that, he blamed me. And for her getting rid of the baby.'

He paused again and Liza took another mouthful of wine.

'So he took the job in America, brooding on his injustices. When I asked if he was interested in helping me get the adventure centre off the ground, he couldn't resist coming to see what it was all about. He hid his resentment and began looking for ways to get back at me. That he found a way to do that by using Natalie felt like poetic justice, I guess, with a last ditch possibility that he'd finally end up with Natalie, too, if she couldn't get back with me.'

'Wow.' Absently, Liza took a sip of wine, voluntarily this time, rather than using it as currency to exchange for information. 'And all the time he was pretending to be your friend.'

He picked up her hand from the sofa and laced his fingers lightly through hers. 'I knew that he thought everything came easy to me and hard to him, which is why he liked it if he could take a girl off me. It must have seemed like a major triumph when he thought he'd taken Natalie off me, too.' He spoke lightly, but she could feel his sadness through his skin. 'He flew to New York when they were both living in America and she was feeling isolated by the end of the relationship. Being in a new country, away from all her friends, intensified that. She didn't particularly like her new job and when Kenny said he happened to be in the city, could they just meet as friends, she was glad enough to. And he kept in touch, waiting to see where it might lead, I suppose.

'To twist the knife he'd already stuck in my back – "his" finance for the counterbid would come from Natalie's share of our house, as well as from the sale of his flat. He had his first meeting with Isabel Jones whilst I was at your sister's wedding.

'And that pretty much brings us to the point where you rang to tell me he was about to swipe the lease from under my nose.'

'And you flew onto the scene like Batman.' She squeezed his hand. 'I was scared that if you'd got into a fight, you would have suffered a cataplexy episode.'

His smile was crooked. 'I took a very light hit, but once I'd leaned on the wall for a minute I'm pretty certain I could have thumped him.' He glanced at her out of the corner of his eye. 'You didn't have to protect me. I know you kick arse when you feel the need. But don't kick the arses that are mine to kick.'

'Sorry.' Liza looked at their hands, entwined, his large and capable, hers small, clean and hygienic. Whilst they'd been engrossed in the story of Kenny's perfidy, Crosswind had skulked up onto the sofa and was lying with his head on her lap, very still, like a dog that wasn't allowed on the furniture and was hoping not to be noticed. He was warm. Comforting. She swallowed. 'Do you still love Natalie?'

Dominic shook his head. 'The betrayal stung like fuck, though. I accept her version of events, and she's so obviously suffering huge amounts of guilt and remorse. And anger over letting herself be manipulated, because being a dupe doesn't suit her self-image. But my feelings for her have gone.'

Liza tried not to feel glad, because it wasn't as if she was in a relationship with him. Although loving a woman who'd left him for his supposed best friend wasn't what was best for Dominic, so she let herself feel glad for that, at least. 'And you threw Kenny out?'

'When I came back here, his room was already empty, the flat and car keys were on the bed. Maybe he's moved his stuff into the hotel, to be near Natalie and maybe make an opportunistic move.'

'So what's happening with The Stables?'

'Anybody's guess. When I told Natalie the figures I was going to go ahead on, and that Kenny seemed to have comprehensively outbid me, she was horrified. I expect she knows that that means he lost his head. But she clammed right up when I asked whether she could extricate herself financially. I suspect she's already put her money in his hands

– and Kenny still wants The Stables. I left them hissing at each other.'

'So between us, we have to fuck it up for Kenny.' Liza squeezed his hand again, relishing the idea of victory over the perfidious Kenny. Then, when Dominic didn't respond, peered into his face. 'Don't we? You still want the place, don't you? Imogen and Fenella are really behind your bid – they were hacked off when I had to break the news that Kenny might get The Stables, not you, in case he wants them out.'

He shrugged. 'I've got some thinking to do. I've been veging here, floating in my own misery, little constructive brain activity going on, consciousness being an annoying time between naps. But I'll start taking my meds again, tomorrow, and get my head round everything.'

Scandalised, she jerked up, unsettling Crosswind just when he'd got back to sleep. 'Shouldn't you take them now?'

He eased her back against him. 'No, that would keep me awake all night. I'll take them first thing tomorrow. And I've told you everything I know about The Stables, so you have to finish your wine.'

Making a mental note to ring him and ensure he kept that promise, then deleting it because that would be Miranda-ish, she drank, beginning to enjoy the coolness sliding down her throat. 'I've never had wine administered like medicine before. One glass and I'm beginning to get a buzz on.' She snorted a laugh and Crosswind jumped to his feet, taking waggy possession of her lap and trying to lick her face.

Immediately, Dominic clicked his fingers. 'Crosswind, bed.'

'He's all right,' began Liza.

Crosswind paused, hopefully.

Dominic clicked again. 'Bed!'

With a sigh and a hanging tail of reproach, Crosswind

eased to the floor and slunk sadly over to a round blue beanbag in the corner.

'Poor Crosswind!' Liza protested, laughing up at Dominic. And their gazes tangled. Her blue eyes widened, lips parting.

He felt the familiar tightness in his jeans at the thought of how those soft lips felt on his. On him. 'I don't suppose that would work with you?' he suggested, softly.

Predictably, she narrowed her eyes at him. 'Click your fingers at me and I'll snap them off.'

He laughed. 'So very Liza.' Then slid his arms around her and scooped her onto his lap, burying his face against her neck, breathing in the scent of her skin, feeling her body soften against his, pulling her closer, closer, as if to absorb her. His lips trailed up her throat, over her jaw line, until they found her mouth. 'Scary, gorgeous, hot Liza,' he whispered, 'come to bed with me. There's no Stables to get in the way between us any more, and I want you like crazy. I want you every time I get within a mile of you. You drive me nuts.' His hand slid up her leg and into the fabulous heat beneath her dress and he went dizzy with the softness of her.

She pressed up against his hand. 'You drive me nuts, too.'

'In a good way or a bad way?'

Her lips brushed his, soft as breath. 'Both.'

'I know that feeling. But I love it. I want us to drive each other nuts all night.' And then, massive relief, he felt her hand slide into his shirt, her palm skim over his ribs. He groaned against her mouth. Instantly, Crosswind sprang on top of them, whining, ears flat, tail beating, as anxious as any self-respecting dog whose human was making strange noises.

Dominic laughed, breathlessly. 'We'd better move this into the bedroom. He's at an impressionable age. Down,

Crosswind!' He managed to dislodge his furry bodyguard and manoeuvre both him and Liza to their feet without breaking bodily contact, though Liza had lost one shoe and her dress was up around her waist. He managed to scoop the shoe up. Those shoes were hot and made her a much more Dominic-friendly height. He had plans for her in those shoes.

'You're not too—?'

He tensed. 'You're not about to ask if I'm too tired, *are you?*'

'Too *hungry*,' she contradicted, indignantly, but not convincingly.

He steered her across the room. 'My appetite,' he closed the sitting-room door, careful of Crosswind's disgruntled fluffy face, 'is not for food.'

She giggled, as they made the bedroom and he slid the zip of her dress sinuously down her back and tugged the straps down her arms. Then the dress was on the floor and she was helping him slide out of his clothes, urgency making her fingers clumsy.

But her hands remembered grace as they glided over his burning nakedness, exploring. Skilled, sensitive fingers, that passed over him as if seeking messages through his skin. He wanted this woman like he'd never wanted another; Liza, who could halt his breathing with a flick of her tongue or a movement of her hips. She rubbed herself against him and he gasped at the pure pleasure of skin on skin.

Her body was firm in his hands as he pulled off her underwear with more enthusiasm than finesse. Smooth. Pulsing. Beautiful in every curve and tremor of her flesh. Then he was discarding his plans for the hot shoes, tipping her backwards onto the bed and was on top of and sliding inside her.

And the world whirled and shrank until there was just

him and this woman, this room, this moment in time. And he needed nothing more.

Liza was jolted awake several hours later, as she found herself being bundled unceremoniously out from under the duvet and into thin – and chilly – air. Crashing to the carpet with a thump. '*Oof!*'

'Get back!' Dominic's words, from the bed above, were slurred, but recognisable.

Rubbing one burning elbow and a throbbing knee, blinking blearily at the first fingers of grey daylight reaching through a crack in the curtains, Liza tried to understand what had just happened. OK, she was lying on the floor beside Dominic's bed. Because …? Because he'd just shoved her out of it. She sighed. 'Think you're having a nightmare, Dominic.'

Silence.

Then Dominic peered over the side of the bed, hair hanging over his eyes. 'Liza?'

'What did you think it was?'

He groaned. 'Scorpion. Sorry. Come here.' Strong arms reached down and helped her off the carpet and back under the warm duvet, snuggling her against the warm ridges of his body, kissing her hair, her eyelids, stroking the length of her spine. 'I chucked you out of bed?'

'It's all right.' And she giggled, snuggling still closer, seeking his warmth.

'There's nothing right about that.' He kissed her hair.

She glanced at the clock then settled against his warmth, head on his shoulder, ready for him to clunk back into sleep until his alarms began their morning fanfare. On the other hand … that was only twenty-seven minutes away.

Experimentally, she let her hand skate over his chest, and down, circling a questing fingertip around his navel. Slowly, sloooowly, down … down.

'Mm, yeah,' he rumbled, his arm tightening around her, his breathing quickening. 'I'm not even going to question whether this is a dream. But it's sure as hell not a nightmare.'

'And if it is a dream, we'd better get busy before you wake up.'

Chapter Thirty-Three

Liza was flabbergasted when Kenny phoned The Stables to speak to her.

'Coming straight to the point,' he breezed. 'If I take The Stables over, will you run the treatment side for me, like you were going to do for Dominic?'

She fought down the impulse to snap, 'Not in this lifetime!' Or, 'So you've managed to keep your deceitful bastard hands on Natalie's funds have you?' Because, with a burst of joy, she saw an opportunity to make things right for Dominic. Spinning her mental cogs, she lied without hesitation. 'Massively interested! Can you come in for a meeting? How about one o'clock? The centre's quiet, then, because most of us take a quick break.'

'Great!' He sounded triumphant.

Liza replaced the phone on a grim impulse to dump him on his arse, hard.

Assuming a beaming smile, she popped her head around Imogen's door. 'I've just had a phone call from the guy who put in the top bid for The Stables, and he wants to talk.'

Imogen's eyebrows went up. 'That's something, I suppose.'

Liza shucked off any guilt at deliberately misleading her friend, crossing her fingers that the end would justify the means. 'If you want to hear what he has to say, be in reception at one.' And she shot off to spin the same strategic arrangement of the truth to Fenella, Pippa and even Nicolas, who'd shown his face for the first time in days.

So, when one o'clock rolled around, not only Liza awaited Kenny King in reception.

He halted just inside the door at the sight of four more people than he'd expected, lined up in an expectant row.

Liza grabbed his hand as if she couldn't wait to drag him over the threshold, resisting an impulse to dig her nails into his flesh, actually feeling queasy at how willingly she'd accepted this guy as Dominic's friend without noticing the craftiness that lurked in his eyes. 'Kenny! Let me introduce you to the other therapists, Imogen and Fenella, and Pippa from the front desk. You know Nicolas.' She turned to her friends. 'Kenny's come to ask me to run the treatment centre side, if he takes over The Stables.'

Kenny smiled uneasily at an exchange of hopeful glances that followed this bald pronouncement.

Liza took a deep breath. 'But I don't work with untrustworthy, deceitful shits.'

Kenny took a second to react. Then his brow lowered with a snap. 'Then I'll have to get someone else to.'

'Fine. Your first port of call will probably be amongst the other therapists in this centre, won't it? But as Imogen and Fenella are my friends, I've already had to tell them that you let Dominic Christy put months of work into a business plan for The Stables, then stole all his ideas and went behind his back to put in a higher offer. And you got his girlfriend pregnant, lied to her about your business methods and got her to put a lot of money into the project.'

Kenny looked slightly panicked. 'Just wait—'

'Eeeouuuw.' Fenella folded her arms and glared at Kenny.

Imogen shook her head in disgust. 'And don't ask me and Fen. Why should we manage the place for you? What's in it for us? How can we trust you?'

'I'll make sure that—'

Liza steamrollered over whatever Kenny was trying to say. 'Nicolas, do you know that, without Natalie, he doesn't have all the money he needs?'

Nicolas paled. 'He hadn't mentioned that.'

Shifting from foot to foot, Kenny popped in, 'Because I am with Natalie, so it's not relevant.'

Liza just smiled, sweetly. 'Oh, don't talk such balls. I expect she's starting action to get her money back from you at this very moment, you lying, cheating bastard.' And she felt a rushing exhilarating whirl of satisfaction at the fury on Kenny's face.

It seemed an endless day, once the excitement of fucking things up for Kenny was over because, no matter how many times Liza tried Dominic's phone, it went straight to voicemail. She knew that he'd taken his meds that morning – as she'd watched from his bed as he did so. Miranda-ish or not, she felt a need to know he was OK.

She sent him texts, but the only messages that popped up on her phone were from Rochelle and Angie sending her ☹s because of her abandonment of the evening before.

Grinning, she returned: *Sorry but did have a reason 4 sneaking off & he was worth it* and received *Whoop!* and ☺☺☺☺☺ in response.

When she finally drove up to number 7, her heart lifted to see a man seated on her wall under the streetlight. But then crashed to her green Chelsea boots because the man wasn't Dominic.

It was Adam.

She sighed. Oh, *Adam*. Caught up with Dominic and trying to fix things for him at The Stables, Adam and his stalky tendencies had hardly been spared a thought.

For his own sake, he needed to stop haunting her and move on with his life. And for her sake and the sake of nights like last night, she needed him out of hers. She'd drunk the symbolic glass of wine.

As she jumped out of her car, he smiled from his perch on the wall. 'Liza, I still think we ought to talk.'

'You're right.'

For an instant, surprise flashed in his eyes. Then pleasure. Triumph. Scrambling off the brickwork, he met her in the middle of the pavement.

Firmly, she took one of his hands in both of hers, and gazed into his eyes. 'Adam, I'm really sorry that I made you so unhappy. I'm sorry that I was drunk when you asked me to marry you and was so rubbish, the way I handled it. But asking me publicly, it kind of left me nowhere to go.'

His smile was replaced with a frown. 'I was showing how much I love you.'

'Were you?' She squeezed his hand. It felt thin and dry. 'Or were you trying to make me feel unable to refuse?'

His eyes shone with sadness. 'Look, you can't just return me like a pair of shoes you've changed your mind about. You made me look like an idiot. You made me ill. You pushed me into a stupid act of self-harm.' He retrieved his hand and yanked back his sleeve, brandishing the shiny pink ridges in his flesh. 'I've lost some of the use of my fingers in this hand, Liza. I haven't got a job, or anything.'

And, abruptly, she identified another emotion in the gleam of his eyes. Anger.

She stepped smartly back. 'I didn't push you into anything.' She tested the words on her tongue. Actually, they felt right. 'Slashing your wrist was more emotional blackmail. To get me back.'

'Even if that were true, it didn't work very well, did it?' He shook his head in sorrow, towering over her, following as she stepped back again. And again. 'You must be such a hard person.'

'Adam—'

'You don't deserve to be happy. And that's why I've been hanging around.' He laughed, but it wasn't a happy sound. A shadow of misery covered his face. 'I realised you wouldn't come back. So I wanted to make you unhappy, like you made me. Like he told me. He was on my side, he said.'

'*Who*?' Liza halted, leaving them toe-to-toe on the pavement like confrontational teenagers.

His smile was un-Adamlike. Unpleasant. 'That day you were on the radio and I met you at The Stables and then you turned your back on me. Kenny stayed and had a chat, said he hated to see good blokes treated badly by bitchy women. *He* didn't turn his back, even though we'd never met before. He was great. He took me for a drink the next night, told me how miserable you were that I'd found you. He said, keep it up. You're getting your own back, mate. She gave you a hard time and so you should give her one.'

'That bastard!' Liza gasped, her blood boiling. 'And you've been making me feel bad to punish me? Kenny just wanted me upset to keep me out of a business deal. He wasn't on your side at all, you stupid arse! He was using you. You've been manipulated. He's been manipulating everyone.'

Fury blazed in Adam's eyes. When he jerked back, Liza leaped back, shocked into thinking, for an instant, that he was going to lash out.

But Adam was gazing in horror over Liza's head at Mrs Snelling's window. 'Who's the scary staring woman?' he breathed, sounding more like the old Adam.

Mrs. Snelling threw up the sliding sash, looking as if she was about to pop a vein. 'Young man, kindly stop your intimidation. Really! That woman is half your size. What are you thinking?'

'I wasn't intimidating her,' Adam began, uncertainly.

Electing not to debate whether Adam entirely deserved such unreserved criticism, as Mrs Snelling was so unexpectedly swinging her battleaxe in Liza's favour, Liza grabbed the opportunity to sidle in the direction of her front door.

Mrs Snelling obviously wasn't in the mood to listen to protests. 'Don't be so untruthful! I've been watching you loom over that young woman and I'm not one to stand by and watch such cowardly intimidation.'

Liza left Adam to stutter stunned objections as he backed away, while she slipped away indoors and danced upstairs to run herself a hot bath, trusting that Dominic would turn up soon, and wanting to be warm, clean and serene when he did.

What she hadn't bargained for was that he'd be spitting with rage.

Chapter Thirty-Four

'I thought,' he gritted when, half an hour later, he had stalked like a lion into her sitting room, 'that we'd had a conversation about me not needing your protection?'

She rubbed one chilly foot on the other. She'd jumped from the bath at the ding-dong of the doorbell and hadn't taken time to do more than pull on her towelling robe and race down to fling open the door. Her hair was dripping down her neck. And now her stomach was sinking.

'And you translated that into, "Please tackle Kenny and turn everybody against him so that Dominic can get The Stables lease after all"? I hate people trying to take over on my watch.' Fury boiled in his eyes. She half-expected them to light up like a werewolf's. Yanking off his jacket, he flung it on the floor. 'Did it ever occur to you that I might have had my own plan?'

Erm … no. She bit her lip, flushing. 'But it was me dragging my feet that allowed Kenny to get his offer in, and everything, and so I— I wanted to help.'

Dominic exploded. 'But don't you think I could have nabbed the other therapists and warned them about Kenny – *if I'd wanted them to know*? How would you feel if I interfered in your plans like that?'

Her face heated still more, but she folded her arms. 'I wasn't interfering, I was helping.'

'If I need "help", I'll let you know. Till then, take it that your fucking help is not what I need. Back off.' He glared at Liza. But, after several moments his gaze flicked to her mouth, her throat, sending a gentle flush of heat through her, and it seemed as if he was beginning to calm. He gave a twisted smile, his voice softening. 'But suddenly Nicolas is keen to sell me the lease and I'm meeting him and Isabel tomorrow morning. Natalie has started making threats and suddenly they're disenchanted with Kenny's proposals.'

Her heart leaped. 'Really? Because my first client tomorrow isn't until two.'

His hand shot out to hook into the belt of her robe and drag her close. 'I suppose that you think you ought to be there to catch any details I miss if I fall asleep?'

'No!' Her palms ended up on his chest, where she could feel his heart beat. 'I want to know what I'm getting myself into, and I'm the right person to reassure Isabel Jones that the treatment centre's going to exceed the hotel's expectation. And Nicolas is a weasel and I know him.'

Slowly, his gaze dropped to her robe. 'I suppose you're naked under that?'

'And because it's not reasonable for you to complain about me meddling in your business, and then try and shut me out of my own.'

'But you are naked under that?' His grey eyes were hooded by dark lashes.

'Entirely.' She smiled her sweetest smile as she glanced at the back of the sofa. 'And it's a lot easier to get me out of this than out of a slutty hornet's costume.'

Slowly, Dominic smiled back. His wasn't a particularly sweet smile. It was calculating, predatory, intent.

She'd never seen him look hotter.

Chapter Thirty-Five

Liza had been impressed with Dominic from the first time they met. But, at the meeting with Nicolas and Isabel, he was mega. Calmly, he began by talking Nicolas's premium down to a level that made Nicolas stutter, and even persuaded Isabel into moderating the rent for the big slope.

Liza supported him by running her well-prepared ideas past Isabel, letting her enthusiasm show, using what Cleo would term 'persuasive language' but keeping it accurate. Dominic watched her, listening closely as she made her vision of The Stables sound like paradise on earth. Isabel seemed impressed. Nicolas looked at Liza as if wishing he had listened to her ideas in the past.

'OK,' Dominic said, slowly, when it seemed as if every *i* had been dotted and *t* crossed. 'Let's all go away and think about it.'

'Eh?' Nicolas shone with sudden sweat.

Isabel looked wrong-footed. 'So am I to get the new lease drawn up, or not?'

'A seven-day cooling-down period should come first.' And Dominic had ended the meeting, snicking his iPad into its case and striding out.

Liza acted as if he hadn't thrown her, shaking hands like a businesswoman, 'Isabel, Nicolas,' and following Dominic through the door. He must have a sleep attack looming. It was the only explanation. He looked strange, distant. Almost shocked. She snaked ahead of him to open the car door. 'Shall I get you home?'

'Yes, please.'

He was silent as she drove back to his flat, but awake.

When she pulled up in his car park, he said, 'Can you come up with me?'

'Of course.'

Crosswind leaped around in frenzied welcome, and Liza took him quickly outside.

When she returned, Dominic was wearing a bleak expression, an echo of how he'd looked on Wednesday when she'd first muscled her way into his flat. Liza felt her heart sink. Could depression strike that hard and fast? Dominic had held everything he'd been fighting for in the palm of his hand, but had jumped on the brake, bringing proceedings to a juddering halt.

He closed the flat door behind her. As if sensing tension, Crosswind skulked onto his beanbag without Dominic clicking his fingers.

'What?' she asked, softly.

'What?' he repeated, absently.

'What's going on? Everything's possible again. Nicolas has come down to a reasonable price for the premium. Isabel is on board. Don't you want your dream any more?'

'I don't know.' He looked pale, unfocused. 'I need to get a manager in to take the role Kenny should have fulfilled.'

'So, advertise. Put the word out. There are always fewer jobs than people to fill them.'

'Suddenly, the adventure centre seems a strange thing to want.'

She was mystified. 'I don't get you.'

'More to the point, I don't get you.' He crossed to her like a man in a trance, eyes empty. 'If I go ahead, we'll be working together. If we're working together, you won't ...'

'What?'

His gaze skewered her, his words deliberate and low. 'Were you running around putting out my fires so that I can go ahead with The Stables, putting us back into a working relationship, so you'll have a lovely fat excuse for blowing me off?'

'Oh.' Truth prodded her accusingly with its iron finger. She hadn't been doing that, had she?

'If I don't get you if I get The Stables but I *do* get you if I *don't* get The Stables, I don't want The Stables,' he said, heavily.

She tried to read his face, the depths of his eyes. 'You've moved mountains to get The Stables and now you're going to throw that work away?'

'If necessary.'

'But—' She struggled to make sense of his logic, her feelings. 'I'm no good at relationships.'

'Or you've only had relationships that are no good?'

'So you'd give up The Stables? For me?'

He moved so that there was no space between them, kissed her forehead, her cheekbone, her ear. 'In a heartbeat.'

Indignation warred with bewilderment. 'But *I* want The Stables.'

His smile was wry, but some of the strain faded from his face. 'I've been trying to work out whether you've been fighting so hard for The Stables – or to rescue me. And I can't decide. But what if I say that we would have to come as a package?'

Her heart kicked up two notches. 'Ergo, if I don't want you, I don't get The Stables?'

He hesitated. 'I suppose that is what I was thinking. But now I've heard you say it … no.' He tipped back his head, closed his eyes. He looked weary. 'No. I'm not going to try to manoeuvre you into it. Either you want me or you don't. That's what's important.'

Relief flooded through her. 'Truly?'

'Yes.' He hugged her, suddenly, hard. Then released her. 'No tricks, no ties, no traps. I'm not going to use the L word.

Need, want, yes. I'm crazy about you, you're in my head every waking moment.' A rueful smile, one last brush of the lips, and he turned and stepped away. Backing off. Setting her free.

Liza watched him pick up a pile of mail from the windowsill and stare sightlessly at the top envelope.

Aware suddenly of an uncomfortable chill in the air, she took a hesitant step towards the cell of warmth that always seemed to surround him. 'When I was, you know, "helping", it didn't occur to me that helping you get The Stables would mean we couldn't be together. I did — I did feel guilty when I thought that dragging my feet had spoiled everything for you. But, mainly … I just wanted to help you make your dream come true. I'm sorry if accepting help to realise your dream doesn't come easy to you.'

His eyes were flat. He didn't move. 'I have a new dream. You're it.'

Something inside her broke away and disintegrated, some obstruction that had always been there, blocking her ability to be part of a couple, like other people. Like Cleo. Cleo was one half of a couple and was supremely, outrageously happy. But wanting what Cleo had wasn't enough. She had to, had to … need it. She inhaled, trying to calm an invading squadron of butterflies. 'You know I haven't been good at relationships—'

'Shit.' He grimaced in disgust.

'—but one of my dreams is that … I am.' She took another step, and another, laid one hand tentatively on his chest, over his heart, trying to convey, with her touch, how much she wanted it. This time. *Needed* it. Needed him.

His gaze searched hers.

Then heat and hope flared in his eyes, igniting his killer smile. He reached for her. 'Mine, too.' He smoothed her jacket from her shoulders, down her arms and onto the floor, fingers walking her waist to the fastening to her skirt, eyes bright and burning. 'I suddenly find I can let you help me realise my dream, if you'll let me help you with that one.'

She managed a strangled laugh. 'We have a deal.' And, remembering the way that he'd removed himself from the business meeting, half an hour ago, 'But maybe you'd better take a seven-day cooling-off period? Because I'll give it my best shot, I really want it. I want The Stables but I want you more. I want dreams to come true. But—'

He pulled her into his arms, hard against the heat of him, and whispered against her mouth. 'No buts. And we absolutely don't need a cooling-off period because they're for people who might change their minds. I'm not going to change my mind and you just had one chance to change yours and I'm not giving you another. We're two people with one dream.

'Take my word for it. Dreams are my thing.'

Epilogue

PWNsleep message board:

Tenzeds: I'm going through a great patch. My new job's out of doors and keeping me busy, brilliant for alertness. And the relationship thing ... wow! Suddenly even N doesn't seem so bad. I want to really thank you guys for helping me out. You've stopped me feeling totally isolated.

Inthebatcave: Even if we all hate N, N isn't all of us, it's just a part of us. Glad to help out, Tenzeds.

Sleepingmatt: Good point, Inthebatcave.

Girlwithdreams: So glad to hear you say that, Tenzeds. ☺ I'm in a new relationship, too.

Tenzeds: So how's that going, Girlwithdreams?

Girlwithdreams: *Blushes* So far, so good.

Tenzeds: Go for it! Rip his clothes off, worship his body. You could even use the L word ...☺

Girlwithdreams: *Sigh* The L word? You know it's me, Dominic, don't you? ☹

Tenzeds: I recognised your own particular way of giving me healthy living tips – even when you weren't talking to me in real life you couldn't resist chipping in to put me right on here. Love you.

Girlwithdreams: I love you, too.

Tenzeds: Whoa, the L word! There's a dream come true, right there! ☺☺☺ xxx

Inthebatcave: Wow! What just happened? Is there going to be a wedding? ☺

Tenzeds: That's a dream for tomorrow. Don't scare her away! I've only just got her.

Girlwithdreams: Actually ... I have been practising writing 'Liza Christy'.

Tenzeds: YOU'RE JOKING!!!??

Girlwithdreams: Am I ...? ☺ You did say you'd let me help you realise your dreams.

Interview with Sue

Q Liza had already made an appearance in *All That Mullarkey*. What made you give her a book of her own in *Dream a Little Dream*?

Liza Reece was too naughty and too much fun to abandon forever in Secondary Characterland as Cleo's sister in *All That Mullarkey,* where I left her looking all loved up with Adam. I know from readers who contact my blog, website, Twitter or Facebook, that they're curious about what happens to characters after the last page of a book and I began to share that curiosity about Liza.

It was an interesting experience, getting into her head a couple of years later when everything had gone wrong for her and Adam. Superficially, she'd changed, but the old sparky Liza soon showed me how she was going to tackle the rest of her life.

Q What made you give Dominic narcolepsy?

It was a whimsical decision, to be honest. Liza was already a reflexologist and I wanted to use a non-PC comment that someone had made to me when he hadn't wanted to pursue reflexology as an aid to recovery from illness. I could see Dominic making that same comment when Miranda dragged him to Liza for treatment. So I wanted to give Dominic a health issue that he didn't think could be improved by reflexology.

In conversation with a writing buddy about the power of titles, on a tangential subject he said, 'Life's not a dream.' And I said, '"Dream" – that would be a good word to include in one of my titles.' And narcolepsy came into my head through association. The word 'dream' is connected with sleep but also with aims and aspirations and both definitions provided narrative drive.

Had I known what a complex and difficult-to-understand condition narcolepsy is, I may have chosen something else! But I became fascinated by it and it soon became a part of Dominic Christy.

Q So how did you set about researching it?
I read a lot – www.narcolepsy.org.uk was a fantastic resource, and also www.sleep.stanford.edu and a number of blogs, message boards and forums. My breakthrough came when, through the message board of Narcolepsy UK, 'the real Dominic', Dominic White, agreed to help me. To meet and chat with someone experiencing what Dominic Christy was experiencing offered me unparalleled insight. It wasn't just facts about consultants and medication that was so valuable but that he was willing to share what sleep hygiene means, how narcolepsy affects career and relationships, how family and friends react or are affected, and how frustrating and difficult everyday things can be – which may be why many narcoleptics suffer from depression.

Q This is another book set in Middledip. Is it going to be the last?
No. There's at least one more, *Is This Love?* And a novella. And a short story or two. So, no. I like it there.

Q Is Crosswind a real dog?
He's a dog I saw skateboarding in Brighton. He skated right into the public library and I thought, 'You're going in a book.'

Many thanks Sue, we know your fans are going to adore *Dream a Little Dream* and we all eagerly await the release of *Is This Love?*.

You can find out more about Sue by visiting www. suemoorcroft.com

About the Author

Sue Moorcroft is an accomplished writer of novels, serials, short stories and articles, as well as a creative writing tutor and a competition judge.

Her previous Choc Lit novels include *Want to Know a Secret?*, *All That Mullarkey*, *Starting Over* and *Love and Freedom*, which won the Best Romantic Read Award 2011.

She is also the commissioning editor and a contributor to *Loves Me, Loves Me Not*, an anthology of short stories celebrating the Romantic Novelists' Association's 50th anniversary and the author of *Love Writing – How to Make Money Writing Romantic or Erotic Fiction*. She is a Katie Fforde Bursary Award winner.

www.suemoorcroft.com
www.suemoorcroft.wordpress.com
www.twitter.com/suemoorcroft
www.facebook.com/sue.moorcroft.3

More Choc Lit

From Sue Moorcroft

Starting Over

New home, new friends, new love. Can starting over be that simple?

Tess Riddell reckons her beloved Freelander is more reliable than any man – especially her ex-fiancé, Olly Gray. She's moving on from her old life and into the perfect cottage in the country.

Miles Rattenbury's passions? Old cars and new women! Romance? He's into fun rather than commitment. When Tess crashes the Freelander into his breakdown truck, they find that they're nearly neighbours – yet worlds apart. Despite her overprotective parents and a suddenly attentive Olly, she discovers the joys of village life and even forms an unlikely friendship with Miles. Then, just as their relationship develops into something deeper, an old flame comes looking for him ...

Is their love strong enough to overcome the past? Or will it take more than either of them is prepared to give?

Visit www.choc-lit.com for more details including the first two chapters and reviews, or simply scan barcode using your mobile phone QR reader.

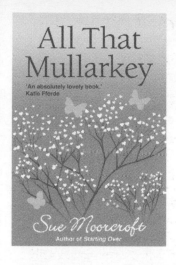

All That Mullarkey

Revenge and love: it's a thin line …

The writing's on the wall for Cleo and Gav. The bedroom wall, to be precise. And it says 'This marriage is over.'

Wounded and furious, Cleo embarks on a night out with the girls, which turns into a glorious one-night stand with …

Justin, centrefold material and irrepressibly irresponsible. He loves a little wildness in a woman – and he's in the right place at the right time to enjoy Cleo's.

But it's Cleo who has to pick up the pieces – of a marriage based on a lie and the lasting repercussions of that night. Torn between laid-back Justin and control-freak Gav, she's a free spirit that life is trying to tie down. But the rewards are worth it!

Visit www.choc-lit.com for more details including the first two chapters and reviews, or simply scan barcode using your mobile phone QR reader.

Want to Know a Secret?

Money, love and family. Which matters most?

When Diane Jenner's husband is hurt in a helicopter crash, she discovers a secret that changes her life. And it's all about money, the kind of money the Jenners have never had.

James North has money, and he knows it doesn't buy happiness. He's been a rock for his wayward wife and troubled daughter – but that doesn't stop him wanting Diane.

James and Diane have something in common: they always put family first. Which means that what happens in the back of James's Mercedes is a really, really bad idea.

Or is it?

Visit www.choc-lit.com for more details including the first two chapters and reviews, or simply scan barcode using your mobile phone QR reader.

Love & Freedom

Winner of the Festival of Romance Best Romantic Read Award 2011

New start, new love.

That's what Honor Sontag needs after her life falls apart, leaving her reputation in tatters and her head all over the place. So she flees her native America and heads for Brighton, England.

Honor's hoping for a much-deserved break and the chance to find the mother who abandoned her as a baby. What she gets is an entanglement with a mysterious male whose family seems to have a finger in every pot in town.

Martyn Mayfair has sworn off women with strings attached, but is irresistibly drawn to Honor, the American who keeps popping up in his life. All he wants is an uncomplicated relationship built on honesty, but Honor's past threatens to undermine everything. Then secrets about her mother start to spill out …

Honor has to make an agonising choice. Will she live up to her dutiful name and please others? Or will she choose freedom?

Visit www.choc-lit.com for more details including the first two chapters and reviews, or simply scan barcode using your mobile phone QR reader.

Why not try something else from the Choc Lit selection?
Here's a sample:

Please don't stop the music
Jane Lovering

 Winner of the 2012 Best Romantic Comedy Novel of the year

 Winner of the 2012 Romantic Novel of the year

How much can you hide?

Jemima Hutton is determined to build a successful new life and keep her past a dark secret. Trouble is, her jewellery business looks set to fail – until enigmatic Ben Davies offers to stock her handmade belt buckles in his guitar shop and things start looking up, on all fronts.

But Ben has secrets too. When Jemima finds out he used to be the front man of hugely successful Indie rock band Willow Down, she wants to know more. Why did he desert the band on their US tour? Why is he now a semi-recluse?

And the curiosity is mutual – which means that her own secret is no longer safe …

Visit www.choc-lit.com for more details including the first two chapters and reviews, or simply scan barcode using your mobile phone QR reader.

Never Coming Home
Evonne Wareham

***Winner of the Joan Hessayon
New Writers' Award***

All she has left is hope.

When Kaz Elmore is told her
five-year-old daughter Jamie
has died in a car crash, she
struggles to accept that she'll
never see her little girl again.
Then a stranger comes into her
life offering the most dangerous
substance in the world: hope.

Devlin, a security consultant and witness to the terrible
accident scene, inadvertently reveals that Kaz's daughter
might not have been the girl in the car after all.

What if Jamie is still alive? With no evidence, the police
aren't interested, so Devlin and Kaz have little choice but to
investigate themselves.

Devlin never gets involved with a client. Never. But the more
time he spends with Kaz, the more he desires her – and the more
his carefully constructed ice-man persona starts to unravel.

The desperate search for Jamie leads down dangerous paths
– to a murderous acquaintance from Devlin's dark past, and
all across Europe, to Italy, where deadly secrets await. But as
long as Kaz has hope, she can't stop looking …

Visit www.choc-lit.com for more details
including the first two chapters and
reviews, or simply scan barcode using
your mobile phone QR reader.

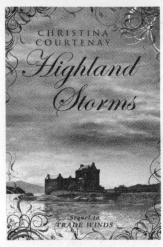

Highland Storms
Christina Courtenay

 Winner of the 2012 Best Historical Romantic Novel of the year

Who can you trust?

Betrayed by his brother and his childhood love, Brice Kinross needs a fresh start. So he welcomes the opportunity to leave Sweden for the Scottish Highlands to take over the family estate.

But there's trouble afoot at Rosyth in 1754 and Brice finds himself unwelcome. The estate's in ruin and money is disappearing. He discovers an ally in Marsaili Buchanan, the beautiful redheaded housekeeper, but can he trust her?

Marsaili is determined to build a good life. She works hard at being a housekeeper and harder still at avoiding men who want to take advantage of her. But she's irresistibly drawn to the new clan chief, even though he's made it plain he doesn't want to be shackled to anyone.

And the young laird has more than romance on his mind. His investigations are stirring up an enemy. Someone who will stop at nothing to get what he wants – including Marsaili – even if that means destroying Brice's life forever …

Sequel to Trade Winds.

Visit www.choc-lit.com for more details including the first two chapters and reviews, or simply scan barcode using your mobile phone QR reader.

The UnTied Kingdom
Kate Johnson

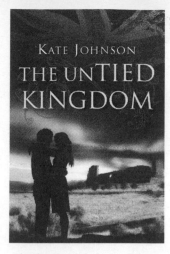

Shortlisted for the 2012 RoNA Contemporary Romantic Novel Category Award

The portal to an alternate world was the start of all her troubles – or was it?

When Eve Carpenter lands with a splash in the Thames, it's not the London or England she's used to. No one has a telephone or knows what a computer is. England's a third-world country and Princess Di is still alive. But worst of all, everyone thinks Eve's a spy.

Including Major Harker who has his own problems. His sworn enemy is looking for a promotion. The General wants him to undertake some ridiculous mission to capture a computer, which Harker vaguely envisions running wild somewhere in Yorkshire. Turns out the best person to help him is Eve.

She claims to be a popstar. Harker doesn't know what a popstar is, although he suspects it's a fancy foreign word for 'spy'. Eve knows all about computers, and electricity. Eve is dangerous. There's every possibility she's mad.

And Harker is falling in love with her.

Visit www.choc-lit.com for more details including the first two chapters and reviews, or simply scan barcode using your mobile phone QR reader.

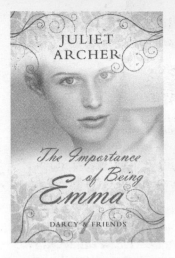

The Importance of Being Emma

Juliet Archer

Winner of The Big Red Read's Fiction Award 2011

A modern retelling of Jane Austen's *Emma*.

Mark Knightley – handsome, clever, rich – is used to women falling at his feet. Except Emma Woodhouse, who's like part of the family – and the furniture. When their relationship changes dramatically, is it an ending or a new beginning?

Emma's grown into a stunningly attractive young woman, full of ideas for modernising her family business. Then Mark gets involved and the sparks begin to fly. It's just like the old days, except that now he's seeing her through totally new eyes.

While Mark struggles to keep his feelings in check, Emma remains immune to the Knightley charm. She's never forgotten that embarrassing moment when he discovered her teenage crush on him. He's still pouring scorn on all her projects, especially her beautifully orchestrated campaign to find Mr Right for her ditzy PA. And finally, when the mysterious Flynn Churchill – the man of her dreams – turns up, how could she have eyes for anyone else? …

Visit www.choc-lit.com for more details including the first two chapters and reviews, or simply scan barcode using your mobile phone QR reader.

The Silver Locket
Margaret James

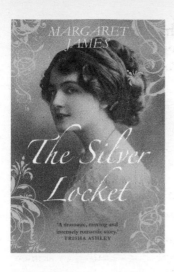

Winner of CataNetwork Reviewers' Choice Award for Single Titles 2010

If life is cheap, how much is love worth?

It's 1914 and young Rose Courtenay has a decision to make. Please her wealthy parents by marrying the man of their choice – or play her part in the war effort?

The chance to escape proves irresistible and Rose becomes a nurse. Working in France, she meets Lieutenant Alex Denham, a dark figure from her past. He's the last man in the world she'd get involved with – especially now he's married.

But in wartime nothing is as it seems. Alex's marriage is a sham and Rose is the only woman he's ever wanted. As he recovers from his wounds, he sets out to win her trust. His gift of a silver locket is a far cry from the luxuries she's left behind.

What value will she put on his love?

First novel in the trilogy.

Visit www.choc-lit.com for more details including the first two chapters and reviews, or simply scan barcode using your mobile phone QR reader.

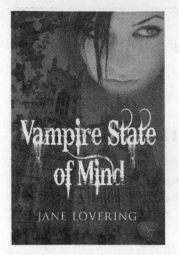

Vampire State of Mind
Jane Lovering

Jessica Grant knows vampires only too well. She runs the York Council tracker programme making sure that Otherworlders are all where they should be, keeps the filing in order and drinks far too much coffee.

To Jess, vampires are annoying and arrogant and far too sexy for their own good, particularly her ex-colleague, Sil, who's now in charge of Otherworld York. When a demon turns up and threatens not just Jess but the whole world order, she and Sil are forced to work together.

But then Jess turns out to be the key to saving the world, which puts a very different slant on their relationship.

The stakes are high. They are also very, very pointy and Jess isn't afraid to use them – even on the vampire she's rather afraid she's falling in love with …

This is the first of a trilogy in Jane's paranormal series.

Visit www.choc-lit.com for more details including the first two chapters and reviews, or simply scan barcode using your mobile phone QR reader.

CLAIM YOUR FREE EBOOK

of

Dream a Little Dream

You may wish to have a choice of how you read
Dream a Little Dream. Perhaps you'd like a digital
version for when you're out and about, so that you
can read it on your ereader or anywhere that you
can access iTunes – your computer, iPhone, iPad or a
Smartphone. For a limited period, we're including a
FREE ebook version along with this paperback.

To claim, simply visit ebooks.choc-lit.com
or scan the QR Code.

You'll need to enter the following code:

Q111207

Introducing Choc Lit

We're an independent publisher creating
a delicious selection of fiction.
Where heroes are like chocolate – irresistible!
Quality stories with a romance at the heart.

Choc Lit novels are selected by genuine readers like yourself.
We only publish stories our Choc Lit Tasting Panel want to
see in print. Our reviews and awards speak for themselves.

Come and support our authors and join them in our
Author's Corner, read their interviews and see their latest
events, reviews and gossip.

Visit: www.choc-lit.com for more details.

Available in paperback and as ebooks from most stores.

We'd also love to hear how you enjoyed *Dream a Little Dream*.
Just visit www.choc-lit.com and give your feedback.
Describe Dominic in terms of chocolate and you could win
a Choc Lit novel in our Flavour of the Month competition.

Follow us on twitter: www.twitter.com/
ChocLituk, or simply scan barcode using
your mobile phone QR reader.